CELESTIAL SPHERES BOOK #3

BLADESUNG

LISA BORNE GRAVES

AUTHORS 4 AUTHORS PUBLISHING

Marysville, WA, USA

Published by Authors 4 Authors Publishing
1214 6th St
Marysville, WA 98270
www.authors4authorspublishing.com

LCCN: 2021940512

Paperback ISBN: 978-1-64477-101-3
E-book ISBN: 978-1-64477-100-6
Audiobook ISBN: 978-1-64477-102-0

Edited by Rebecca Mikkelson
Developmental and Copyedited by Brandi Spencer

Cover design ©2021 Brandi Spencer. All rights reserved.
Interior design by Brandi Spencer
Scene break icon by Lisa Borne Graves

Authors 4 Authors Publishing branding is set in Bavire. Titles and headers are set in Mr Darcy. Handwriting is set in URW Chancery. All other text is set in Garamond.

CELESTIAL SPHERES BOOK #3

BLADESUNG

LISA BORNE GRAVES

Authors 4 Authors Content Rating

This title has been rated 17+, for older teens and adults, and contains:

- moderate language
- frequent intense violence
- intense implied sex
- mild alcohol use
- domestic abuse
- forced abortion
- forced marriage
- attempted suicide

Please, keep the following in mind when using our rating system:

1. A content rating is not a measure of quality.

Great stories can be found for every audience. One book with many content warnings and another with none at all may be of equal depth and sophistication. Our ratings can work both ways: to avoid content or to find it.

2. Ratings are merely a tool.

For our young adult (YA) and children's titles, age ratings are generalized suggestions. For parents, our descriptive ratings can help you make informed decisions, but at the end of the day, only you know what kinds of content are appropriate for your individual child. This is why we provide details in addition to the general age rating.

For more information on our rating system, please, visit our Content Guide at: www.authors4authorspublishing.com/books/ratings

DEDICATION

To my own draca bearn, Squire Draca D,
you completed our world.
You're a hero in your own story,
which made me realize I can do anything in mine.

Works by Lisa Borne Graves

Celestial Spheres

Fyr
Draca
Bladesung

The Immortal Transcripts

Quiver
Fever
Shudder (February 2023)

Stand-Alone Titles

Apidae
"Dare"

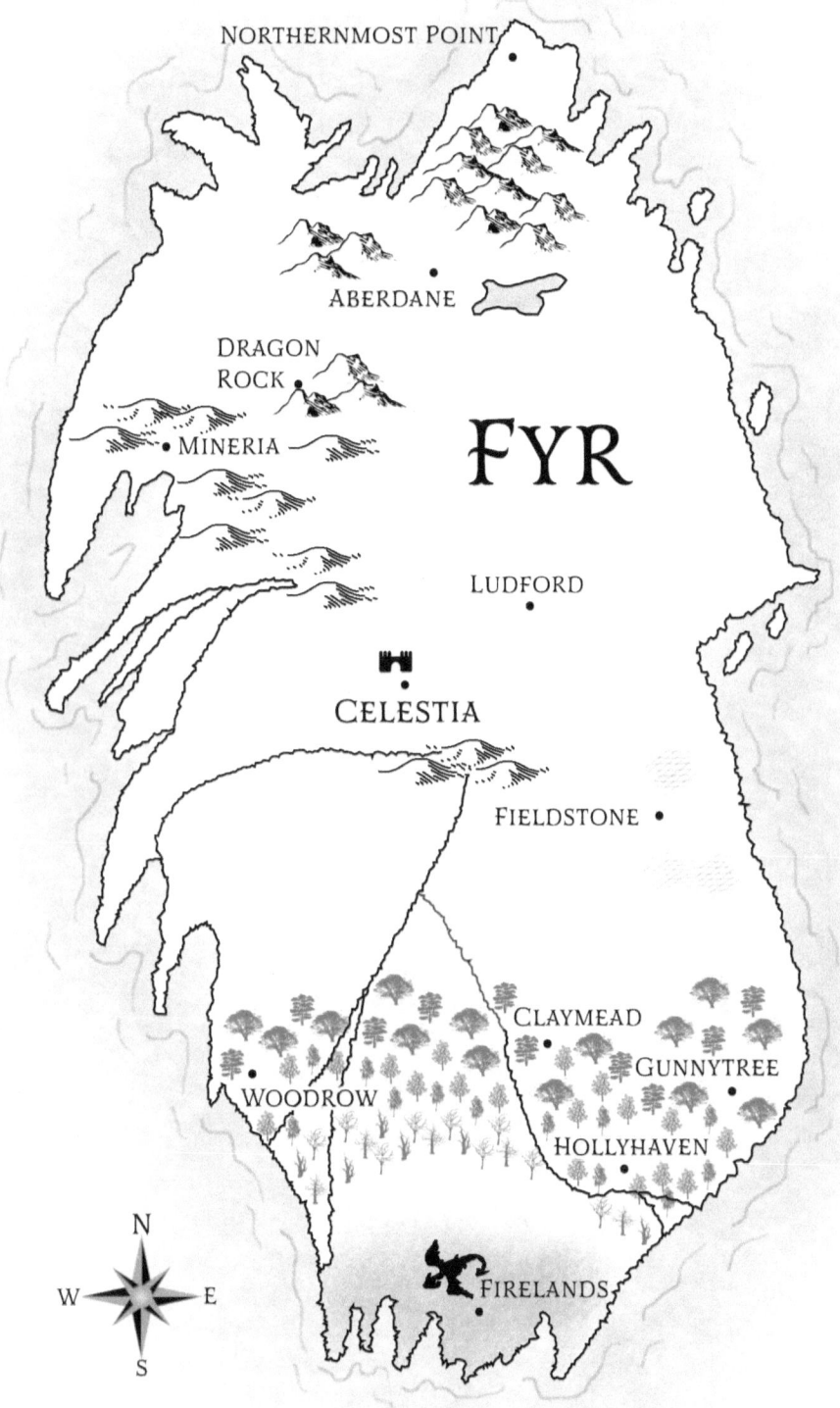

TABLE OF CONTENTS

1

FORSAKEN

The morning after her wedding night, Toury woke up to a cold, empty bed, the fire having gone out. She blushed recalling what had ensued only hours before. Her embarrassment turned to rage when she rolled over to see a letter sitting atop the book of royal edicts her husband had asked her to finish reading, resting on the pillow in lieu of him. She picked up the letter, hoping in vain he hadn't actually left the castle. King Alex, her lifemate for less than a day, surely wouldn't abandon her hours after her parents were killed, hours after their wedding, breaking his promise not to leave until they had an heir on the way.

She picked up the rolled missive and broke the seal of a crown with the outline of fire behind it—although the King of Fyr wore a silver medallion with a dragon instead these days. An array of emotions from anger to despair to anxiety warred over her. Why had he left? More to the point, how dare he?

My Dearest Toury,

I don't expect you to ever forgive me, so I won't even dare to insult you with an apology for leaving, or to beg for the forgiveness I don't deserve. Please read the edicts, and you'll understand. Only I can bring my uncle in. The sooner I pursue him, the sooner this can be over, and I can come back to you, where I desperately want to be. If I wait and he leaves the sphere, this threat will loom over us. I will return as soon as I can, if only to transport back to see you for a moment. I cannot stand the thought of a lengthy separation. I never thought I had enough power to transport so much, but our recent battle showed me otherwise. Expect me within a couple days. I cannot stay away, and I know you need me. And before you get ready to scold me about broken promises, I did not break my word. I will happily continue to fulfill my duty to the crown. I can think of nothing else, if truth be told.

Your lifemate, now and forever,
Alex

He was a...her distracted brain couldn't think of appropriate insults. Her emotions settled on desire, ignited by his last few words. She lost her anger, and memories of his touch made her heart race. The melding of their magic when true love destroyed Alex's curse was nothing compared to becoming husband and wife—or lifemates, as this sphere called it.

Originally raised on Earth, Toury still had a lot to catch up with. She was very studious when it came to the magic of the land—stones, fire, light, and blood magic—and she understood the gist of it all, but there was so much more she would have to know to be a great queen by her lifemate's side. He had announced to an entire patriarchal sphere she would be his *partner* in everything. Almost a year had not been enough time to learn all of this, especially when kidnapped by necromancers and then her own rebel parents. They were dead now, and her husband had left her to grieve—alone. He was hunting down his own uncle.

Toury growled. She threw away the covers, slipped out of bed, and donned her self-warming robe, the first gift Alex had given her. The matching nightgown had been destroyed by the necromancers, but thankfully, the robe had been spared. At least he didn't insult her or underestimate her anger by thinking he could persuade her with a gift this time. She pulled the bell for Madge, her bodyguard-waiting maid. Distance from the bed allowed Toury to find her ire again.

But her servant was terrible for Toury's resolve to stay mad. Madge pampered her with bath salts, oils, and lotions, and let her soak in the tub for an entire hour, despite the many things that needed to be done. Madge dressed her, even indulging Toury by leaving half her hair down on her shoulders since she wasn't fond of the tightly pulled and pinned updos. She weaved Toury's circlet into her hair atop her head and pinned it. The physical feeling of it was awkward, but the figurative weight was staggering. "Queen" was just a word, but the circlet made it real. Toury examined the headdress in the mirror: the stones were grouped in the center like a giant engagement ring, and Alex had treated it as one, proposing to her on her birthday. It was his third proposal. She'd said no the first two times, but he had deserved it. He'd refused to admit he loved her, and she refused to get engaged without being in love. Plus, their relationship had been marred by mistakes—mostly on his part, but she wasn't exactly blameless either.

When Madge urged her to eat more food to fortify her, Toury became suspicious. "Why are you being weird?"

"Am I acting strange?" Madge asked. "I am simply taking care of my queen. If I'm using extra care, it is due to your kidnapping, loss, and wedding night. You are a strong woman, but now as Queen Tourmaline Sapphirian, you need to let me care for you, to embolden you, and help you be the best you can be."

Okay, "queen" with her married name was a bit more than just a word. In her head, it wasn't a huge shift in titles from Queen Proxy-to-be to just Queen, but hearing it gave her imposter syndrome. The novelty of her new last name, combined with how lost she felt—grappling with this official shift in her power and in her relationship with Alex—made her feel weaker than ever. She would let Madge lead the way...for a day. She would relax and be pampered, and tomorrow, she would don her circlet with pride and pluck.

At breakfast, the queen—wait, the queen dowager now—inquired where Alex was. Toury's anger rekindled. Not only had he left, but he hadn't told anyone else, leaving her to fulfill that duty. She might just murder Alex when he returned.

"He has left for a couple days to oversee the capture of Lord Emerald. He says the edicts proclaim he must bring him in." She stuffed her mouth so she could say no more, but tears started to prickle her eyes, unwanted emotion rising.

"That is true..." the dowager said. "But I thought he might delegate for a little since you just married. He didn't say he was leaving so soon, but he did pen a note to me that you married yesterday. I did not get to see you or congratulate you, but we must have a celebration once things are stable."

Mary and Toury both emitted a simultaneous scoffing laugh, then met each other's gaze, and giggled.

The dowager frowned at them, and her eyes narrowed. She clearly was not happy Toury and Mary laughed at the thought of stability. "This kingdom will settle. Alex will be the best king this sphere has seen in a thousand years—"

"Mother, stop," Mary chided. "Alex has been handed a mess. It'll take a long time to straighten it out, so you should plan your party accordingly, despite my nefarious uncle."

The dowager sighed. A lifetime of doing what she was told had obviously conditioned her to accept whatever fate handed her. She should be as equally mad at Alex for leaving as Toury was. Instead, she simply accepted it, just as she'd turned a blind eye to the same behavior from Alex's father. Toury would not be that kind of queen.

Mary dropped her fork and gave her mother a censorious glower. "And *my* party, but you better not make it a joint one for their wedding and my birthday, because their marriage will be all that matters to the people. I'm always an afterthought. Alex just leaves without helping any transition of power. I guess the already scheduled grievances are all up to me today?"

Neither Toury nor the dowager spoke. Mary had taken a liking to scolding spoiled nobles and righting wrongs, but Alex forcing her to pick up his slack without warning was wrong. Toury was too exhausted and hadn't expected to deal with it because of her parents.

Her parents' deaths were a huge blow since she had hoped for some kind of compromise, for her parents to give Alex a chance, to help him stop these rebels. It would never be. It was a strange feeling to miss people she hardly knew, whom she'd dreamt of as being perfect, only for them to disappoint her. It was hard to grieve what never was but easy to grieve what could have been.

That too-familiar choking feeling of loss crept over her, so she shifted her focus onto whom she had. The Sapphirians were her true family, and she had her Aunt Edwina, Uncle Gareth, and brother Aschen. And Alex made promises of a large and loving family of their own one day. But for that to happen, she needed Alex here.

And she had Mary and Alex's mother. The queen dowager appeared tired, with bags under her eyes, more wrinkles than Toury had noticed before, and a few streaks of gray in her hair. It marked her grief and stress. She had seen her lifemate die and almost lost her son only a week ago. Then the dowager didn't even get to see him marry, since their real wedding had been interrupted by her rebel parents, and Alex and Toury made the hasty decision last night to elope. No wonder the woman couldn't respond to Mary's complaints.

"I think a party for each is a necessity," Toury commented. "It'll bolster the people after the rebel and necromancer nonsense, help them see unity and a hopeful future." *And keep Alex here for more than a couple hours.* "We could throw Mary's first to not outshine her birthday, then ours later." Alex would have to be present for both.

The dowager seemed pleased and launched into ideas about each party. Toury only listened carefully enough to agree or disagree. She didn't want a party, really, but seeing how happily distracted it made the dowager, she'd go through worse to ease the woman's suffering. Once the meal was over, Toury feigned fatigue, wanting to mope alone.

"Must've been a looooong night." Mary giggled.

"Mary!" The dowager's mouth dropped, and her face grew pale due to Mary's lack of decorum.

"That's your brother you're talking about," Toury reminded her, taking glory in watching Mary's face drop, cringe, and then feign retching. "Yeah, so no girl talk, Mary."

"No girl talk," Mary repeated.

Toury was all too aware the two women at the table were inadvertently thinking of her and Alex sleeping together, so she stood suddenly and excused herself, which made them hastily stand in respect. Tory nodded for them to sit again—another custom her marriage instilled—and then she bolted from the room as fast as propriety would allow a lady. She would visit the rest of her family.

After checking if her aunt was on the mend and listening to her babble on and on about how Toury had made such a great match, she sought out Aschen to find him with their Uncle Gareth, who was tutoring the young boy. They were the good part of her family. Her aunt had risked her own life to save Alex, removing poison from him. Even Aschen had known their parents' actions toward Toury were wrong, and he'd helped her escape. Their sister Racine was another story altogether.

Toury told them her news. Gareth congratulated her. Aschen grimaced to tell her she'd committed a grievous sin. To an eight-year-old boy, marriage was probably the most unappealing concept imaginable. She marveled over how Aschen appeared unaffected by their parents' death, at least outwardly. Toury wondered what kind of parents they had been to him. She doubted abusive but could easily see them neglecting the boy for their radical cause.

Toury let Gareth and Aschen get back to the lesson and spent the rest of the day lounging on the settee, reading the royal edicts, which was a "thrilling" combination of boring and bloodthirsty with an overwhelming stench of ancient patriarchy. The rules for royalty were easy. Madge had taught her half, and Ruby's knowledge—which Toury gained through the stone that had brought her to Fyr—remembered it all.

After reading about types of execution from stakes to beheadings, Toury put the edict book down in favor of a nonfiction book about taming men, which Mary had given Toury as a joke gift on her birthday. Sadly, because of Alex's most recent action, she needed to read it. The book was actually fascinating, and she was making study of the artful ways women could control men, since she needed to put her foot down and get Alex to stay and delegate until his uncle was captured.

Her mind kept drifting back to everything she had experienced since she'd arrived in Fyr, and she could read no longer. She wouldn't trade her life here for the one back on Earth, for she wouldn't have Alex or a family at all, but she longed for just a couple mundane days of school. She longed for peace.

A knock at the door sounded. Peace? Apparently, she wouldn't get any. She had let Madge retire to the servant's room across the hall, so Toury hid the book quickly under the settee cushion, luckily before the door opened. Mary entered.

"You should wait until I answer the door," Toury said. "You can't come waltzing in here."

"Alex here?" She surveyed the room.

"No."

"Then no harm done." Mary flopped onto the couch and slumped in a most unladylike posture.

"And if Alex were here?" Toury challenged.

"I'd wait."

"He transports, as you do, so he could've been here without you knowing it. And we are married now, so..."

"Eww. Point taken. I'll wait for permission in the future."

"Why are you here?" Toury asked to divert the conversation away from the topic of interrupting a newly married couple.

"Ouch."

"I didn't mean that in a bad way, just trying to start the conversation. You came here for a reason."

"I wanted to see if you were okay." Mary took up Toury's hand and squeezed it. "And mother didn't want to bother you, but it did come up because it wouldn't be appropriate to have any parties yet...I'm here to ask about your parents."

They were dead, so what was Mary asking?

"I mean, the funeral pyre. It could be a private affair—probably best—or public, but for public, you'd need Alex to pardon them. It's a complicated situation. You wouldn't want to embolden the remaining rebels, but you wouldn't want to anger them either."

"My aunt surely can decide—"

"Toury, you are Queen, not your aunt. It should be done within three days after death."

"Public," Toury choked out. "Schedule it for me. If Alex isn't here, I will pardon them myself. I will speak."

Mary hugged her tightly. "I'm so sorry, Toury." She got up, and Toury tried to hide the tears that formed. "Do you want me to stay?"

Toury shook her head.

"He's a cad leaving like that. The least he could do is have breakfast with us, spend the day with you, make it a celebration so you aren't here sitting on your own with nothing to do but think. What would a one-day difference make? Cobalt is the best tracker there is, and he's already after my uncle."

It stung. Mary just had to open her mouth and make things worse. The dam holding back tears started to spring leaks. Toury kept choking down her anger at Alex, but it wanted out.

"A day could mean a lot," Toury said hotly. She was defending him, and she shouldn't. She knew, though, Alex wanted to be home, but he wanted their safety foremost. What she had not let herself think about was the possibility that Alex was distancing himself to protect her. If his uncle was trying to get to the throne, the path there was through Alex, Mary, and then Toury if she carried the heir. Could she already be pregnant? What a thought.

"I suppose." Mary allowed, knowing better than to argue. "Just so you know, my cousin is coming to the palace. Mother thought it best to summon him to see where his loyalties lie." Mary hesitated on the threshold. "If Alex shows up, make sure he stays long enough to deal with all this nonsense."

Sadly, Toury resorted to reading more of *Tame the Dragon: How to Control Men* to figure out how to keep Alex home. Although an interesting read, nothing artful would work on Alex. They were honest with each other. Toury would be herself, or perhaps a more assertive version of herself.

At some point, not long after she had taken supper in her room, she fell asleep fully clothed on the bed. She slept better than ever until a swishing noise woke her. Groggily, she sat up and rubbed her eyes. Alex was there with David, the latter practically running to get out of the bedroom. Alex simply stared at her and she at him. Once the door closed behind the servant, Alex rushed toward her, pulling her up by her forearms and kissing her until goosebumps rose all over her body.

He pulled away to run his hand down her hair. "God and goddess, fifteen hours away from you is far too long."

She was ready to argue, to yell at him, to duke it out. He had left her when she needed him most. Instead, "You left me," came out in a pathetic feeble voice she hardly recognized as her own. She shook with unspent emotion from her parents' death and everything that had happened since she'd arrived on this sphere.

"I'm sorry. I'm being torn in a million directions, but I want to be here the most." He punctuated it with a kiss, and Toury unraveled.

Emotions overwhelmed her, and logic went out the window. The fight and anger left her, replaced with overwhelming relief and desire for him to hold her and kiss her and make her whole again.

2

A TRAITOR

Alex left before Toury was awake, again, in the wee hours of the morning. She would kill him—maybe just maim him—but he could not afford to get stuck there. Breakfast would lead to time with his mother and sister, and then he'd want to spend time alone with Toury, lunch would suddenly show up, and then he'd be bogged down with kingly business. He had to get out of there and back to his men who were marching south, awaiting news from his scouts. His men had already searched and swept the north and could not find a trace of the traitor: his uncle. Lord Emerald had married into the Sapphirian family through Alex's aunt and had been the mastermind behind the curses, hoping to overtake the throne for his son.

Henry Sapphirian, Alex's cousin, was another concern. Alex needed assurance of Henry's innocence in all this. Henry had been a young child when the curse happened, but where would his loyalty lie now? He could not imagine his cousin being associated with anyone who would want Alex dead. But Alex had thought that about his uncle, clearly a mistake. Memories of his uncle's kind tips to help with sparring, his corrections when observing their lessons about warfare, and his compliments at Alex's ingenuity when it came to problem solving flooded Alex's thoughts. Lord Emerald wasn't what one would call a loving or doting man—not even to Henry or Ruby—but Alex had never seen him cruel or malicious. He had been strict and assertive, yes, but never deeply unkind. The only inkling Alex got of his uncle being uncharitable was hearing of how he'd treated Toury when Alex was gone. Back then, though, Alex had written it off as Lord Emerald being set in his ways and against the progress Alex wanted to instill.

"How is my Mary?" Cobalt shook Alex's hand, wearing a goofy grin Alex had never seen before.

Alex cringed. *His* Mary? Alex still wasn't used to the idea of his best friend being engaged to his sister. He doubted he ever would adjust to the very idea. Cobalt was still far from proving himself worthy of his sister's heart.

"I'm sure she is well. I didn't have time to see her."

"Of course you didn't," Cobalt said knowingly. He laughed. "How is our queen?"

"Well." Alex's cheeks burned.

Cobalt gave him a slap on his back. "You dog."

"The north?" Alex redirected his womanizing friend's thoughts—formerly womanizing, he hoped. Other men were joining them, and he would not have the queen besmirched or, worse, lusted after by other men.

Cobalt cleared his throat and stood straight, physically shifting his role from best friend to advisor. "No signs, no sightings. However, we have a lead toward the southeast. The scout saw him unobserved. He's tailing him incognito and will send messages."

"Your Majesty," Captain Agate greeted. "We think we have him and are maneuvering to discreetly surround him and push him back toward us. If you want to review the plans, my tent is over there."

As Alex walked toward the tent, his men stopped and stared at him. He didn't glance at them, but he imagined they regarded him with a cross between intimidation and reverence. This troop was the very one he had transported out of a hopeless battle—all of them at once—something unheard of for any Sapphirian to ever do. Toury had freed Alex from that curse by stealing his heart, but she'd also unleashed this power he had in him that had been dormant or suppressed by the dark curse. Or perhaps she increased his power with light and fire melding in that curse-breaking kiss. Regardless, the dragon in him had risen, never to be restrained again.

Alex tried to get away after Agate apprised him of plans, to get back to Toury before she woke, so he could explain why he couldn't have stayed. That became impossible when a message arrived about a sighting of his uncle in Mineria, which was due north past Celestia and contradicted what his scout had seen. This lead came from a civilian who tipped off one of his captains there. It could be a trap or an attempt to throw off his search, but every lead had to be examined. Sending some of his men might be in vain if his uncle wasn't there, and it would take too long on horseback. An entourage would also send his uncle into flight again.

If the man got ahold of a labradorite stone, he could escape to Earth. Alex knew his uncle couldn't escape to Lyft or Water. The vessels used to transport to either sphere were a rarity on Fyr, expensive, and there were peace treaties with both spheres dictating that the reigning monarch have sole possession of them. The first thing Alex had checked before he left was his inventory: not one was missing. Even if his uncle had managed to get to one of the spheres by some miracle, he stood no chance against the strict matriarchal society of Lyft nor in the war-torn Water, which had beasts that made dracas look like kittens. No, Emerald would hide and bide his time here or escape to Earth.

He had to stop his uncle's escape at all costs. Alex donned a simple cloak to conceal who he was, then envisioned himself in Mineria and used his fire power to transform matter and slip through space, taking Cobalt and his new bodyguard, Percival, as well as Alex's own, David. He remembered the times back when Toury was in school and he'd used transporting, or dragon's trapdoor, to surprise her by showing up in her room. Those days seemed a lifetime ago. Ever since that girl entered his life, it had been utter chaos through no fault of hers.

Alex cleared his mind of Toury and focused on his objective: the rich opulent city center of Mineria, the only part he had ever been in before. It had been a while, but it still was a beautiful city. Mineria was named aptly for what it functioned as. It was a sprawling metropolis that thinned outward to the mines, which excavated the majority of stones the land used. If Celestia was the finest city in Fyr, Mineria was a close second.

The three of them waited on Alex's orders, but he had no idea where to go.

"He was seen in the slums," Cobalt prodded.

"Slums?" Alex asked.

Cobalt met his gaze and nodded.

Alex hadn't a clue there were slums anywhere in Fyr until Toury told him. Yes, he knew there were wealthy people and there were the poor, but helping the poor had been an unfashionable idea to his father. Alex needed to fix things instead of chasing a murderer. It would get the rebels off his back if he could change his kingdom into one where few suffered. He longed for a day when grievances from citizens were the only thing that he'd deal with in a day; even better, he envisioned a schedule only filled with opening buildings that would help his people—orphanages like Toury's, free healer centers, and modest dwellings given free to those who could not work.

Wordlessly, Cobalt led the way. Of course he would know where the slums were since that was where desperate women who traded pleasure for coin resided. He tried not to think of how many girls his friend had used when Alex had only ever been with his lifemate. He never cared what dalliances his friend had indulged in, but the idea bothered him for Mary's sake. She knew whom she was marrying, though. If it happened from here on out, Alex would put a stop to the marriage. He would not see Mary regret her choice in spouse, no matter what she thought the flames foretold her.

Sensing where Alex's thoughts lay, or at least his mood, Cobalt brought their attention back to Mineria. "I believe the report came from the same area the rebels kept your lifemate. It would make sense if they were working together."

"No, Toury's parents weren't working with my uncle. They were hiding from him all these years. They knew it was him, but no one would have believed them after Toury's mother had jilted my Uncle Alfred and he wound up dead."

Cobalt nodded. They walked on. An older woman in threadbare, risqué clothing winked at Alex and beckoned him hither with her finger. His gaze darted away, trying to hide his distaste for a woman selling her body, even though he knew most likely a man had driven her to this last resort. That was another conundrum he was sure his feisty lifemate would solve: more jobs for women, and especially more assistance when a man left them with child and no resources to feed them.

Cobalt stopped and watched her walk into an alley.

"No. We don't have time for that, Cobalt."

"Eww, no. She's old. I don't need to *pay* a woman to—"

"Because you wouldn't dally with anyone, considering you're engaged to my sister?" Alex saved Cobalt from himself.

Cobalt froze, his face reddened, and he muttered, "Of course." Again, he quickly changed the subject. "Don't you recognize the resemblance?"

"No."

"She looks like your...uh...the firelasher." Cobalt had almost said brother.

Great. Now Alex was uncomfortable and worried about coming here without an army. "It's a trap."

"Could be, but you can transport us out of the alley, no?"

How was Cobalt so at ease about following a strange lady down an alley?

"I don't like this," David said.

"I'll check it out," Cobalt said.

"You can't. They will want to capture you to get to Mary. And Mary—"

"Will do something stupid. Ugh, being a royal is not fun!" Cobalt actually stomped his foot.

Alex was beginning to think Cobalt and Mary were either meant for each other or would annoyingly throw tantrums regularly. Toury would tell Alex "both." Instead of sharing his thoughts, Alex said, "Now you understand all my complaints."

"I never wanted to be. I wasn't born into it. To be honest, I never even thought about it. I just had to fall for Mary and her fanciful visions."

And that was the point. Those who weren't desperate for power were the ones who deserved it.

"If we could get out of plain sight, get moving," David hedged, nervousness in his voice.

"Her *real* visions of the future, you mean," Alex said. "You only believed them because you wanted to. David is right. Let's just do this. Follow her."

"I didn't say that, Your—"

"Shh," Alex cut David off.

David bit his lip to prevent Alex's title from coming out. David knew better, but old habits were hard to resist. "I didn't say that..." he paused to avoid his title. "I didn't say follow her. I just wanted us to move along."

"Too late," Alex said with more bravery than he felt as he followed Cobalt, who was already fearlessly heading around the corner. David somehow made Alex relax a little, knowing the man would do enough worrying for both of them.

Alex stopped right inside the alleyway so he could have a quick escape and assure they wouldn't be boxed in. David had the same mindset and watched the mouth of the alley with his keen attention to detail. Satisfied David would have his back, Alex turned to see Cobalt talking to the woman. She pointed to a door. Alex crossed his arms and gave her a challenging glower.

"No way. The informant must come out," Cobalt insisted without even needing to ask Alex.

The door cracked open, and the woman was handed some coin. Then she scuttled along by them, stopping in front of Alex for a moment. Keeping her head bent low in reverence, she whispered, "Our paths will cross again, Your Majesty. Until then."

"Wait, what?" he demanded.

"I see things in the light. There will be a time when all seems lost, but I can guide the way. Not to worry, I will call upon you when the time comes."

"Why are you helping me?" Alex asked.

"Because you have my son and will do what is best for him," she assumed, making Alex feel guilty. He hadn't even properly met the firelasher yet, discomforted by his baseborn brother's existence.

Cobalt had been right about her familiar features: The eye color, the hair, and the lip shape all matched the firelasher's. This woman—Irene, Alex thought Toury had told him—had been his...was his brother's mother. Irene and her sister had helped Toury escape her rebel parents.

"And if others win this war, my son will die." The last part was so quiet, he barely heard her, but the honesty in her statement amplified his trust in her.

She had sent her son with Toury to protect him, and Alex could do that. In turn, she would give him information when he needed it. A reader of fire himself, he knew trusting the visions might be the difference between life and death. And he sensed this woman was full of light magic. A lightreader was rare and deserved distinction. How could his father have let her fall into this state of poverty when she had raised his child? Done nothing for his baseborn son?

Alex pulled a few golden sapphirians out of his coin pouch, ones with real sapphires in them, and handed them to her. Her eyes went wide as she snatched them up. She curtsied deeply and then rushed out of the alley. Too late he realized she had said "war." Would things get that bad?

Alex turned back to see Cobalt talking to someone in the door. He recognized the eyes at once: Racine. "Seize her!" he commanded Cobalt.

"Shh," Cobalt chastised. "She demanded *sibb*."

Alex growled. A fugitive could evoke this claim for peace if they had important information to gain a pardon. He was never going to pardon her for killing one of his dragons and plotting to overtake the throne, not to mention emotionally abusing Toury. He had never seen sisters so drastically different in appearance, manners, and mind.

Unafraid of this girl, he pressed the issue. "What do you know?"

"I know the identity of the commander, and I know the direction Lord Emerald fled. He was here but left."

"Why should we believe you?" Alex demanded.

Her jaw set. Stubborn as ever, he figured she must be weighing how much the truth would cost her dignity. Perhaps he was inadvertently projecting Toury's personality onto her sister. "Because they turned on me, betrayed me in more ways than one. They made allies with the necromancers, the very people who framed my parents, destroying my family. That was never the plan." She paused and stared down at her worn boots. Her voice came out faint, without the touch of unpolished bravado she used regularly. "Emerald killed my parents. I don't believe in a cause that will cut off its own feet. My parents and I were the only link the rebels had to get to Toury and, in turn, force you into a bargain."

Racine continued, her voice finding its strength again but not its brazen confidence. "I mean, why make an enemy of me if I could get rebel demands right to her? I'm thinking now they don't want her alive anymore, and my parents would insist on her living. As much as I dislike the queen and loathe you, I don't want my sister dead. My parents only ever wanted to bring us home and free us from their pasts. I lived with them for barely two years, but they were my parents. Emerald was never part of the rebel plan."

Her thoughts aligned with his. They would go after Toury at some point; her parents had been a buffer that had preserved her life in the rebels' plans, one that was now gone. They might've been the only rebels who would object to Toury's execution.

"We have to go." David drew his sword.

"Go due east for Emerald. Rebels abound here. You're not safe." Racine said.

"Come with us?" Alex impulsively asked.

"No. I have to finish up here first. Go," she whispered.

Soldiers blocked the alleyway now. "Good job, Racine," one of them said.

Was this a trap, or was she honest in saying she was leaving the rebel army? She did warn him to go. Alex grabbed Cobalt by his collar as he moved toward the rebels to attack. Cobalt, realizing what was going on, grabbed Percival's arm. Alex could transport, but he needed David. He couldn't leave him behind. Three rebels spanned the alley entrance, but David was battering them back. Fighting their way out would draw attention, and who knew how many men the rebels had out there. Alex threw out fire, knowing it would expose his identity, but he had to split David off from the rebel fray. Percival grabbed David's cloak. Alex turned to see if Racine would change her mind and go with him, but she was gone.

15

Alex transported back to camp, scaring his men half to death when the four of them popped into existence in front of them. The few eating dropped their bowls or their mead.

"Sorry men, but pack up camp. We head east immediately."

David cleared his throat and gave Alex a nod. Alex walked away from the group with his valet, who needed some kind of counsel. "Your Majesty. You must go home, the queen—"

"Will understand. I'll send a letter."

David raised his brows and crossed his arms, unknowingly making a Toury-esque pose. It reminded Alex of how angry she would be. "It will take the men a few days to even get there. There's not much in the way of bustling cities out there except Fieldstone. Send the scouts ahead. They can report when he is found. You can always be there in a split second. And you know the queen will never understand, because she hates being second best to your politics, and you promised—"

"You're more of a nag than her, David," Alex ground out.

David blushed red, making Alex realize how terrible he was acting.

"I'm sorry. You are right, and it is your job to nag me until I see reason. We'll leave momentarily."

He took a moment to discuss Racine's motives and trustworthiness with Cobalt. Alex did not want to trust her, but if she could be turned to their side, she could be the key to defeating both the necromancers and rebels. She had told him many things, including the most dreadful one: his enemies had joined forces. This was not good. What other ways had Racine been betrayed? Who was the commander? He could not tell Toury about this either. Hiding things from her had caused strife in their relationship, but he couldn't stand to see her get her hopes up that her sister was changing to have Racine dash them away by betraying them.

3
QUEEN

Toury was furious. Alex didn't stay *again*. This time, he didn't even leave a note! He merely returned to be with her physically, and that was it. No apology, no discussion of when he would be back—not much talking at all, actually. She felt used and no longer important or a priority. He had gotten what he wanted, and now he no longer had to try to make her happy.

She would show him she was a force to be reckoned with. Toury wouldn't waste her time being angry or despondent about Alex. She would push the feeling aside, be a good queen today. When he returned, she would unleash her anger and not let him touch her until she had fully chastised him, put her foot down, and gotten a real apology.

Unable to fall back asleep, she picked up the thick book of edicts. She had finally gotten through the execution section. What would be next, though? Something worse? She opened to her bookmarked page and saw "The Tales of King Edward I." Some stories about Alex's ancestor. Odd that his stories would be in an edict book. Curious and hoping this would be more entertaining, she read on.

> *After King Rowland III died of the dowsing fever, his brother ascended the throne. Being the best firebrander in Fyr since man was born from draca flames, King Edward Alexander Sapphirian had foretold his brother's death. Some had been skeptical of his claims, but as time went on, many of his prophetic visions came to pass. Here, in this section, we include both the ones that have happened and the ones that may occur in the future. King Edward I was the only firebrander to this day known to be able to see past his lifetime...*

Toury paused. The man's middle name could be Alex's namesake, which rekindled her annoyance with her husband. She needed to ask Alex or Mary how far into the future they could see. Mary was more powerful with the firebranding, but this ancestor with excessive and unheard-of power might explain Alex performing such feats as transporting entire troops. Fyrians believed in magic, not science and DNA, but Toury wondered if there were any studies on a power-level gene, similar to how eye color was usually a dominant gene passed along the paternal line.

Now interested in the material, she pressed on with her reading. There were many tales of events coming true even when people tried to defy their fates. For the section of ones that hadn't occurred yet, she'd have to ask Mary. Maybe some had; this was an old book. Some of these prophecies sounded ominous, but she enjoyed the one predicting a golden age with hundreds of years of peace. She noted one in particular that made her pulse quicken with fear and eagerness. It described the Sapphirian line dwindling down to "the brink of extinction" before being "replenished bountifully."

There were four Sapphirians alive altogether; surely, this was "the brink." Did that mean she and Alex, and Mary and Cobalt, would all have many children? Perhaps this cousin Henry would remarry someone as well. Not ready to think of possible motherhood, she glossed over a couple more boring tales too vague to link to anyone she knew. As Mary and Alex reminded her often, visions didn't have dates on them, so these weren't in chronological order. Right before she put the book down, she had the urge to read one more. It ended up being a longer, thrilling tale of the Bladesung, a savior who merges the powers together to create one never before seen and saves the realm by liberating all of Fyr from evil. Sadly, the tale lacked detail.

Madge came in, surprised to see her up but not shocked to see her alone. She would know Alex was gone because David was with him. Toury tried not to be grumpy about Alex and didn't complain when Madge readied her, again weaving the circlet in her upper hair with the bottom half trailing. It would be her fashionable move toward a style more of her own. She was tired of corsets and dresses and updos, and would murder for a pair of yoga pants.

She had breakfast with Mary and Queen Sapphirian—err, Queen Dowager Sapphirian. This title shift would take a while to get used to. After breakfast, Toury saw her aunt, who was now venturing out of bed for a few minutes at a time. Later, she found her uncle playing with her brother in the orchard. She saw Craig there too, the baseborn—Alex's half-brother—and mentally added it to the list of things for Alex to take care of when he returned. He must do something for his kin to keep him happy, safe, and away from the rebels. Being older than Alex, the rebels could back his half-brother, despite his mother never marrying the late king and Craig not inheriting those Sapphirian eyes. She also knew Craig's presence hurt the queen dowager, who didn't need a constant reminder of her lifemate's premarital track record.

Once Toury was satisfied that everyone was comfortable, she summoned the dowager and Mary to the princess salon. She went to pour the tea, but Mary stayed her hand. "Queens don't pour tea." The princess took over the tea service.

"Thank goodness for that," Toury muttered. She had hated the tea service, which was an artform in itself of carefully displayed moves other women judged emphatically. "Queen Dowager, I wanted to start taking care of things, to discuss how things will work around here."

"Your Majesty—"

"No, please, don't do that." The title was weird coming from the former queen. "Call me Toury. I hate this shift in...everything."

"We have to." Mary scoffed at the notion.

"You don't. Alex told me I could call him his nickname instead of his title before we were engaged because he gave me permission."

Mary let out a whistle and shook her head. "He's either a fool or a conniving, manipulative brat on so many levels."

"Mary," the dowager chastised.

"I knew enough at the time not to. He was not conniving...*then.* Anyway, the point is, I know if I ask my family, of all people, to call me Toury, then they can and should."

"Um, did you forget you said his name without title after he kissed you at the infamous ball that propelled you into this marriage?"

The dowager groaned at Mary's comment but made no attempt to further chastise her.

Toury could not believe her nerve, but a bratty sister was better than a groveling friend. How to deal with this shift in power? Toury knew just what to do. "The reason we forgot ourselves and the propriety of names will be something you learn soon Mary, if you haven't already." Toury lifted her tea cup and took a scalding sip. No one could drink until she did, and Toury couldn't let Mary's milky tea go cold because Toury preferred hers black. "I shall be Toury when with only immediate family then."

She had to change the subject, for Mary's face wasn't blushing with affirmation, but sulking at Toury's comment. Perhaps Cobalt was behaving himself for once. She had not caught Mary and him alone yet nor seen him kiss more than her forehead or cheek. Mary's sixteenth birthday was fast approaching, blighted out by the recent drama. Perhaps Cobalt realized fifteen was too young or that Alex would torch him for touching his sister. Knowing Cobalt, possibly just the latter.

The dowager smiled at her, eyes glistening with pride, something she'd never gotten from her adoptive Earth parents or her biological ones—well, maybe a tiny bit. Just losing her Fyrian parents, she was allowed to romanticize how they had cared about her despite everything. Regardless of whom they were or could have been, she had a different family here now that loved her.

"I'm glad you broached the subject." The dowager squeezed Toury's free hand in her own. "I didn't want to bring it up first. What will happen, per custom, is I will move from the king's tower and allow you and my son to take it over, as well give you the Queen's Room for entertaining. I can walk you through the household duties at your convenience—"

"Queen Dowager, I don't wish for any of that. I meant with certain arrangements with family members and my parents' funeral. But you are right. We should discuss everything upfront."

The queen dowager nodded with a soft smile of relief, awaiting Toury's commands, which was a strange shift as well.

"First, I don't see a point in moving everyone and everything just for distinction's sake. If it must be done, change the names of the rooms. Surely, having servants calling them differently is all that is necessary."

"That would make sense, I think," the queen dowager began. "But the king's quarters and the Queen's Room are larger and more lavish. Plus, you'd be sharing this entertaining space with Mary."

"I don't want to change quarters. Alex and I only use the first two floors of our tower, so I can't foresee needing more space. As for this room, it is large enough. I can't stand droves of people at once. And I like sharing it with Mary." She turned her attention to the princess. "I feel more confident with you by my side in company." It was true, and she didn't want to give up the quarters that had become her and Alex's home, the place she'd fallen in love with him, Fyr, and her future.

"But you need to keep up appearances," the dowager pressed.

"Alex hasn't used the King's Room either. Cobalt says they keep going to the Prince's Room," Mary told her.

"Well, if you insist, we must at least redo this room for your tastes, make it more luxurious." The dowager gestured around, caving in. "And the King's Room too."

"If that is the compromise you need to let things stay this way, then consider it a deal."

"Deal striking by the fairer sex. I'm astounded, ladies," a male voice said from the doorway.

Madge and Lucy had moved to block the intruder from entering, and the dowager's servant-bodyguard was by her charge's side. Toury could see Madge hadn't drawn her dirk, so the person wasn't a stranger to palace servants. Toury couldn't see his face, but the voice sounded pompous and arrogant.

"Henry?" Mary stood, her face animated and full of joy.

"The one and only," he said with a laugh.

"Let him enter." The dowager's gaze darted over to Toury's, wide-eyed with concern.

Toury should be the one to invite him in but shrugged to show she was not insulted with the poor woman continuing her role out of habit.

Their protectors parted for this Henry to enter. Decidedly, Toury hated the man. When arrogance rang in a greeting, it wasn't someone Toury could befriend. The fact his father had killed her parents for some ridiculous conspiracy involving Henry taking Alex's place on the throne solidified her hasty judgment. She would never trust him either.

Her stomach plummeted when she saw him. She was taken aback by his appearance, stunned as the man swaggered in and scooped up Mary in a bear hug. His wavy brown hair had hints of auburn in it, and with those sparkling Sapphirian blue eyes, a cleft in his chin, dimples, and a dazzling grin, he looked much like Alex—if Alex's face had been overdosed with cheesy manly gusto. Henry was fit with broad shoulders, but his height elongated him, making him more wiry than brawny. Women at court proclaimed he was attractive, but not Toury. He was Alex gone wrong, reminding her of Earth caricature drawings with exaggerated features. That was it: he was definitely a caricature of Alex in appearance and lofty tone.

"My baby cousin is all grown up." He twirled her around and put her down.

Toury glanced at the queen. She was smiling. Did no one else find his behavior absolutely offkey? His father was wanted for treason and murder, and he could be an accomplice. He had been missing, supposedly undercover with the rebels, but during interrogation, Craig and Aschen had never mentioned a man matching this description. They had seen many rebels, true, but no one would forget Sapphirian eyes.

Toury wanted to avoid him, but she needed to see his eyes. Necromancers were still out there. If she could get a little emotion out of him, she could see if they turned black as her enemies' had.

"Auntie," the guy almost purred. Was he for real? He pulled the dowager so hard into a hug, she yelped playfully before he let her go. She fixed her hair afterward while he whispered condolences for the king. He was an Emerald, technically, despite the fact anyone born to a Sapphirian in wedlock became a Sapphirian in name. He had fire magic—a dominant trait—but he might also have Emerald magic. Growth and peace came back to her, but there were other powers connected to it dealing with the heart, the infamous ability his father had inverted to kill her mother.

"And this..." the man stood in front of her, grinning widely, arms wide in hopes he'd scoop her up next.

Everything about him was off. She didn't want him to touch her. Her back stiffened, and she did not stand to greet him, but offered her hand to shake.

"...must be the queen." Sensing her trepidation, he put his hands back together and took up her hand in his warm ones and bowed his head. He branded her hand with a wet kiss, and she suppressed a cringe.

She couldn't place it. Most girls would say he was charming, but his greeting dripped with superficiality. Of course, the court had been absolutely saccharine, so he would've been the cream of the crop. Alex would change all of that—if he were actually here.

She took her hand away.

"They did not exaggerate your unique beauty." He flashed her a plastic smile.

"Nice to finally meet you, Lord Sapphirian." She must've sounded cool, because Mary shot her a confused glance. Toury ignored it. "Why don't you join us?" Toury motioned for him to sit. He had planned on joining them without invitation anyway, so she might as well point out she was in charge of this room and conversation.

His smile faltered slightly, and she raised her brows in challenge. This cousin, Henry, smirked in response—which at least was genuine—thanked her in a more subdued tone, and sat across from her, his eyes scrutinizing her the entire time. Mary poured her cousin tea. Toury felt safer with Madge behind her, the dowager and Mary sitting adjacently between her and Henry. She had no reason to fear him but irrationally did.

"Does my appearance displease the queen?" His tone was sarcastic, proclaiming he was fully aware most Fyrian girls found him attractive.

Toury took a sip of her tea to think over her response. Mary's quizzical gaze met her own. "I don't judge people based on the way they look, Lord Sapphirian, but on their behavior." Not exactly true. Toury could see the evil in the necromancers' eyes, so she judged on that score, but the principle was true.

"And my behavior offends you?" His gaze locked on hers in challenge. Was he egging her on or truly lost? He was an actor through and through, and she couldn't find the real him underneath to read the truth.

"Not offensive, no, but extraordinarily confusing, considering the events of this past week."

The façade fell. His smile went limp, his posture rigid, and his eyes went cold and narrowed on Toury. There was definitely emotion, but she did not see blackness in his eyes. Either he was no necromancer, or he was talented enough to hide it from her—something no necromancer she'd met could do.

"Toury," Mary chided and then covered her mouth and peered at her with bug-eyed worry. They had just agreed she shouldn't address Toury that way anymore in front of others, but Toury wasn't worried about Mary.

She broke the staring contest with Henry to reassure her friend things weren't changing that much. "Goodness, Mary, I'm not going to punish you."

"I just don't...understand what is going on," Mary managed, with some difficulty, to form a sentence.

"His father is accused of high treason—implicated in the curse that caused the late king's death, your uncle Alfred's, and the one that could've killed King Alex. Lord Emerald also murdered my parents and is wanted for all these crimes. For his son to come in here with smiles, pretending this was a friendly visit, is beyond my comprehension." She knew she was being cold and regal, which was unlike her. It must baffle Mary, since she saw this man as family, but Toury saw him as a threat.

"Since we're being so candid, my queen," he said in a quiet and subdued voice, "what kind of visit is this? Do I leave this room in shackles?"

Now it was her turn to laugh lightly, play the part to show him she was in charge. "I don't think we're there yet, Lord Sapphirian, and hopefully we will never be. Considering what is going on in this kingdom, one can never be too thorough to question everyone's loyalty—even family."

"My loyalty is to the throne." Henry said. His eyes did not waver, and his voice was firm. He seemed so genuine, but then Toury realized what he actually said.

"When who is sitting upon it?" Toury fired back.

He laughed, covering his mouth, then met her gaze. "My, my, Alex has chosen well. Where is the little whelp?" Henry surveyed the room. This was the real man under that polished courtly veneer.

Toury kept her temper in check, reminding herself this was all a game she had to play. Part of the charade was figuring out what he was up to, just as she had to with some of the courtly ladies. She processed his words. Henry was only concerned with the throne, showing no loyalty to his king by undercutting Alex as a "little whelp" while complimenting her power, insinuating Toury would rule in Alex's stead.

She wished her husband wasn't MIA. "I do hope that is a pet name left over from childhood. Our king is no whelp, and he is away on business. When he returns, you can assure him yourself of your fealty." That was enough. She wanted to get away from the man as soon as possible. As a master actor, he might see through her own performance. She rose, which surprised him. Her rising dictated everyone else do so, and they did. Being queen was so weird. "Mary, will you join me for a moment before you go down to listen to grievances?" Toury asked.

Mary, still bemused, followed.

"Women listening to grievances?" Henry's eyebrows rose.

"Henry," Mary scoffed. "There have been queens and princesses who have done so in the past. Plus, I like it."

"Maybe I'll join you." He smiled.

"Except lords are not permitted." With exceptional effort, Toury withheld the smirk trying to rise, all too happy to wipe the smile from his face. Proud of herself for remembering that particular edict, she considered thanking Henry's sister for that barb. She no longer felt Ruby's presence, but the hostility and the knowledge of that edict possibly came from the late Fyrian. Ruby hadn't trusted her brother, and wanted Toury to know that.

"Queen Dowager, Lord Sapphirian, good day." Toury left the room, Madge flanking her, Mary and Lucy trailing behind. Typically, she should be polite and give an excuse, but she didn't think Henry needed a false one.

Once they were upstairs in Toury and Alex's sitting room, Mary rounded on her. "What was that? My cousin is a Sapphirian through and through. He'd never hurt us or lay a finger on Alex. I can't believe you were so mean to him when he was being so nice." Mary crossed her arms and frowned, tapping her foot like a spoiled princess impatient for servants to fulfill her every whim.

"Nice?" Toury's mouth dropped. "You've been in this court too long. He was exceptionally fake and had no reason to come in here acting so happy." Toury tried desperately to be patient, but her irritation was overpowering.

"He was happy to see me!"

Patience: gone. "Mary, open your eyes!" Toury paced and added his crimes up on her fingers for emphasis. "His manner was completely wrong for the occasion. He was summoned after his father was just branded a traitor and murderer. He had to know it could be a bad visit or simply one to check which side he belongs to. Just pretend he isn't family for a moment, and think about it."

Mary opened her mouth to speak but stopped, and her eyes pensively stared off, just like Alex's did when puzzling something out. Her shoulders slumped. "It would be stupid to assume he's innocent, I guess. He's not...a necromancer, is he?"

Toury took a deep, calming breath. Mary had backed down, listening to Toury as she should—by rank and by rational proof. "Not that I could tell, and I did get some emotion out of him. That doesn't mean he's innocent, though. How do you know the necromancers or rebels aren't backing him to take the throne?"

"But I'm next in line."

"I'm worried about you too, Mary."

"He'd never—"

"Are you willing to bet your life on it?"

Mary wrapped her arms around herself, seemingly chilled, despite the fact Sapphirians didn't get cold easily. She bit her lip and gazed at Toury anew. "Henry is right about one thing."

"What?"

"Alex did choose his lifemate well."

The compliment was not lost on Toury, coming from Mary, who was her best friend and now sister. Toury just hoped she could live up to that reputation. Being queen felt like a new shoe that needed to be broken in; she just wasn't used to it. At times, her role was daunting and overwhelming, but part of that was due to a certain missing person.

4

A TRAP

Alex appeared in a flash. "Be ready to go in about two hours."

David beelined for the door. Alex had to get back to his men. He only stopped long enough to pass on what happened in Mineria and to continue on what he hoped was a real lead in the east.

"Forgive the king, David, he means you are off for the evening. Get some rest," Toury said.

David stopped, his gaze darting between Toury and Alex the way a child does when getting conflicting replies from parents. Toury's arms were crossed, and Alex saw the hard lines of her face, the pain in her eyes, and he knew she would turn into a dame draca if he disagreed with her. Yet she needed to know David was his servant, not hers. He loved the strength of his lifemate, but this butting of heads would get them nowhere. She had to know she did not rule him, just as he would not rule her—even though that was the way it was supposed to work. Times were changing, but Toury had to realize change must be slow to be accepted.

"Be ready in two hours' time, David, unless I otherwise notify you." Alex raised his brows at Toury, crossing his arms too.

Alex heard the door shut behind him. They were alone.

"Toury," Alex moaned, dropping his feigned anger. He ran his hands down his face, frustrated. She would be furious about what he had to say, and a fight would ensue. "Don't ever, for the love of god and goddess, directly question my command in front of my servant or anyone else. You will make me look weak, which means I'm easy to overthrow."

Her face turned red, and her arms tightened, inadvertently accentuating her bosom. She was about to explode and blast him with her white light. He crossed over to her, wanting to kiss away her anger.

The moment he touched her chin, she yanked away. "Don't touch me!" There was the explosion he had expected, verbally and physically. White light shot out of her hands uncontrollably, shattering a vase on one side of the room and the other smashing into the mantle across the room, both lightballs dissipating quickly after. Thankfully, her batting his hands away kept Alex away from her light, for those things hurt.

Alex frowned. He knew she would be mad, but to not let him hug her or kiss her?

"I'm not some booty call!" She glowered at him, frozen in a rigid stance, her fists balled up again, trying not to zap him to smithereens with her light magic.

"Right..." he stalled. What? "I don't even know what that is, my little Earthling, so you'll have to help me out."

She growled, frustrated.

He remained silent as her agitation grew. It was better to wait for her to get whatever was bothering her out, and he didn't want to risk getting hit with her light.

"It means when someone meets up with another person only to have sex, and that's it. They use them for gratification."

"We're married!" Alex protested. "You made me promise to fulfill that part of our marriage—not that I'm complaining." At least he was fulfilling the deal. There would be no lengthy separation this time.

"I didn't mean to only come back for that and leave! Two hours, then gone? You sneak away in the night without saying goodbye—last time without a note or explanation—and don't come back all day!"

Alex flopped onto her bed, frustrated. This was the last thing he needed on his plate right now. "I was needed. I didn't leave a note because I fully intended to check in and then come back to bed, I swear. And then I found out there was a possible lead, but I didn't want to risk sending a bunch of men when I could check it out quickly. Things went awry. It's a long story I'm sure you couldn't care less about right now, but I came back as soon as I could."

"Then *stay*. You have duties here. Your men can find your uncle and send word after they capture him. You can transport! I read the edicts. They can imprison him on your orders, but you have to be the judge of him and dictate his punishment. Your mother needs you, Mary needs Cobalt, and you are not here for me at all!" The last part started her tears.

Great, he'd done it again, put the kingdom before her. He thought he was fairly splitting his duties, but she was grieving and needed him more. He should've known. She was strong, but he was expecting too much of her too quickly.

Alex pulled her into his arms and held her. She tried to push him away, but it was a halfhearted attempt, so he held her fast. "I'm sorry, Toury. I'm so sorry. You're right. Please don't cry."

She pulled away, wiping her tears. "I have a list—"

"Not now, my love. In the morning." He kissed her.

"Your mother and Mary need to talk to you, and your cousin—"

He disarmed her with a deeper kiss. She became putty in his arms, and her hands weaved through his hair. His lifemate was as weak as he was when it came to their attraction for each other. As much as he couldn't get enough of her, she needed him likewise. He was foolish for not staying home with her every day, but he had worried about other duties—beyond her—consuming his time.

When he awoke the next morning—he didn't dare leave her in the middle of the night—Toury was no longer in bed. He went to sit up but couldn't move his left arm. His gaze followed his arm up to his wrist, and he saw it was bound to the post by metal.

"Did you know I can weld metal with my light powers now? On Earth, we call those handcuffs." Toury sat in a chair by the bed with a superior expression on her face.

"Toury, what is this?" His wicked mind thought of some kind of amorous game Cobalt had once spoken of, but he shook the thought from his mind. Toury was angry, clearly more so now he'd seduced his way out of dealing with other duties at home, which hadn't been his original intention. His lifemate was completely distracting. He had kissed her just to stop her angry tears, and then he just could not help himself.

"Law enforcement on Earth use them to detain criminals."

"A criminal?" She was really calling him a criminal? The comparison confounded him.

"You were going to leave again. To me, that is a crime; ergo, you're a criminal." She just stared at him in challenge, a smug smile on her lips.

It clicked. Great, he'd not only hurt her but lost her trust. Not the best start to a marriage, but he hoped she'd give him leeway to learn. "I wasn't leaving."

"I don't believe you, so just in case, I kept you trapped. I'll let you out once you listen to everything you need to take care of before you go again. First—"

"Toury, let's do this in a more civilized manner. Can I at least put some clothes on? Eat some food? I'm starving."

"First," she continued, pulling out a square of parchment.

God and goddess, she had a list written out! And it looked long. He had better just listen and let her have her fun at his expense.

"My parents' funeral pyre is today. I've gone public with it, so you will need to be there and speak at it. I could pardon them, but I thought it would mean more coming from you."

He was such a cad, triple cad. He'd forgotten about the arrangements for their funeral, forcing Toury to figure it out. He must pardon them since he married their daughter and didn't want her fealty questioned. "Toury, I'm such a—"

"Yes, you are. Second,"—she moved on, not even glancing at him—"something needs to be done about your half-brother. His presence here is grating on your mother's already frazzled nerves. Talk to him. He doesn't want much from what I can tell. Third, we're trying to have a birthday party for your sister, but you need to be here..." and on she went, making him feel like a terrible human being until she finished after ten complaints. This was worse than hearing the people's grievances. When she was finished, she finally peered up at him.

"You did excellent without me, by the way. Half of those problems already have been solved by you, but you are right. I'm supposed to be running the kingdom, and I'm making you do it. I promised partners, not you doing all my work. I wasn't here when you needed me either, and I'm sorry I wasn't. Yes, I had to go and give my orders, but I should've only been a couple hours there and the rest here." He didn't want to concede that much or let his lifemate call the shots, but she was right, and to fight her on this would be willful ignorance and not an assertion of power.

"Thank you," she said, unable to hide the surprise in her voice. She'd expected him to fight her, he supposed.

Then he heated up the metal around his wrist, catching the molten metal with his other hand as it began dropping away until he was free. He molded it into a ball as one would with clay and pulled his fire back in. The sphere cooled, and then he placed it in the hands of Toury, who was wide-eyed, her mouth agape. He got out of bed and slipped into yesterday's clothes.

"You could do that the entire time but just sat there?" she asked.

"Well, you desperately wanted me to listen."

"You said I wasn't allowed to command you last night."

"In front of servants, yes, but when we are alone, you are my queen, and I can be your lowly subject," he said as he pulled her up out of her chair and kissed her. He didn't let his mind wander too far on what that could mean on other levels, but focused on the tasks he had been casting aside. "I'll go deal with my half-brother first, then my cousin, and then I'll prepare myself for the pyre. Of course, I'll do a speech. I can't let you do that on your own."

"Thank you." Toury wound her arms around his neck.

He was concerned he would allow her to command him in everything if he let her. He hoped she'd never realize the power she held over him.

"Just so you know, I was pretty cold toward your cousin."

"Of course you were." Alex smiled. He wouldn't expect any less from her.

"And what is that supposed to mean?" she challenged.

Oh, she was a lot of work sometimes, but he'd hate life any other way. He had wanted that sass he saw in that dress shop, a woman with a spine, and she was back, despite everything she had gone through. Butting heads in a marriage was not something most Fyrians would see as a positive, but Alex needed it and desired it. He hated fighting with her, but he wanted her to always push boundaries to remind him he was human, not a god like his father and grandfather insisted they were. It was time to bring Fyr back to what it once was, and Toury was key in checking the selfishness and arrogance his father had tried to instill in him.

"I meant he's the type of man who would not at all appeal to your nature." Despite his explanation, Toury stared at him, her brow furrowed, so he elaborated, "He is full of false modesty, is popular with the ladies, and has a way with spinning words. You prefer truth, openness, nothing artful. And these honest attributes, my love, are what should be in our new court."

She seemed satisfied with that. "His behavior was deplorable. All smiles and charm when people are dead and his father is ousted for treason."

"You have every right to distrust him. His father killed your parents. But understand that it is his way of dealing with things of this nature. He tries to pretend them away. But I'm glad you were. He needs to know we question his involvement. But, my lifemate, I beg you: please, today, let me take the lead with him."

"Of course," she said demurely.

He prodded her chin up, wondering where her spark had gone.

Her gaze met his. "He called you a little whelp, so I'm going to enjoy your pissing contest. Helping you would only let him win."

Alex laughed wholeheartedly and kissed her. Funny how some of her Earth terms translated to Fyr. Little boys proving their worth by how far they could project their urine transcended realms. It must be an innately human thing to do.

"Come, lifemate of mine, the day awaits." Alex let her go so they could get ready for the long day ahead.

5
KING

Toury let Alex bathe first, while she ate her breakfast. Then they switched places. She had Madge finish readying her downstairs because trivial things, like being dressed by a servant, were now weird in front of Alex, who never remembered servants were present until things became too intimate; the lines between domesticity and intimacy had become so scrambled that pleasant greetings turned into lewd stares and comments in front of Madge. When Toury walked upstairs into their sitting room, Alex's eyes roved over her, and his mouth dropped. David chuckled at him, which pulled Alex out of his stupor. He silenced his valet with a glare.

"You..." Alex moved toward her, lost for words and needing action. His one hand pulled her waist in closer to him; his other hand toyed with the loose hair Madge had left half down per Toury's request. "...look amazing wearing that. I mean...amazing all over, but I'm not used to the circlet." His lips crashed into hers, and Toury was all too aware of their company.

She pulled away. "Hardly the time, Romeo, and I only wore it once in front of you because you left, only coming back when it was already off my head for the evening."

"Who's Romeo?" His brow wrinkled. He was cute in his insecurity.

"A hero in a play on Earth. He died for the woman he loved, due to ridiculous circumstances," Toury told him. "But he was a very charming speaker when it came to Juliet."

"Oh, I remember hearing about those plays. Some Earthling brought them here, and my ancestors got rid of them. They thought violence and killing would inspire others to do so. As if they need to read about what they innately are to act upon it."

"So book burning and blaming the arts for causing the violence is not exclusive to Earth?"

It had been a snide remark, but Alex answered her rhetorical question anyway: "No, little Earthling, unfortunately not. My father was not a patron of the arts or books, but we can be. Fancy going to a play?"

"Yes, when it is safer." She knew he would not let her be in a massive crowd in the open until the heir was born, so it was pointless to take his question seriously. Long ago—it felt that way—this place had been a beautiful prison. It was different now; she deemed it was safer within its walls than outside them, but the idea of being pregnant was daunting. It would constrict and confine her to the castle for her protection as if the idea of a child made her weaker. Stupid, but she knew the moment she started showing might be her last outing for a long time. The only way to stop that would be to stay away from Alex's bed, and that wasn't about to happen.

He changed the subject. "I like the hair loose." He ran his fingers through it.

"I thought I'd start making being comfortable a trend. You said the ladies would follow me, so I intend to take advantage of that. You just wait until I make ladies' pants fashionable."

"No," Alex moaned, covering his face. "I will be forced to execute every man who stares at you."

"Fine. Baby steps. Hair now, wardrobe later. And you need to focus," she scolded. Then she ran her hand through his hair to tame it. He needed a haircut again—according to the sphere's tastes—but she kind of prefered it growing out past his ears, since longer hair on men was more laid back than the court's strict tastes. After a couple more stolen kisses, she finally convinced him to get started with his duties.

They were told Craig was in the armory, a place Toury had never been. They walked past where the servants and soldiers' quarters were located, near the back of the castle. They passed a servant who was polishing Alex's armor, and the walls had rack after rack of all kinds of weapons. They exited the room, went down a hall, and then suddenly were momentarily blinded by sunlight. To their left were the orchards, and to their right were outdoor work stalls, connected to the castle with more weapons in various states of completion. Smiths, armorers, and bowyers were glancing up and bowing their heads at Alex and Toury. Craig was sparring with a servant in a little dirt clearing where the soldiers must train. They stopped and knelt when Alex approached.

"Ugh," Alex said. "Stop that. I changed the law for that; bowing will do."

"Sorry, Your Majesty," a man said, getting up. He was covered in soot: a blacksmith.

"Firelasher, you craved a word?" Alex said in short clipped tones, not angry, but annoyed. He was busy and must find this to be tedious. Or he was trying to intimidate.

Whatever his motive was, it was working. Craig, although older, looked frightened out of his wits. "Yes, Your Majesty." Craig got up as well.

"Come." She thought Alex would turn and walk away from them, as his father would do—show them less respect and affirm who was in charge. This Toury did not like, but she'd sworn not to intervene, not to challenge him except in private. Although that rubbed her Earthly feminism the wrong way, she understood this land needed things to shift at a slower pace and very well might take her lifetime for patriarchy to dwindle into true equality.

Instead, Alex offered her his arm and led her inside, with Craig, David, and Madge following them. Toury thought they would go to the assembly chamber, which was used for grievances, but he turned and made his way to the Prince's Room. This was an honor for someone of Craig's station. Toury was confused now, and she hated not knowing what Alex would do next. He was intimidating the guy but showing him respect. Why?

In the Prince's Room—King's Room she should start calling it—Alex deposited her on the settee and motioned for the servant to get drinks. Alex sat next to her, leaning back, his arm across the top of the settee behind her, his leg crossed with his booted foot resting on his knee. Their bodyguards stood behind them.

Craig still stood in the doorway, staring into the room in awe. Alex didn't seem to notice.

Realization dawned upon his features. "Come in. Sit," Alex commanded.

Craig walked in and obliged.

"We're here to talk about what we're going to do with you, your future."

"My future?" Craig was dumbstruck. Prior, he had told Toury easily enough exactly what he wanted, so she wondered why he couldn't freely answer Alex.

"Yes. People know about you now. You could be used as leverage if they think I'd want to save my half-brother, or you could be scooped up in the rebel cause."

Craig moaned. "I didn't want any of this. My seer mother and my aunt forced me into this, and I felt bad for the new Queen Sapphirian. I wanted to do something profoundly good."

"You have, and I thank you for that. But think of the situation from my perspective. You lived in Mineria—the former hotbed of rebels—and you managed to save the queen and get her back to safety. It is suspicious."

34

Alex leaned forward, attempting to appear more intimidating. She wondered if all his delegating moves were done consciously or if the court had ingrained itself in him. The latter concerned her. She would not have children forced to hide their emotions and fake their actions.

"Why would I want to harm you or the monarchy? I have no interest in ruling." Craig answered and then seemed lost about what to say next.

Alex patiently waited for more. Toury wanted to say something to fill the silence or to at least end the tension being drawn out, but she knew Alex would get upset again about her not staying in her place in this moment. She swallowed the rage at such a thought and rationalized Alex needed this. He had to go through this tête-à-tête with his half-brother to be able to trust him. No matter what she said or did, that didn't matter. Alex and Craig had to work this out themselves. Toury was there as an observer.

Craig put his hands up in confusion, his eyes darting wildly in thought. "I wouldn't know how to rule at all. I know how the world works and have no qualms against my—our—father. He gave my mother money to raise me. What ruined her life were lesser men who jilted her with my siblings, ripped apart her business, and made her destitute. The man who started all that was Lord Citrine. I thank you for taking care of that."

"So, you have no interest in court life?" Alex pressed.

"None. I'm afraid to go anywhere near the queen dowager. I've been waiting for her to order my execution. I shouldn't be here, but the queen told me to stay until you decided."

"Then what is it you want?"

"What do you mean?" Craig's mouth was agog, the shock of Alex's possible kindness too much for him to believe.

"Queen Sapphirian told me you had some ideas of what we should do with you," Alex prompted him.

"I...I—"

"Relax, Firelasher. We're negotiating so you stay loyal to your blood. And I would not have a relative of mine—even baseborn—living in the slums. My father never told us about you."

Toury wondered if there were more relatives Alex didn't know about from his father, but remembered the queen dowager said the curse had taken a toll on the king's fertility and how they had been lucky to get Mary. Toury doubted there would be many others, if any.

"I want the name. I don't like being marked as a baseborn."

Alex sighed, and Toury knew it was a sign he'd deny him. "I cannot. You cannot be a Sapphirian without the eye color foremost. I believe you are my brother, and in some cases, it isn't unheard of for the eye color to not come through, but I cannot change the edicts. Plus, you were born out of wedlock; even if I reinstate you, the eye color is everything."

Oh, Toury detested the edicts. It wasn't fair. She wanted to speak, beg Alex to do something. Knowing her well, he grabbed up her hand and squeezed it. She understood to wait, to not say anything. It irked her, but she had agreed. Most business in the King's Room did not include women, and her being there was a step in the right direction. Next time, she was going to demand to know the business beforehand so she would discuss it with him in private and not react after *their* decision was made.

Toury took a deep breath. She'd almost spoken up when she was in the wrong. To go against the edicts would nullify the monarchy, giving more reasons for the rebels to attack a king who wouldn't be curbed by any law. Some of the edicts were silly or unfair, but some were good for the people and served to protect.

"I understand." Craig's shoulders slumped, and he stared at his hands.

"However, I do have a few smaller former necromancer estates left."

"But only lords can own estates." Craig's brow wrinkling reminded her of a confused Alex.

"I know." Alex took a sip of his drink to let it sink in. He was making Craig a nobleman; only Craig was still confused. "Baron Firelasher sound good to you?"

Craig's mouth dropped. Then he closed it and stared at the floor. Alex gave him time to process it.

"As much as I appreciate the offer, I'm no baron, and no one makes a cunning folk a baron."

"I assure you it is legal. It usually is only done when a lord's lifemate is barren and there is no sibling, nephew, or niece to inherit, but there's no edict limiting a monarch from raising cunning folk to noblemen. Speaking of the Citrines, they had been cunning folk until a hundred years ago. They simply took on the father's stone name, but as I already said, without the eye color, I have to improvise. You'll be the first of your kind." He leaned back into the settee, more at ease.

Toury sipped her drink and coughed. Wow, it was strong. She guessed the men didn't water it down much during business.

Craig was lost in his thoughts.

Alex continued. "We can give you a small estate without much land or tenants to deal with. Your siblings and mother could live there, or the income from it could put them in a house, set your mother up in business again, so she can sustain herself without your help. Seers can make a fortune if they know the right people. I'm sure if we had a reading done by her, she'd be set for life." Although Alex mentioned it, he seemed tense when talking about the woman. Was he annoyed at a woman his father had been with before his mother?

Craig chewed his lip. His dreams were coming true, but he was still worried about something. "I had my heart set on becoming a soldier."

Alex frowned. "Barons usually would start high-ranked, but we can't do that. Number one, I'm still learning to trust you. After this past year, I cannot trust anyone but a handful of people, so you'll lead no army. Second, I just saw you with a sword. You will either not be respected or get yourself killed. You can train to be in the regular militia and earn your way up."

"I wouldn't have it any other way, Your Majesty." And for the first time since he had walked into the room, Craig smiled and picked up the beverage he was probably too nervous to have drunk prior.

"I'll decide on a property and sign the documents, but for now, collect your family and put them up in an inn." Alex took out his coin pouch and took out three silver Sapphirians, the ones embedded with emeralds to up their value. Toury measured it against the costs and realized this would put them up for ages and was more than Craig had ever seen in his life.

"This is too much."

"I was told you had an aunt who helped Toury as well?"

"Misty," Toury confirmed.

"Help her and her family in whatever way they need as well with this money."

Toury knew Craig could not deny that. Help his siblings and cousins as well as the women who raised him? She was sure he'd agree to do anything.

"After you settle them into their new home, report back for duty," Alex said.

Craig finished his drink, noting it was a dismissal. Then he got up, bowed, and offered Alex his hand. Alex stared at his hand for a moment, then shook it. Craig bowed to her too and then left them alone.

"That was wonderfully done," Toury commented once she knew Craig was out of hearing range.

"See, overbearing lifemate of mine, I *can* perform my duties fairly and all by myself." He smiled to show he was teasing, but she still wanted to smack him.

"I cannot argue with that," she allowed. "But when we're alone later, I still might smack you for gloating about it."

"You are murder, you are," he grumbled, but he pulled her to him and kissed her not so innocently, belying his comment completely. There were still three servants present, and her face heated. She would never get used to ignoring the fact they were there like the rest of the royal family had out of a lifetime of conditioning.

When she saw his admiration for her in his eyes, she regretted ending the kiss and pushing him gently away. She knew he loved her, but to see it and acknowledge it was staggering. The neglected and unloved girl from Earth had found love finally. And she was never letting it go.

6
A WRANGLE

Alex hoped this feeling would wear off. It was a heady combination of love and lust rendering him senseless. Oh, he never would ever want to stop loving his lifemate, but the lust compounded the issue. Just one kiss, and all thoughts—except those of being with her, alone, behind bedroom doors—left his brain. He needed to focus on more important things.

He had to talk to Henry next. Had to see how things were between them, and Alex needed to ask him to leave the army, to abandon the spy business Lord Emerald and he had done for Alex's father, and limit him to the castle or his estate only. It felt very much like sending a child to their room when they did wrong even if they denied doing so. And Henry being older than him had always intimidated Alex a little.

As he heard the servant approaching with Henry, Alex grew a bit nervous. He whispered to his lifemate, "Stay strong. I need you. Now pretend I said something funny, and laugh."

"It *is* funny, and I'm so going to say I told you so later," she whispered back. This made him laugh since she already said it, which made her laugh, and they were genuinely laughing as Henry crossed the threshold.

God and goddess, he loved her, so much so that it took Henry clearing his throat to make Alex realize he had been lost in Toury's eyes. As soon as Alex noted the smirk on his cousin's face, all familial nostalgia left him. Toury was right. Henry should be worried right now, groveling, distressed about his father, but his expression was mocking Alex and Toury's relationship. He would treat this Henry separate from the hero-image he'd had of him growing up. Henry had changed. He looked tired, eyes slightly sunken in—stressed or overtaxed.

Henry bowed so slightly, it was merely a nod of the head. "It appears to be a love match after all. I should've known better than to believe rumors about your friend and the queen." The smirk never left. He wasn't even trying to be civil. He wanted Alex to react and to do or say things out of anger; otherwise, he wouldn't mention the time Cobalt had abused his powers to kiss Toury.

What was Henry up to? Was he seeking banishment for some other plan? Alex studied him, not telling him to sit.

Being the hostess, as they had planned, Toury motioned for drinks. God and goddess, he hadn't thought about how she was not used to that much firewhiskey, but one didn't order tea in the King's Room, and women usually weren't invited. The drink might help her relax, and him. It was the day of her parents' pyre, and he needed to say some words. He'd wing it like his speech after he had almost been killed; surprisingly, he had done well that way, his emotions guiding him to say emboldened words that showed strength, power, and passion.

"Sit." Alex didn't let any emotion show. "And yes, you should know better than to believe tavern gossip."

Henry sat and sighed a breath, running his hand down his face. Here was the man he expected, worn out by his spying, lying, and his father's crimes. "Shall we skip the pleasantries and get on with it?" Henry's eyes were cold, dead. The man Alex had known to be his cousin was gone.

Alex wanted to get this over with too, but Henry was trying to overpower him and lead the conversation. "As much as I'd love to quickly get on with preparing the funeral pyre for the people your father murdered..."

Toury twitched next to him, and Alex regretted the shock factor, but he had to get the upper hand over his cousin. Henry, however, didn't move a muscle. He hadn't been expecting Alex to be so bold, so when the stoic Henry feigned surprise, it was a beat too late to be believable.

How had Alex missed this growing up? True, he hadn't seen Henry much in the last four years—last year not at all—but still, Cobalt had warned him. Alex had been a naive boy, and his cousin had been expecting a naive man. "Civility is best. How is your mother fairing?"

The question set something off in Henry. His fists tightened, his posture went rigid, and his eyes slightly widened. "Is that a threat?"

Alex had no idea how to respond. He was being civil.

"And why would that be a threat, Lord Sapphirian?" Toury asked, filling the silence. She said it in a calm, befuddled tone, but Alex knew her too well. She was faking. Then his mind caught up to his clever lifemate's. Henry's mother was involved with the curses. Of course Henry thought Alex would punish his mother. This was almost a confession of knowledge of his mother's crimes. Toury's father had been blamed because one could inverse one's power—light could evoke dark—but the same went for fire. And Toury's mother had named his uncle and aunt, Henry's parents, but did Henry know this? If so, how?

"His Majesty doesn't sound very civil." Henry was floundering.

"It was you—was it not?—who told me I was too serious growing up. I remember it repeatedly. I'm simply being serious. Is my aunt well?" Alex would leave him on edge, play into this game of feigned ignorance his lifemate had started.

"She is fine," Henry said.

"Good."

The conversation lagged until Toury picked it up, asking about his health and estate. "Fine" were the responses. Henry took turns looking back and forth between Alex and Toury like a caged and wounded animal who was unable to flee. Good.

Alex cut to it. "Down to business. I need your information. You left your father's company while posing as a rebel because...?"

"I had a lead to get into the unit closest to their leader—"

"The commander," Alex interjected.

Henry froze. "Yes, you've heard of him?" Henry was fishing for information, probably lying right now. Because Alex was beginning to think his uncle was said commander.

Alex nodded and simply motioned for him to continue.

"What do you know of him so far?" Henry asked.

"I thought it was the king who asks the questions," Toury said, starting to show signs her patience was wearing thin.

"Funny, because to me it seems as if the queen is running the show here. You let yourself get sucked in by a girl, Alex? There are plenty of them who'll show you a good time, but let me guess: she was your first, so she is leading you by a leash now. How very noble of you to stay pure for your lifemate." Henry gave Alex a knowing smile as his eyes darted to Toury and lingered there.

God and goddess, he was angry at those mocking and condescending comments. Alex pressed his fiery rage down, something much easier to do without the curse feeding off that emotion. He needed Toury to be quiet, because even the small seemingly innocuous comment had given Henry a weapon.

Alex glanced toward Toury, who was turning red with rage, her fists clenched, and a furious outburst might ensue. "Toury," Alex warned. "I required you here as a witness. If you cannot handle it, you may leave." He chose his words carefully as to not set her off, while showing Henry he was utterly wrong.

Alex and Toury exchanged a glance, and she took a deep breath, calming herself. She stared down at her hands, and Alex knew she wouldn't speak again. Even through her rage, she realized what she had done. "Sorry, Your Majesty," she used his title instead of name to show her inferiority, something he knew she must despise as much as he hated hearing it from her lips. Despite her candid and honest manner, she was becoming an outstanding politician.

Henry again had a lost expression, as if there were sand shifting beneath his feet.

"Henry, I have barely seen you in the last four years. I was fourteen when you married and moved to Ludford. I don't wish to speak about my conquests in front of my lifemate, and frankly, I don't need to list them to prove anything. I am a king who chose a partner to help me. It doesn't make me inferior or less of a man. It makes me smart."

Henry said nothing. Toury stayed quiet.

Alex sipped his drink. "You will write up an official report and present it to me tomorrow about everything you know concerning the rebels. You will attend the funeral today and present solidarity of the family and your separation from your father. You may even speak a few words at the wake dinner about your allegiance to me and the breakaway from your father if you want to remain here and protected. Show them you are a Sapphirian, not an Emerald."

"You're letting me stay?" Henry's brows rose.

Toury went rigid next to Alex and took a big swig of Firewhiskey. He had wanted to send his cousin away, but this conversation changed everything. He was too dangerous not to watch.

"Do you need to leave for something?" Alex challenged.

"Am I staying as prisoner or guest?"

"Guest...for now. Honestly, cousin, there's only one room in this house I could keep you prisoner in, and I'm giving you a choice here. No matter what your father's plans were or if you knew of them, you can make the right choice now."

Henry paled in reference to the room they had locked his mother in. The walls were lined with alumina bricks, which were fire resistant. And the Sapphirian power didn't work in there. Alex's aunt, so he'd heard, had been moved to Fort Emerald once a similar room was built. She had gone mad overnight and then tried to burn the castle down twice right after the curse situation. Things were coming together. Alex knew the room would affect Henry emotionally. It was a threat, and it worked.

Henry met Alex's gaze, and there was nothing there—no anger, resentment, or fright, but blank. "As you wish, Your Majesty."

"That is all." Alex took up Toury's hand and transported them to his room. He envisioned David's concern as he would race through the castle to catch up to him. David despised being left behind. Oh, Madge would be livid too, he was sure.

Toury examined their whereabouts and then flopped inelegantly onto the settee. "I told you I didn't want him here."

"I know, but Toury, think about what will happen if I let him go."

"Even if he can endanger me? Mary?"

"He can transport, Toury. There would be no way of stopping him from coming and going. If I send him away and he is involved in this, I am letting them plan and gain power over me. If I make him stay here—"

"Keep your friends close and your enemies closer."

Alex mulled over her words. "Perfectly understood, my love."

"It's a saying on Earth. I understand, but I don't like it."

He knelt before her and took her hands in his, kissing them. "I promise you this: I'm staying. I will leave only when my uncle is captured. I will bring Cobalt back, who will stick to Mary's side, and you and I will do everything together. It's time you understood all the politics anyway. You and I do not part, as you wished."

She sighed in relief.

How had he overlooked how much she needed him? She was the strongest woman he knew, but god and goddess, if he needed her, then she needed him likewise. He needed to be stronger with her and for her, which turned his thoughts to the logistics of protecting them. "In the meantime, I'm thinking of opening our upstairs bedrooms to have Madge and David stay in here with us. Across the hall does not protect us from a transporting Sapphirian. Which makes me think. I'll move Cobalt out of Mary's quarters; he's one of the best trackers of whereabouts and moods, so he can detect Henry's comings and goings. I'll lodge Cobalt right next to Henry as a sort of guard far away from all of us. For Mary, we can move my mother and your aunt in with her. Your uncle and brother should be of no concern to my cousin, but we can lodge them on this side of the castle."

She smoothed her hands down his shoulders, telling him she was pleased with his plans, but it momentarily distracted him.

He shook his head to focus, trying not to get lost in those slate-gray eyes. "Keep those we trust by our sides, and there is safety in numbers. I implicitly trust Cobalt's elder brother and father and will keep them here running security as well. Henry will be a prisoner with a larger cell, technically, and he knows it." Alex inadvertently thought of the time Toury had called the palace a gilded cage. Although he was sure she no longer saw it that way, Henry now would feel its sting.

"And if he transports away and doesn't come back?" Toury asked.

Alex hadn't thought about that, because it would mean Henry was waging war, choosing his father's side. "I don't think he will, but it would be just the same as letting him go now. I'll have him watched. Luckily, there's the perfect room in this castle for spying, and no one knows about it but me. My father left it in a letter he had locked in his study. You know him, lots of instructions to order me around posthumously."

Toury yanked his hands, making him fall against her, and she hugged his head to her abdomen and leaned down to kiss the top of it. He gazed up at her to see her eyes swimming with tears. She was going through a lot, but her empathy would be the breaking of her one day. She loved everyone so much. Alex leaned up and claimed her lips.

Then David and Madge burst in, huffing and puffing from the effort to catch up. He reluctantly pulled away from Toury and stood quickly to issue all the orders he had just gone over with Toury. He wanted to kiss her more, hold her, make her feel safe, and make her smile. But things needed to be done, he knew, and immediately. And in the back of his mind, he knew at night he could steal as many kisses as he wanted because they would not part and would never sleep separately again.

7
PLANS

Toury wanted to scream. If they walked through every scenario of impending doom one more time, she was going to lose it. Wasn't three walk-throughs of six scenarios enough? She didn't want to think about emergency plans for if the castle were invaded. All the memories of necromancers and rebels getting in and taking her resurfaced. Yes, they needed better security and plans, but she was reluctant to think about it ever happening again. Couldn't they do it in meetings without her and simply brief her later?

And to do this the day after her parents' funeral pyre was heartless. It wasn't Alex's idea but Cobalt's. Alex was all kindness. He had been so strong for her yesterday. She had been numb; it had been surreal, and she wondered if her sister had been out there in the small crowd that came out of respect. There had been more guards actually, because of the concern over a rebel presence. She wondered what the rebels thought when Alex read out the pardons. He was always so eloquent and made her parents sound loyal to him in the end, realizing he would forge a new age of progression and how there was no cause left. Not that she really had taken in his words properly at the time. He'd used her parents to undermine the rebel cause, but in turn, he was allowing them to be remembered with dignity. She knew this was some kind of reparation he'd concocted for all the evils his family had done to them through no fault of his own.

Something along the lines of "their greatest legacy and accomplishment was the queen" had brought tears to her eyes. As soon as Alex's fire had begun to consume them, her little brother started bawling, and she held him, losing her control too. He cried over losing the only parents he had ever known, while she cried over what was and could never be. She had no parents, no real ones ever in her life, the kind who loved and sacrificed things for their children.

During the wake meal, she had been in a daze, as well as that night. Alex had held her silently as they both fought to try to sleep after such a busy and emotional day. Sleep had eventually come...

"Enough!" Toury didn't realize she had said it aloud until every head whipped in her direction—Mary, Alex, Cobalt, the dowager, and Aunt Edwina. She was lost in thoughts of yesterday and annoyed about being bothered with this safety drill today. No one said a word.

"Let's adjourn for today. Talk about this after supper this evening," Alex said.

"I would feel better if we actually attempted a drill after supper, Your Majesties," Cobalt insisted.

Toury was about to burst. "What's the point?"

"My queen, with all due respect, if we're prepared, we can stop them," Cobalt spoke down to her as one would a child. She wanted to punch him in the face.

"She knows that, Cobalt," Alex snapped before she could. Alex met her gaze in understanding. He knew she was overwrought, and Cobalt was an unsympathetic cad. "What were you saying, my...queen?" Alex had almost slipped up and called her "love" in front of others. She would laugh at the blush on his cheeks if the conversation weren't so serious and her mood were better.

"What's the point when the person who's the largest threat cannot be controlled? He can get to any of us at any time."

"Not this again." Mary rolled her eyes. "Henry is—"

"A threat, Mary. Anyone who can gain power in Fyr is a threat," Cobalt cut in.

"Just because you don't like him—"

"Mary." Alex held up his hand as a shut-up order. "You must think with your head. He could be a danger."

"Yeah, apparently *so* dangerous, you stole my engagee from me," Mary cattily muttered.

Toury wanted to yell at her but knew Mary's attitude was really doubled in crankiness because her birthday party would be limited due to safety concerns, and Alex had made Cobalt move out of Mary's quarters. She pretended none of it bothered her, and Toury knew deep down, the shrunken guestlist didn't truly matter; when it had to turn from all nobles in the land to just her closest friends, she'd selected Toury's waiting maids and a couple of their younger sisters. Toury suspected Mary's lack of friends was the real problem, and it was due to Mary being so sheltered and not making an effort to befriend anyone, particularly at school. Cobalt and Toury were all Mary had, and they were both busy and living away from her now.

Properly chastised by her brother and king, Mary sulked, crossing her arms, scoffing. Toury should talk to her, but what could she say? Anything would make Mary more upset.

"There's no way to escape him. There's no point in discussing anything. Until you cave in and lock him up in that alumina room, I refuse to bother with drills and plans." With that, Toury got up and stormed toward the door, Madge opening it for her, anticipating her mood and retreat.

Mary gasped, offended. "We're *not* locking him up."

Great. Toury just pissed her off more, but she couldn't regret it. Mary had to get this innocent image of Henry out of her mind.

"She has a point," Alex said. "Who wouldn't go after her to get to me? They have already tried twice. They know it will work, that I would do anything to get her back. Think about it. Who wouldn't go after Cobalt to get to you, Mary?"

Toury could hear no more as she was out of earshot, walking briskly through the castle toward their quarters. It was the only place she felt safe, even though she was loath to admit she wasn't safe anywhere. Even her protective shadow Madge wasn't enough comfort. Madge had failed before, not from a lack of abilities but because these enemies were tricky, tenacious, strong, and everywhere—even among them. It was like the necromancer nonsense all over again.

Once they were in her quarters, she asked Madge to bar the door. It made Toury feel falsely safe. Flames burst in front of her, and Toury pulled her dagger out of the pocket Madge had sewn in for that very purpose. She held it up toward the flames. Madge was at the ready behind the figure with her dirk unsheathed.

"God and Goddess!" Alex gasped and staggered back away from Toury's blade, which had been mere inches from his face. He backed into David, who had used his dirk to block Madge's. Shocked at the noise of weapons behind him, Alex ducked out sideways, staring at them all in shock. Realization spread across his face. "You thought I was him."

Toury didn't respond.

"Your Majesty, we must prepare for everything," Madge broke the silence. She and David sheathed their weapons and backed away against the wall as shadows in the room, present and protectively looming.

Alex glanced at the barred door, then Toury, his brow crinkling in puzzlement. She let him collect whatever thoughts he was having trouble formulating into words by hastily sheathing her dagger and putting it away in her pocket. This skirt was so confining. She would do something drastic that would make her feel safer and able to fight back, to run, to get away. She would make her own superficial clothing plan to also do something rather than simply wait for an attack.

"I see," Alex mused.

"See what?"

"He could simply transport in here, but Toury, any impediment to keep him out would prevent me using any of my power. If I could lock him up, I would, just so you didn't have to live in fear, but..." His eyes darted over to the bookshelf.

"The freakin' edicts!" Toury threw herself on the settee in a very unladylike manner. "I want to burn that book."

"Technically, that's treason, and it can't burn so..."

"Not a time to joke," she chastised.

"There is an option to make you safer, but neither of us will like it." He came over to her and pulled her into his arms, his eyes dancing across her face as they always did, unable to pick a feature he adored most. She was sure her eyes did the same until they locked on his. They were full of sadness.

"No." She knew what he would suggest.

"If you were in the alumina room, it would block out fire magic as well; then he could never harm you."

"Locking me up?" she challenged. Henry was the problem not her. He should be the one imprisoned.

"It wouldn't be locked. You could come and go as you please."

"And you couldn't be there with me, or if you were, you'd be powerless?" She was trying to understand this irrational thinking. Why would Alex ever want to do such a thing, even if it meant her safety?

He nodded, frowning. He hated the idea, but still he had dared to say it. How could he suggest such a thing?

"We don't part. This wasn't your idea. Cobalt's?"

"Of course. Toury, I can't be away from you for a moment. I'm stuck here. What can I do aside from protectors in here and our families clustered together? I need Henry to do something—even trivial—to lock him up, as an excuse. I've got nothing. He's blameless."

"He's not. He's a snake." Toury started thinking of things that might set Henry off. He didn't seem to prefer strong women, yet Toury acting out could weaken Alex in Henry's eyes. Toury laughed aloud at her new idea.

Alex cocked his head, perplexed, his arms still loosely holding her. "What?"

"Nothing. Just an idea."

"Dare I ask?" He let her go.

"No. It's a secret."

"I'm sure I can coax it out of you tonight," he said suggestively.

"Maybe I'll let you." She knew she'd given him whiplash with such a forward comment, but she didn't want to spoil her great idea or have him try to shoot it down. He was so easy to distract. She sauntered away to his bedroom and stopped in the doorway, leaning on the frame, hand on hip.

He was standing there staring at her, his eyes drinking up the sight of her. He muttered to their servants they were dismissed. David and Madge awkwardly hurried upstairs to their new quarters, close by to protect if needed.

Alex met her gaze, an intense heat in his eyes. He went up in flames, and he crashed into her, his arms wrapping around her, his lips urgently on hers. Then that odd pressing sensation squeezed her, and she was falling, landing on a soft bed. Unable to even wait a moment to cross the room on foot, he had transported to collect her and then again to the bed. He had landed on top of her but pulled back and propped himself up on his elbows. "Toury, I love you so much."

Her heart leaped with joy each time she heard it. "I love you too."

Alex beamed; his happiness was so rare with all this stress that it made her realize she needed to say it more often. She would stop living in fear, and she would fight that horrid cousin in parlors, through ladies and rumors. She would oust the traitor in him and force him to make a move. Anything was better than waiting like a sitting duck.

They kissed madly until Alex pulled away with that sigh. Having learned how to read him, it was a reluctant duty-calls sigh.

"You have to go."

"Oh, but we'll continue this later, my love. I'll be back as soon as I can get away to bring you down to supper." Then he was gone in a ball of fire.

Alex must've collected his servant, for Madge came down instantly.

"Madge, could you bring me paper and a quill. I will summon my friends. Henry accused me of wearing the pants in this relationship. So be it, I will."

8

A SHOW

Alex wanted to be anywhere but here, listening to spoiled nobles' grievances, but his sister had done so much in his absence and during his busy schedule that she deserved a break for her birthday. His mind was still behind in bed with Toury, waking with his arms around her and talking about far-off future plans when things would hopefully be peaceful. Two weeks of her daily morning optimism bolstered him, and her realism made him acknowledge there was a lot of work to do before they could be free from enemies. He knew he couldn't live without her, and yet part of him regretted pulling her into this mess he'd inherited.

A servant opened the door and handed a note to David. Thank the god and goddess! No matter what it said, he would say he had to leave. He had stopped listening to the noble who was disputing a half acre of useless land the cunning folk wanted to build on since it was part of a former necromancer's land Alex had made public to buy. The snob was insistent the "slums" must be far away enough that "he would not see the filth from his windows while dining." Alex knew not how people got such airs when he himself didn't act as such, even as the highest noble in the land.

David handed him the welcome distraction. Alex unfurled the missive stamped with the wax seal of Toury's emblem—fire, circlet, and lines representing light. He suppressed a smile and pretended it was serious.

> *Lifemate of mine,*
>
> *Your presence is demanded in the Sapphirian tea room immediately upon receiving this missive. Failure to comply will result in the queen gracing her own bed instead of yours until further notice. Come in haste, and stop listening to spoiled brats complain about their "poor" luck in life.*
>
> > *With very conditional love at the moment,*
> > *Lifemate of yours*
>
> *PS Keep a brave face for your sister's sake. It's her birthday after all.*

Alex failed to withhold his smile. She was adorably witty and made him laugh in the times he needed it most. He had always been called grave and serious, and she lifted his mood. "Brave face" was a bit alarming, though. He knew there was a dinner and ball planned for later, but Toury was always full of surprises.

"I must go," he simply told Lord Serpentine.

"Go?" The man was flabbergasted. "What of the land lying next to mine?"

Alex stood and flippantly shooed the man with his hand, eager to leave. "The land is public domain. There is nothing you can do. I suggest building a wall if folks living in quaint cottages is so displeasing for your sensitive digestion. But please, do not call the lovely houses they will build slums merely because they are smaller than yours. You're dismissed."

And with that, Alex vanished into a ball of fire—David in tow—appearing where his tenacious lifemate commanded. He entered the serpent's den. He was surrounded by half a dozen girls, who were giggling messes when he arrived. He retreated to the back of the room, where Cobalt stood equally uncomfortable.

"I'm glad to see you. Mary tricked me into coming here, and now I'm trapped."

"What's going on?" Alex asked.

"He's here!" his mother singsonged to a large folding screen that hadn't been there before today.

He gave his mother a quizzical glance, but she was all smiles, clapping her hands, full of youthful jubilance he hadn't seen from his mother in...ever. The hard lines in her face and brow were gone for once, along with the tension in her shoulders; one would say she was almost...slouching in relaxation. Alex hated how awful her life must've been with his father and full of guilt for not fully noticing her suffering until the last couple years, more so when Toury entered his life.

"Your Majesty, I present the latest fashion to sweep Fyr. Women's trousers!" Alex heard his lifemate's voice call out like a host at a ceremony or play.

"God and goddess, tell me she didn't really do this." Alex moaned. He rubbed his hand down his face, his mind whirling with the implications this could make. Would it be a good progression? Show he was committed to change? Or would it be bad? Show he was weak and his lifemate held the power?

Cobalt slapped him on the back. "You wanted change. You're getting it."

He gave Cobalt a glare. "Mary's going to be wearing them too, you know."

Cobalt's smile slipped into a scowl.

"And it is her birthday, so if you say anything—"

"I'll be dead," he said, followed by the telltale sigh of giving in. The positivity his friend exuded due to his magic was nonexistent. Cobalt was agitated. "I once made fun of you for falling in love, but I was right in that it makes us brainless."

"There is so much more good than bad, my friend, you'll see."

"Say that to me again when your lifemate comes out here wearing your trousers."

Alex had no retort for that. It was his very fear. Would people mock him and say she was the leader? He could not afford for Henry to see him as weak.

His focus was directed to observing the first girl who walked out: Toury's bold friend, Lady Deanna Tiffany. Overly confident, she strutted across the room to the queen dowager, who covered her mouth but then clapped her hands, smiling.

"I didn't even notice at first, so subtle," his mother said.

That's when Alex noted the skirt the girl wore was split in the middle, yet the material was so loose and baggy, it hung like a dress. One might not even notice, and it was the perfect subtle change toward trousers Toury had promised. The lady parading in them gave Alex a couple ineffective seductive glances as she pranced. The leveled glare he returned wiped off her little grin.

"Palazzo pants," Toury called out from behind her screen.

What an odd name for them, so it must be an Earth term.

The next girl came out: Lady Delphine Opal, one of many daughters of Baron Opal. She came out in skin-tight leggings of some sort, the same kind as the olden days a hundred or so years ago when men wore hose. But she had on a dress of sorts or—he didn't know what to call it—but much like a tunic that had an upper corset, or a very short dress. It modestly covered areas on a woman that should remain hidden, and yet it flattered her more than a poufy dress would; it was slimming for the heavyset girl. She blushed under his and Cobalt's gazes.

"Leggings and a knee-length princess-cut dress," Toury supplied.

Princess-cut dress was a strange Earth name as well. He guessed only made for princesses? What a strange sphere it must be to make clothes for a role and not for everyone.

"Not so bad," Cobalt mused. "Practical. I can imagine riding horses, sparring, and exercise would be much easier for them."

Alex didn't point out that women—aside from the ones in this castle—didn't normally spar with weapons. Cobalt was right in that it was a change but still modest. Alex was on edge. He knew his lifemate well; there was something up Toury's sleeve. She'd push past some boundary. After all, she had her secretive "plan."

"Will some men see this as an attempt to usurp their control in the home?" he asked Cobalt as a girl came out in baggy pants that gathered at the ankle. She wore a dress that split and was missing the front; again, Alex noted, good for riding a horse astride. That was something he would prefer Toury wear after that accident falling from her horse in the orchard, something that only occured because she had to ride sidesaddle.

"The old sad sort, yes. Young men, however..." Cobalt trailed off, allowing Alex to realize the perk men would get from seeing women's legs, even clad.

He thought of Toury in her boy's trousers, her legs bare, when she was sparring with Madge. This was a terrible idea. He wanted no one to see the outline of his lifemate's legs.

Girl after girl came out with varying loose pants of different material, some billowy, some tight, but Toury had been careful to keep them modest. Then Mary came out, strutting in what seemed to be men's trousers, neither loose nor tight, but the same width all the way down. Instead of a dress, she wore something that appeared to be a peplum top, like a doublet where it tapered in at her waist and flowed out before it cut off. Not bad, but when he glanced at Cobalt's expression, he grew tense. It must not have left enough up to the imagination, because his friend was undressing his sister with his eyes.

Alex gave him an elbow to the stomach, a little harder than he'd intended, for Cobalt doubled over, holding his side, before righting himself, earning Alex a glare from Mary and him. Of course she'd seek the wrong kind of attention from Cobalt. In Alex's estimation, Cobalt needed to prove himself steadfast, and Mary was much too young to marry. She was only turning sixteen, after all. Alex just realized another bonus in tearing Cobalt away from his sister's rooms: less private time together meant less time for his friend to take advantage of his sister.

Then Toury came out. The air left his lungs as he drank her in. From the circlet upon her head, half lost in her wild tresses, to the hair falling onto her shoulders in her new style, she was beauty itself. His eyes moved down her body to see her top was tight, so she was still wearing a corset that flattered her curves and heightened her bosom. She wore fitted sleeves down her arms that went to the wrist, and of course, it was purple, complimenting her skin and making her gray eyes appear to be a tad purple.

When he roved his eyes down farther, he saw it cinched at her waist with a sash tied into a loose bow, with a gray skirt of gauzy material that flowed behind her as she walked. It didn't wrap around her front as it should, but split open in subtle ruffles, exposing her legs clad in the gray fabric. It looked so soft, he wanted to run his hands up from ankle all the way up to the top of her legs. And when she moved, he could see up to her...

"What do you think?" She posed, hand on hip, raising her brows at him.

He was speechless. Alex's mind hardly found words to form bawdy thoughts of her, let alone explain what he thought about her garment. He rushed to her and tugged the material closed in the front. "Toury, everyone can see up to your...your crevice."

Hurt flickered in Toury's eyes, but then she bit her lip trying not to laugh. He could see the suppressed mirth in her eyes.

Mary started laughing hard, and everyone followed in suit.

Toury covered her mouth, trying to hide her laughter, but gave up instantly. "My...my...what?" She guffawed in an unladylike fashion and then pulled herself together.

Then her gaze met his. He backed up a step to transport out of there, being a coward, feeling his face flush with embarrassment. *Don't go*, her eyes pleaded.

He was annoyed, embarrassed, angry even. "Look! Everyone will see what is mine. Some things are better left private, Toury."

Her laughter vanished. "*Yours?*"

The giggling around them stopped. A fight in front of everyone was about to ensue. He had no choice but to show her in equal terms how he felt.

"And all of me belongs to you, Toury. How would you feel?" He started to unbutton his doublet.

"What are you doing?" She scanned the people in the room, worried about their reactions.

54

The girls were getting giggly and whispering. The outgoing flirt was making whistling noises. Toury gave her a pert expression, but that didn't stop the lady.

"Yes, what *are* you doing?" A pompous voice he recognized said in the doorway.

Toury went rigid but scooped up a shawl that had been lying about and wrapped it around her shoulders, pretending to cover up a chill.

Alex couldn't stop making an example of her now. Knowing Henry well, he had been listening and watching before he entered and spoke up. Henry would run with the idea of Toury being the ruler of him, the ruler of Fyr. Henry could spread that, while using Toury's parents against them. All could be ruined if Toury's fashion party went any more awry. Alex did what he must and unbuttoned the rest of his doublet and devested it.

Toury's friends turned into silly messes of blushing and laughter as he stood there in his linen shirt, his neck exposed. Toury's eyes drank him up, and she rolled her eyes at her friends. Then she met his gaze in understanding. He could see tension in her face, not wanting to admit the reaction from her friends when he was on display made her uncomfortable, but then she smiled mischievously.

Oh, god and goddess help him with her: what was she up to now? Did she realize how much rode on her obeying him in front of a potential usurper of the throne?

"Your Majesty, I shall endeavor to please you as always." The innuendos were apparent to all in her tone. She came closer to him, taking up his hand in hers.

He had no idea what to do or say. She was burning his brains to ashes with her legs and eyes.

"I shall have Madge sew a few stitches so nothing much can be seen above the knee when I walk." Then she kissed him gently, but her lips made him want more.

"Your queen seeks to please her king, but you'll deprive all men of the sight of such beautiful women's...legs," Henry dared to say.

Alex wanted to throttle him, but Toury's gentle squeeze on his hand warned him to stay in control.

"You approve of trousers for women?" Toury said in her cold austere voice that Alex thankfully rarely heard directed at him.

"Of course, my queen." The way Henry's eyes ran all over Toury made Alex livid.

Instead of letting the anger build, he traced his lifemate's thinking. She was giving him a hint, a line of thread to sew further. "I didn't think you a progressive." Alex said. His uncle had been a staunch for tradition and noble blood over all others: women had no voice or role but to procreate and be useful.

"I do not hold the same views as my...as Lord Emerald." Either he was fantastic at playacting, or he was seriously upset about his father's notions. "The new rulers know best." He bowed his head.

Alex's eyes darted to Cobalt's, whose gaze narrowed on Henry. Just as Cobalt could spread certain emotions, he could also sense them, "taste" them as he described it. Alex had grown up with Cobalt and could read every expression on his face and what they might mean. Henry was lying.

"No, the medallion knows best," Toury purred, running her hands down the chain, driving Alex crazy.

The giggling of her friends told him their intimacy was on display for all. And suddenly, he didn't care. Henry's trying to belittle him, Toury's silly girlfriends ogling him in his shirt, Toury's female trousers—none of it meant anything, only her and him. That was all that mattered.

"Transport," she said only for his ears.

"I'd hate to be rude, but we must be off," Alex addressed the room. "Well done, ladies. You all look fetching in the new styles. I must go and chastise the queen about these trousers she wears and dictate where the stitches will go."

"King Alexander, I crave a word." Henry stepped forward.

Madge and David came between him and them. Henry took a step back, his face clouded.

"It can wait." Alex commanded.

Henry held his gaze as Alex placed his hand on David and Madge to transport them. As soon as they were in his bedroom, David and Madge beelined for the door, closing it behind them.

Alex kissed his lifemate. "What are you playing at Toury?" His hands touched her waist of their own violation and moved downward, moving the dress away and marveling over the soft material that clung to her legs.

Her fingers dug into his biceps. "Playing at? Are you threatened by my changes, worried about Henry—who I did not invite, by the way—or are you really turned on due to these trousers?"

"All three? No." Alex shook some sense into his head, trying not to let his lifemate distract him. "No, not threatened, not at all. But my god and goddess, the last." He kissed her but pulled away before he was lost in her.

"I love these." He bent down and ran a hand from her ankle up to her thigh, sighing. Then he pulled the front together. "Perhaps some buttons here a girl can undo for horseback riding. But Toury, please, keep this prototype, for us."

She giggled, throwing her arms around his neck and kissing him soundly. "I will make you jeans next."

"Will you find me attractive in them?"

"Oh, yes."

He kissed her toward the bed, and when she broke their kiss, it was to remove his shirttail. With her hands on his chest, he had a hard time thinking. "I want jeans—no, no. Don't distract me. You cannot—"

"Seduce you? Oh, I did, in front of your family and my friends."

He moaned before he pulled himself together. "Henry must see me as ruler—"

"While I show I'm no one to mess with in my own way."

"Is this what the trousers were all about?"

"No. I'm more comfortable in my sparring clothes than these. If I have to ride a horse sidesaddle again, I might scream. And when I said the idea to Mary, it was all she wanted for her birthday. She helped me design them."

"You miss Earth." He pulled away from her, kicking off his boots. He stooped down to pick up his shirt.

"I honestly don't. Not the people, not the place, but the culture. Food, comfortable clothes, and most importantly, women living equal to their men."

This rubbed him the wrong way. "I've given you everything, Toury." He had given her a kingdom and more control over it than any non-Sapphirian born queen ever had before.

"Please," she protested, yanking the shirt from his hand. "I know. You have done so much for me compared to how this world treats women. But when your cousin is around, you revert back to the arrogant, controlling, cursed Alex I knew. Please," she interrupted Alex's potential protest. "I know you have to, but it is so hard for me to handle."

Alex frowned and then sat upon the bed. He had to explain it in a way she would understand without angering her. "As I said before, change must come slowly. It isn't me with the problem. It's the old-fashioned-thinking rich and powerful sorcerers out there who would love to usurp a young king who they think is under the power of a woman who had connections to rebels and ordered many nobles to their death." He knew the words would strike a chord in her, so he pressed on. "Yes, we know you have no allegiance to the rebels, and yes, we know those dead necromancers were guilty, but think of the lies they could spin anyway."

Her silence was admittance of agreement.

Alex took up her hand, kissing it. "I have enemies enough. Seeming weak is not a worry of my pride, but for my life. I'm asking you not to take things too far to create more enemies for me." There he practically begged her to be slightly less empowered in front of others.

He awaited backlash, but she didn't speak for a moment, so she was thinking and not lashing out. She had this adorable expression on her face every time she was pondering something. "Tell you what? We plan to wear the pants to dinner and the ball, so I will have Madge put in the buttons so you can prove to Henry you're in charge but give me my little freedoms."

"Do what you will," he gave in, but it was a good compromise. "I'm tired of this game. I need him to react, to act. I'd rather anything but this tension."

She kissed him. "So much tension," she sighed, digging her fingers into the knotted muscles of his shoulders. Everything, including tension, was soon forgotten. He was no ruler at her touch; he was hers.

9
ACTRESS

Toury woke to an empty bed. Alex said they would not part for a second for their safety, and he had always been in bed every morning for weeks now. When she sat up and surveyed the room, she saw him sitting at his desk, staring out the window to the orchard below. His face was pensive and brooding. Would he ever gaze out that window with a look of languid contentment? Would there ever be peace to allow them to live happily ever after like in her Earth fairytales?

A fire was burning in the fireplace, and from the warmth of the room, he had lit it earlier. She did not remember one burning when they went to bed, but then again, she hadn't been paying much attention, being absolutely exhausted from all the dancing. All the ladies danced too much. The freedom of pants made movement so easy. Mary had a lovely birthday, and even though she drank very little firewhiskey, she still kept up her partying night owl routine, and the ball hadn't ended until what Toury believed was the middle of the night.

"Can't sleep?" she asked.

Her voice made Alex jump a little, and he turned toward her, sadness in his eyes.

"What is it?" She sat up farther, clutching the sheets to keep herself warm. She wondered for a fleeting moment if he was disappointed she had told him she'd been too tired for his advances last night.

Alex was in his robe, but his hair was wet, fresh from a bath. The sun was hardly up yet.

"How long have you been awake?"

"I hardly slept," he admitted. He got up and came over to sit on the bed next to her and leaned in to give her a peck on the lips. He smelled of peppermint, soap, and that tiny bit of soot-type scent he emanated due to his fire power.

"How? Last night was exhausting."

"I am tired, but when the festive spirit left me, I began to worry. I decided to firebrand and try to foresee through our troubles."

"Are you grave because you saw ill tidings or couldn't see enough to help us prevent anything?"

"Both. I'm not sure." He sighed, running his hands down his head, mussing up his wet hair.

"You need a haircut."

He chuckled at this. It had to be one of the last things on his mind. She waited for him to continue, "My uncle will be captured. I saw it in the flames. My cousin is guilty of something, and he will side against me. I'll have to fight him, Toury."

"You will win." Toury hid her worry at such news and focused on bolstering him, to be strong for him so that he would win.

"I don't know. Things were unclear. Sometimes the future isn't set in the flames; it changes, remember? I don't see you or Mary. I'm sure I'll get a message soon about my uncle. I will have to leave you. Today, I will do something about my cousin."

"Lock him up, Alex. You cannot let him go." She was frightened of the idea of disappearing from the future; it felt like an omen of death.

"I know. And yet, if I let him go, I can find out who he is working with, what he is up to. I need an insider to spy, someone my cousin doesn't know, someone we can trust."

Finally, a problem arose she could solve, a way she could help to protect them both: "Your brother."

Alex cringed.

"Half-brother." She corrected herself, withholding an eye roll at Alex's childish reaction. "You sent him away to be trained. Even if Henry has heard about him, he's never seen him. If Craig doesn't shave for a couple days, he won't look very much like you or your father. And he doesn't have the eyes." She wondered if his mind turned to the eye conversation he'd had with his brother.

"They were here at the same time, though." He fidgeted with a quill, not meeting her gaze, obviously distressed about her proposal. He did feel guilty and was uncomfortable at the thought of asking this of Craig. It meant his brother was growing on him.

"Your brother had been lodging among the servants before he left. Craig wants to prove himself so much to you. Don't you see that? Make him some military spy or something."

Alex dropped the quill and stood. When he met her gaze, she saw the gears turning and his melancholy mood melting away. "It could work. Henry has always been searching for fireproof folk to help with his mother. I'll send the firelasher there. Just maybe he can find something out before anything happens. I'd hate for anything to happen to my...Baron Firelasher, though."

He still couldn't name him as brother or with his father's name. Interesting. She supposed that would take time.

Toury wanted to slip out of bed, but her robe was across the room. She didn't want him distracted by her body—as he so easily always was—in the middle of the conversation, so she stayed put. "I wish you could lock your cousin up, but I understand why you can't and want to banish him from the castle. I think, without him here, I'll relax."

"I fear banishing him too early will provoke him. I need a solid reason." He started pacing, still agitated.

"Can I banish him?" She took pleasure in the idea and wanted to see the look on Henry's face when she did it. The man hated being commanded, even more so when it came from Toury.

Alex thought it over. "Legally...yes." He was hesitant, wary of her massive grin.

"What? You don't want to appear weak?" She folded her arms under her chest, which made his gaze flicker down at the slipping sheets. She uncrossed her arms, pulled the sheets up higher, and gave him a chiding glare. He sure was weak in that way.

"It's not that. I don't want you to appear so strong to him. Don't get mad at me. Hear me out." He cringed, and his hands went out as if he needed to tame a wild dragon.

Good, he knew his comment was infuriating. She stared daggers at him instead of responding.

"If there is to be a war between him and me, you being too powerful might make him rash, act out."

"Meaning?" she prompted, still a little annoyed and not understanding what he was trying to impart.

"Meaning, he'd only view you as an obstacle to the throne if you were with child. If something happens to me, and you are with child—"

He was being too morbid. She didn't want to think about a baby or his death. Becoming a queen was enough right now. Toury had to stop him.

But he knew her too well "—no Toury, please don't interrupt; it has to be said—per the edicts, you can rule by proxy until our child is born and reaches the age of fifteen, and you succeed over Mary. If Henry sees you as a powerful queen who could take over and prevent him from taking the throne, he will want you dead."

He let the fact soak in and then gave her a sad look, one she wanted to kiss away. "In fact, he might want that anyway. It is clear to anyone with eyes in their head—so much more so after today—that our relationship is a loving one. He commented as much."

She hated to hear about a possible future without Alex, but she needed and appreciated his honesty. She did remember reading that rule in the edicts but had glossed over it, never thinking about possibly losing Alex. The thought struck terror in her, but if it happened, she had to prepare herself to take over the monarchy and not give it up to Mary if it occurred; otherwise, she would forfeit Alex and her child's legacy.

What was she thinking? She wasn't pregnant, or it was way too soon to know anyway. She had to dismiss Alex's what-ifs and think of now. How could she get Henry to show his true nature, to get himself banished? Then it came to her. "We should have a fight."

"Huh?" He gaped at her, bewildered, and she realized her logic made massive wild jumps he couldn't follow.

"A fake one. Ignore each other today."

"I don't like playacting, Toury. I'm not good at it." He shook his head, but the bewildered expression on his face told her she must expound on her wild scheme.

"And your cousin is an actor through and through. If he sees a split between us, he will act accordingly." She was excited about this idea. Finally, she could do something useful rather than just sit there and wait for an attack.

Alex flopped onto the bed in an undignified manner, making the top of his robe open. Her gaze flickered to his torso before she yanked her focus back to his face. He gave her a cocky smirk that told her she had been caught. So, yes, she was weak too, but that made it all the worse. Everyone in the palace knew that, including Henry.

"What do you think he'll do?" Alex asked.

Toury shrugged. "Befriend me and talk bad about you, or he'll go to you and badmouth me."

"Okay, I think that makes sense, but what does that do?" Alex not understanding how women's court politics fully worked was another weakness, but it did warm her heart in realization that he had never cared to learn about it before she came along.

"Either way—for lack of better words—it makes us look weak, divided, conquerable. His intentions will be clear."

His eyes narrowed on her in a shrewd expression. "You're so good at this; it's quite frightening, Toury."

"It's called high school on Earth, more political and, at times, more cut-throat than your court." She was being sarcastic, but she should have foreseen Alex would take it literally.

"Seriously?" He frowned.

"Well, high school doesn't often kill people, but people can be inherently cruel, and being popular is everything. It's emotional and mental warfare." Toury did not want to get into how a Coast Guard kid had to move often and people never were nice to the new kid, never accepted her, and how she had always felt out of place on Earth.

"I don't like this." Alex mused.

"Then leave the acting up to me. Just stay busy and make a flippant comment in front of him. We'll figure him out."

When Toury went down to the bathroom, she knew her acting would need to be good. It looked like there was no child on the way. She was relieved and disappointed all at once.

She and Alex had sworn to share everything, but she was positive Alex would not want to talk about his wife's period—not in this squeamish patriarchal world.

Toury was glad she didn't tell him. The next day, it was gone, and so was the cramping sensation. Her mind turned to other reasons, but she pushed them from her mind. She would not think about this right now, not with Henry around.

Before Toury could even invoke a plan of attack against Henry, an opportunity arose a few days after Mary's party. While she was having tea with Mary and the queen dowager, the dreaded Henry invited himself. Toury drank her tea, being quieter than usual, forcing the dowager to pick up the conversational slack.

"Is something troubling you, my queen?" Henry asked, giving her a confident smile. Apparently, his talking to her was a gift. The man loved himself.

"What isn't troubling?" she retorted.

"I'm sorry. It was a ridiculous question used simply to spark conversation."

"No, I am sorry," Toury made herself say. "You are being kind, Lord Sapphirian. I am not in a great mood. So many pressing concerns, but most of all, your father's fate weighs heavily on us all."

A darkness clouded Henry's face, and he stared at his tea, giving himself plenty of time to rebuild his façade. He took a sip. Parents were one of his weaknesses.

"Must we talk about this?" Mary moaned.

"When do you suggest we talk about it? After your uncle is caught and brought back in chains? Lord Sapphirian, we must discuss your fate."

"I had no idea what my father had done until I was told by King Alexander. I have nothing to do with Lord Emerald. I've sworn fealty to my cousins and have broken off with my father publicly—"

"But what of privately?" Toury cut off what might've been stage five groveling, which she could not bear.

Henry gawked at her, shocked, too reactionary, like he had whiplash. "You do not believe me?"

"I don't know whether to believe you or not." Then she leaned forward a little as she had seen many ladies do to engage a man's attention. It felt wrong and gross; Toury was never a flirt—not with men she didn't care about—but one way to make Henry think she was inferior was to remind him of her femininity.

He took the bait and ogled momentarily before his eyes snapped back to her face, and he shifted uncomfortably in his seat and crossed one leg over the other. It was a pretty unmanly way to sit in this sphere, but she supposed he had to hide the evidence of his lust. He would rather not have women clouding his thoughts—interesting.

She whispered, "If you were in Alex's situation, and Alex's father had committed high treasonable offenses, would you believe him innocent?"

Henry smiled at her appreciatively. "I would be honored to have such a queen as you to counsel me on whom to believe."

This was getting creepier, and yet he was avoiding the question. Was he onto her game, or was he imagining himself with her? She could not react to that, but it had opened up the perfect opportunity.

"Me counsel Alex? I think you have the wrong idea of our relationship."

"I'm sure he listens to your thoughts, my dear," the dowager interjected to defend her son.

Of course, Alex did, but Toury needed to put a wedge between them.

Perhaps she should've told the queen about this plan, but she didn't trust the dowager's or Mary's love of the guy.

"He listens," Mary scoffed. "Doesn't mean he comprehends it." There. Dependable Mary with her scathing sibling rivalry.

"He is the king, so who am I to argue?" Toury raised her brows.

Henry's eyes studied her, trying to puzzle her out.

"Did you two have a disagreement?" The dowager asked. The concern in the woman's voice made Toury feel terribly guilty. She would tell her later one day, when everyone was happy and safe, that it was all smoke and mirrors, but not yet.

"Nothing major. Do not worry yourself." She wanted to call her "Mother," but she hadn't had the guts to do so to the woman's face. It was too much, too overwhelming a notion.

A note entered as planned. Madge brought it over to Toury, who frowned and opened it, acting her part. She read the note she had instructed Alex to write, crumpled it up, and tossed it down on the table flippantly. Then she sighed. "Alex cannot get away, as I figured, so I'm to dine with you. I hope that doesn't inconvenience you?" She directed her question to the queen dowager, who was all flattery and happiness that they would be graced with Toury's presence, but it rang false and obvious she was trying to cover up the oddity of it.

"It will be nice to have your company as King Alex always steals you for private luncheons," Henry said, masking the barb as a compliment. He was trying to wound her, and had she and Alex been in a real fight, this would have acutely stung.

She examined her tea, pretending to be lost in mopey thoughts while the others changed the subject. She retired to her room briefly before lunch to "be alone."

Of course, Alex had transported there prior and was lying on her bed, smiling. "Well?"

"He's taking the bait. What he said about me dining with them would've hurt, had we really been fighting."

"Good. I want this over with. Come here. Kiss me," he said.

"So demanding," she teased. She kissed him once; then he transported back to his study, and she plotted for lunch.

10
A SIBLING

Alex despised pretending to ignore Toury. What he liked even less was the missive in his hand. It was from Lord Rose Quartz, who was stationed in Mineria. A fire had burned down an entire block of slum buildings. A grey-eyed girl had been seen fleeing the scene. According to his general, the building had been the supposed headquarters of the rebels that they had planned to storm the next morning. Fifty bodies were found inside. This definitely meant that a lot of rebels had died—conflictingly, he hoped it was true.

He had forgotten about Racine. All his energy being on his uncle and cousin, he forgot about Toury's sister. She had warned him about the two forces of rebel and necromancer banding together... Depending on their numbers—resurrected bodies included—they might be able to overtake his kingdom. He had forgotten Racine because she was a lesser evil and possible ally.

It was all so frustrating. When firebranding, the flames showed him many contradictory things. What drove him the craziest of all was that he could not see Toury's future. Mary's neither. He sought Tobias Firebrand's help, the best firebrander who was not a full-blooded Sapphirian, and he, too, had been unsure of what the future held. It was ever-changing. Mary was no help. She apparently was only seeing happily-ever-afters with her lovestruck eyes, unable to see the near future. All would be well, according to her, but he knew better. Futures changed as frequently as the flame flickered. He wondered when the firelasher's mother would make her promised appearance, because now would be as good a time as any.

A knock sounded on Alex's study door. He called the person to enter, and Cobalt did. Alex sighed. He had thought it might be Henry—Henry, who was busy eating lunch with his lifemate instead of Alex. He would not get jealous. He knew how much Toury loathed the man and how frightened she was by him. He hated this plan, truly, but he hadn't listened to Toury before, much to his detriment. Their lives were on the line, enemies everywhere. He had to let her fight what battles she could—in parlors, with clothes and words as her weapons, she had told him.

"Why is Toury eating lunch with everyone else lately?" Cobalt asked.

"Is everyone talking about this?"

"Well, yes. You steal her away for private time, your luncheon lasting a couple hours, and suddenly you don't have time for her? Friend, shall we ride and talk man-to-man, not advisor-to-king?"

What a welcomed suggestion. Alex needed to clear his head. The safest place to talk without being overheard was out in the fields. He was up and heading for the door, David stumbling at his sudden change of plans.

Once the fresh air hit his face, Alex rode hard, David, Cobalt, and Percival following. Cobalt despised being pampered by the servant, and it was quite hilarious to watch that battle. By the lake, they dismounted. Alex sat on the grass, annoyed his concerns came back so fast. For a few moments, he had been free from worry.

"What is it?"

"You cannot tell Mary," Alex cautioned.

Cobalt took a deep, shaky breath. "She's tenacious, though."

"Never mind then." Alex shoved his friend.

Cobalt laughed hard. "No, I won't speak of it, even to her. Now, tell me. What are you two fighting about? Henry? Please tell me it's him. Any excuse to punch the braggart in the face, please. Let me."

"It is Henry but not what you think. It's a scheme, not a fight." Alex explained it all to him.

His friend was much too enthusiastic, wanting to join into the scheme too. He planned on a sly comment here and there, pretending to be on Alex's side. Cobalt enjoyed courtly games too much, but at least he gave up ones with women for political ones. "How are things really, with the queen, I mean?"

"Aside from worrying Henry would appear at our bedside and butcher us on a daily basis, just dandy." His sarcasm wasn't lost on Cobalt.

"At least Toury senses the danger. Mary sees nothing but sincerity and goodness in him. It makes me sick. Honestly, I have to watch out for her life foremost since she doesn't have the sense to preserve it herself."

"Cobalt, what are we going to do?" Alex's voice caught at the end, exposing his vulnerability, but someone had to know. He could not hold everything together in this entire torn-up world by himself and pretend he was able to easily bear it.

Cobalt met his gaze, and his friend used his magic to ease Alex's tension. He couldn't even scold him for it, because he needed relief, just for a moment. As much as Alex wanted to avoid conflict, waiting for it to happen was even more stressful.

"One step at a time, Your Majesty. Your uncle, then the rebels. If we meet some necromancers along the way, we'll take them out too. As for your cousin, once your uncle is captured and confesses, you have every right in all the laws and edicts to imprison Henry. If you let me go back to tracking, I could—"

"You chose to enter an engagement with my sister over a military career. You are a liability out there. Plus, I need someone watching our backs inside the castle."

"I know." Cobalt sighed. "It is an honor, I assure you. I'm just not used to being idle, but I'll continue to watch him. Speaking of watching, I already got the firelasher in place. Very easy to get him into the fort. Apparently, the mad princess bit the ear off her last 'handler,' so they were desperate. No questions after the fake references were handed in."

"How will he communicate?"

"Coded messages slipped to the grocer's delivery man. His route takes him to Tobias Firebrand's home bi-weekly. Since Firebrand visits you after the weekly Magician Guild meetings, him showing up that often would not raise alarm."

Alex nodded.

"The grocer's deliveryman? We trust him?"

"He's a...relative of sorts. A cousin."

Alex gave him a dubious look.

Cobalt's mouth dropped, and then his ears turned red. He was ashamed at having low relations, not that Alex would care, but Cobalt was so prideful. "No, he's not a baseborn brother or anything. My mom had an older sister who kind of ran off with a magician, okay? I promised him a nice position at the palace once I marry if he does this."

Social ladders, bloodlines, how they dictated who was loyal to whom, and yet Alex's family had been the worst. He didn't trust this random grocer's assistant, but he had to put his faith in Cobalt because he had no more energy to worry about this intel mission.

Literally sensing Alex's mood, Cobalt squeezed Alex's shoulder. "Let me take on some of this burden, Brother."

All he could do was nod. Alex was overcome by overwrought emotion. He and his friend had been through so much together. The good times, and the bad. There was a time when Alex couldn't do without his best friend and a time he had wanted to kill him but, in the end, he loved him as a true brother. Yes, they butted heads, disagreed often, and they checked each other's egos frequently. Yet Cobalt was steadfast, true, dependable, after Alex's best interests. Sure, they had a few bad spots, but Alex imagined this was the exact relationship brothers had.

Alex took the missive he had inadvertently slipped into his pocket about Racine and handed it to Cobalt.

He read it and whistled. "I'll deal with this. Don't even think about it. Once she is captured, I'll inform you. Let me take this burden from you."

Alex nodded. He had too much to bear. He needed the help. One half-brother through blood, one brother through a future marriage; the firelasher, Cobalt, and Alex would exemplify what family should be. After he cut out the Emerald disease slowly killing them.

11
CORNERED

Toury and Alex walked into their chambers. As soon as their servants barred the door and then retreated upstairs for their luncheon, Alex yanked her to him, devouring her lips, murmuring sweet nothings of missing her between kisses.

"Stop," she giggled as he kissed her neck, trying to convince her other things overrode what she had to say. "Alex. Seriously."

He groaned and pulled away, his hands cradling her face. "I'm sorry. I miss our lunches. I hate pretending to distance myself from you."

"I think it's working."

"How?" His whining tone told her he was thinking the wrong thing, that Henry was courting her. Henry wasn't that dumb.

"With the tone, I can tell you think the worst. No, he's starting to say cavalier things. Called you 'Alex' to me instead of 'King Alexander' or 'His Majesty.' And 'little cousin' was one I had to bite my tongue not to snap at him. He hasn't dared to use 'whelp' in front of me after I chastised him for it. I think, given any opportunity, he will choose the side against you."

"And this is supposed to what? Make me feel better? I think I'd rather he flirted with you."

She scoffed. "No, you wouldn't." Did he really think she was doing this to torture him? He was acting like it. "Alex, you need to know these things."

"Can we make up now?" he asked, frowning. He was too adorable when he did that. "He's not stupid enough to reveal some sinister plan to you."

"A little more time is all. I think he'll slip up and say enough to incriminate himself. One only has to badmouth you to get in the dungeons, as you loved to remind me when we first met."

He kissed her and wrapped his arms around her. "When we first met, you had a viper's tongue, woman."

"Are there vipers in Fyr?" Toury asked.

He leaned his forehead against hers with a huff. "You still haven't read the Great Book, have you?"

"Busy reading your millions of edicts, wasn't I?" She scoffed. "And you guys don't even practice the religion anymore. Give me the CliffsNotes."

"Earth term there, I'm guessing?"

"Means the short of it."

"Dragons killed the serpents back before the age of man. Serpents were evil, and dragons were good. And there aren't millions of edicts. Just about two hundred. And don't lie, you were too busy reading *Taming the Dragon*."

Toury pushed him away, feeling her face flush.

Alex laughed lightly. "Under the couch cushion isn't the greatest hiding spot." He was so smug, she wanted to smack the look off his face.

"Well, I wouldn't have had to read it if you hadn't abandoned me." Her embarrassment fleeting, she went for a guilt trip by giving him a full puppy-dog pout.

"The book said nothing about tying a man up to get what you want," Alex protested.

"You read it!" She laughed wholeheartedly.

"That's it, woman!" Alex grabbed her up and threw her over his shoulder.

She squealed out in shock. Then she was flopped onto the bed.

"We're making up." He lay down next to her and kissed her gently.

"Only in this room," Toury challenged.

He kissed her but then sighed and lay back on the bed, folding his hands under his head and staring at the ceiling. Something was wrong. He'd always made lunchtime about being intimate. The number of advances he had made on her daily to be physical meant that him avoiding an opportunity was tantamount to him pushing her away.

She wondered if she had done something wrong. "What is it?"

"Huh?"

"You have me in a bed, and you decided to brood instead. Not that I'm complaining. It takes Madge ages to set my hair right after our lunches."

Alex was back up on his side, running his thumb along the seam of her lips before he kissed her. Again, it was a chaste kiss when compared to Alex's normal behavior. "I'm preoccupied."

"Obviously." She wouldn't let him evade her.

He sighed.

Uh-oh. It was going to be bad news.

"We swore to always be honest with each other. I hid something from you—well, at first—and then with all my concerns about Henry and Emerald, it slipped my mind."

71

"Tell me now," she demanded, trying to keep her tone light. She didn't want to react until she heard the news. If it was a big deal, she might just smack him. Once upon a time, that would've landed her in a dungeon, but not anymore.

"I didn't want to say anything until I heard more, but today I have."

"Just tell me, Alex. You're building it up, and now I'm worried."

"I saw your sister in Mineria."

Well, he just mentally slapped her instead. The shock rippled through her, and she couldn't process it for a second. Then bitterness overrode the shock of him hiding something so big. "That did kill the mood." Toury sat up. It was the truth couched in a bad joke. "Did she try to kiss you or kill you?"

Alex sat up as well, trying to mask his flinch at the barb. Truly, she was over the his-letting-Racine-kiss-him debacle, but anger lashed out of nowhere. She and Alex were solid, so her catty remark was ridiculous in hindsight. She couldn't undo it now. It was said.

Alex frowned, making him adorably angerproof. She couldn't hold a grudge against those eyes in that dignified face, even more a man than when they had met. "Neither. In short, I thought she was luring us into a trap, and so did other rebels, but she warned me to go a second before the rebels showed up, told me where my uncle was headed, and professed she was breaking away from the rebels."

"You believed her?" Toury didn't know what to think, but she was unhappy with how easily her husband had been led into an ambush, and she didn't trust her sister one bit.

"I was unsure. Listen, she said the rebels and necromancers joined forces—"

"Oh my god," Toury breathed out. They had bested the necromancers but barely escaped the rebels. Together, even though a large number of necromancers were snuffed of power or dead, a dozen necromancers could defeat even Alex's great armies. When one could raise every fallen soldier, the army would grow exponentially.

"My scouts are telling me her warning might be true. I tried to get her to come with us, but she had something to do. I just found out someone killed fifty rebels in a fire."

"Which will look like you did it," Toury concluded.

Alex's face scrunched up, and then he raised his brows, an epiphany, but of what? "Which is good. It would show I'm onto them. I was seen in

Mineria; within a few weeks, fifty rebels died. I wasn't quite sure she was on our side, but the fact she chose fire might be a signal to us."

"But why would she turn on them and the cause? She was practically married to it. She hates me."

"Oh yes, she admitted to disliking you and loathing me, but Emerald killed your parents and is in cahoots with the necromancers, isn't he? If the rebel cause joined with the necromancers because they want power, meaning me dead..."

She gripped his arms; the thought of him gone was too much. Her eyes prickled. Was she really going to cry over a hypothetical situation? She blinked them back, but Alex had noticed and stopped talking.

He pulled her onto his lap, and she rested her head on his shoulder. "I'm not going to let that happen, Toury, but either your sister wants revenge for your parents' deaths, or she sees a greater evil than me—"

"Or it is an elaborate trap."

"Or that," Alex allowed. "I took her sentiment as genuine, but trusting her? Absolutely not. There was something else that made her give up the cause, but she never got to say what. And, Toury, she knows the commander. If they can capture her, we could get information."

Toury thought for a moment. Alex didn't press or say anything, but ran his hands soothingly down her arms.

"No." Toury paused thoughtfully before switching into regal-planning mode: "Don't spread your resources thin. If Racine is performing some scheme, we'd play into it. Concentrate on your uncle, then Henry, and then Racine. Unless something happens to change things, we know your uncle is the most dangerous. One at a time."

"I agree." He sighed.

"You don't sound like you do."

"I wish I could go after all three while protecting us here. It's just impossible."

"And you spreading your armies out might be what they would want too."

"I know, my love. I just need some kind of closure with one of them."

Toury pulled back and saw the lines of displeasure around his mouth. She kissed them away, which made his face neutral as those eyes—so eerily bright, they sparkled like sapphires—stared into hers with warmth, love, fear, and anxiety. Would it ever be over? Would they always have these intense extremes of love and impending doom clashing over their lives? But wishing for an end to it all could be good or very bad: normalcy or death.

Alex distracted her with gentle kisses down her neck, but she knew their pressing concerns were too sobering for him really to be seducing her. A rapping at the door pulled him away from her. He gazed at her sadly as he said, "Come in."

That would never change, the constant interruptions, duties, the kingdom. Still, she chose this. She loved Alex, and if this was what came with him, so be it. She'd pay him in return with a lot of hell from her.

They got up and went into the sitting room. David came hurrying down the stairs to answer it, Madge trailing. A servant handed David a missive. Madge barred the door behind him as David handed it to Alex. He opened it, reading, making no move to screen it, so Toury saw it too.

Your Majesty,
We have Lord Emerald in our custody. Please come at once.
—Agate

Dread crept over her. There was the closure Alex had asked for. As much as she wanted one enemy behind them, she hated that Alex had to leave her side. Apart, there was fear for both of their safety.

Alex gave Toury a halfhearted smirk. "To Fieldstone, David. Pack my ceremonial armor, and ready my battle armor at once."

David nodded and left the room.

"For safety," Alex added for Toury's sake. It did not put her at ease. "I'll be back, and we'll—"

"Don't say it."

"Say what?"

"That we'll never part after that. It will happen now and then. Plus, you'll jinx it."

"Jinx?" Alex was adorably confused. "Earth term?"

"Yeah. It means if you say it, it won't come true."

"Sounds like a ridiculous superstition to me."

"Kind of," she allowed. In a way though, she had never given up that sentiment. Things had a way of coming true or not happening when you want them to as if there were a higher power controlling things. On Fyr, it was a god of fire and goddess of light that these people used to believe deeply in. Seeing actual magic happen in front of her eyes and sensing the energy coming from the planet was intense. When it was used and returned back to the core, it was tantamount to a religion, a spiritual transmission. If that was all true, then superstitions could be as well. She wouldn't dare chance it.

During her ruminations, Alex had left to get ready and now was back in his armor to give her a good long kiss goodbye. Immediately after, he and David vanished in a ball of fire.

She sat in silence for a moment, melancholy sweeping over her. Then an idea swept over her. "Madge, let's spar. I could use some activity."

"Is that wise?" Madge asked.

Toury narrowed her eyes at her. "I'm not...I don't think I am...not yet..." Saying "pregnant" aloud might make it true. Maybe she was unhealthily superstitious.

"Women in Fyr do not partake in too much physical activity while they are trying for children either, Your Majesty. They do not wish to exhaust the body."

"Well, on Earth, their studies say exercise leads to easier and safer labors, but I'm not—"

"No, of course you're not." Madge interrupted. "And when you are, I'll hide it in your clothing as long as possible if needed."

"I will spar."

"I will take it easy on you...somewhat." Madge cracked a rare smile.

"You better not."

Minutes later, they were in the crystal courtyard to train, something Toury hadn't been doing much since the wedding. She was taking over many queenly duties, save for running the house. Toury had no desire to do so, and the poor dowager had lost her husband, so Toury let her continue her role of running the household. Toury had bigger things to worry about than dinner menus. Her mother-in-law was so eager to please that she often read Toury well and adjusted things to suit her. It truly made her feel this castle, which not long ago had been a gilded cage, was home.

Madge flew at her with her dirk. Toury, lost in her thoughts, just got her own up in time to deflect it. Out of practice, the dirk felt strange in her hand.

"You know what they say when a woman's mind is woolgathering too much?" Madge taunted.

Toury was sure this was Fyr's reference to preggo-brain. "Or she is simply tired of everyone saying certain nonsense about her," Toury huffed out, throwing in an attack.

Madge stumbled back, not ready for Toury's sudden resolve. The feel of the dirk in her hand came back to Toury. Anger built up in her—at Lord

Emerald for taking Alex away and forcing him to make hard decisions, at her sister for wedging herself in her life again with her shady ways, at the pressure and speculation of being pregnant, taking over the duties of queen to boot, and frustration with necromancers and rebels who just needed to let Alex prove himself first. With every annoying thought, she swung wildly until she realized she had backed Madge into a corner. Madge yanked Toury's dirk wrist past her, and it clanged into the wall behind Madge.

"Don't turn. We have an audience now," Madge whispered. She pushed Toury away.

Toury swung back. They fought back and forth until they were drenched in sweat. Both holding their own, equal in combat, she and Madge finally gave up, the servant calling it as they always did in custom to make the royal triumphant. For the first time, Toury thought she could almost be as good as Madge in real combat.

Madge bowed deeply, and Toury put her dirk away. Madge sheathed hers on her belt.

"That felt—" Toury began.

Clapping from the balcony above stopped her in her tracks. Madge had warned her about an audience, but she had figured it was Mary and the dowager. It was Mary and Henry. The latter was clapping and walking down the steps, his sparkling sapphire eyes full of wonder and appreciation. He stopped in front of her and drank her in, even though she must look frightful. She didn't know what to make of him.

Creepily, his eyes scrutinized her ponytail, her boy's clothing, all the way down to her naked ankles and bare feet. "You are a conundrum, Queen Sapphirian. That's all I can say."

She thought the same of him.

Madge handed Toury a towel, discreetly placing herself a step ahead of Toury and adjacently between her and Henry. If Henry saw her protective maneuver, he didn't react.

"That doesn't sound at all like a compliment." Toury laughed so he'd know it didn't bother her, because the truth was that a real compliment would bother her more than a snide remark from him.

Mary was by Henry's side, lacing her arm in his. Had they not been cousins, Toury would wonder if the girl loved Henry, but Fyrian royals never married close relations—one of the few edicts that didn't make her mad. The stars in Mary's eyes weren't born of love; they were idol worship. It was still annoying, though, that her sister and best friend was blind and couldn't see the real man underneath.

"Henry," Mary nudged him. Mary's waiting maid Lucy watched everything with restrained terror. Good. "That does sound like an insult."

"My dearest queen." Henry bowed. His lips quirked with secrets and lies he'd never tell. Toury could see through him but not the matter behind the façade. "I would never insult you. I'm impressed, in awe, flabbergasted, and full of intense admiration to see this spectacle. A noblewoman fighting? I'm astounded and yet, dare I say, pleased?"

"My, what overtures you have. I did not seek to please anyone but to learn to defend my own life. Is that not a good trait for a woman?"

"Not if she has a good man to protect her." Of course he would try to measure swords with Alex while he wasn't present.

"A woman doesn't need a man to protect her. Men underestimate us. How amazing would it be if both the man and woman in a relationship could defend themselves and each other?"

Henry cocked his head in contemplation, but the intensity in his eyes was alarming. Toury had the inkling he was interested in the idea but also hated it. Like other noblemen, he probably wanted to keep power over women yet was turned on by a powerful woman. Gross.

"I think that would be a match made by the god and goddess," he replied.

Toury gave him a dismissive glance. His face went blank at her disbelieving rebuff. "Any woman who is taught can wield a sword. I only learned after coming to the palace."

"Where is the man who taught you to wield it? The two of you are so odd, I thought the king was fighting you."

"Toury and Alex sparring? Are you mad, Henry?" Mary giggled.

"My bodyguard taught me. Who would be better to do so?" Toury said.

Henry gave Madge a quick glance. He was not the type to even notice or acknowledge the hired help. "Where is Alex?"

"On business, which is none of yours," Toury retorted.

"Tou—I mean, Queen Tourmaline," Mary chided.

"You dare to scold me?" Toury shot at her.

Mary frowned.

Toury didn't want to hurt her friend's feelings, but Mary's love for her cousin and refusal to see the truth was grating. She needed a strong front when it came to Henry. She turned her attention to the man. "Does King Alexander need to tell you where he's going?" She corrected his use of Alex's nickname.

"He's left?" Henry guessed.

Toury wanted to kick herself for not being careful with her word choices. "Is it really leaving when you can disappear and reappear in seconds?" Toury tried laughing it off.

"I could help him," Henry offered, "if you told me what it was about." My, he was prying, desperate even. It was insulting he thought Toury was that gullible.

"No, you couldn't." Toury could tell the prying was to ascertain if it was about Lord Emerald.

"You don't know that," Mary said. "Both of us could help. Alex doesn't need to keep everything so secretive when there are others who can help. He needs to delegate."

Mary was clueless, and everything was over her head. How could Toury get her to stay quiet without offending her or telling her what was going on? Mary probably would tell Henry, thinking she was doing what was best, and get them all killed. Toury loved Mary, but her immature and naïve nature was a chink in the Sapphirian armor.

"He does delegate," Toury said vaguely, "but not to people who might be involved." She raised her brows at Henry, whose face went devoid of emotion, frozen and unable to react. She had cornered him while also exposing why Alex had left. Alex hadn't permitted her to tell anyone, but neither had he said to keep it a secret; Henry would learn soon enough.

Henry had no options left on how to react to her multifaceted barb. A smile would ring false. Anger would show he might have something to hide. Confusion was too late to feign now. Acknowledging his father could be imprisoned would make Lord Emerald look guilty. Henry had many things to hide, and that blank face attempted to do so.

Toury gave him a sly grin to show she was onto him, even though she was unsure of what he was up to. She left the bewildered Mary and shocked Henry behind and returned to her rooms. She had won the day, and Henry would need to act soon: swear fealty or flee.

12
A REQUEST

They had captured Alex's uncle in Fieldstone, which was due east of Celestia, a farming district and the last place they'd expected him to be. It made sense only for that reason. Otherwise, the choice was nonsensical; there was no dissention noted out there, despite the drought-induced famine. Alex had recently sought out and handsomely paid Water immigrants. Most people from other spheres had been stripped of power, but Alex knew of immigrants who were able to assist in such things, and Fyr never turned away refugees from Water. He never told Toury, but someone in her maternal line was from the Water sphere. Her mother's dark skin showed that—a grandparent of Toury's most likely. A Sapphirian ruler would be stupid not to take in Waterians. Due to the planet being made from fire, water evaporated too quickly, droughts often occurred, and using water magic was cheaper than transporting snow and ice from the north. Only, as of late, his father had driven the Water folk toward the rebel cause. Alex's scouts had found one family willing to help, and he rewarded them handsomely.

When he had time, he'd listen in detail to Toury's description of chemistry and something she called desalinization. She had said there was a way to make seawater into freshwater. There were so many more important things Toury and he could be doing for his sphere than chasing down people who wanted to stop it merely for their own benefit. He fantasized about a time when he and Toury could laze about in bed or the orchard, planning how to improve their world together. Now, unfortunately, was not that time.

Regardless, the deal he struck with the Waterians had been a great investment. The east was happy with him; crops were starting to flourish again, and the civilians turned in his uncle right away. Lord Emerald had been there but a day before Alex's troops were informed. Alex transported there with little reservation. The only thing that had his nerves on edge was facing his uncle and hearing what he had to say. Would he lie, or would he tell Alex truths that would be much worse?

And Racine. She had told him the truth about his uncle's whereabouts, which helped them capture him. What was her motivation if it wasn't to help? What did she wish to gain?

The steadfast Captain Agate met Alex. "This way, Your Majesty. We have him in a cell with bars full of alumina." Wise, Alex thought. His cousin couldn't transport in or out to save his father, nor could a rebel with the remaining dragon's blood, which should have been losing its potency at a high rate by then.

Alex pressed down his nervousness at the prospect of seeing his uncle and made sure his face remained the cold, aloof mask he had been raised to bear. He would not let his uncle get to him, not outwardly at least.

Agate led Alex into a tent. Inside was a cage with nothing but a wooden box. His uncle sat upon it, his head in his grubby hands, stained with dirt. His oily wisps of hair clung to his bald head, and his clothes were worse for wear. He had been running since he'd fled the palace, since he'd murdered Toury's parents, trying to forever hide his secret. How many more secrets were in his head, and how much could Alex pry from him? That's all he was, a man full of secrets that Alex needed. He had to be the cold, rational, strong Draca King.

He observed the man—he would not think of him as uncle any longer—and saw his posture was slumped in defeat. Alex would bring him back, put him on trial, and end up burning him at the stake. It would be a long, awful process he did not want to put Toury through, yet she deserved to see the man who had killed her parents be punished.

Lord Emerald peered up, his green irises vibrantly clashing with the bloodshot area around them. His lips tweaked up for a moment upon seeing Alex—a familiar face in this situation—and then it fell in realization. "I wondered if you'd come."

"If?" Alex walked farther into the tent. "A royal has to retrieve another royal. You think I'd send someone in my stead?"

"No, Your Majesty. I should've known better." The title rang false on Emerald's lips. "If you were smart, you'd stay snug in that fortress of yours."

"Is that a threat?" Captain Agate was at the bars, his sword poking through, making Lord Emerald fall off the box onto his bottom to avoid the blade.

"Back off, Agate. There's nothing he can do to me now. The question is, who outside of this cell can?"

Emerald stayed sitting on the ground, his face reminiscent of a sullen child. "And you expect me to tell you everything? Why bother? I die regardless."

"And you leave behind a lifemate and son who will be implicated and stripped of everything for your crimes."

Emerald blanched and then stood, dusting himself off. He forced out a laugh. "What have I supposedly done?"

Alex crossed his arms and started pacing, withholding his temper, knowing his uncle expected him to be weak or temperamental. Like Henry, Lord Emerald expected a boy. Perhaps Alex had been one not so very long ago, but so much had happened that forced him to grow up in more ways than one. "I tire of parlor tricks and games. Unlike my father, I'm direct. You killed Lady Angelica and Baron Aschen Hematite."

"Lady and Baron," Emerald scoffed.

"Pardoned in death for telling me *everything*." Alex stopped and glowered at the prisoner. He let some of his power out, warming the air within the tent up just a touch to make the man sweat from the heat. He doubted his power could breach the bars if he tried, but the increase in temperature would make his uncle think otherwise.

Emerald swallowed hard and tried to loosen the collar of his filthy doublet. The man's eyes darted around, reminding Alex of a cornered animal. "You can't know everything, because I've done nothing. I have no idea what you are talking about."

"Right." Alex clapped his hands. "You've locked up an innocent man, Agate. Should we set him free?"

"Your Majesty?" The captain was confused.

He knew Agate wouldn't take him seriously, but Alex needed to unnerve Emerald. "He says he's innocent, so that must be the truth, no?"

"That is for you to decide, Your Majesty."

"But all lords are truthful, are they not?"

"Err..." Agate uncomfortably shifted. "Not in my experience, Your Majesty."

"Hmm," Alex exaggerated. "See how these tricks are tiresome, Lord Emerald? Wait, not a lord anymore, I fear. No, *Mister* Emerald."

The insult hit home. Emerald slammed into the bars, rage Alex had never seen before etched on the man's face. "You cannot! Henry is innocent!"

Alex withheld the flinch at the man's pain-filled words and the stench of his body odor. "It matters not. He will lose title and estate, along with his mother, both to be known as Missus and Mister Emerald from here on out. Your crimes carry over to them."

"You still haven't told me what else I'm accused of."

"Oh, you're not accused of anything," Alex said quietly.

Emerald was confused. The anger left the man. He was truly lost. Had Alex not known the truth, he would question the man's guilt. He would enlighten him to how much he really knew. The fire in Alex wanted blood, revenge, but he pushed it down. He had to stay calm.

"You are guilty. There was a witness...to both your crimes." Alex let it set in.

Emerald's eyes scanned the air, ferreting out meaning, and then they came to a halt. Realization flickered across his features, and then resignation. He sat on his box, head in hands, as Alex had found him. "One of the Hematites lived?"

"The mother, for a bit, long enough to tell us all she knew. And from the cause of her death, the way her wounds could not heal due to her heart becoming a weapon within her, I knew instantly that only an inverted Emerald power could do that. As the Emerald line is almost nonexistent these days, and you were the only one in the vicinity, within the walls of the castle...well, there is no other possible suspect." Alex paused for effect. It was satisfying to watch this conniving man, who sacrificed his family for power so offhandedly, realize he had been caught.

"And I know you're capable of dark magic. You, who had so long ago tried to slaughter me in my crib, were interrupted by the Hematites. They saw my aunt and you cursing me. You killed my uncle but could not quite kill my father, could you?"

Alex waited. Surely, the man could not deny it now. Even if he did, Alex knew the truth. The healers at Toury's mother's deathbed had heard it all and could testify. There was no way of denying it.

"Your father was extraordinarily powerful. Like a boar that wouldn't go down. The curse got him in the end, though. It just took much longer than I had hoped." Emerald said this on purpose to get Alex angry.

He could not take the bait; he wouldn't give his uncle the satisfaction of breaking his mask. He had to keep him talking, get a full confession. Alex urged him on: "Long enough for your child at the time to grow up, to be able to take over the throne. But you didn't plan on Mary, a miracle child, considering the curse sterilized my father after a while. You could not get near her, and my aunt had lost her mind by then."

The man looked away at his words. Remorse and regret were coming to him much too late.

Alex tried to feel sympathy for him but could not. He just needed to push the man a bit further to crack him. "And, little did you know, the Hematites tried to save me, limiting the curse to only my heart. Little did you know your darling Ruby—"

"Enough!" he shouted, his eyes full of fury. Then he started to weep, crumbling in on himself, a shell of a man destroyed by greed and lust for power.

"Ruby found you out. She fled for her life so you would not kill her to keep your secrets. She was more faithful to the crown than to you. Did you have your own daughter killed?"

The man continued weeping.

"She fled to Earth and by happenstance or providence found the Hematite child and gave her her powers. With the strength of a Sapphirian and the combined healing and light powers of her parents, she was able to eradicate the curse, destroying it for good. Your daughter defied you, sacrificed herself, to save me."

Alex waited for the man to speak, but he could not own up to it or even react to the bitter sting of truth.

With the tale told and the man broken, Alex needed information. "So, what were your plans now, Emerald? Kill me, my lifemate, and my sister and hope not to get caught?"

Alex was shocked when the man began to speak, expecting him to be uncooperative. "I was working with the necromancers, although I'd never taint my own self with their darkness. They have failed, thanks to some trick you figured out in identifying them. I was on my own trying to salvage lost plans, but I'm done." He stared down at his hands and shook his head. The man wiped his eyes. "I wish to request *beheafdian*." He used the old word found in the edicts for a gentleman's death, a beheading.

Alex froze, his pacing stopped, and horror crept over his skin. He had not thought of that. If a noble asked for a quick death after confessing guilt, Alex was to honor that. Could he do it? He had to stall, delay things until he could come to terms with it. "Only a gentleman gets such a privilege, and you have been stripped of that. Unless...you have more information about your son, rebels, and necromancers that would aid me in keeping my kingdom safe?"

"My son is not involved, and I have reported all I've known about the rebels." Was he saving his son through his own sacrifice? Alex couldn't prove it yet, but Henry was definitely involved.

"And yet your lifemate was a necromancer, so..." Alex left the comment in the air and turned to leave. To Agate, he said, "He is to be thoroughly questioned about all three. Let me know when your men get something. Otherwise, we head back tomorrow, and he stands trial."

"Thoroughly?" Captain Agate pressed, making sure he understood his meaning.

"Do what is necessary." Enforcing such a harsh command made Alex feel guilty. He reminded himself Emerald had tried to kill him when he was an innocent baby and would kill him now if given the opportunity. "He is a gentleman no longer. I might reinstate it for his death if he's forthcoming."

Then Alex left. He hated himself for ordering it, but he needed answers. Alex and David retreated to the tent the soldiers had set up for him. He flopped onto the fur-lined pallet, brooding. It was midday, so he could not sleep, nor did he dare transport back. He longed for the comfort and council of his lifemate, but he knew he could not become dependent on her, nor could he ask her how to sentence the murderer of her parents.

"Your Majesty seems troubled," David commented.

He moved about, and Alex heard liquid being poured. He handed Alex a glass of ale. He could use something stronger like firewhiskey, but troops were not allowed spirits. He could ask to get it from an officer such as Agate, but he needed to be stronger, hide his weaknesses.

"Pour yourself one, David."

"Your Majesty?"

"I need a friend, a confidant. I need to talk this out, and you looming over me will defeat that purpose."

"I cannot drink and keep you safe."

"Have you never?" When the question left his lips, he realized the ridiculous fate of his servant. Always watching over him every moment Alex was awake, taking over for Alex's former bodyguard and David's master when David's apprenticeship ended at fifteen. "Stupid question. Perhaps another time." He noted to try to give David and Madge a day off a week without offending them. They deserved to have lives outside of watching over theirs.

David sat.

"Well, you obviously know what is wrong, but what are your thoughts on it?" Alex asked.

David opened his mouth but then closed it.

"You never had issue telling me when I was being stupid before, particularly when it came to my lifemate. Speak plainly."

"Forgive me, Your Majesty, but what am I to say? A gentleman requested his death. I don't think there is a way out of this, although I wish there were for your sake."

Alex looked away. His servant's eyes were full of sympathy, which made Alex realize David was right. "But there has to be a way. What if I strip him of his title so he can't ask for it? I mean, some could argue I stripped the title after his request, but only you and Agate were there to know the truth."

"It goes to trial then, and you would ask a servant and a gentleman to lie in a court for you," David calmly pointed out. His ease with making that statement meant David would lie for Alex but would hate doing so, or David would never have pointed it out in the first place.

"No, I would never ask that of you, and I'm not the type of king to circumvent the court's laws to avoid what I clearly must do. But, David, *how* can I do this?"

"Think about who he is and what he has done. You read his charges aloud. He helped kill your uncle, drove your aunt into madness, could be implicated in his daughter's death, killed your lifemate's parents, and cursed you and your father, which caused his premature death and forced you to rule at an age where you should be happily starting a family without all this pressure on your shoulders." David shifted forward, and Alex could see the formal servant crumbling away and the man taking on the role of a more casual friend.

David continued, "Every worry and task you've had to do, everything you and the queen have been through, is because of this man. Focus on that because, if it doesn't raise enough hatred in you to do the deed, it will at least make you apathetic to his demise."

Alex was taken aback by David's powerful advice. He had proved a great listener and advisor—completely unbiased and saying all the right things Alex needed to hear. Alex had always depended on his counsel before Toury came along, and he would make sure he always took David's too in the future.

David's reaction at first to Toury never had to do with David having feelings for him as Alex had falsely believed; as David so bluntly told him, although David preferred men, Alex just wasn't his type. Now, though, Alex understood David had been jealous in a much more platonic way. David's knowledge and opinion should not be cast aside in favor of Alex's lifemate; instead, he should've taken more people he trusted into the fold. Knowing the man wouldn't accept an apology or bear hearing Alex ask forgiveness without being severely uncomfortable, he let the issue go, making an oath to himself to listen more to those he trusted: David, along with Mary, who had finally taken up her responsibilities.

A grim-faced Agate came in three hours later. "He's asking for you."

"What has he said?"

"The commander of the rebel army's identity: Racine Hematite."

A chill crept down Alex's spine as he followed Captain Agate outside, trying not to think about the repercussions if this were true. Alex was married to Toury, so if she lost favor due to her family connections, he would as well. Pardoning her parents was one thing he could spin politically, but a draca-slaying rebel-leader sister? Never would happen. But was it true? Alex could not believe it. Was his disbelief founded upon not wanting to accept it, though?

When Alex entered the tent, Emerald was slouched against the corner of the bars, a bit roughed up, but the torture didn't seem to have been too extensive. Alex would not feel guilty about it.

Alex crossed his arms and gazed at Emerald skeptically. "You'll have me believe a teenage girl who recently just returned to Fyr is the commander of the entire rebel army that has been working since the days of my grandfather—albeit underground until recently?" It was ludicrous once it was said aloud. How dumb did Emerald think Alex was? A child, that was what he thought of Alex. He must. He saw him as the soft, naive boy in his cruel father's shadow. Despite proving himself and saving their world at the age of seventeen, living through a poisonous attack by the rebels at eighteen, the Emeralds still didn't believe he was a ruler to fear.

"The Hematites took over as the leaders; their daughter was just an emblem pitted against your queen."

"Then, without them, there is no commander, according to you. I have spies too, Emerald, and they are telling me the commander is still issuing orders."

"It's her, I swear it!"

"And why would the rebels work with the necromancers?"

Emerald floundered at Alex's accusation and peered up at him, his gaze frightened. "I don't know what you're talking about." The lie was obvious. Emerald may have faked his persona at times, but he was no leading actor. Staring into the man's eyes, before his gaze darted away first, Alex could see the fear and rage. The face was plastered into confusion, but the eyes didn't match the sentiment. Memories came flooding back—his uncle fishing with him, giving him archery lessons, giving him books about war to read, praising him. They were now tainted by falsity. He'd never remember his uncle the same again, but that was good. Alex was vanishing, and the draca in him would see him through this.

The Draca King sighed in annoyance. "The Hematites were never in charge. They couldn't be. They recently came back to Fyr, and this pathetic rebellion has been ongoing for ages. Second, they left the realm to hide from *you*. They even gave you up to protect their other daughter, despite their misgivings about Sapphirian rule. You see, they would never work with you, even if it were to bring me down. And Racine would never work with your people after you killed her parents. I know enough about Hematite women—having met four of them—to know that although they have light magic, they have fiery tempers." He let it sink in that he had spoken to both Toury's mother and Racine. "So, who really is the commander?"

Emerald's terrified face went slack, becoming devoid of emotion. His green eyes went cold. The way he stared at Alex was unnerving, not with hate or fear anymore, but completely apathetic. "I will die without telling you."

"There's only one person in this kingdom whom you'd die for. Thank you for telling me who the commander is."

"You cannot arrest a Sapphirian for treason without cause." The man spat out. Then, realizing he just confirmed Alex's suspicions, he talked faster, spinning tales, "If you arrest him, the real commander will act. My son is a usurper, yes, but by proxy; he doesn't know the plans, but he's the one who will rule after they win their rebellion and you're dead."

Alex wasn't sure he believed him. Emerald pressed his face to the bars, but Alex didn't dare back up and show weakness. He held the man's intense gaze, Alex's face devoid of emotion.

"And Henry is completely ignorant of my dealings. No one knows, save the commander. Everyone's too fixed to their cause for you to stop it all now. That silly little Hematite girl will be killed if she tries to divide up forces. Oh, the necromancers and rebels alike will get you, my boy. There's no way you can stop that now. You're facing a draca made of decades of fire, fueled by the spirit of hate. You can't put that out."

Alex wanted to make him stop talking, but Emerald was revealing so much without realizing it. All Alex's fears were true. The rebels would join with the necromancers to try to usurp the kingdom. And his cousin was this commander. This meant all the information Emerald and Henry had given them about the rebels when they had been "undercover" had no validity whatsoever. They hoped to make Alex a draca flying blind into a storm.

"You forget one thing. I can simply fabricate what you have said here right now. I can say you named your son the commander of the rebels and necromancers and you professed your innocence before I took your life."

"There are witnesses. You wouldn't. You're disgustingly all that is noble and honest." Belying his calm words, Emerald pressed his reddening face against the bars as if he wished he could force his way to freedom and rip out Alex's heart. The hatred in the man's eyes was palpable.

"Agate, who has the prisoner named the commander and head necromancer?" Alex challenged.

"Lord Henry Sapphirian, Your Majesty," Agate came forward to proclaim.

"You revolting little cad! My son is innocent. I will scream it out as you kill me." He shook at the bars and thrashed like a caged animal. The man was at the end of the line and coming to terms.

"Shall I take out his tongue?" Captain Agate asked.

Alex was happy to have an ally such as Agate who would pretend Alex would expect such a request. For the first time, Emerald appeared genuinely stricken.

"It matters not. He can scream all he wants or die a gentleman," Alex said.

"You haven't the constitution to murder anyone. You're a spineless little whelp." The man snapped insults at Alex. He was the one pacing, and Alex had found peace. Alex had needed this show of open hostility to kill the man. It was easier to take out an enemy who hated you than one who was just ambitious. "Nothing like your father. I rejoiced in the news of his poor health and celebrated his death. Craig was powerful, like felling a tree, but you will be like snapping a twig."

Alex had enough of the madman's nonsense. No new information was coming, just repeated insults. He was done. "The Citrines underestimated me, and look at them now. Oh wait, you can't, not yet, at least. The worst thing your son can do is underestimate me. And the sad thing is, you won't live to warn him. Without this curse, I am more powerful than any

Sapphirian I have ever heard of. I can open the ground, transport entire armies—what you believe to be tall tales are facts. My father chose a powerful bride, as have I. What can your son do with your diluted Emerald blood? What will my children become?"

Alex turned to leave the tent, determined to have the last word: "Unstoppable." To Agate he then said quietly, "Prepare for the beheading at dawn."

A gentleman's death. Alex had put it off, partially to make his uncle suffer the anxiety of waiting and to also help himself gain the courage to do this. Somehow, he had slept a few hours, wondering if David had slipped him a mild sleeping draught. He was thankful for that but wished there were something for his nerves now.

Alex was dressed in ceremonial armor by David, trying not to think at all about what he must do. David was grim. If there was a way out of this, David would urge him to take it. Emerald was a gentleman. To deny the request would be pathetic and prove he couldn't do it. Plus, it would torture everyone over a long trial. Yesterday, he had berated Emerald with a speech worthy of a king. Where was that strength now? He chided himself to pull it together. Moreover, Alex needed to silence Emerald to cut him off from those whom he had been leading before he could warn them.

The entire troop of soldiers was there to watch it. Great, a live audience for his barbarous act. He wished it were a law he could change, but it was a damned edict. His ancestors made sure he would take someone's life thousands of years after they wrote them.

Alex inhaled deeply and took in the scene. The army was parted in a semicircle. In the center was his uncle on his knees, his hands bound behind his back. Helpless. Head down. Defeated. Alex couldn't do this. He mentally pleaded for his uncle not to turn around and look at him.

The soldiers quieted their murmurs. His uncle's shoulders tensed, knowing the quiet was due to Alex's presence. His uncle, thankfully, didn't turn his head.

Alex moved to stand behind his uncle. He unsheathed his sword, trying to do so quietly, but the *schwing* sound of the sword tip flicking the brass throat of the scabbard disrupted the silence in a cringe-worthy, foreboding way, announcing what was to come. Alex gripped the hilt tightly to hide the trembling of his hands. "Any last words?" Somehow, his voice came out strong and devoid of emotion, although Alex was going through every feeling possible.

"Yes." His uncle's voice was brittle, panging Alex and tearing away at his resolve to do this deed. But then Emerald shouted out, "*Acwelan, draca!*" It was a death threat; there was no other way to interpret the ancient words for "die, dragon."

Alex almost expected an ambush of rebels to come to his uncle's rescue as they had come and attacked him on his wedding day, but Alex was unafraid and surrounded by his men. One of the soldiers spat at the ground near Lord Emerald. The prisoner flinched. Others followed in turn, disgusted by the man's last act being in rebellion against Alex instead of asking for forgiveness. There were boos toward Emerald from the men too far to show their resentment physically.

Alex put his hand up to silence them. "On this day, I sentence this man, Lord Humphrey Emerald, to death for conspiracy to practice dark magic and to usurp the throne, and the murders of Prince Alfred Sapphirian, the late King Craig Sapphirian, Lord Aschen Hematite, and Lady Angelica Hematite. As an act of mercy, I grant him his requested *beheafdian*. May the god and goddess grant you eternal peace."

Alex placed the blade of the sword in his palm and let all his emotions filter through his magic—anger, resentment, grief, panic, sorrow—and it lit the blade up red hot. He pulled his hand away lest he start melting the blade down.

"What is taking so long?" His uncle fretted and almost turned.

"I'm heating the blade, *Emerald*. Unlike you, I am merciful."

"Thank you," his uncle whispered and bowed his head, at last giving up the fight.

The blade was cooling, so Alex had to act fast. He hefted the blade over his shoulder and swung down, leveling his sword sideways, with all his strength, hoping he could truly grant a quick death. When he knew it would make contact in the right place with enough strength to bring instant death, he closed his eyes.

13

BEHEAFDIAN

Alex didn't return right away. His uncle was captured, so she expected it to take him a few minutes to transport the man to their dungeon, an hour or so if he got held up. When he didn't return, she realized she didn't know what to expect, what it meant for Alex to bring him to the castle's prison. This worried Toury. Her emotions were everywhere.

Worry followed her all afternoon. Would Alex have to travel back with his men for his safety? She was concerned, and after the nuisance known as Henry became too anxious over what Alex was doing and whether his father would be put on trial fairly, she was about to lose it. Oh, and the man's pacing! She couldn't blame him for his concerns, but she loathed the man, so much so that she just renamed the princess salon, christening it as the Queen's Room. No one could enter the Queen's Room without her invitation. Toury had intended to share it with the dowager and Mary, but if it kept Henry out, she refused to share. The old Queen's Room was renamed the Sapphirian Tea Room, where any female of the family could entertain. And today, to stop Mary's whining, Toury had joined them there and tried to ignore Henry's pacing.

Cobalt insisted on joining them, and that did make Toury feel a bit safer and much better for Mary's sake because she still believed her cousin was innocent.

"I think, Queen Dowager, you look quite done for. Shall you retire to your quarters until supper?" Cobalt asked, taking up her hand.

"I think my mother knows her own mind, Cobalt," Mary huffed.

The two of them. Toury wanted to roll her eyes but reminded herself Mary was younger and her relationship of butting heads might be good until she was mature enough to marry.

Toury noticed the dowager was tired and saw the chance of escape. "You do look tired, as am I. It has been a trying day for everyone. If you'll excuse us." She stood and started to leave the room.

The dowager did not protest and let Cobalt lead her from the room after he made his excuses to Mary. He ignored Henry, which he now could do as the prince-to-be, but Toury knew Henry would see this as an affront.

Toury didn't intend to retire and headed to the Queen's room, realizing after a turn that Cobalt and the dowager were following and whispering.

Toury stopped by the doorway.

"I was wondering, Queen Sapphirian, if the dowager and I could accompany you. She has said she isn't tired but is glad I got her away from her nephew, which was my goal for all of us."

Toury nodded and entered. She was bewildered by Cobalt's presence, his behavior, and she hoped he hadn't had a fallout with Mary or worse—he better not be here for Toury herself.

"No more tea, please. Something stronger, perhaps, since Mary isn't here," Cobalt muttered when Toury motioned for another cup of tea. He didn't wait for her approval but went to the decanter and poured himself a glass.

"Don't say it as if it's a sin to abstain. She's been so supportive and active in her duties," Toury said heatedly.

Mary had done well with stopping her wild drinking habits, allowing herself one watered-down firewhiskey with dinner and that was it, but still no one wanted to drink in front of her and spark her drinking problem if they could avoid it.

Cobalt's head whipped around at Toury. "You misunderstand me, my queen. I'll explain my rash words, but before I do, would you ladies like one?"

"God and goddess, yes," the dowager breathed out and sank onto the couch, her head in her hands—defeated, exhausted—and Toury was terrified since she had never seen her this weak before.

"No thank you, and sorry, Cobalt, I'm worried about Alex." Toury sat herself on the settee next to Alex's mother and took up her hand.

The former queen met Toury's gaze and smiled sadly. She squeezed Toury's hand.

Cobalt handed the dowager a drink, Toury a water, and sat across from them. "I'm glad Mary rarely drinks now. I meant I needed a drink and didn't want to do so in front of my engagee. I don't want to lie to you. Alex's absence is frightening. I wish he hadn't left me here."

"He needed you here because of me," Toury admitted. Cobalt stared at her, astonished again, so she had to explain, "I am very sorry, but Henry frightens me. He's scheming and seething with something I can't see. He's not a necromancer but just intensely ambitious."

"Thank you!" Cobalt shouted. He took a swig of his drink and then said, "I've had an argument with Mary about Henry, so I'm very happy someone agrees with me. I don't trust Henry; I saw his falseness as a child. I hated him, while Mary and Alex idolized him. He was this charismatic hero to them, but to me, he was just an ordinary boy—less than Alex and Mary. I saw them as real people, friends, but he was this...I don't think there's another word except a puppet."

"Yes," Toury agreed, relieved that not everyone was blind to Henry's false persona.

"I wanted to go with Alex. He shouldn't take on his uncle alone. Alex is stronger, of course, but he's too nice to do what needs to be done. I'm worried this will break him."

"Alex will be fine. He has us here to support him. As for Henry, sending him away might be worse than keeping him here," the dowager began.

"I see your line of thinking, Queen Dowager, but I'm not willing to bet Mary's, Alex's, and Toury's lives on it," Cobalt said.

Toury froze. Someone was confirming her worst fears. "You think he would go as far as to..."

"I know you hated the safety protocol, and I backed down, but you must be more observant, Your Majesty."

"Excuse me," Toury chided. She wasn't an idiot, and he was talking down to her as if she were merely inconvenienced by safety drills when truly she had been close to an anxiety attack—not that she could use that term here; they'd tell her she needed some silly stone to calm her. Nothing can calm you when you're on edge because someone wants you dead. "I have been *very* observant. I just wanted to know how he let it be so obvious he wanted to kill me, and confirmation of that is always shocking, I'll let you know."

"Forgive me, Your Majesty. Surely, you noted Lord Sapphirian's interest in why you weren't hungry this morning? He thinks you're with child," Cobalt said.

Toury had thought Henry's overconcern was odd.

Cobalt's eyes met hers, expecting her to answer with affirmation or denial. When neither response came, he continued: "Mary and I had a very different take on his inquiries, which led to an argument."

"I'm glad you and I see things the same," Toury commented, never before thinking she would join sides with Cobalt on an issue rather than Mary. "If I were with child, this would've been frightening news."

Cobalt's eyes narrowed on her, and he met the dowager's, but she sipped her drink. Cobalt thought Toury was pregnant. Just great. She thought she'd had her period, but it could hardly count as one. Could it have been something else? With their magic stones, the healers could tell if she was pregnant, but Toury was afraid to find out. With what Cobalt just said, she was even more worried now. She'd feel safer if Alex were here. If he'd banish or imprison his cousin, she'd relax, even though she knew he could still get to her via Sapphirian-powered transport if he were banished.

Since Alex hadn't returned that evening, Toury took supper in her room alone, not wanting to face that wretched Henry watching her appetite. She was not with child—or more that it was too early to be put off her food from it if she were. She was sick with worry and glad she was alone, for she barely could eat. Throwing up in front of Henry would be a huge target on her head. The nausea was caused by nerves from this situation, nothing more. Where was her husband? Had something terrible happened to Alex?

After supper, she read until she fell into a fitful sleep, waking often from terrible dreams she could only vaguely remember. They all seemed to gravitate around Henry killing Alex or her.

In the early light of dawn, a flash of bright light woke her up, and Alex stood in front of her in battle armor. His face was grim, pale, and covered in what Toury instantly realized was blood spatter. David stumbled but righted himself, his hand on the edge of Alex's cape—ceremonial armor then. They had left in a hurry, the servant grabbing on at the last second before a rushed Alex left him behind, as usual. David's face was horror stricken.

The sword Alex had been holding fell to the floor with a clang. It was covered in dark—blood.

She gasped and gave him a frantic once-over, her heart racing, unable to speak, before her stomach turned in a very different fear. It was not Alex's blood. She had a good suspicion of whose it was. "Alex?" She was hesitant. She slowly slipped out of bed so as to not startle him, for he was staring off in shock, unaware she was there.

His eyes snapped up to meet hers, and her heart broke. His gaze was wide and lost, full of desperation, and shattered. His shoulders were tense, mouth grim, and brow wrinkling in confusion as if he was piecing together what just had happened. Alex fell to his hands and knees with a clinking of armor scales hitting one another.

"Let's get you cleaned up, Your Majesty," David whispered. The servant's hands shook as he reached out to touch Alex's armor. She wasn't sure if either man could support the other.

"Leave us. I will ring for you," Toury said when Alex did nothing. "Madge, please ring for someone to take his sword down to be cleaned."

The servants obeyed, David reluctantly leaving Alex and Madge taking the ghastly weapon out of sight.

Alex just knelt there staring off, his breaths coming out in deep jagged pants. She had no clue what to do, and there was nothing she could possibly say, so she sank down onto the ground next to him and pulled him into an awkward hug—the armor in the way—and pulled his head down onto her shoulder. He burrowed his face into her neck and squeezed her so tightly, she could barely breathe.

His body shook with silent sobs, and he pulled her even tighter, searching for some kind of comfort no one could give. The state he was in, she couldn't help. All she could do was be present, to try to hold the pieces of him together.

"Alex?" she asked, needing to get him back to himself. He had to talk about what happened, to process it.

He pulled his face out of its hiding spot and loosened his grip on her. She took up his face in her hands to make his tear-filled eyes meet hers.

"My uncle. I killed him. I had to." Then he looked away from her in shame.

"Had to?"

"He asked for *beheafdian*." He paused to take in a ragged breath. "Please tell me you finished the book of edicts, because I don't think I can bear to explain."

"I have finished it," she said quietly, running her hand through his hair. They called it a "gentleman's death." There was nothing gentlemanly about it: beheading. She withheld her cringe. The rigidity of Alex's posture told her not to shower him with sympathy and condolences at the moment.

"I've never... I'm a murderer." He pushed away from her and stood quickly.

"No, you're not!" Toury's forceful tone stopped Alex from fleeing, and he peered down at her, lost. She got up off the ground, crossing her arms across her chest to hide the blood smears staining her ivory nightgown. "You were doing your duty and sparing your uncle long trials, shame, and a public execution. You had to."

Alex said nothing, but it was clear he was debating whether she was right or not. An awkward silence formed, so she knew he could speak no more of it at the moment. She crossed over to him and unfastened the buckle from his shoulder and then repeated the other side to remove the shoulder plates of his armor that were etched with scales. He did not object, and they did not speak as she dropped the armor to the ground in a clatter, ignoring the fact she should be more careful with the silver-plated and jewel-encrusted gear.

Next, she moved to each of his sides and then his shoulders again, freeing him from the breast- and backplates. It was ceremonial armor, not battle, so his helmet and leg armor must've been left behind at his camp. She dropped the breastplate, staring at the imprinted emblem of his medallion covered in blood droplets. All that was left were the arm plates, and she made quick work of them, wanting to distance him and herself from the armor that symbolized how duty demanded bloodshed. Then she tried to lift his scale mail, but it weighed too much when she lifted it above their heads.

Alex finally snapped out of his trance and helped. He tossed the scale mail onto the ground. She went for his shirt, and his hands stopped hers. "What are you doing?" he whispered. The vulnerability on his face was staggering, and she couldn't meet his gaze because it pained her. She did not want to see him so weak, sad, and frightened.

"We have to get you cleaned up," she told him.

He nodded slowly. "Can you draw me a bath? I'll be down in a moment."

She hurried downstairs, wanting to distance herself. Toury needed a moment to hold herself together for him because he needed her to be his rock right now. Her emotions were everywhere because Alex's emotions had become hers. They truly were like one, which made the situation doubly devastating. What was worse, there was nothing she could say or do to make him feel better. That hurt more than anything she had ever known.

Alex came down a moment later in his robe, the scent of smoke wafting down with him.

"Is something burning?"

"My clothes," Alex said sheepishly. "I could never wear them again."

Toury nodded and went to leave.

Alex caught her wrist. "Stay," he pleaded, the need for comfort so raw.

They were married, but seeing Alex naked without it being sexual, in an intense emotional situation—what the heck was she supposed to do? Distract him? Talk to him? She didn't know what he needed. Those eyes, though—richly blue, sparkling, and full of agony, pleading for help—banished her awkwardness.

She nodded and sat in the chair Madge occupied when she insisted on washing Toury. After he climbed in and dunked himself, she began to do that, wash his hair. He laid his head back against the tub, his hair all sudsy, and closed his eyes. She kept running her fingers over his scalp, creating a rich lather, because it made him relax. She watched the tension slowly leave his shoulders and face.

He seemed at peace, so she got up to leave. She wanted to have David bring Alex something to eat. She was sure Alex hadn't eaten much the last night, knowing what he had to do. His uncle had asked for a dignified death, and Alex would've needed to process that and then do it. She was positive he needed food, even if he didn't want it.

"Don't go," Alex pleaded.

She stopped. She wasn't used to Alex being needy, asking instead of commanding. It was a strange shift in their relationship. She turned to him. "I'm getting some food sent up for us." When he was about to protest, she hurried out the rest: "I know what you'll say, but you need it. We'll eat a little, talk this out, and let it go. Tomorrow will be a new day. Focus your energy on other things."

"Like telling my cousin I beheaded his father?"

Toury cringed. "Fine. After you tell him that and make him leave this castle, it'll be a new day."

"You want me to kick him out after I tell him his father is dead?" Alex was confused.

"Alex, he's definitely conniving and completely fake. You know this. He was studying my diet and asking questions. He thinks I'm pregnant because I haven't eaten well. I'm too worried for my life with him around."

"Are you?" Alex turned around to face her.

She tried not to watch the water run down his chest and focused on the task at hand. "Your hair. It needs to be rinsed," she reminded him, grabbing a towel.

He turned back around and slipped back down into the water to wash out the suds and gasped a breath when he resurfaced. She heard the water running off of him and brought him the towel, focusing on his face. His hair was longer than it had ever been. Toury wondered if it had been cut at all since their wedding day—the first wedding that never finished, where her father had almost killed Alex.

"You need to have a haircut."

"Huh?" He wrapped the towel around his waist and pulled her into his arms, finally himself again—somber and exhausted but the Alex she knew.

"You haven't cut it since that horrid day," she said.

"Our wedding day?" His brows rose. "Horrid?" The fact he was joking was a good thing, considering.

"It was. Our second wedding day was amazing, though." As soon as she finished saying it, he kissed her vigorously. She pulled away after a moment because she was determined he'd eat something.

He cradled her face. "Are you?" His eyes drank her in, and in that moment, she felt like the most beautiful woman in the universe.

"Huh?" It was now her time to ruin a moment with that word.

"Are you carrying our child?" he asked, his hand running down to her lower abdomen.

This was the last thing she wanted to talk about. She pulled away.

"Toury," his voice broke.

It was wrong for her to hide anything from him. "No. I dunno. Maybe?" She was confused on how to proceed. He was looking for a way to not face his uncle's death, searching for something to eclipse the feeling he was trying to evade instead of face. And if she told him her suspicions and was wrong? He was barely holding himself together.

"Apparently, we need to talk. Order the food you want, and I'll be up in a moment."

Needing to escape, she fled upstairs and rang the bell, ordered David to get some bread, meat, and cheese, then poured Alex a firewhiskey with water. She didn't make one for herself. What if she were pregnant? Wouldn't she know? Wouldn't there be signs? Her chest was sore, but that could be a sign of the opposite of pregnancy as well.

Alex was upstairs in his robe, and he approached her. She really wished he would put on a nightshirt or pantaloons or something. The thin silky robes in Fyr didn't leave much to the imagination, and there was a serious talk about to go on. Alex took a sip of the drink and put it down. He drew her into his arms, giving her that look that made her feel like a goddess. "Are you? I mean, girls figure this out by their courses, don't they?"

"Courses?" All Toury could think about was school. Did he mean they were taught about it in school? "Yes, they teach us about having babies in school."

Alex's brow wrinkled, confused. Then his mouth opened and closed. He blushed furiously. "Not school, Toury, um..." the conversation reminded her of how shy he had been when they'd first met when talking about anything dealing with intimacy. "I don't know what they call it on Earth, but girls, you know how they bleed when—"

"Oh, stop! Okay, I know what you mean." He was talking about her period. How awkward. "I'm not...regular. I've never been, so I wouldn't know. I thought I did have it, but it was short-lived." She was so embarrassed, her face burned with the sentiment.

He affectionately rubbed her cheeks with the pads of his thumbs.

"But I refuse to find out through the healers and refuse to wear the prince medallion until it's obvious." There was no way she was going to wear that bullseye on her body.

"Why, my love? If you were, it would make me the happiest man in Fyr."

"Your cousin and others. They're speculating and hoping, I think, that we won't have a child. I'm scared, Alex. They'll want me dead if I am." There. She said it, the truth as they always promised to tell each other no matter what.

His face fell, and she felt wretched for ruining with the brutal truth this blissful moment that had brought him cheer. "If you are that scared, I will get him out of here." His hand moved down and touched her stomach again. "I bet you are. The stones foretold our high fertility level." Alex's face spoke of something else: knowledge. He must've seen snippets of their future.

"You've seen it!" she accused.

"No—yes. What I mean to say is, visions don't have dates. There's no way to know when." He was terrible at hiding anything.

"Good. We won't find out. We don't tell anyone. We figure it out when symptoms occur." She was putting her foot down. Because, knowing him, he'd be too excited and announce it to the world.

He nodded. "You're right. We should hide it, just in case, unless everything with the rebels dies out with my...the former Lord Emerald."

Toury won a great victory, telling a king what their plans would be. Partnership was what he'd promised, and at least in this, she got it. She took his hand and led him to the sitting room, trying to take his mind off his uncle and her own mind off what could be going on in her body.

14

A DISMISSAL

Alex woke to David shaking him. He sat up scanning the room, frightened at first, and confused about where he was and where Toury was. His room. Toury was sound asleep, curled up next to him. He had been dreaming—having a nightmare—that he had cut off his uncle's head. And then it hit him hard. He had given his uncle a gentleman's death. It was real.

"Your Majesty? It is almost four hours after the dawn. You needed rest, so I didn't wish to wake you, but there's a high probability of this morning's events spreading across the land to the palace..." David hinted, trying not to command but to suggest.

Groggy, it took Alex a second for David's words to register. "Henry!" Alex was out of bed and covering his lifemate in the warm blankets. She murmured in her sleep. He kissed the top of her head. Then he left the room quietly and whispered, "Madge is to stay in this room with the queen every moment I am not, starting now."

David nodded and hurried up the stairs to where the two now resided. Alex started to dress himself, which annoyed his valet when he returned. Madge was clad in a robe, but she wore a belt that held her sword and daggers. Good. Madge entered the room and closed the door.

Alex hurried down the hall, contemplating whether to have Henry summoned to the study to show this was business or to the Prince's—no, King's Room—to show it was a family matter. He veered left as soon as he hit the main building toward his study. He could afford no kindness with the commander if that was truly whom he was dealing with. There wasn't enough proof to arrest Henry, and knowing but pretending he wasn't aware might give Alex an edge. He must do as his father instructed about hiding his heart and emotions—at least when it came to facing his enemies.

Once he entered his study, he nodded.

David rang the bell for servant. "Do you want food as well?"

"Not yet. But have the servant who summons Henry come and pour a couple firewhiskeys. My cousin will need it." More like Alex might need it.

"So, the poison taster too," David added.

Alex rolled his eyes at the thought of someone tampering with the firewhiskey he never drank in this room, but David knew best.

Too soon, his cousin entered. He appeared exhausted and probably hadn't slept. Alex was signing a bill to waive taxes for the year for those who had taken in people from Hollyhaven, the town burned to cinders by a rogue dragon. It hadn't been Dame Draca B's fault. Racine Hematite was to blame for that. Racine, the dragon slayer the rebels had rescued from his dungeon, could be the commander as his uncle had proclaimed. He could not rule her out. Yet the man who stood in front of him was the better candidate. It would be much easier to replace royalty with royalty than to rebuild an entire government overnight.

Had Henry and his father ever realized Henry was a simple pawn—a placeholder—to be taken out once the rest of Alex's loyal subjects settled down if he ever was usurped? There were still so many believers around, according to reports, chanting about the Draca King reborn, musicians singing of his feats, and children heralding him as a hero, their parents hoping he was this hero who would fulfill their own and future generations' dreams.

"Sit," Alex commanded Henry. He motioned the poison taster to serve the drinks. "Have a drink."

The servant came over and handed Henry one glass and then tasted the other, swishing it around in his mouth before swallowing. Alex tried to ignore him as Henry spoke.

"A bit early, cousin, no?" He smiled, but it was feigned. Henry was tiring of this game of being in the castle and being watched.

"I have bad news," Alex said.

The poison taster, satisfied it was safe, handed the drink to Alex. He drank just the littlest bit. It was too early by any standards, and he didn't want to seem like he needed intoxication to be courageous.

"My father has been captured?" Henry said.

"He is dead." Alex decided to get right to it, not torture the man. Also, he wanted to gage his reaction to the news. If he was the commander, this would be a heavy blow. His partner would be gone, and this he would have to hide. Or would Alex see a son grieving for his father instead?

Henry's eyes went wide. His hand trembled so much, he used two hands to steady the glass and then drank it back in one go. Alex politely took another very small sip, waiting for his cousin to say something.

"How did it happen?" Henry managed to ask, staring down at his hands and the empty glass.

"He was captured in Fieldstone. I went to bring him in, and he opted for *beheafdian* instead." Again, Alex wanted this over with and to not drag it out for both of them.

"You mean to say you chopped off my father's head?" Henry asked incredulously, glaring at Alex. His jaw clenched, and his face flushed red, indicating the infamous Sapphirian temper had been triggered.

"If that is how you wish to phrase it, yes," Alex shot back. "But the truth of it was, he wanted to spare you the trial, the shame, and the stripping of your title and estate."

Henry went pale, the anger leeching to shock.

"He was trying to spare you, Henry. You know the edicts." Alex reminded him he had to do this, that if Lord Emerald had been found guilty, he would've lost everything—his life, title, estate—and by proxy, Henry would have become a stripped gentleman, something seen as worse than a cunning folk in the social sphere.

"What were his last words?"

"That is between him and me." Alex didn't want to repeat the words about rebellion, particularly if they were a coded message for Henry to enact some diabolical plan.

"I have every right to know!" Henry was upset now, unstable.

The door opened, and a few soldiers entered the room, weapons drawn. Henry had stood in haste, and weapons froze him in place.

"What is this?" Henry's gaze frantically searched for a way out.

"Sit. You raised your voice to the king and arose quickly. They are merely doing their duty to protect me as trained." Alex did not call them off. All gentlemen carried a dagger on them at all times, so one dive across the desk would be all it might take for Henry to end Alex's life. Fire would protect Alex, but it wouldn't harm Henry. To calm him further, Alex admitted. "Your father said, 'Thank you' because I heated the sword for him. It was quick."

Henry fell into the chair then, stunned. He stared at Alex as if he had never seen him before. Alex looked away, not wanting to keep staring into those probing Sapphirian eyes so similar to his own. Henry had expected the Alex of two years ago, and he was realizing Alex had become a man. Your father dying, ruling a kingdom, almost dying yourself, taming dragons, facing necromancers, almost losing the woman you love *twice*, marrying—all these things make boys men. Some of these things can break men as well. Alex was beginning to believe he was seeing this before his eyes with his cousin.

"Did he say anything? Did he confess to killing the Hematites? I can't believe he would do that."

"Yes, he admitted it, and he said much more than that, things I already knew or suspected." Alex began to write on a document to show Henry he was too busy for questions.

"Like what?" Henry was tense but hiding his emotions again; trying to stay in control meant he was fishing for information. The actor might be back in command, but his façade could not last in this emotional state.

"His crimes will be published in the paper, but it might be best you don't read them, to be honest. It would only hurt you." Alex signed the document.

"I have a right to know what he told you."

"No, you don't actually." Alex clipped at him. He also felt a very many things at the moment—guilt, anger, regret—but he too had to hide it. The thing that would hit Henry hardest was Alex being calm and in control—not the whelp. "Here is the decree that allows you to remain a lord despite your father's treason, but you are banished from the palace and to remain at Fort Emerald for the time being. If you return here without invitation from myself, you will be killed on sight. This is until further notice."

"Further notice?" Henry now seemed lost. Whether fishing for Alex's next move or forgetful in his grief, Alex could not determine Henry's motives.

Alex pressed on, wanting to see the back of his cousin. "The guilds decide these things. You know the edicts. Normally, you'd be stripped of title, lands, and name, but since I let your father die a gentleman—"

"Let him?" Henry laughed sardonically. The misplaced smile left Henry's face when a soldier held a sword to this throat. Henry froze.

"Do not interrupt the king," the soldier ordered.

"Stand down. He is not himself with grief. Yes, I *let him*." Alex cracked a bit, letting his anger through. He raised his voice, "Do you think I wanted to murder my uncle, the man I had believed cared for me as family my entire life? I gave him mercy, what he asked for, in exchange for information." Alex sighed, trying to subdue the anger. "I will have the guilds meet to decide as soon as possible to put you at ease. The decision is out of my hands since you are family."

"But it wasn't for my father." Henry scowled at Alex. Was he trying to get Alex to attack him?

103

"Because it was treason with a witness, confession, and request for mercy. Henry, you and I were schooled together. I know you know the edicts. You haven't been accused of anything..." Alex left the 'yet' unsaid, but Henry's eyes met his in understanding.

Neither said anything and continued to stare at each other. Both awaited the other to attack, the tension building between them. The guards' hands tightened on their weapons, feeling it as well.

At length, Henry said quietly in a tone of submission, "I want his...remains."

"They were boxed and sent to the fort so you could have your pyre."

"Thank you," Henry managed to get out, although Alex knew Henry couldn't see the kindness he was bestowing at that moment. His grimace said as much.

Traitors were normally buried into the earth against custom, not allowed a dignified ceremony—or much worse was done with their remains long ago as a lesson to obey his ancestors or else. He needed to end the practice of traitor burials lest the necromancers use the bodies as they had up north when they'd resurrected all the dead necromancers from their mass grave.

"Am I to transport home now without my things?" Henry asked in a quiet voice. Alex wished he could believe Henry was struck down by this and finished, but he knew better. Henry would be back for revenge.

"No, these soldiers will help you pack up and take you through the gates. Once you are outside the walls, you may transport home. Remember not to return until summoned by me, for your own safety." He meant it as a threat.

Henry smirked, knowing well it was for Alex's peace of mind and safety as well. He stood with a sigh, giving Alex a measured look. "I guess this is goodbye then, cousin."

"Goodbye?" Alex peered up at him, twirling his quill. He studied Henry. "Only if you want it to be or the guilds dictate so. I suggest keeping your head down, not leaving the fort, and perhaps they shall see you as innocent."

"Innocent of what?" Henry asked, aghast.

Alex studied the man's face. This wasn't the cousin he'd grown up with. Henry was a stranger, an actor. Cobalt had been right all these years about Henry's false charm, his fake charisma. Henry was not taken aback at all by Alex's comment. No, he was pretending to be to ferret details out of

Alex. How low the Emerald men had thought of Alex. They had underestimated him, and Henry's father paid the price. Alex would show Henry who he truly was.

"You and your father were pretty close, in each other's company often, assigned together in the same troop by my father. It's quite unbelievable that you—being as shrewd and knowledgeable as you are—would have no clue what he was up to. Or at least the buzz in my ears from the guilds are seeing it this way."

"I had no idea what my father was up to, and I...I still don't believe you."

"Are you calling the king a liar?" Alex asked, standing. He couldn't care less whether Henry believed him, but he had to put the man in his place. Show him he was the king.

The soldiers shifted uncomfortably.

"No, Your Majesty." Henry ground out.

Alex wanted to gloat in Henry's restrained anger. No matter how good of an actor he was, bits of the real man got through: shrewd, ambitious, and he wanted that medallion around Alex's neck. His eyes flickered to it often. How far would he go to get it?

"You're dismissed."

Henry bowed his head with effort as if it killed him inside to do so and retreated into the middle of Alex's soldiers, who escorted him toward the door.

"Send in my breakfast while I finish up my correspondence," Alex said to David. Alex's nerves were rattled, and he was far from hungry, but Henry was a showman, so Alex put on his own show of ease, that informing his cousin of his father's death was perfunctory task number one of the day's business, and he was moving on without worry to the next.

After the food arrived and the poison taster was satisfied, the smell did get to him, and Alex ate heartily. Soon, the threat would be gone, and even Henry wouldn't be stupid or rash enough to enter the palace and risk his life. Henry would need a foolproof plan. And once he was out that door, Alex would enact a plan of his own for all their safety.

After his breakfast, Alex caught up on his correspondence. His next task was a more private matter, so he cleared the room except for his bodyguard. "David? Your queries into staff?"

"No one was seen talking to Lord Sapphirian, save three servants: a chambermaid, a laundress, and a stable boy. It was quite noticeable as he is the type to ignore servants' existence. These were quiet, secretive conversations, suspicious. He talked to the laundress a lot, but some say she is pretty, so he might've been making some arrangements."

Alex thought for a moment. "Our chambermaid?"

"Yes, the one who tidies your rooms, and the laundress does the palace bedclothes. You suspect foul play or intel?"

Alex thought for a moment. "Have someone search our entire apartment for anything out of place or dangerous, have the three servants questioned, and if they have been up to anything, imprison them. If they are innocent, let's still redistribute them away from our rooms. Only the most trusted are allowed in our rooms. Select one chambermaid, the head laundress shall do all of Toury's and my clothing, and the stablemaster is to check every saddle, horse, every inch of that stable."

"Yes, Your Majesty."

"David," he said before the man could go ring the bell. "From my quarters."

They transported to Alex's sitting room, where Toury was eating breakfast at the table. David rang the bell. Alex leaned down and kissed her, making her giggle tightlipped because her mouth was full of food.

"Henry is leaving, right now."

Toury swallowed her food, sighed with relief, and leaned her head against his stomach since he was standing and she sitting. He loved when doing the right thing made her happy. She was so easy to please. She smiled up at him then, and he took her chin in his hand, just admiring her lovely face.

The door opened, and David dictated Alex's orders. Toury gawped at the two servants who began cleaning and searching through everything. She stared at him, perplexed, awaiting an explanation.

"Just being careful about servants, moving some people around, and now we truly make an emergency plan with Henry gone and no spies to report to him."

The worry left her face quickly. "Cobalt will be in high form."

Alex laughed. "He deserves his day in the sun, no?"

"I'll behave and try not to yell at him too much." She smiled, her eyes alight with mirth and mischievousness.

Alex doubted that, but he would never tire of seeing his lifemate scold men like naughty children. Well, perhaps he could deal with her not reprimanding himself that way. "Not too much, but maybe a little."

The worst was over, at least for now, so Alex felt on top of the world for once. Toury made all his troubles fade away. She pushed the terrible memories away. They had happened hours ago, and yet, without even trying, she made them feel distant. Toury was his lightbearer, banishing the dark from his mind as she had with the curse. He marveled over how they had found each other and what he must've done to deserve her.

15

FIRE LIGHT

A dark cloud had been lifted. The palace was light and airy when Toury woke, and she had a spring in her step when she got ready. Alex was all smiles and happiness. Henry was gone. They both knew Henry was still a threat—not that they said it aloud—but not having him under their noses gave them a snug feeling of security, even if it might be false.

Cobalt broke their little bubble with all the security plans: two soldiers outside each tower, two inside their sitting rooms, barring the door every time they were inside. Madge and David's old quarters directly across the hall from their quarters were now to house four more soldiers. The heads of the guilds—Cobalt's father and Tobias Firebrand—were moved to the castle to keep the government intact while minimizing who could enter the castle. The poison taster would now test the "core four" as Cobalt donned them to save repeating names: Toury, Mary, Alex, and Cobalt himself. They would be the targets. The "core four" were not to leave the palace. What was new? Toury hadn't left since her wedding. That had been seven weeks ago—yeah, she had been counting. Then he said they couldn't even go outside.

She drew the line at not being able to visit the orchard. "Whoa, no. Absolutely not. The orchard is in the back of the palace, away from the center city, well protected and far from any walls," Toury cut in.

"Our enemy can transport anywhere at any time," Cobalt said, treating Toury as a simpleton.

"Stop calling him an enemy. Maybe suspect?" Mary, stubbornly determined not to think ill of her cousin, added.

Cobalt rolled his eyes, and Toury couldn't blame him. She was also tired of Mary downplaying and disbelieving that Henry was after the throne. Toury was worried this would get Mary killed in the end, but she wouldn't listen, and Toury was tired of arguing with her.

"People need fresh air," Toury said before yet another Cobalt-Mary spat started. "As you pointed out, he can get to us in the palace anyway, so how is outside the building any different?"

"She's right, Cobalt. We can't hide indoors. The back of the castle is the safest, as the queen points out. A retinue of twelve out there should suffice." Alex joined her side after neither Mary or Cobalt spoke up at first.

Toury thought she had won until Cobalt opened his big mouth. "What if he brings fifty men as you did, King Alex?" Cobalt challenged.

"No one in the history of Fyr could do that. Alex is an anomaly. Henry is not that powerful," Mary said.

"True, although I'd rather not be referred to as an 'anomaly.' It isn't very flattering." Alex mused. "Twenty-five men for outdoors then. Surely, our finest soldiers can defeat two rebels in a fight, and that's if my cousin were powerful enough to transport as many as I did."

Cobalt conceded. Then for fun, Toury protested each demand after that. The grievances would be postponed, all balls banned, visitors one at a time if approved. Alex smiled at her and winked, so she kept at it. It was silly that Cobalt actually thought she wanted to hear grievances. Mary caught on, and then all three of them were making Cobalt irate. When he realized they were messing with him, he stormed off. Mary went after him, half giggling, half pleading. In the end, the only additional success Cobalt had, aside from the retinue for the orchard, was banning any large gatherings and halting the grievances, but Alex shifted to having them done via missives as he preferred anyway.

"We'll be safe." Alex folded Toury in his arms.

"No, we won't. He's not the kind of man to give up." She leaned into him for warmth after her chilling statement.

"Okay, as safe as we can be." He kissed her.

"Thank you for the orchards." She gazed into those sapphire eyes, seeing the love she had for him mirrored back. It had been kind to take her side, even though she would be safest locked up.

He grew pensive. "Your points were logical. I'm angry about not being able to hit the stables every time I need to think, to be honest, but the orchards are a pretty safe compromise. I can imagine picking fruit with the love of my life is even better." He could not resist another peck on her lips.

"It better be," she teased him, eliciting a full-bellied laugh from him.

Only, when she invited him to join her in the orchard the next afternoon, he was ensconced in his study with the guild heads. She found Mary and the queen at leisure, who desired to get out of the castle. The twenty-five soldiers were picked up on the lower floor, and they went outside. Duric, Toury's personal dracaberry forager, handed them baskets and trailed behind to help.

They worked their way far into the orchard because the nearest fruit had been picked already. The soldiers set up a perimeter, the bodyguards staying by the royals' sides. They picked fruit and spoke of trivial things, mostly news and gossip other ladies had sent to them via post. Duric insisted on climbing the tree and not allowing Toury to use ladders. She was guessing the little pipsqueak had a special order from the king not to let her risk her health. She'd hate to see what restrictions Alex would try to instill once she was sure she was pregnant. He would have a fight on his hands from her if he dared. She took a deep breath. She needed to check her anger—getting mad at little Duric for no reason was so not her.

A flash of fire made Toury's heart jump. Alex wouldn't be stupid enough to surprise his own soldiers, who were ordered to hack to pieces anyone who appeared out of nowhere. She thought the worst: Henry was here to kill her. Toury was drawing her light power into her hands to be ready when she saw not Henry but Racine standing there, holding a big jug of reddish-brown liquid. Madge's dirk was at Racine's throat, while four of the closest soldiers had spears pointed at her back. Seeing how light magic wouldn't help her against another Hematite, Toury pulled in her magic.

"I'd stand back if I were you." Racine's face contorted. "This stuff is off." She held up the jug of what Toury now realized was dragon's blood, taken about eight months ago when Racine and their parents had slain a dragon. Apparently, there was some left, even after the rebels used it to almost kill Alex on Toury's disastrous first wedding day.

Then Racine fell to her knees, vomiting up red liquid. Toury turned away, more than disgusted. Toury wretched and held back the sensation by pressing the back of her hand to her lips. She held her breath and took a couple steps away from the bloody vomit. Mary, the queen, and the rest of the soldiers closed in around Toury.

Racine wiped her mouth off, her lips stained crimson. "I came only to talk. Have the soldiers cuff me and search me for weapons if you like, but I need to tell you something privately, and it needs to be fast."

Toury didn't trust her, even if Racine had helped Alex in Mineria. However, if she could tell Toury anything that might save their lives, the risk of talking to her might be worth it.

"Not privately, no." Toury decided. "Cuffed, with Mary safe inside."

"Hey," Mary protested.

Toury shot her a commanding look, and Lucy led her away. Toury would keep Mary and her separated so both couldn't be taken or hurt. The queen dowager came to Toury's side, touched her shoulders with a soft squeeze, then took the jug of blood from Racine and held it tight, preventing an escape. A soldier cuffed Racine, and Toury took the key from him. Then he backed away.

"I stay with her," the dowager told Racine.

Something crept over Toury's skin, an invisible film. It didn't distress her, though; it made her feel safe and emboldened. It had the same sensation as Cobalt's eerie seduction powers, but unlike that time, it made Toury feel in control, powerful. Any anxiety she had over Racine's presence waned. Toury was calm and collected.

Racine frowned. "You were once a Jasper, were you not?"

"That's right." The dowager held her head high.

"You're protecting her."

"Of course I am."

That explained the weird sensation cocooning Toury in a strong, protected, invisible bubble. She had heard the dowager possessed incredible blood magic, and the stone jasper was one of protection, but Toury had never seen the queen practice it. She was sure the dowager had to be very powerful; the former king would've only married the most powerful, beautiful woman he could find. Not only that, she could see the appeal the dowager had as well. If she had made the former king feel this powerful, he would've wanted that fix daily. She finally understood her in-law's relationship more knowing this, and sadly, Toury had been used by Alex just as Lady Jasper had been used by her lifemate. But Alex was a much kinder man, a more malleable man when it came to Toury. He would try not to command her and would put her before the kingdom. If only the latter could be true once and for all.

Toury commanded the soldiers to set the perimeter again so they would be out of hearing range but able to see and be close enough to respond if anything went awry. The queen's bodyguard and Madge were ready with dirks pointed in case.

"Speak, quietly," Toury commanded.

"I'm glad you're being so cautious, and you and Mary should stay apart as much as possible. You're too much of a bounty together."

Although Racine was right in a way, Toury felt safer with the "core four." She would not admit this to her sister. "You said you had little time. And why would you help? You hate Alex and me."

"I know I've done bad things."

Toury gave her a leveled glare.

"Okay, terrible things. And I knew you wouldn't believe me, but I had to come tell you. The commander will attack and soon. He leaves me out of things now. He became suspicious after I trapped Alex in Mineria and didn't help detain him." The way she spoke of the commander was with spite and pain. Toury could read Racine well, despite not knowing her long.

"The commander is Henry, and you are in love with him." Toury said to gauge her sister's reaction.

"No," Racine said too loudly and quickly. She went on, not even realizing, or perhaps not caring, that she confirmed Henry was the commander. "That is...he promised to make me queen. He promised me so much, but I know now that those were empty lies. It wasn't love, maybe admiration under false pretenses—it doesn't matter. Listen, he suspects me already for a lot. I went mad on him when I found out his father murdered our parents." She paused, blinking away tears Toury could tell were genuine.

The irony was not lost on Toury. She had said Racine had been married to the cause—technically, Racine would've been, had Henry kept his side of the deal and his father not killed their parents. Toury didn't trust her sister, but as always, she wanted to comfort anyone who was unhappy. "Stay here, then."

"In a dungeon? No. I'm no help there."

"You'll be safe, alive," Toury begged, knowing well her sister would not obey. She was a Hematite, after all.

"Don't pretend we're best friends, Toury. I was insanely jealous of you. Power, savior status, and a prince in your pocket, all without trying—it angered me, but when our parents died, it made me realize—"

"That if you could have a real family, you would?" Toury cut in with her own sentiment. How she longed for her family to have been different, the long lost fantasy of a loving and accepting home she'd had while growing up without them on Earth.

"No, but wow. Earth must've been as rough for you as Water was for me if you'd want me as family. No, I realized that if Mother and Father were still alive... They had a cause, but that cause was born of needing to protect us—you, Aschen, and me—and they thought it was with the rebels, as did I. Opinions are turning." She paused to make a face of displeasure. "Apparently, your king is doing good within a couple months of his coronation. Rebels are leaving the cause."

She sighed and crossed her arms; her gesture and darting eyes showed she was no good at sharing, and she was about to get as emotional as her hardened heart could get. "The point is, our parents would never join necromancers, and neither will some of these rebels. I know if Mother and Father were alive, they'd have left and joined forces with you. In fact, Father did speak of some term he said you'd understand. Before they were captured, he said it might be time for us to turn 'double-agent.' I've realized now that means pretending to stay loyal while actually switching sides." She uncrossed her arms and pointed to the jug in the dowager's arms. "That is my last supply of dragon's blood. It's so old, I'm lucky it worked. I cannot return to you this way again." Then she added hastily, for she had not been dismissed by her queen, "That's if you let me leave. If you let me go, when you see me again, it will be at the siege. I will do what I can to stop him."

"When. When will it happen?" Why wasn't she telling her more? They could prevent it. What was the point of Racine making this effort to warn her about something they already knew would happen eventually?

"I'm sorry. I don't know. I will try my best to protect you and Aschen. It would be what our parents would expect of me. Look, I'm not good at this feelings stuff, but please take care, and I actually hope we see each other alive at the end of all this."

Because Racine did care, Toury's heart warmed with the belief her sister had changed. Perhaps it was a foolish indulgence, but Toury did not care. She would believe. "But wait," —Toury tightly clutched the key that would free her sister— "how will he do it?"

"I have no idea, but use your head. Fire cannot fight fire. He will somehow incapacitate the king, try to kill him, and take you and Mary..."

Toury ignored the dowager's gasp.

"He won't hurt Mary if she allows herself to be called unfit to rule. I truly think he doesn't want her dead. And Toury, he doesn't want you dead either. I think he plans to wait it out to see if you are with child. Because if you aren't, you're no threat without Alex."

"The hell I'm not," Toury ground out.

Racine tilted her head to examine her sister. "I think, had we met in better circumstances, I would've really liked you. You don't take squat from men either. Please, I do have to get back before I'm noticed gone." Racine held up her cuffed hands.

Toury hesitated. Her sister had garnered no information from them, except that they were in the orchard, but she knew that already to have appeared there. She learned Toury would go down fighting, but Henry had to know this about her already. Racine had given information. She had confirmed the commander's identity and his plans. She had given, and Toury hadn't reciprocated. She had to believe Racine.

She gave the key to Madge, who unlocked the cuffs. Without needing to ask, the queen gave the jug of blood to Racine so she could escape.

Toury painfully watched her sister drink the horrible stuff to gain enough power to escape. "Promise me something, Racine. If it comes down to my life or Alex's, choose him."

Racine shook her head. "Our parents—"

"Promise me!" Toury shouted.

Then her sister gave her a sad smile and a nod, acknowledging it could be the last time they would see each other. "I promise." She closed her eyes and disappeared into a ball of fire.

"I should've imprisoned her," Toury said quietly.

"No, she wants and needs to redeem herself," The dowager said.

"If she dies?"

"It'll be on her terms. Locking her up might save her life but not her soul, Toury." The dowager stopped to brush hair off Toury's shoulder in a loving motherly gesture. "I was not given the courtesy my benevolent son bestows upon you. Freedom to do as one wishes is the best gift of all."

Toury's eyes teared up at what her mother-in-law had gone through, what most women or servants of Fyr went through. She would help take Henry down in whatever way possible, because he represented the false, conniving court of men controlling anyone whom they deemed lesser. Alex was the future who wanted everyone to have a chance, the man who esteemed honesty above all. She would fight for Alex, and if letting Racine do her bit to make things right and losing her made sure the kingdom would be good for all people, Toury had to let it happen. This mentality made her finally understand how and why Alex had gone dark with the necromancers and gone as far as almost killing her in hopes she could save them all. This was her kingdom and bigger than her wants and needs; the people were more important.

Once they entered the castle, Mary stood there cross-armed, foot tapping. "You let her go? I'm sorry for saying it because she is your relation, but next time I see her, I'm going to at least punch her in the face or burn her. Sorry."

"Don't be sorry," Toury mused. "Now you know how I feel about your cousin."

Mary's mouth dropped in shock.

The dowager laughed and put her arm around both of them, giving a gentle squeeze. "Ah, girls. You cheer me up in a time of woe."

Mary appeared lost still, but Toury understood. Their innocuous banter made the dowager forget the threats and the loss of her husband. The comment meant much more to Toury. Although she and Racine shared the same blood, Mary was her sister—their disagreements worked exactly how they would between siblings—and the dowager's comments and affection seemed like a mother's should be. These two, and the people inside the palace, were her true family. She had one at last and would not let Henry take it.

16
A LAUGHING MATTER

Threats were looming, but an amazing month of bliss passed them by where Alex passed new laws that upended the rebel cause. Toury began to get moody and less interested in nighttime and lunch pleasures. She ate less but was in complete denial there was a baby. He'd let it slide until this morning, knowing she just was too scared to face it. Almost three months since their wedding night? Even if she hadn't conceived instantly, she would know by now. Of course, she evaded his question yet again, this time distracting him by the very pleasures she had avoided recently.

His day had been busy, and he didn't see Toury again until supper. Even though he wanted to talk to her alone, it was still nice to have the family sit around the table in the dining hall together. Hematites and Sapphirians were dining together in peace. What would his father have thought? How would Toury's parents have reacted? This was the very picture of Fyr he wanted to show his people: peace and coexistence. There was just the matter of Henry and his impending attack. He believed Racine. She could've hurt or taken Toury, but she hadn't. The information was useless until they knew exactly what Henry planned and when, but they were at least warned. Alex had maximized the guards outside the dining hall and even had six stationed inside, in addition to the valet-bodyguards.

Lady Edwina was fully healed and doting on Toury's little brother as if he were her own son. The boy would grow up spoiled, but there were worse things for a poor kid whose parents had been unstable, destitute, and unloving. The rebels lived in squalor, so this kid was finally getting real food and education. Lady Edwina had found out he couldn't read and was remedying that. Being almost nine, he would need a tutor to catch up in education. In powers, of course, the Hematites trained him well. He had strong light magic but not the healing kind like Toury's.

Toury grasped Alex's hand in hers and gave it a loving squeeze. With Henry gone, she was glowing. She was a bit more relaxed. He wished Henry's absence relieved him as much as it did her, but this impending trouble loomed over him. As much as he didn't want to face his cousin's possible fight for the throne, it would almost be better to get it over with. He instantly regretted the thought. His cousin's attack could mean the death of him or his loved ones. If only the edicts didn't prevent Alex transporting Henry to another realm or imprisoning him.

Mary and Cobalt were engaged in a whispering conversation, a smile on her face for once and sweet words between them. Henry had been a wedge between them since they believed the opposite about him and stubbornly refused to see each other's side. They would learn to compromise and that there was no clear-cut line between right and wrong, but an overlapping blur full of personal subjectivity. It was Mary's age. Alex wished they hadn't impulsively agreed to be engaged. It meant they'd marry in less than a couple years, and the sheltered and spoiled Mary—Alex had to admit he, too, had been at that age—needed time to figure out whom she was before she could realize whom she loved.

Alex's mother sat next to Alex and across from Toury. His queen had refused to sit at the other head of the table as tradition dictated and insisted to be at his side. He found he much preferred it this way as well. Toury's Uncle Gareth raised a glass in Alex's direction as he was oft to do, needlessly blessing them. A baseborn by nature, elevated by Toury, he hadn't quite gotten over the need to grovel. At least he was silent and subtle about it.

Alex spoke low to Toury as to not be overheard, "You still haven't answered my question from this morning."

Toury avoided his gaze. "And what question was that again?"

Alex turned her chin to make her meet his gaze. "You know what I'm talking about. I know. Just please tell me. I want to hear you say it."

Toury didn't answer him, as Cobalt inadvertently interrupted, asking what the guilds had said about Fort Emerald. Since it would raise everyone's spirits, Alex explained to the group that Henry had pulled his soldiers off his perimeter into the fort, but it seemed a tactical protective move. Citizens were harassing the soldiers in town. The people had turned on the Emeralds after the deceased Lord Emerald's crimes went public. This was good, as it meant the general population wouldn't back Henry. He had a crumbling rebel army and few necromancers on his side.

The topic changed, and Alex was able to escape the conversation to give Toury a loaded look to impart that the baby conversation was far from finished.

"I don't want to know or you to know. It will stress us out more," she snapped.

He would not let her rule him in this any longer. He had a right to be told his suspicions were true, to hear the best news of his life. "But you would know by now, Toury. God and goddess, it has become obvious to me."

"What is that supposed to mean?" Here came the moodiness.

How to deflect her query? "We agreed to share everything. This would be a blessing, not a burden. Please?"

She met his gaze and tried to press down a smile. Her hands involuntarily touched her abdomen as women instinctively do when they are with child. "I think so."

Alex broke into a huge smile, and euphoria and pride that he had never felt this strongly before flooded over him. He could imagine how this feeling might intensify when he got to stare into their baby's sapphire eyes for the first time, their love having been transported into a living being. It was the greatest magic he could ever fathom.

"I'm not certain, but it has been a while, and I am tired lately, and I've had some other signs."

"The stones, just to double—"

"No one can know, not even the healers. I don't trust anyone. The way servants gossip, all of Fyr would know by tomorrow."

Alex wanted to protest, but they did love to spread information and rumors, often twisting the truth as they had about Toury and Cobalt's kiss. Alex didn't want to put Toury in more danger, but soon there would be no hiding it. "Toury, people will notice soon enough."

"We said hide it as long as possible."

Alex nodded. "I will sneak in the infirmary later and grab the stones. We'll check ourselves." Alex had to be certain. Only he wasn't a healer or a great stone reader, his magic being fire. "Madge will know how to read the stones."

Toury nodded, for David and Madge were not the gossiping type.

"I need that affirmation, my love." Then he leaned over and kissed her before she could protest. It was not an innocent kiss, considering they had family around. Someone cleared their throat, and he forced himself to pull away.

Cobalt was trying not to laugh. Mary was wearing an expression of disgust like she would actually vomit. Gareth and Edwina were red faced, looking anywhere but at them. His mother suppressed a smile and stared at Toury as she picked at the meat and cheese appetizer.

Cobalt oozed out his magical charm to relax the room and spoke of courtly gossip his younger brother and sister had written to him about. His elder brother and father remained in the castle, but Alex could tell Cobalt missed seeing his mother and siblings. Hopefully he could one day soon.

When the second course came out, soup, Gareth toasted aloud to Toury and Alex again, red-faced and laughing. Alex thought it odd. Was the man so deep in his cups already? He wasn't normally a heavy drinker. But then Alex smiled at the idea of Gareth being silly. Alex was giddy, not in a good way, but in an uncontrollable way. Maybe he was just so excited about the baby, an overwhelmed joy.

The conversation turned to stories, funny ones, about people and gossip. They were having a grand time. Alex hadn't laughed so hard in his life. A weight had been lifted off of him. Life was beautiful. Why had they been worried? Alex couldn't remember.

When the servants brought in the salads, the conversation dwindled. Once they withdrew, Little Aschen Hematite burst out in a peal of laughter, hysterical, nonstop giggles; apparently, something was really funny, only nothing was going on to elicit such a response. His head swayed back and forth, almost as if he were drunk and trying to realign his head to steady double-vision. Toury was perplexed, her brow wrinkled. Something was wrong.

"Aschen?" she asked, getting up and moving to him. "What is so funny?"

"My head is spinning in the opposite direction of my body, and I'm floating through space," her brother managed to get out before turning into a giggling mess.

Toury's expression was horrified and confused. Something was very wrong indeed, for Alex had to suppress the urge to laugh, although he was panicking inside.

"What's that smell?" Toury sniffed the air.

"Stop being so paranoid. I don't smell a thing." Mary rolled her eyes and let out a giggle.

Then Toury laughed, apologizing, and everyone started laughing. He had no idea what was so funny, though. Everyone was hysterical, Gareth coughing from laughing so hard. Alex had trouble squelching the need to giggle, and then he became lightheaded, like he was floating up into the air.

That's when Aschen, who was making long, slow blinks, didn't open his eyes again. He slumped over, his face falling into his food. Only, he didn't sit back up after he was face down in his salad. They all went silent. The laughter stopped. His aunt picked up Aschen's head and wiped his face clean. She shook him. There was no response, even after she slapped his cheeks.

"Poison!" she shrieked.

Everyone dropped their forks.

"The poison taster is alive." Alex pointed to the man across the room.

He came over, his gait a little uneven, clearly light-headed too. He resampled the food and shook his head at Alex.

"Not poison," Alex concluded. "But I don't feel right either."

"I'm dizzy." Toury yawned. "And tired."

Cobalt was out of his seat, searching the room, smelling the drinks, when pandemonium broke out.

A fiery ball lit up the room, and masked men appeared. Alex's soldiers had their swords out, but they seemed just as lethargic as him, and they were a step behind these invaders. The masks covered most of their faces, but he did recognize a pair of sapphire eyes next to grey ones: Henry and Racine.

Alex drew Toury into his arms and transported. They reappeared right where they started. Twice. Whatever poison was in his system was preventing or slowing down his magic. He tried to cast a ring of fire to protect them with success, but he doubted it would be a match against Henry right now. Mary was doing the same around herself, but Cobalt was already into the fray. His sword was swinging much slower than usual. His best friend was going to die. Alex blasted his magic out to separate Cobalt from his enemy. Doing so was a gamble, for Alex had left an opening, but Toury protected them with a ball of light that blasted men back. She lurched, almost falling into his fire ring. Alex grabbed her and helped her to the ground. His own eyes were heavy. His body felt heavy as solid metal, and he sank to his knees.

His mind tried to focus. He held Toury close and concentrated on keeping the fire ring up. Soldiers tried to get in but couldn't. Mary slumped down with Cobalt. Her fire ring protecting them flickered. His mother was on the ground, as well as a few others—asleep, he hoped. *Don't let them be dead.*

Things were hazy. It was difficult to stay alert, let alone keep his fire up. He was helpless. What could he do?

Racine was there in front of him, her eyes wild and pleading. "Toury! Stay awake!" Racine's voice sounded like she was underwater, either muffled by the cloth covering her mouth and nose or because his head was swimming. "Put your fire away; it will be useless," Racine hissed. "Save your strength. Stay awake."

Groggy, he let the fire fall. He let Toury go and clumsily withdrew his sword. He forced his numb limbs up, leaving Toury on the ground. She was nodding off. "Toury, blast him," he pleaded.

Toury sat up, swaying, and threw light out at the figure approaching them: Henry. He was blasted back, caught by his men. Henry then scowled at Toury, heading straight for her, enveloping himself in fire. Fire wouldn't do anything to him, so Alex swung his sword. Henry was surprised but parried it off with a muffled laugh behind a strange cupped-shaped mask over his nose and mouth. Henry swiped the blade toward Alex's head, and Alex blocked it but barely in time. His body wasn't reacting as fast as it normally would. As his little brother-by-marriage had said, his head and body were floating and spinning.

Swords flew out, and Alex deflected one that would've hit him in the face. Alex fell down, unable to fight, to hold a sword, to use his limbs. His eyes wanted to close. He would die here, and so would Toury with their unborn child. He saw David fall next to him. Was he wounded or sleepy like him? Someone was battling Henry, preventing him from getting to Alex. He saw a flicker of gray eyes, light brown hair, and men's clothes. Was Racine truly defending him?

"*Traitor!*" Henry shouted.

Alex's eyes closed. He was lost in dreams of space and floating between the spheres of the universe, seeing Earth, the moon, Water, Lyft, and Fyr among the cosmos.

17
FORTRESS

Toury was shaken awake. Her head was splitting. Her heart beat madly in her chest as if she had just run a marathon. Her chest was tight and constricted. She took in a deep breath with difficulty and pain. She moaned and opened her eyes to see she was in a darkened room. Mary was shaking her, looking in just as much pain as Toury. Mary's eyes and nose were red and irritated, and Toury bet hers were too, based on how they stung. She swallowed, and her throat was sore.

What had happened? They had been eating. Then she'd grown dizzy and disoriented. There were people. Henry! She had to get away from him. She sat bolt upright and then moaned in agony as her brain seemed to sway in a mismatching rhythm to her skull. "Transport us! It's Henry."

"Too late." Mary's voice was hoarse.

Toury took in her surroundings. A barred window had a drape over it, but the sun still shone through enough to dimly light the space. The room was devoid of furniture or any belongings, except pillows, cushions, blankets, and books. A few of the latter two were torn to pieces, the paper and stuffing scattered across the floor. Between them and the fourth wall, with the door, were metal bars up to the ceiling. It was some kind of cell within a room.

"You can't transport?" Her mind was working slow as sludge.

"No. These are made of alumina, the fire-resistant ceramic-coated stones. They are keeping me from performing any fire magic." Mary scoffed. "Used them long ago to contain dragons."

Toury tried to puzzle it together. Her mind ached, and it was slow working. The stones kept dragons locked up back in the day—she assumed—and the same stone worked on the Sapphirians as Alex sort of explained when he referred to the room his aunt had to be locked in at the palace because she had been trying to burn the castle down. Were they in that room? "But how? What makes it work?"

"Alumina. It's the same stuff used to make all our clothes fireproof, except much lower doses on the clothes. The fibers are carded with a light dusting of alumina before they're spun into yarn. These are a thousand times stronger."

"How do you know it's alumina?"

"Because we're in Fort Emerald, I already tried to transport us out as soon as I woke, and that is my aunt over there, Princess Anne."

What Toury had thought was a pile of pillows in the corner was a woman huddled and wrapped in a blanket. She lifted her head, revealing black hair streaked with gray. It was undone and wild, knotted, and matted—probably because it hadn't been washed or brushed in ages. More like a frightened child than a grown princess, she gave them a childish wave of erratic enthusiasm with her bony hand. That's when Toury noticed how deathly thin the woman was. Her cheek bones were hollowed out, and her blue Sapphirian eyes were wild with an uncontrollable energy. Henry's mother and the state of this room spoke of years of use. How horrible. No wonder she was crazy. Maybe it wasn't the necromancers or curses that ruined the woman's mind, but the Emerald men. Even if she were dangerous, how could they lock her up in these conditions?

"Why didn't any of you tell me exactly how this stuff works? I will one day—if we get out of here—be a mother of children with your Sapphirian powers." And right then Toury's heart sank. *If* they got out of here. She had wanted to hide and pretend it wasn't there for this very reason, but there was a baby inside of her, another life, one that would die with her if they didn't get out of here. She could not ignore the baby anymore, but might double her efforts to get out of here alive for both of them.

"You never asked. You were satisfied it would work and asked no more."

Toury could just smack Mary's smug face. After all this, she would point fingers at Toury rather than Henry. "Regardless, why hadn't rebels used it against you before?"

Mary sighed, dropping her petty anger. "Alumina, or aluminum oxide, is an extremely rare chemical compound on Fyr. Few these days understand things outside of magic, mixing natural elements, and the like. We Sapphirians mined it excessively through the ages. It's kept in a secret place." Mary gave her a loaded stare that said, *Don't ask, the walls could have ears.* "In our times, it is pricey. You saw your own rebel family slay a celestial beast to gain power rather than suppress ours. Don't you think the rebels would use this against us if it were easy and cheap to find?"

Mary's barb stuck. It hurt. Not only was she dragging her parents into this as an attack of Toury's naivety, she also had to point out Toury's

123

ignorance and lack of logic. Of course her parents would've gathered this stone or compound before they would take the life of a majestic creature.

Toury opted to change the subject from her and her family's shortcomings. "How do we get out of here, then?"

"No one gets out." Princess Anne's voice was brittle from disuse. "I will die here. So will you. No one gets out."

"We'll get out, Aunt Anne," Mary said.

"Aunt?" the woman asked.

"I'm your niece, Princess Mary Sapphirian, remember?"

"Lies!" she bellowed and then fell over into the blankets. "Lies!" she screeched. Then her shouts turned into sobs. "I'm the last Sapphirian. I've killed my brothers and the baby. And he killed my daughter. Why else would she stop seeing her mother daily, brush her hair, and read to her?"

"You're not the only Sapphirian left. I'm your niece. I was born after you left the palace, and my older brother, Alex, is alive and king. And there's your son, Henry. He's a Sapphirian too." Mary talked to her, creeping closer. Mary purposely skipped over the fates of the woman's brothers and Ruby.

"Henry is an abomination!" She leaped up and grabbed Mary's arms, shaking her hard. "He's an Emerald through and through, no son of mine."

Despite the frail appearance of the woman, Mary was unable to pry herself away from her intense grip. "Aunt Anne, let go of me."

"I am not your aunt." She shook Mary harder.

Having enough of this exchange, ignoring her horribly aching head, Toury intervened. The woman reeked, making Toury's delicate stomach churn, and bile rose. Mary was struggling, though, so she held her breath as she gripped the bony hands in hopes to pry them off. The moment Toury touched Princess Anne, something sparked—literally—and the woman backed away, leaving Mary alone. Anne pushed herself into the wall as far away from Toury as the room allowed.

What the heck was the spark about? Toury had never short-circuited her light magic before.

"Lightbearer," Princess Anne growled in one of those demonic voices Toury had heard in Earth horror movies. Then she hissed at Toury like a feral cat. Even in the dim light, Toury could see her eyes were now inky black voids, dark ovals of evil.

She backed away, pulling Mary with her. Mary clung to her, a bit frightened too.

"Still a necromancer," Toury whispered. Her heart pounded. She pushed horrific memories away.

"But this cell blocks magic." Mary's voice shook. She held onto Toury as if she were a lifeline.

"Or just fire magic?" Toury drew her power into her palm, and the room glowed in a brilliant white light.

The woman across the room screamed and clawed at her eyes, slipping down into her pile of blankets and screeching.

"Don't let anyone see you can do magic in here. Pretend to be powerless," Mary told her.

Toury withdrew the magic, not only because Mary instructed her, but also because Anne was screaming loudly. Once Toury's magic was hidden, Anne calmed down.

Footsteps headed their way. There was no knob on the inside of the door of the room, which didn't matter because they couldn't reach it anyway; the cell bars cut them off from that part of the room, reminding Toury very much of the cages zoo animals live in, except this cage did have a cell door.

The outer door swung open, groaning in protest. A middle-aged man with a slight limp entered. He hit the bars with a stick, making Princess Anne cover her ears.

"Let us out. I command you," Mary tried. "I am Princess Mary Sapphirian, and if you don't let us go, I'll have you burned at the stake."

The man was squinting at her, bemused. Then he shrugged and turned away.

"Hey!" Toury shouted.

The man didn't even hesitate or respond. She thought about attacking him with a light ball, but they were locked in a cage, and that situation wouldn't change with a knocked-out guard.

"He can't hear," the aunt said. "Or talk. And can't see very well." She giggled eerily like a child. "He only comes in to beat the bars to make sure I'm still here and alive. But I have a new handler now after I burned the last one. He is special, and he is kind."

Could it be Craig? Dared she hope Alex had enacted her plan in time? She'd never followed up with him about it. Why hadn't she asked more questions? Why hadn't Alex and Mary told her everything, knowing she didn't see snippets of the future in the flames as they could? If Craig was this new "handler"—such a derogatory term—they could escape.

The door's latch locked ominously behind the man after he left. Mary sank to the ground. Toury joined her. This was pretty bleak, but they couldn't give up. Surely, Henry had some ridiculous plan for them. He hadn't killed Mary or Toury so—

Alex! Was he alive? Henry had been attacking them when she lost consciousness. He could not be... She refused to finish the thought. "Alex?"

The desperation in the question made Mary's face crumble into a strained expression of despair. "I don't know about him or Cobalt."

"No," Toury said with determination she didn't feel, but then she let logic take over. "If they were...you know...would we be locked up? If Alex was gone, he would've killed you too, Mary, and taken over—"

"Henry wouldn't."

"Stop thinking he is good, Mary!" Toury clutched at her hair, her fingers digging into her circlet, very much wishing she were instead ripping Mary's out of her updo. How could she be so stupid? "Open your eyes, and take a look. Your cousin attacked us, kidnapped us, and tried to kill Alex." She hoped her theories were right, that he was unsuccessful. Then it hit her: kidnapped yet again. Was it a ridiculous Fyrian custom to kidnap people? Did it work? Because it hadn't the first two times. She hoped this was their strike three.

Mary grumbled. Chastising her further in a situation where they needed to work together would not be beneficial. Toury let her anger shift toward the one more deserving: Henry.

"He would have killed you too. I know Alex is alive, because Henry is holding us as bargaining pieces. He thinks Alex would give over Fyr for both of us."

Neither of them said aloud whether they thought that plan would work, but Toury knew Alex just might. He'd chosen his kingdom over her before and still lived with the guilt. He wouldn't again. No, Alex would be planning ways to get them back. He had an army at his disposal.

"Who are you? What are you doing here?" Princess Anne's face was now blank, like nothing had happened.

"We are friends, stuck here the same as you," Toury said quietly. Toury hoped being vague would prevent setting her off.

"I didn't know I had friends. When we get out of here, let us have tea together."

"That sounds lovely." Toury managed to sound chipper.

"Where are we?" Anne asked.

"Locked away in a castle. We're princesses waiting for the king to save us."

"Of course, I remember." Princess Anne hummed to herself, toying with her hair, now in her own world.

Toury was wrong. This wasn't bleak. This was downright catastrophic. They had no hope, except who was left at the castle. She hoped Alex was all right and that he had a plan. She had saved his hide and his kingdom; it was his turn to return the favor, two-fold, for both her and their child.

18
A SEER

Alex's head was pounding in tandem with the fast pulse in his ears. His mouth was dry as if he had eaten sand. His body ached and felt heavy. He had never overindulged in firewhiskey, but the descriptions Mary had given him prior to her sobriety sounded exactly like what he was feeling right now. His mind also wasn't clear.

He tried to open his eyes, but the light hurt. Something flat and solid was under him—stone. He rolled off his side onto his back. He tried to breathe, but his chest constricted, so he took quick shallow breaths. He opened his eyes slowly, very slowly, blinking until he saw the ceiling come into focus. He stared up at a still-lit wooden chandelier, one that reminded him of a wagon wheel with spokes. He had always imagined it was a wheel as a boy, one of the things that had annoyed his father about him when he had been young. He remembered saying it at dinner and his father rebuking him for not thinking of more important matters. Having an imagination had been a sin to his father. Alex disagreed and found having one should lead to progress and innovation, but his father mocked him for saying that. What an awful and torn emotion to both despise and love someone so much after they passed away.

Alex focused his mind as it had been listlessly drifting. He was in the dining room, but it was daylight, with the lights on. Odd.

He sat up and instantly regretted it; his head spun. He closed his eyes and pinched the bridge of his nose, which relieved some of the ache momentarily. When the room was righted, he opened his eyes. Bodies were strewn across the ground, but their chests rose and fell. They were breathing, asleep somehow like he had been.

Alex got up and staggered to the table, thinking only of drinking some water. He heard a sigh behind him and turned quickly, regretting the movement as pain laced through him.

Racine sat in a chair, in front of the door, sword in hand. She had a scarf tied across her face, covering her nose and mouth. "Good. It must be clear now," she said, her voice muffled. She pulled the cloth down.

Alex surveyed the room, still disoriented. "What happened?"

"You were gassed."

"Gassed?" What did that mean?

Racine sighed impatiently. "Look, it's called nitrous oxide. Henry pumped it into the room to knock everyone out. He was going to slit your throat, but I protected you. I couldn't stop him, though; I'm sorry. I had to make the best choice for the kingdom."

"Toury!" He wildly scanned the room for her.

"He took her and Mary. I'm sure they're okay. Since you are still alive, he'll want to use them to bargain with you. I foiled his plan, but I couldn't stop him from taking them and protect you at the same time. My sister made me promise you were the priority."

"Of course she did," he ground out. As always, she had put him before herself, which she shouldn't be doing, particularly because she believed she was carrying their child. What had she been thinking? He was fuming. Of course, Toury had told him every detail of her and Racine's conversation, except that. Or was there more Toury had hidden so he would survive this night?

Cobalt started to stir, as well as his mother. How would he tell them Mary had been taken as well? How could he keep Cobalt from going mad and storming Fort Emerald? Because Alex wanted to as well and depended on his friend to stop such rash actions. This needed planning and cunning.

Racine broke the silence as people started to wake. "I disconnected the apparatus—don't know what it is, from Earth apparently—so it should be harmlessly blowing outside if there is any left in it. Henry abandoned his men, of course. Most are dead. I opened the windows to air out the place and dragged the bodies into the corner there. I tied up his two men who are alive over there. Everyone outside of here has been trying to get in, but I kept it locked. I didn't know who to trust, and I didn't want the gas to get to them."

Alex's gaze followed the places she pointed to, and he nodded, half comprehending her. All he wanted was Toury and Mary here, safe, with him. He unlocked the doors to see worried soldiers and barked out commands he hoped made sense. When he turned, Racine was picking up her little brother and handing him to a soldier, watching with concern, her hand brushing his forehead, the only loving gesture he'd seen the girl make that wasn't feigned. Another two men hoisted Cobalt onto his own feet. He was groggy but awake.

"Take everyone to the infirmary until they wake. Those two are to be locked in the dungeons and questioned about Henry's plans," he told the soldiers.

"And her?"

"Lock her up," Alex said.

"What?" Racine demanded, incredulity etched in her face.

"You're not pardoned yet, Hematite. I only have your word you saved my life. This could be an orchestrated plan to do more harm, having you in my palace."

"I put my life on the line for you! For my sister!" She shouted, those Hematite fists balling up. He had to be careful. In his state, what would one of those light balls do to him?

He calmly explained, hoping she could be rational, "You killed a dragon, helped the rebel cause attempt to overthrow me, and sided with my cousin—also known as the commander."

She appreciated someone listing things on their fingers as much as Toury did, indicated by the glower she pinned on him.

He crossed his arms to show her he was in charge and in case she decided to chop off one of his fingers. "Toury told me what you said, but I have doubts. I'd be stupid not to. You had to know he was the commander, and your parents had to have told you Henry's parents put the curse on us."

Racine had to back away to let some healers through who were carrying out more injured. Cobalt lumbered over, using his sword more as a walking stick, his eyes on Racine, ready to defend Alex if needed, but the way he blinked his eyes to focus proved he was no match for anyone at this point. Alex placed his hand on his shoulder to tell him to stand down.

She shook her head, disagreeing with the accusations—which ones, the god and goddess only knew. "No. I mean, yes, I knew Henry was the commander, but he hated the necromancers. They ruined his mother, drove her insane. My parents never told anyone about the cursemaker until they told you."

Could he believe that? The way the Hematites had held that secret so close told him it was a strong possibility.

Fervor filled her looks, that familiar and fierce determination on the wrong face. "I didn't have a clue. Listen, I want vengeance for my parents." Her vicious tone spoke truths, but he had to be careful.

"The ones you abandoned to my men?" It was a low blow, but Toury would've never given up on them, never left them. Horrible images of pulling her away from her dying mother, covered in blood, flittered through his mind.

Racine's mouth puckered slightly before she continued, her voice pleading now. "I know I've done terrible things. I had hoped to free them later. Lord Emerald took everything away from me, so I cannot side with Henry now. I can help you. I don't need a pardon. I want to end this. If I survive, I will leave. I'll try Earth out. You can even snuff me before I go. I cannot be trusted with these powers, not that they'd work well there anyway. The things I have done with my light go against the very nature of the magic. I'm tainted and just want to feel clean again. Just give me a chance."

He had heard all this before, that candid whining voice professing innocence, taunting him with promises of knowledge, when instead she had tricked him into getting close enough to kiss him. He had almost lost Toury due to it. He could not trust Racine and risk losing Toury forever.

"Lock her up in a guest room, at least for now," Alex finally compromised. He wanted her out of his sight and secured, but it was best to separate her from the two men she had betrayed.

She was taken off, shouting nonsense he ignored.

"Your Majesty." Another servant entered, out of breath. "There's a seer here demanding she speak with you. Said it was highly urgent, and we tried to drive her off, but she spooked us, telling us stuff she shouldn't know." The man was rambling and pale-faced.

There were frauds in Fyr but also the real deal with seers. One could brand with light just like Alex could with his fire.

"A seer?" Alex asked. As soon as it was out, he realized. A cold chill shot down his spine. The seer in Mineria—Craig's mother, Irene—said she would come to Alex in his most dire hour to help him. He almost fled from the room, but David said his name. He didn't have time to wait for his valet. "Stay here, David. You're of little use at the moment."

David woozily glared and splashed his face with water from a glass on the table to wake himself up more. His valet then wiped his face clean and, in an overly dignified manner for the circumstances, insisted he was fine. Instead of pressing David to remain behind, Alex caved in but ordered two more coherent soldiers to accompany them for extra protection.

The woman was in the Sapphirian Tea room, formerly the Queen's Room. She was better dressed than before, her hair clean and the upper half twisted up in the latest fashion, modeled after Toury's new hairdo. Fear of what this woman would tell him crept over him. If she told him something would happen to Toury...

The seer stood waiting to be invited to sit, her pale eyes scrutinizing him. She had the appearance of a lady, and the noble turn of her nose and high cheekbones told him she must've been before her fall from grace,

131

possibly due to his father. He would not feel guilty for his father's crimes. He had already righted the situation by elevating Craig and in turn gotten her out of the slums in Mineria.

"You've come as you promised you would in my time of need, but had you told me what would happen, I could've prevented it. Sit." The last part he barked at her.

He shouldn't get mad. He knew it wasn't a perfect science. Seeing bits and pieces and trying to decipher when they happen, while lacking the info about how an event would occur, was the maddening plague every seer had to deal with. Hell, Alex should've seen it too. He'd lashed out at her for no reason, but he had needed some kind of outlet for his rage.

She was unfazed by his accusatory greeting. He sat across from her, his head still pounding from whatever gas had knocked him out—nitrous something or other; he couldn't remember the name Racine had given it.

"The sight is not all-seeing at all times, Your Majesty, as I'm sure you know. Do you think I would've led myself into ruination had I seen properly how men who professed love would treat me?"

"My father."

"Among others. Time is critical. I didn't know what would happen to you, but I knew your queen and sister would be taken—"

"Then why—"

"Time is critical, Your Majesty."

He scowled at her for daring to interrupt him, but he didn't reply. If time was so important, he had to hear her out.

"What many don't understand about the gift of seeing—I'm sure you get this due to it being your gift as well—is that things must happen in a certain way, in a certain order, for the future to happen. The queen and princess *had* to be taken. I'm sorry. Henry needed the upper hand so he will act, and it will be his fatal flaw."

Alex wanted to know, wanted to beg her to tell him what that act was or, more importantly, that he got to kill Henry. As much as he had dreaded executing his uncle, Alex wanted to kill Henry. No one took his lifemate or sister and held their lives in his hands as a bargaining chip to get to Alex. He would make Henry suffer for it. But he didn't dare interrupt, allowing the woman to continue.

"You must attack tonight. I've seen several scenarios. You must do it at night and from within. Surprise him, and you'll succeed in half your endeavor."

She was saying Alex would use darkness to his advantage, tonight because Henry wouldn't suspect Alex could be ready. He might even think Alex was still unconscious at this point. "From within" meant Alex must transport an army inside the fort. Although Henry had heard Alex could do this, Henry's pride was his fatal flaw. He would see it as a myth spread by supporters or Alex himself; no one had ever done it before in the history of Fyr. Henry himself had only been able to transport about ten men and Racine inside the castle, from the low number of bodies and prisoners Alex had seen. Henry would've sacrificed his best men against Alex's army, who had been less skilled under the influence of the sleeping gas. Attacking him right away was ingenious and something Henry would never expect.

Wait, she said "half"? Did Alex not get to kill Henry or not save the women in his family?

"Your Majesty, there will be a time when you will be forced to make a tough decision."

What was new?

"You must think with your head and not your heart. It isn't something I can prepare you for nor what you are used to. If I tell you why, the repercussions could be far worse. If you choose your heart, all of Fyr is lost, including yourself and everyone you love in it. If you choose your head, you save Fyr from a horrible fate. I've seen the scenarios, but the future is unwritten and hinges on your decision."

No pressure, not that Alex wasn't used to life-or-death decisions by now. Alex knew instantly what the seer meant. A decision of the heart would involve Toury, doing whatever it would take to save her. Choosing his head would be using logic, and if that resulted in his inability to save her, he had to let her go. He knew deep down, facing that decision would be impossible. He was led by his heart in everything ever since he had first kissed Toury. No, not true. He'd chosen his kingdom over her. God and goddess, though, he never wanted to do it again. If her life was on the line, he could not think rationally. He needed her, alive, safe. "Let me guess: I won't be able to save the queen."

"A woman is capable of saving herself, Your Majesty. It is something men often forget."

Of course, Toury was capable, but he didn't know if he would be able to put her in danger again for his kingdom or his life. She could never either. Toury had been taken because she insisted her sister save him first. He knew the seer was telling the truth about not seeing any more. Even

Mary couldn't see the actions of Henry coming, and neither could Alex. The fire was just not telling them much at the moment because the future was too much in flux. It would ride on the decisions made in the near future.

It didn't seem like she would expand, so when he was interrupted by a servant saying Tobias Firebrand requested a word, Irene stood and went to leave. Alex walked with her to the door, telling the servant to show Tobias to the King's Room.

He took out his pouch of coins to pay her, but she waved her hand. "If we survive and Fyr blossoms into a golden age, you could help me then by inviting me here to do a reading for your friends. I simply want to work and help others again. Now is not the time to worry about such things. My sister Misty foresaw your elevation of my son, and now we live comfortably and quietly."

He nodded as a servant escorted her out. She was a strange woman indeed. Alex transported to the King's Room because he was impatient to plan his evening attack. He would trick fate and the future. He would make decisions of the heart and head. He would save everyone, no matter what it would take.

Tobias arrived moments later, providing interesting information about his aunt, how the firelasher had ingratiated himself into the fort, that there were plans made and men gathering to act on something. He had tried to warn of the attack—too late—but he had done his best. On the back of his note, Baron Firelasher provided a map of the layout of the fort. Alex imagined his mother or aunt had prepped him to send that. Even though Alex knew the fort, he now knew where his aunt would be kept, which meant Mary would have to be with her. The quarters would be made of the same stone as the room outfitted in the palace to block fire power. Mary would be powerless in his aunt's quarters and unable to transport. The question was, would Toury be with Mary, or would Henry have separated them?

Regardless of where Toury was imprisoned, he felt a tad better remembering his half-brother was there. If he knew his bloodline well, Craig would have a plan of his own once he saw Toury and Mary imprisoned and try to help them escape. It did have to happen tonight. The seer wanted her son safe as well, so he had faith they would thwart Henry's plans in some way. He ordered the servant at the door to fetch Cobalt and others. They would plan a siege for the history books. Henry would die tonight by Alex's hand.

134

19
DINNER

As soon as Toury pulled herself together, she tried to think of means to escape. After checking out the cell's door, she found a lock and tried to pick it with a hairpin. She'd used to pick her Earth mother's filing cabinet searching for her adoption papers, but they were obviously never there since she hadn't been born on Earth. These old fashioned pin-tumbler locks wouldn't budge under the pressure of a flimsy hair pin. She really needed to convince Fyrians to use these keylocks on other room doors. She had only seen the old-fashioned locks on chests, boxes, and dungeon cells like this. After a while, she was persuaded by Mary to give up since they had no way to open the outer handleless door even if they got out of the cell.

What felt like hours later—having nothing to do to pass the time—the servant entered, carrying clothes and a note. Toury wondered if Henry had cut the man's tongue out. She didn't know how much of Henry was a façade or whom he really was—was he also sadistic? The aunt wailed upon seeing the man and started scratching the walls again, while Mary stared out the window. This betrayal hit the princess hard, and Toury knew Mary was still trying to process that her "loving" cousin was holding her life ransom for a kingdom. Toury didn't dare tell Mary the truth. She knew the end of this scenario was the death of her, Mary, and Alex. Henry would leave no loose ends.

Since no one made a move to go near the bars, ones Anne had said made her body ache from them apparently being filled with the fire-resistant stone dust, Toury grabbed the items. The man backed away from her, scared, knowing well that if the bars didn't bother her, her magic was not diminished. No wonder Princess Anne was half-starved. Only the brink of actual starvation would drive a Sapphirian near bars that caused them pain, and there wasn't a slot or opening for food to be slid through.

Toury glared at the man because words were useless. As she'd noted before, there were no weapons, no keys on him. Hurting this man would do nothing to aid in their escape. Not that she could get out of this cage.

"What is it?" Mary asked.

"Clothing and a note," Toury responded.

"What does it say?"

"Dress for dinner."

Mary yanked a dress from Toury. "I'm starving."

"How do you know he won't poison us?"

"He'd never," she said so matter-of-factly, it was clear she hadn't yet digested Henry's true character.

"Mary, stop it!" Toury shouted, her emotions and hormones getting the better of her, tears streaming down her face. She was a hot mess now. "Stop believing there is anything good in this man! He will kill us. He wants the throne. Alex can't give it up. Henry will kill Alex, you, and me for good measure."

Mary turned away, her hands shakily trying to unlace her soiled and crumpled garment. Toury hadn't wanted to be so cruel, but the girl had this delusional—and dangerous—belief that her cousin was a good person somewhere deep inside. Even with their lives in danger, she was in denial.

"You don't understand, Toury. When we were little, he was the kindest cousin one could ever have. He looked after me, protected me." She stared off, lost in memories, a soft smile trying to take flight but failing. She turned to let Toury help her with her dress. "There was a time when Alex, Cobalt, Ruby, and the few other kids who were schooled at the palace excluded me. Henry would take me fishing, horseback riding, swimming. He never let me feel lonely. Seven years older than me, he had no desire to play with a little girl, but he did it out of the kindness of his heart."

Toury helped Mary unlace. "I don't doubt you, Mary, but that boy is gone, replaced by a man who will stop at nothing to take over Fyr. If you trust him, you will end up dead." It had to be said.

"Let's see what he has to say at dinner."

"No." Toury shook her head. Toury softened her voice, realizing that if the combative stance would not work, perhaps sympathy would. "Mary, I know it is hard, but you must prepare yourself that we may never come back from dinner."

Mary turned, blinking back tears in her eyes. She hugged Toury. "I'm sorry. I'm trying not to give up hope."

"The hope lies in us. We cannot let him win. I will go down fighting." And she hoped Alex had a plan or was on his way, because she knew she could not depend on just herself to make it out of here. Toury could never fight her way through Henry's men and live. Now, too late, Toury realized Alex had been right. It had been safer to keep Henry in the palace, under surveillance, without his fort soldiers and his rebel and necromancer armies. "Mary, unlace me please."

Mary undid Toury's laces and then proceeded in getting dressed herself. "Ugh, I feel ill." Mary clutched her stomach.

"The dress." Anne pointed to Mary's dress. The woman was being strangely lucid again. "They sew the powder into the gown, see? No magic. Otherwise, I'd burn the fiends to ashes as I tried to again and again."

Toury examined the inside of the dress and sure enough, there were what looked like thick boning channels inside the gown. When she touched them, instead of steel boning, she could feel the powder sealed inside. These were Anne's dresses, used to control her when she was allowed out of her cage. The Emeralds were sick people. Toury wanted to vomit. At least there was only one madman left to deal with.

Toury experimented and was able to light a small ball of light in her hand. The dress felt heavy on her but did not block her light power. There were so few lightbearers left, she doubted Henry would've tested the stone's effects on one.

"Lightbearer," Princess Anne said in awe. She grasped Toury's shoulders painfully tight. "You must kill them. Set us free." She was not afraid of Toury because the necromancer didn't seem present. She wondered if Anne had a split personality type thing going on, for now Toury saw no darkness in her eyes.

"Who?" Toury asked, not sure if the woman was as lucid as she seemed, if she were with them in the present, understanding who the real enemy was.

"My lifemate and son. They are demons living in the flesh of men. They turned me into this monster. I battled the darkness until it took over my mind, and I lost. I battle it always." The woman was now suppressing it as Alex had during his curse, as Alex's father had.

"Aunt Anne?" Mary asked in awe.

"Are you my niece? I never got to gaze upon you, child, but I heard of you. So pretty, like your mother. You have her coloring. Tell her I miss her and that I'm sorry. We had been the best of friends when she caught my brother's eye." She touched Mary's cheek endearingly. "I'm sorry. It's too hard for me to stay. I hope you kill them before they destroy you as well."

"Your lifemate is dead," Toury said quickly, hoping the woman heard it. She hoped if they kept her talking, the princess would keep the necromancer away.

Princess Anne's body contorted and writhed. "Good," she muttered before her eyes went full black and she stalked the cage the way a tiger or lion might.

Toury backed into the corner of the cell. Not seeing a necromancer in a while had softened her, and with the entire situation she found herself in, Toury found the woman's eyes downright terrifying.

Then a man entered. "Hey!" he shouted, but Toury kept her eye trained on the necromancer version of the aunt. "You play nice and go back inside, or Anne doesn't get dinner."

"No!" a strangely deep and terrifying voice boomed out of the woman. This was identical to some demon-possession-type crap Toury had seen in Earth movies. In person, it was terrifying.

"Pull it together, Anne. You've got company," the man chided, all jokes and calmness, which made Toury relax a fraction. The personality and the voice were both familiar. She peered to see Craig Firelasher half obscured by a beard. Mary's sharp inhalation of breath confirmed that what Toury was seeing was real. He held his finger to his lips for silence and winked. Alex had sent him after all. Could he truly help them? Did he have a plan of escape?

Craig unlocked the gate and entered.

Anne hissed like a cat at him.

"Come, come, where's my sweet Aunt Anne?" he crooned. He held his palm out, prompting Mary and Toury to stay put, his eyes trained on Anne.

Toury had an urge to bolt for the door, but how far would she get? Craig hopefully was here to help them escape.

"I need Anne to show up today, not you. If you want freedom, you need Anne to run the show, and you know it."

There was moaning and contorting before she breathed heavily with bright blue eyes again.

"There are two of her in there, you see. The princess is stronger than the darkness, but being abused and neglected all these years makes her forget who she truly is."

"I'm a Sapphirian," the woman said with dignity. "Set me free, nephew. Please, just kill me."

"No," Mary said. "No."

"Real freedom, Princess Anne. Real freedom." Then he took out a knife, cut her laces and threw a shawl over her shoulders. "But I need you to perform. Huge wonderful distractions, only when the time is right."

Toury realized it was for the aunt to free herself from the dress and use her fire. A lot was banking on her being lucid enough to do so, though.

This was not a solid plan, and yet Craig had only said "distraction." If that was all that was needed, Toury could create one if Anne failed.

"And me?" Mary asked, turning her back to have her dressed undone or cut open.

"He will check you, Your Highness, not his mother."

"He's impatient!" someone called from outside the room's door.

"Come on, we must suffer through the dinner, but help should be on the way."

"How soon?" Toury asked. This wasn't a plan at all. A distraction? Then if help didn't come right away, what? Death?

Craig shrugged as he took up the rear, pushing them forward toward the guard who was at the doorway.

"Better not wait on them then," Toury whispered.

"Wasn't planning on it, Your Majesty. Just keep him distracted and occupied by being your willful self."

"That won't be hard," Toury mused. She should be offended, but she knew when it came to Henry, she'd take pleasure in being disagreeable.

They entered a dining hall lavishly set up for an important dinner party for honored guests rather than prisoners. Henry was dressed in his best, clad in a maroon doublet embellished with gold-embroidered vines and shiny black boots with gold trim. Even his cream britches had gold buttons on them. It was a gaudy display of wealth that contrasted so much with Alex's plain, commanding style.

Henry spread his arms with that arrogant smile on his face. "Welcome to my home!"

Toury's spine prickled. He had to be insane, but not like his mother; there was no good to battle the evil. There were evil and delusions of power in a shell of false normalcy. His mother's own description was not far off: a demon in man's skin. Toury's demand about what happened to the others back at the palace died on her lips. There would be no truthful answers, and who knew how'd he react if she dared to mention Alex.

Henry took Mary by the hands but then pulled her in roughly, checking that the back of her dress was laced up. Then he let her go and told her where to sit.

"Henry, why am being held prisoner?" Mary frowned. She was playing into the childhood memories Henry had of her. Perhaps Mary finally understood and was being as manipulative as she could, for she didn't demand answers about her family either.

"Prisoner?" His brow wrinkled in confusion and then frowned, offended. "That is a horrible accusation. You're my guests, but I have to take precautions for my own safety." He put his hand to his breast and contracted his brows, wounded. "What a—"

"Guests can leave," Toury said bitterly. "Guests aren't kidnapped from their homes."

Henry gave her a strange look, a glare and smirk combined, like she annoyed him but he sadistically got turned on by it. "You are a lovely and interesting creature, Queen Tourmaline. I wish we would have had more time to get to know each other."

The threat in his past tense made her go sit as instructed. When she did, he touched the back of her dress in a weird caressing manner that made her nauseated. His pungent cologne made it worse, and had she eaten earlier in the day, she would've lost her stomach's contents.

"Mother," Henry said with warmth. It was the first genuine emotion Toury had seen come from him. The shell of a man loved his mother still. He went to hug her.

Oh, no! He'd know her dress was open and would be onto the escape plan. Toury started pulling light into her hands until she saw Craig subtly shake his head and prod Anne's back. It was enough.

"You're no son of mine!" she wailed, her eyes dark but not quite black, and she went to attack Henry, her hands out reaching out, swiping like claws.

Henry's face fell, and then he put up a wall of fire that she struggled to claw through but couldn't. Craig yanked her backward, whispering things that made the woman calm down.

"How mortifying." He gave an embarrassed little smile, but he did not blush, nor did he seem surprised by his mother's response. This had to be a common occurrence. "My apologies for my mother. She is...well, mad." He shrugged. "There's no other excuse for her ill-manners. But as you see, we found a new fireproof handler who works wonders calming her down." He looked to Craig, and Toury wondered how he did not see the resemblance even with Craig's beard, but men always relied on the eyes, overlooking the rest. Craig's head was bent low too. These noblemen often ignored those beneath them. A cousin under his nose, and Henry was ignorant of it.

Henry clapped his hands, rubbing them together. "Speaking of ill manners, my apologies that we will be eating with our hands. Mother cannot be trusted with silverware after the other night."

"I was only trying to cut the demon out of my son," Anne said demurely. She was seated at the other end of the table, far away from them. Her calm tone was creepier than her outbursts. She was acting her part and coherent.

Ignoring her comment, Henry motioned a servant to bring forth beverages. "I thought, for all of our safety, we eat with our hands, like mother, tonight."

Because he knew Toury would stab him with a butter knife the first chance she could get.

Wine was poured in front of her. It was a test. Henry wanted to ascertain whether she was pregnant. Even though Toury figured a single glass just this once would not likely hurt her baby—especially since refusing it might be a death sentence for both of them—her hand hesitated on the glass.

"Would you prefer water to wine?" Henry asked, his eyes boring into her.

"It's poisoned," Toury accused with a spur-of-the-moment believable excuse to avoid drinking it. And yet, it might be. How easy would it be to get rid of them at dinner in one go?

Henry laughed. "Contrary to what you might think, my queen, I don't want you dead." He lifted his glass and toasted. "To Queen Tourmaline." Then he downed the whole glass of wine, although no one else raised their glasses.

Toury took up her glass and took a tiny sip. Henry's eyes twinkled as he smiled at her. What was in his eyes? Triumph? Admiration? Had her schemes backfired to make him care for her? Not her intention, but if it was enough to spare her life, should she tolerate him? The idea sickened her, but pretending could be her way through all of this.

The food came out. Ravenous, she ate. If it was laced with poison and they all would die, she could not help herself. The upset stomach of early pregnancy—thankfully, she was blessed not to actually be sick yet—was now replaced by intense hunger since she hadn't eaten in about a day if it was truly suppertime. She paced herself in case her appetite was obvious, but the way Mary picked up the roasted chicken leg and in an undignified manner went to town on it put Toury at ease. She tried to ignore Henry's eyes on her. Toury risked a glance at Craig, but he stood behind Princess Anne, staring at the wall above Henry's head. What were they waiting for?

Toury only drank a few sips of wine throughout the dinner. There were only three courses; soups and salads weren't practical without silverware. When the dessert came out, Toury had enough of the tension.

"Drink up," Henry raised his glass.

She was suspicious.

"Toury can't abide by wine or firewhiskey. She never took to it," Mary said.

Toury was thankful for a way out of drinking more but couldn't voice it.

Henry frowned, disappointed.

"You *have* poisoned us," Toury said, aghast.

Mary dropped her cup, spilling the wine on the table.

"No, not all of us. Just the nasty problem growing inside your belly." He grinned. His eyes met hers. "I told you I don't want you dead, Toury. If that whelp's spawn is gone, you can live, and I want you to live." Then his face hardened, and he stared off, imagining. "I want you to see him die, to see what a powerful and righteous kingdom I will create, and I have no wish to strip you of your title." His eyes darted back to hers with intensity. The fact they were Alex's but not made that fervent gaze even creepier.

She felt nauseated, her stomach whirling. Her head spun. Instinctively, her hand went to her stomach. The baby moved for the first time—just a tiny fluttering—and she knew her child was distressed, perhaps dying. It was too early to feel it move, so her healer instincts had to be feeling extrasensory, searching out how to heal the baby's suffering.

No.

No, she wouldn't let him take her baby. She fell onto the floor, pain slicing through her abdomen. She pulled the healing white light back inside of her, even though she wanted to blast Henry to smithereens. Toury heard Henry bark at Mary to remain seated. She heard Anne scream, and fire blasted across the table. Henry was on the floor now too.

Stop. She closed her eyes, hearing noise all around her, but channeled her white light to her abdomen. She enveloped her baby in white light, and the pain stopped. She had no idea what she was doing, if she just put her poor child out of misery with too much of her magic or if she protected it. She sobbed.

She was yanked up off the floor and opened her eyes to see absolute chaos. There was fire, smoke, soldiers, shouts, and screaming. Toury didn't fight. She kept the light magic running around her unborn child, hoping desperately she could continue the circuit of magic, that the baby was still alive and this would keep it safe.

When she saw Alex's face across the room, she thought she might be saved. He reached out to her but glanced over his shoulder at something, then back at her, his face torn. Before he could make a move, strong arms tightened around her, and the sensation of dragon's trapdoor magic overtook her.

Henry had taken her away from Alex.

20
A RAID

When they transported to Fort Emerald, Alex had to envision the motte and bailey of the fortress just inside the barbican. He was bringing twenty men, counting himself, David, Cobalt, and Percival. Although the fort itself was a decent size, most of it had smaller rooms not safe to transport a group into.

His cousin's men faced the outer walls, not expecting an attack from the inside. They'd heard the swish of Alex's magic, and Henry's men on the curtain wall trained their weapons on Alex, and a volley of arrows went flying. Alex threw a huge wave of fire up into the sky, burning the bowmen's arrows to cinders. Only the arrowheads and a few arrow splinters rained upon them. His men raised their shields to deflect it. Alex had his battle armor and helmet on, so all he felt were little taps.

Murmurs went through the bowmen. Some renocked their bows. "It's him!" Someone shouted.

"It is I, your king! Lord Sapphirian is a traitor to the crown. He has taken the queen and princess hostage. Anyone caught protecting him will die. Stand down, drop your weapons, and leave the fort, and you will not be harmed."

"What are you doing?" Cobalt hissed.

"Changing plans as always to unnerve us," David scolded quietly.

"Too many lives to go to waste, too many men to fight through. We need the element of surprise. If there's a war out here, he'll know. If they vanish into the night..."

Alex didn't need to finish as several of the men put down their bows, retreated inside and came outside on the ground level. They simply walked by him while bowing out of respect, opened the outer gate, and left the fort. Swords were sheathed as footmen around them paid respect on bended knees and walked out the gates. A fortress that had priorly been protected by about thirty men was down to about ten.

Cobalt looked at him, astounded. "How about us four go in, unlock it." He nodded to the inner gate as the remaining few loyal to Henry closed in on them with swords drawn.

"We'll clean up this mess with pleasure, Your Majesty," Lord Rose Quartz said with confidence.

"Let's do this," Alex agreed. He had to admit, it had been too easy to persuade them, but he knew his people wanted to support him, to believe he would make things better.

He transported Cobalt and their bodyguards just past the front door. David's sword was up, parrying a blade away from Alex's head. His helmet would've saved him, but it could've knocked him right out of the battle. Thankful to have David covering his back, Alex made quick work of lifting and throwing aside the wooden bar. Cobalt threw the doors open. Outside, his men were dispatching the last of Henry's men, pulling the barbican back down to stop any reentry, and positioning themselves in a guarding setup. Ten remained on guard, the other six hustling inside to aid Alex's crew. He turned around to see a pile of incapacitated soldiers in the hall.

How many more soldiers roamed the halls was unknown. Where his cousin had Toury was also an unknown. He knew Mary would have to be in the Princess chambers with his aunt to prevent her from transporting. "Work your way from the dungeons up and stay together," he commanded. "We will begin from the top and meet you in the middle." He had to be ruled by logic, not his heart. He'd send his men below where Toury might be and seek Mary and his aunt out first. Logic, right? Saving two overruled trying to save one who might not even be down there.

The men hustled down the hall toward the dungeons below. Counting the dungeons, the fort was four stories but not massive in area. The top was the sleeping quarters, and Alex knew from the map where his aunt was kept. He transported them there, in the hall, for he had never seen his aunt's chambers before, and the worst thing he could do was trap himself in her room and not be able to get out or use his power.

"You must go in, Cobalt."

He nodded, unlatched the door, and went in. Alex hardly called that locked, and if the princess was a danger to others and herself, where was the lock for nighttime safety?

Cobalt and Percival entered but quickly hustled back out. "No one's in there. Alex, it's like a *cage*. There's a dress in there, the same color Mary had been wearing and...a women's pants-gown—whatever she's calling it."

"Let's go." Alex tried to push away his worry and disgust. What was Toury wearing then if she didn't have her clothes? And kept in a *cage*? He flared with anger but tried to withhold it.

Cobalt's jaw tightened, and the emotions emanating off him were the opposite of his nature.

They worked their way down the halls, opening doors, finding most unlocked and empty. Startled servants hurried out of the way. There were no guards. At the end of the hall was a locked door. Cobalt tried to kick it open. They were wasting time, but splitting up could be a death sentence. Percival surprised them all by kicking the door open on his first try. David let out an impressed whistle. It was Henry's quarters. They were empty, but there was possibly something hidden if he had left it locked and transported out.

"Yes." David knew his thoughts. "We'll have to come back and search, but we have more pressing matters."

Alex growled but nonetheless led them out of the room, down the steps, and to the third floor. Throughout, they found no one but servants. He grabbed a few and demanded to know where Henry was. One servant said the second floor. Alex let the man go and stormed toward the second floor.

"Alex, we have to check," Cobalt insisted.

Alex knew the servants could lie or be misinformed, and they could walk right by where Toury and Mary were trapped, but he wanted to race down to the next level. "Then be quick, damn it!" He pulled in his angry energy so he wouldn't lash out fire in the wrong direction by accident.

The three men raced from room to room, running, but Alex kept his quick pace toward the stairs. He couldn't wait. That's when they heard screams from the floor below. They threw open the last two rooms, and satisfied no one was in them after a cursory glance, they rushed down the stairs. At the mouth of the stairwell, a sword flew at Alex's head, and he ducked. The stairwell was too cramped to unsheathe his sword, so he blasted the man with a fireball. The man slammed down the last couple steps, knocking three more men down with him, then skidded across the wooden floor to the opposite wall a dozen feet away.

"Whoa," Cobalt said in awe and squeezed by Alex.

Alex shook off the shock, reminding himself he needed to find Toury and Mary. He had control over his increased power, but perhaps his emotions were adding a bit of fuel to his fire power. He followed Cobalt, drawing his sword enough to slam the hilt into the face of the guard who had been trying to get back up off the floor. He heard David disarm him and the other man behind him. In the open space, Alex drew his sword, ready for anything.

146

A scream sounded again, but now he could hear her words: "I'll kill them all! Every Emerald left!"

Aunt Anne. Smoke drifted out the archway down the small hall where the family privately dined. Alex almost crashed into his other men at the entrance of the hall.

"All clear below, Your Majesty. The place is almost empty, but we checked every fleeing servant. He has not escaped through the doors."

No, he wouldn't; Henry would transport out and was probably gone. Alex could not think that, could not give up. The seer had said he'd be half successful tonight. Alex had won the fort with hardly any opposition, but he would only be comforted when his cousin was locked up in the fireproof cell or dead and Toury and Mary were safe.

Alex led his men into the dining hall. It was hard to see what was happening. The firelasher—Craig—was throwing around an arc of fire, trying to keep some fort soldiers at bay. His aunt—he hardly recognized her—ran about in her underclothes, igniting anything flammable. It wasn't clear whom or what she was fighting.

"Mary," Cobalt breathed out. He lunged into the room, and a sword came flying down at his friend, ready to strike him at that vulnerable spot right between his helmet and armor.

Alex tackled Cobalt to the ground, and the sword glanced off Alex's helmet, hurting like mad as it was prized from his head and clattered behind him. His ears rang and head throbbed, disorienting him momentarily. Cobalt yanked him in and rolled them away as two bodies hit the ground with the clatter of metal. He peered up to see David and Percival looming protectively above them, swords bloodied. Cobalt scrambled up with a sheepish expression on his face as Percival chastised his rash actions.

David offered Alex a hand and yanked him up. David rubbed Alex's hair out of his face, which he found weird until the man sighed with relief. He had been checking for a head wound. "Once this is over, Your Majesty, if you don't agree to attempt to stay safe, I'm going to hand in my resignation," David said as he went back-to-back with Alex, blocking attacks behind him.

Alex dispatched a man in front of him. "No, you won't." Alex teased back. He knew David loved him, and he loved David just as real brothers who'd grown up close would. He would not let the man resign, and David would be offended at the suggestion. Family did not always mean blood, and blood could be foes.

The smoke grew thicker, and it was hard to tell which soldiers were on his side until they were right in front of him. That's when he saw her: Toury. She was lying on the ground, curled up in a ball. His cousin was standing above her when he noticed Alex. The shock on Henry's face proved he had not expected Alex to come himself or so soon. He expected him to be incapacitated and then remain safely in his castle to preserve his kingdom. To not foresee Alex would come after them confirmed Henry was a fool who had never known love. Hadn't he realized there was no kingdom for Alex without Toury?

Henry yanked Toury up. She was wounded, or something was wrong. She was terrified, in pain, and didn't fight back like she normally would. Henry pulled her in and had his arm around her shoulders. Alex couldn't use fire because it would hurt Toury and not affect Henry. He was too far away to attack him with a sword. If he closed the distance between them, Henry could reappear anywhere.

"Al-lex!" His sister's piercing scream made his blood run cold.

He turned and glanced back to see Cobalt and Percival on the ground, wounded. Mary was scrambling over Cobalt, sobbing. They were surrounded by Henry's soldiers. Craig was throwing everything he had to try to protect the three of them. Behind Alex, David was trying to break through two men at once. Men lay on the ground everywhere.

Alex turned back to Toury. He couldn't save her, but he could save his sister. Logic over his heart. This was the decision he would have to make, according to the seer, but both involved his heart. How does one choose between his sister and his lifemate?

Craig shot Alex a significant look that screamed, *Do something!*

Craig, Cobalt, Mary, Percival—four lives in the balance versus one and perhaps an unborn one. That was logic.

"Down," Alex's voice boomed with all his strength and pain balled up in one.

David dove to the floor. Alex aimed his fire high to avoid Cobalt and his bodyguard. Alex went crazy with the rage boiling in his breast, for he knew before turning around when he was done vaporizing the enemy that Henry had transported Toury far away.

Sure enough, they were gone.

21

UNRAVELING

Unbearable heat wafted over Toury's face, that feeling of baking out in the sun on a hot beach. She opened her eyes to see a little square room that had no windows and one door, with two bare cots on opposite walls. It was tiny, the size of her palace closet.

Arms let her go, and a curse word was screamed in her ear. She backed away, turning against the wall by the door. Henry grabbed his hair in his hands, tugging the strands as he screamed again in frustration. He covered his eyes and bumped into a little table and two chairs that were in the middle of the back wall, pretty much up against the cots. Henry was losing it. She had to take advantage of that.

She noted the door was next to her. She yanked it open and stepped outside. Henry's arms pulled her back in against his chest just as flames crossed her field of vision. She struggled in his arms, and he turned, shoving her back into the shack, blocking her path to the door.

"Stop!" The desperation in his voice was baffling, making her freeze. He was scared and vulnerable. This was not playacting either but the man underneath who had lost his mind. He was fraught, dangerous. "We are in the Firelands, where the dragons live," he growled.

So that was a dragon breathing fire she'd almost walked right into.

"They kill any intruder and eat them on sight if they aren't a Sapphirian. They think Sapphirians are one of them in a way, so I am safe, but you have no escape. The shack is fireproof; the wood is covered with flame-protectant, much like they treat our clothes to not burn. You must stay put, or you'll die, Toury." He squared her shoulders. "I'm not lying. Don't try to leave. Promise me."

She ignored the intimate use of her nickname without title. Now was the time to pick and choose her battles, not that she was able to protest. His strange distraught pleas and seemingly genuine concern stunned her into silence. She nodded. Alex had told her about the draca before. This shack was where his father had taken him to teach him about the dragons. She could not leave. Henry had taken her to the perfect prison.

He sighed and let her go.

Toury sank onto one of the bare cots. She had to plan, strategize. She could not give up, and she could not escape. She had to keep playing Henry so she could figure out who he really was and what he wanted with her.

He screamed a curse again out of nowhere, hunching over and balling his fists in pure unadulterated rage.

Apparently, the gravity of the situation had just caught up to him.

She'd had enough of his childish screaming and needed to figure out what his plans were. "What did you think would happen when you took us? That Alex would just let us go?" Toury demanded. She could not play it safe and be demure. The hot, thin air did not help her temperament.

He stared at her with those beautiful eyes in the wrong face. No, even the eyes were wrong, not just the lids, but the erratic intensity in them. He was lost and unstable. "I never thought he would dare leave the castle to save you. It goes against all our education and training. When royalty is captured for ransom, the reigning monarch and next in line are to stay put. Otherwise, it risks the entire monarchy. I thought I had time. The gas must've malfunctioned. And a siege from outside the gates would've taken days, months after my reinforcements came. But he came himself, bringing the battle inside."

Toury wanted to tell him Alex ruled with his heart and not logic, but then Henry could use that against him. She had to think fast and craftily. Instead of wise words coming up, something else entirely did: the contents of Toury's dinner splashed all over the floor. She fell over, writhing in pain, her stomach full of razor blades. It was the same pain as earlier. She searched her light magic and found it was lower, still encasing her womb. The pain was in her actual stomach. Her body was giving her the hint. She needed to keep being sick to get the poison out to save her child.

Henry screamed curses, pacing as she kept vomiting until it was all out and she was dry heaving. Not caring, she lay on the floor by her pile of sickness and closed her eyes.

"You're not dying on me, Toury!"

"Why do you care?" She laughed, and it bubbled into a cry before she reined in her emotions.

"Why didn't you tell me you weren't with child? I just thought..."

"What, that Alex and I were alone too often?"

When she opened her eyes, his jaw was clenched. Jealousy? Surely not. She studied him.

"No. I bribed a chambermaid in your staff. Lots of laundry with evidence that you two were...*coupling*." He said the last word with distaste and stood, annoyed. "And no clothes stained with courses."

Courses? It took a moment to remember that was what Fyrians called a period. Henry had used spies and guessed right that she was pregnant.

"We have things on Earth to prevent dirty clothes each month, not that my hygiene is your concern." Toury ventured. She so did not want to describe sanitary products to this guy—or any man in this sphere. Thankfully, he didn't press.

"This is good."

"What is?"

"Black draca tree root only makes you sick if there isn't a child. Otherwise, it attacks the womb and aborts what's in it. I never wanted to hurt *you*, Toury."

She heaved again, this time from his words. Killing her child would've scarred her for life. The only response she could muster was "Why?"

"The only problem I had with you was the fact you might carry *his* heir. I never wanted to hurt you. You will make a great queen."

He used the word "will," insinuating she would still be queen, but how? He had hinted prior that he didn't want her title to change. He wanted Alex and Mary dead. Her stomach lurched again at what he meant, but her stomach being empty, nothing came up.

His hand touched her hair softly. "You were the last thing I expected. You saw right through me, Toury, to the real me. I can be myself around you." Then his hand pulled away. "This entire situation is a mess."

"Just let me go, then."

"I can't do that. I just found out you aren't spoiled by him." His mouth quirked at that, and she did not want to know what he was imagining. "You can be my queen once I kill the whelp. You can have my child." A wild look came to his eyes as he planned on into a future she would rather die than be included in. "I know this time my lifemate will live through it. It can't happen again. And you can be queen as you always wanted. You're ambitious like me, weaving your way into our family with your uniquely bold charm."

She laughed sardonically. She knew accepting his advances would be too false, and rejecting him outwardly might end in her death. The entire idea of her marrying him was disgusting. She couldn't deny his false accusations about her desire to be queen either, although he had her pegged wrong in that respect. She'd always wanted Alex, not the throne. Nothing was safe to say, so she stayed silent.

"Do not try to leave. They'll kill you."

"Where—"

He transported away before she could ask where he was going. Toury clambered up and opened the door again. She waited. She heard a piercing shriek, and fire shot in front of the shack, making her scramble back onto the cot. With the door open, air was now wafting in, although they were waves of heat. At least it lessened the strong odor of her vomit.

Minutes later, Henry reappeared. Foolishly, her heart leaped at the idea of a burst of flame, thinking of Alex. Then disappointment set in.

Henry wore a cloak and scarf, covering much of his face. He was the most wanted man in Fyr. "Here." He set down a bucket, a bunch of cloths, and two jugs of water. "Clean this up. I need to get you some food and drinking water. This stuff is...questionable. Drink at your own risk."

Said the man who'd fed her herbal poison. He was absolutely unhinged.

Toury nodded and dumped the cloudy water into the bucket. She could not bear to thank him and didn't dare tell him to clean it up himself. He walked out the door this time. The dragon shrieked.

"Calm down, calm down. You think you could hunt down some dinner?" He paused. "No? Fine. I'll do it myself."

He was communicating with the dragons—but not the way Alex had described it—so maybe he was talking to a voice in his head? Anything seemed possible. He walked away into the smoky terrain, and she worried for his welfare, not for him but with the stark realization she would die here if he never made it back or told anyone where she was. To busy her anxious mind, she dipped a towel into the water to start wiping up the mess.

Cleaning occupied her time, but when the bucket was full of more sick bits than water, she had to dump it. Warily, she looked to the door. There was no way she was getting fried over it. She set it by the door, peering out. All she could see were scorched earth and trees, smoke, and shadows flying through it in the distance. How big were the dragons?

To experiment, she pushed the bucket out into the door frame a couple inches with her foot. No flames. She attempted it again to the same lack of a response. Then she pushed the envelope and moved it a good six inches. She heard a strange noise like a growl and purr combined, guttural. It was close, right outside the wall. Toury backed up away from the door, worried the dragon might break the shack to pieces and she'd be torched and eaten.

A thud made her jump, as well as the reverberations under her feet from it. Another one followed. Giant footsteps. She held her breath. Maybe it would think she was gone. She could not live through necromancers, rebels, and evil family members' schemes to be eaten by a dragon in the end. She surveyed the room. There was nothing to fight with, nowhere to hide. The walls were bare, not even a lantern on the table. Toury realized Sapphirians must bring all their supplies with them when visiting the dragons. If she lived through this and Henry was defeated, Alex would one day take this baby to the Firelands. She shook away her ill-timed fantasies. She must focus on this dragon walking onto the little porch to inspect the bucket.

A snout five times the size of a horse's came into view. And its mouth was much wider, with teeth protruding over the bottom lip slightly like a dinosaur back on Earth. These teeth were on the smaller side but appeared sharp. She was sure they could tear her to shreds easily.

The snout leaned down over the bucket, and the nostrils flared. A large feline eye came into view, bright vibrant sparkling blue, the exact hue of Alex's. As she stared at this majestic creature in awe and terror, she realized why Sapphirians were fabled to have descended from them. The eye color, fire power, and strength had carried onto them, even if they weren't biologically descended. The myth said Sapphirians were born from draca flames.

Its eyes dilated. It shuddered and huffed a breath out. A large claw swiped into view and knocked the bucket off the little porch onto the charred ground below. The eyes narrowed on her, and the draca turned to face her. Its head filled the doorway but couldn't fit inside. It sniffed the air, and Toury felt a pull of magic swirling around her. The dragon cocked its head, seemingly perplexed, and then growled, apparently annoyed, and walked away.

Toury let out a sigh of relief. She couldn't leave, but this trial meant they would not kill her as long as she stayed put. And inadvertently, the dragon had gotten the messy bucket dumped for her.

The smell was still in the room, although the heat dried the floors in minutes. Toury dumped the other jug of water on the floor and scrubbed again. She let it dry. And then repeated cleaning twice. The water was almost gone, so she dumped the rest onto the floor. The smell was almost gone completely, with just a tinge in the air that would soon hopefully dissipate.

She was thirsty but glad she'd dumped the tainted water out so she couldn't be tempted to drink anything else that could hurt the baby. She hoped it was okay. She indulgently held her tummy; it was just a tiny bit firmer and fuller down low than before, thankfully hidden by the dress. She let go. Henry could transport back at any moment, and if he saw her touching her belly, he would believe there was a reason to kill her.

After all the trauma, she plopped onto the bare cot, exhausted, parched, and starving. She tried to clear her mind for sleep, but despite how much rest she needed, sleep didn't come. She pondered on how this might play out—ignoring the depressing idea Henry would be caught or be killed, never telling anyone her whereabouts—and it kept coming down to Alex's guess, or maybe a vision?

Alex might fight Henry. Who would win? There was no way Henry was as powerful as Alex. Without the curse, Alex's power was unheard of. Madge had told her of progeny, powers, and how intensity of powers carried down and combined. The dowager had strong blood magic. Her power could intensify her children's, whereas the Emerald family was influential through their name and money, not power. By default, Alex could kick Henry's ass in fire power. Yet fire couldn't harm either of them, so what would it come down to? Brains and battle? She'd seen firsthand how great Alex was in fighting multiple men off, but Henry had a military career. As for brains, Alex was a natural and just leader, but he was not as nefariously conniving as Henry or others in the court. Toury preferred his honest manner, but it could get him killed. It would be up to Toury. She had to tip the scales. But how?

Her mind tried futilely to plot until sleep finally overtook her.

22

A BLOODBOND

Alex screamed out in fury. He wasn't sure if the fighting was done or if his rage stopped everyone, but they were gaping at him like he had lost his mind. He was afraid he had. Toury taken—again—this time by a sadistic man who would stop at nothing to kill him and do whatever it would take to rule the kingdom, including killing Toury. No, Henry would hold her as ransom. Using logic to try to calm himself, Alex pressed on. Henry wouldn't kill Toury. Only, Alex didn't fully believe that. She was carrying his child. If Henry found out, he'd kill her. There was no way he'd let Alex's heir live.

He screamed again.

David's hand on his shoulder grounded him. "Your Majesty. The fort is won. Dispatch your commands."

"My commands?" he asked numbly, letting David pull him away from where Toury had vanished.

Mary was on the other side of the room, weeping over Cobalt.

"Perhaps send the wounded back to the palace, station some of your men here. You could have someone search his quarters for plans and evidence, while you and I return to the safety of the palace. There, we can figure out where he might've taken our queen?" David suggested in hurried whispers.

Alex wanted to crawl up in a wailing mess on the floor beside Mary, but he could not. Yet his mind was having trouble formulating a coherent thought. "Delegate my commands for me, David, and return post haste so we can go."

David's eyes went wide with surprise and concern at Alex's inability to rule at the moment. Mary was in no state to take over command either, so he had to let David.

"As you wish, Your Majesty." David squared his shoulders with pride and hurried off.

He shouldn't let his servant rule and decide what was to be done, but Alex was too busy keeping himself together. When Toury had been taken before, he had been wounded, lost his father, and there had been so much going on. He had made it through that, so this time, he should be seasoned and stronger. Instead, he was useless.

He had loved Toury back then, but now what he felt for her after becoming her lifemate—their souls were entwined. He needed Toury more than the air in his lungs. To be so close to saving her and failing...he couldn't bear not knowing where she was.

Alex wouldn't see Toury again. It was his worst fear come to life. And if he didn't see her again, he would die. He would be foolish, reckless, and bloodthirsty, but at least he wouldn't leave this sphere without taking Henry's life. He would ensure Mary would rule on.

Alex went over to Mary and touched her head.

She peered up into his eyes. Tears streamed down her face. "I didn't see this in the flames!" She wailed.

Alex examined Cobalt. "Because it is a small wound, and he's unconscious from getting smashed in the head. He just needs healers, silly girl. Take him back to the castle. I'll follow shortly."

Mary looked to Cobalt, then Alex in disbelief, and back to Cobalt as she examined Cobalt's head. Finding the bump on his crown, she half laughed and half sobbed. "This dress. It limits my magic." Mary started ripping at her gown, pulling down further to free more than her already bare arm.

Alex got up and searched the room for his wounded men. There was no way he was helping his sister out of that debacle. He dragged four of his incapacitated men over to Mary. Mary was in her shift now. Gross.

"Take them back to the palace infirmary, and stay there. Alert the Guilds as to what has happened. Increase security."

"What are you going to do?" She clutched his hand, telling him he could not go after Toury, that he must return with her.

He had no idea where his cousin would head. He was sure there were safehouses hidden all over Celestia, but he would send men to Mineria first. He'd scour the entire sphere until he found her.

Alex pulled his mind out of the future. "I'm going to find our aunt and get her out of here."

"Be careful. She's like two people—a necromancer and herself—fighting in one body." She closed her eyes and pressed her mouth shut, probably trying to stave off the horrific memory of the encounter with their aunt.

Alex knew the feeling of dealing with dark necromancer magic firsthand. He squeezed Mary's hand. "I will. Now go."

Mary nodded. He let go, and she vanished in a blaze with his men.

Alex pulled the fire raging in the room back into himself. The burning stopped, but it didn't dissipate the smoke quickly. Everyone left in the room was dead. Alex checked again. He had lost one soldier. He sighed. He didn't know him, but any loss was too much.

Alex ventured half-numb into the hall, where he found Craig talking to his aunt with his hands out, placating her as one would a startled draca.

"Please, no one will lock you up. I promised you freedom but only as Anne, not the other part of you. Please stop burning things, and let's get you away from here." Craig was speaking to her soothingly, and she responded.

She placed her hands in her underarms, trying to squelch her powers. Alex hadn't seen her in years, but she was unwell—physically and mentally—frail, bony, and pale, with wild eyes.

Alex pulled in all the raging fire. It was a lot. His aunt was strong. He pressed the fire down and was able to subdue it, although he wondered if bottling up this much fire inside himself might backfire. He didn't know. The curse had prevented any overload, but he had done amazing feats with more magic in him since Toury had broken it.

"Craig?" his aunt said in awe, staring Alex down.

"I'm here, Aunt. That is the king," Craig told her.

"My brother has finally come to free me. I knew he wouldn't blame me for it all. I knew he would eventually realize I was forced to do it and that I needed saving. My brother." She smiled and raced toward Alex.

Instinctively, he put up a wall of fire between them. It stopped her.

"I'm not him. He didn't know. He died never knowing who had cursed him." He hoped his honesty didn't set her off, but he wasn't able to pretend to be his father to placate her. Maybe it was better for her to know his father had died thinking well of her.

Anne's face dropped, and then her eyes seemed to clear; they grew brighter, more vibrant. Her hand went through his fire, and she touched his cheek gently. He dropped the fire, having forgotten it was pointless against her.

"Forgive me Alexander. My lifemate made me dark and controlled me." She withdrew her hand, shocked. "It is gone from you, the curse. Bless the god and goddess for sparing you. Let them save me as well." She ran from them.

Craig shouted for her to come back. That was when Alex realized she was running full force toward a large window, one that had been smashed out for fresh air when the fires began. His Aunt Anne leaped out of it.

"No!" Craig screamed in horror.

Alex acted, not even thinking about it. He transported. He slammed into someone and was falling through the sky, barreling toward the ground. He transported back to where he had come from. Craig was standing at the gaping hole of the window and then spun around to see them. Alex had his aunt safe back inside.

"David!" Alex shouted. "Craig, come. I'll transport us."

His half-brother came and took hold of their aunt, who sobbed wildly on him. He shushed her, quietly whispering things to sooth her. Strange. Alex had sent him to spy, and he had grown attached and useful for Princess Anne.

David hurried back to rejoin him. "The fort is secure." He placed his hand on Alex's shoulder, while Alex grabbed Craig's wrist as he held tightly to their aunt.

Then Alex transported back to the palace. He opened his eyes in the entrance hall of the castle. His mother stood there waiting, already alerted by his sister. His mother threw her arms around him, hugging him, which made him cringe. What grown-up king has his mother hugging him in front of his men? Sure enough, when he scanned the hall, soldiers were trying to avert their eyes and hide their smiles. Alex shirked her off. His mother noted Craig with an impassive face, which was better than her prior thinly veiled revulsion, and gazed at who was in his arms. His mother's eyes grew wide. Then she smoothed the hair out of Princess Anne's face.

"Anne?" His mother was astounded.

His aunt clutched her arms, smiling. It was awkward, as if she hadn't smiled in years. "Jane," she returned to Alex's mother. They embraced.

Alex took his leave, knowing his mother would get her settled. He heard his mother ask where Toury was; Alex walked faster to avoid hearing the response while trying to swallow the lump expanding in his throat. David was on his heels. He walked the entire way to his study, taking the time to think, to list, to prioritize.

"Your Majesty, perhaps you should bathe, lie down, rest?" David said.

Alex flopped into the chair at his desk and took up a quill. Without looking at the man, he returned, "You give me any more ridiculous suggestions, considering the circumstances, I might just light you on fire."

After it was out, Alex felt guilty, but how could the man—knowing Alex as well as he did—ask Alex to take comfort and indulge in relaxation when his lifemate was in the hands of his enemy.

"Silly of me, Your Majesty. I sought to do what was right for your health without thinking of your mind."

Not wanting the man to grovel more for Alex's own rude behavior, he launched into command mode. "David, you are never to leave my side, even if I am stupid or reckless enough to tell you to do so. We have no idea when he'll show up to try to kill me. I need you to ring for servants to summon a few people. First, I need a couple scribes and several messengers. I will dispatch orders for every fort in every city to send out scouts to find Toury or information about Henry. Also, summon Toury's aunt and uncle. Get me updates on Cobalt and my injured men. If Mary will leave his side, I need her here."

David went to the wall and pulled the bell chains to alert some of the staff. Alex set to penning his missive ordering scouts. He would not send armies into cities and leave forts unprotected. It would be covert to quietly locate Toury. Then they'd hatch a plan to save her. Henry could not know Alex was coming, or he'd act rash and desperate. And so might Alex himself. Planning helped ease the ache in his heart momentarily. It would be back. He did not know how he would go to bed alone tonight.

The first scribe showed up, groggy and hastily dressed. Alex realized for the first time that the hour was late. It mattered not. This could not wait. "Twenty copies." He handed the scribe his missive, and the man took it to one of the small desks on the side of the room and started at once.

Two more scribes joined him a moment later. Messengers arrived, and as the wax dried on the copies of his orders, they took them and headed to the stables. During this, Alex paced the room. Out the window, he saw the first messengers ride off on their horses. Some would take a day to get to their destinations, changing horses, which worried him, but Henry would not act tonight. He had been surprised Alex came so soon. He wasn't ready. Henry would be plotting, and Toury would be giving him a hard time. He smiled at the thought of how his lifemate would make Henry rue the day he had taken her.

Lady Edwina and Lord Gareth showed up next, together. Lady Edwina seemed to finally accept the man as an equal, or tolerate him being treated that way.

Alex got right to it. "Lord Sapphirian escaped and took Toury."

Lady Edwina gasped and sank into a chair.

Lord Gareth straightened his shoulders. "What has been done to find her?"

Alex pointed to the last few messages going off and explained, "I was hoping you could help."

"Blood magic," Gareth said. "It doesn't work as well with light as it does with fire. You could seek your blood all over Fyr. My radius is maybe fifty miles, but I will try."

"Ride out in the morning. Maybe by then we'll get an indicator of what area she could be in. Or you can rule out areas for us." It was wishful thinking, and it was a fool's errand, but there was the slim chance he would find her, and if it took long, he could find her through the process of elimination. It was a backup plan.

"I will go too," Edwina found her voice. "My blood tie is a bit stronger...no offense," she added hastily. It was true since she was Toury's full aunt instead of half.

"No. Lady Edwina, there could be danger. Lord Gareth is trained to use his light as a weapon. You are a curse breaker and practiced in healing arts. We will need you here. I have a very important assignment for you here at the castle. We managed to rescue Princess Anne..." He paused at the other lady's astonishment. "She had been imprisoned and ill-treated by the Emeralds. Despite her crimes, I'd like you to pull the darkness out of her and free her from the necromancer inside her. Try, but if it will kill her, halt until we know what else we could do for her."

With that, he dismissed them. He dismissed the scribes as well since all messages were sent. He was itching to do it, wanting to see if it would work, to find Toury, but he couldn't leave the castle until he spoke with Mary. David tried to ply food onto Alex; he took a couple bites to please the man and then gave up.

Mary finally arrived, her skin tinged with green.

"Cobalt?" Alex froze, afraid he had been wrong and his friend's injuries were worse. *Please don't be dead.*

"He's fine. I'm not. I was sick from something Henry fed us." She kept her eyes downcast. She sat quietly in the chair across from his desk.

"I need you to take over if I leave now."

"You can't leave, Alex." She finally met his gaze.

"No, I must. Toury is...with child. I can trace her through blood magic."

"Oh, Alex." Her voice broke.

He wasn't used to this weak, sickly Mary. He wanted his spitfire sister back, giving everyone a hard time.

"Don't try it, please." Her eyes welled up, and she avoided his gaze. "The healers told me Henry gave us black draca tree root. That's why I've been sick. You vomit it out if you aren't with child, and if you are..."

Alex's stomach dropped. His child. His poor Toury was losing their child far away from him with a sadistic murderer holding her hostage. No; he wouldn't believe it. He'd find Toury and get her back safe, get healers to help her. It wasn't too late.

"I have to try," he said quietly.

"I will be here waiting," was all Mary said.

"Wait, weapons, men..." David said, exasperated.

Alex must've given himself away, for David raced over and grabbed Alex's arm as he transported onto the roof of the palace. He closed his eyes, concentrating, branching out his mind in search of the sensation of his blood throughout the kingdom. There was Mary downstairs, Aunt Anne on the first floor, Craig a few blocks away, a bit fainter in pull. Then Alex branched out farther and farther. There were tiny blips here and there, pulses of magic from distant relatives, descendants of baseborns from his ancestors. Then there was the largest pull of all: the Firelands. The power of the dragons was a thousand times stronger than his and a hotbed of Sapphirian blood. He gave up on the south and tried north. He checked the land again and again. Nothing. He transported out of desperation, but he opened his eyes to his study and Mary, not Toury. If there had been a child, it was gone. Even worse, maybe Toury was gone with their child.

It was all too much. He fell to his knees, his legs too weak to stand.

"Oh Alex." Her hands touched his chest, pressing him back up to kneeling before his head hit the ground. She knelt too and hugged him.

He buried his face in her hair and silently begged for his sister to hold the pieces of him together.

"Stop, stop. Look at me." When she pushed him away and held his face in her hands, entreating him to focus, he had realized he was crying out in a mixture of pain and rage. "Alex, listen, if he tried to kill your child, he's not trying to kill her. He will keep her alive for some purpose. And you came back here to me, not where Henry was. Why couldn't you find him?"

His faculties came back to him, and he got himself up off the floor. He offered his hands to Mary to help her up. "Thank you, Mary." His cousin didn't register on his blood search. What did that mean? Had he left Fyr?

"It is okay to be human, Alex."

161

"Not when you're the Draca." He discreetly wiped the tears out of the corner of his eyes.

"You aren't a dragon. You're a man. It's okay to show emotion. Father never let us, please don't…" She broke down crying.

He sighed, pulled her in, and hugged her. "I know. I know." He soothed her. "Cobalt?"

"He's fine. He's trying to get cleared to be here, but they aren't happy with his wound and are keeping him." She wiped her tears away, and they just stood there staring at each other for a moment, understanding each other's pain.

"Tell them I command his presence. Transport him to my sitting room. We need to plan."

"Have you thought that if we can't see Henry, he might have left the sphere?"

"Yes," Alex said. "I'll have Tobias send a messenger to each sphere to warn for a fugitive. I can't see him leaving, though. I can't see him giving up what he wants most: Fyr in his control."

Mary took a deep breath. "Alex, I'm starting to wonder if his goal has shifted from the throne to Toury."

He went rigid.

"Alex, listen." She put her hands on his shoulders, pressing against them, bracing him. He didn't want to listen anymore. "Why would he try to make her lose your child if he planned to kill her? You don't want to hear this, and I don't want to say it, but anyone who wants to end your line and has seen how much you love her would kill her. He wants her alive for some reason, and I think it's more than ransom." Her eyes bore into him, entreating him to meet her gaze.

When he finally dared to, he couldn't speak.

When she realized he refused to think further down this path, she sighed. "She reminds me of Henry's late lifemate—without the false exterior and manipulative mind. Remember how Lady Emily was resilient, intelligent, and crafty? Toury is more honest and overall a better person, but I see similarities. I realize now how fake she and Henry were. Toury warned me. Cobalt and I fought about Henry." She let her hands drop, and Alex had to right his weight not to fall forward. "I believed he was good. He had always been kind to me, growing up. I couldn't see through his lies."

"Father's lessons, remember? Keep your enemies close so you know everything about them. That's what Henry and Emily did: learned our weaknesses and used them against us."

"You think even as children he was scheming? I cannot believe that."

Alex's jaw clenched. Mary was young, but she could not be this naive. Yes, Alex had been blinded as a child too. Henry had been the older cousin they looked up to, but it was clear once they were adults that he was false to the core, almost inhuman. Yet badmouthing Henry could set off her Sapphirian temper. He chose his words carefully. "Our uncle and aunt planned this before you were born. I'm sure he was conditioned from birth. It's all clear now. Our aunt wasn't well enough to curse you, so Henry watched over you." He was the one to sigh and brace her shoulders, hoping she would not take this the wrong way. "I love you, dear sister, but you never had an interest in politics. Then you went a bit wild. You were never a threat. Had you challenged his leadership, he could've discredited you. Henry wouldn't worry about you until now with your engagement with Cobalt and your recent involvement in politics."

She was pensive, not angry. He knew she was grasping what he said, actually listening. Then she backed away, and he dropped his hands. She shook her head and her jaw jutted out—angry, but at what?

"How can such a man exist?" She was growling.

Good. Back to the spitfire girl he expected and needed her to be. Because, god and goddess, he was falling apart.

23

TOPAZ

Toury woke up soaked in sweat. Sapphire eyes watched her. Not Alex's, but ones intensely wild and haunted. She sat up and backed against the wall. It was daylight, and Henry was sitting at the table only feet away from her cot, staring at her. How long had he been there? How long had she slept?

"Were you watching me sleep?"

"You remind me of her." He avoided the question.

"Who?"

"Emily Topaz."

Not good; that had been his wife. "Do I look like her?" Toury asked, severely freaked out this madman had watched her sleep, but desperately trying to hide it and stay calm. Reminding him of his dead lifemate was not much better. Bunched against the wall was worse temperature-wise. She couldn't last long here.

Guessing her thoughts, he offered her a jug of water. "Here, drink. We don't want you to dehydrate."

Toury took the jug and drank it down in big gulps.

"Slow down." He pulled it away from her. "You'll throw it up. Small sips." He handed it back and watched her drink. "No. You are beautiful, Toury, unique with your tan skin, but she had been fair and delicate." He stared off in another time and place, the corners of his mouth turning up in a small attempt at a smile. It was one of those smiles of happiness and grief fused as one. "She was not a fighter with swords as the whelp indulges you in, but a fighter of the mind. She was clever and could outwit any person I ever met. She fought with words. You two would've been friends, so alike in wanting women to be equal, for the poor not to suffer, both with great hearts."

"If she were so great and clever, why did she marry you?" It came out so fast, Toury didn't realize how insulting it would be.

Henry sat up as if she'd slapped him across the face, but then he smiled. She was unnerved when he smiled at her like that. It was oddly misplaced affection. This could not be happening. Henry could not be interested in her that way.

"That's something I'd often say to her. You know what she would always reply with? 'Because everyone needs a savior.' So intelligent and sly, yet she married someone she thought she could save." His face fell, and he was staring off, eyes no longer focused on Toury. "People don't ever change. Never. They stay the same, or they die on you. She's lucky she died and didn't see what I've become."

"What have you become?" Toury ventured. Him talking was good. It could possibly prolong any actions. She drank more water, her mouth no longer dry.

"Let's eat, huh? I hope you're not picky. Not much around these parts, except rabbits, goats, and deer. The stores will be open now, so I'll venture out again and get necessities after we dine." He ignored her harder questions.

Toury was beginning to think Henry would not have become this unstable monster if Lady Emily had lived.

Toury watched him pull two hares out of a sack she hadn't seen behind the table. Under them, he pulled out sheets for the bed, and a dress with shortened sleeves. "It is far too hot for that garb with its magic-blocking layer too. Change, and then make the beds. I'll be back." He walked out the door, whistling for a dragon.

Toury wondered how many there were out there and about their colors. The one that approached Henry was blue. No longer frightened, she examined them now. Their scales shined almost like a fish's, but the scales themselves didn't appear slimy or dry like a lizard's. They were glassy, reminding her of polished precious stones.

She should be changing, for she was sure Henry would watch her if she waited. She undid her laces with trouble, shucked off the gown, and slipped the nice cotton material over her body. Instantly, she was cooler. The sweat stopped trickling down her.

Henry had his eyes closed as the dragon breathed fire all over the hares he held aloft by the ears. It was fascinating to see him being immune to the flames. She tucked the first sheet around the cot as she listened to him speak to the dragons.

"No, you can't eat one. They're for me and my lady friend. No, you can't eat her. She's the queen." Then he huffed out a breath in annoyance. "He will not have the throne or her much longer. I will be king." Then he stomped across the ground. "Well, you might prefer me being king. I might just let you eat my enemies." He laughed. "I thought you'd like that. Tell Draca B she can eat the dragon slayer for all I care. She's a traitor."

Toury's sister. She had told the truth. Toury made the other cot up quickly, her mind churning. Henry was the rebel commander, and his father had been the orchestrator of the necromancers. They had joined forces in the end, so now Henry had an army and a way to raise his soldiers once killed. This was bad.

Henry entered and placed the charred carcasses on the table. "Forgive me. I didn't think about the laces." He turned her around and started pulling the laces tighter for her.

Thankfully, she had a corset on, preventing him from seeing any of her back. Despite the heat, she had left it on. It was her safeguard if Henry became too attracted to her. When he got to the top, he swept her hair out of the way and tied a bow, his finger lingering, tracing a pattern across her neck. She moved away from him, the chill creeping down her spine from fright. The look in his eyes was terrifying, filled with want. His mouth was in a predatory grin. She had to wipe that expression from his face.

"Where can I use the facilities?" she asked.

That worked. He frowned. "There's an outhouse, but I don't think you can make it there on your own. Can you wait until after we eat? I don't have any soap yet either."

Toury couldn't stomach the idea of being in an outhouse and then eating dinner with her hands, especially because there wouldn't be plates and silverware or anything convenient here. Henry pulled out the chair for her, being a gentleman, which was odd, considering she was being held against her will and they were in a shack, ignoring all other etiquette. He sat much too close to her, his leg rubbing against hers, but there wasn't any room to really move away. Henry dug his fingers into the burnt hare and pulled out a hunk of steaming meat. Under the layer of charcoaled skin, it was tender, and she was ravenous.

"What are you waiting for? Would you like me to feed you?" Henry asked her in a flirty tone.

"Absolutely not." She scowled and dug into the other hare. Her fingers burned, but she refused to give him a reason to actually feed her.

Henry laughed, enjoying her disgust. He was a weird one, unhinged, which meant difficult to read.

She ate slowly and deliberately, despite being ravenous. She didn't want to give Henry any indication she was pregnant. "What will you do?"

Henry scrutinized her, trying to read her. "Is this you trying to fetter out my evil plans so you can stop me? I'm not the bad one here, Toury."

She wanted to punch him in the face and tell him he was nuts. She filled her mouth with more meat to stop her comments. After she swallowed and repressed her anger, she spoke carefully. "Some would say that taking someone against their will, planning to assassinate one's cousins is a bit evil."

"Some people must do terrible things to save many. Did that whelp not almost kill you? He chose to let the necromancer's magic overtake him, and he well knew it would try to kill you. I grew up seeing that magic and the damage it can do. I'd never go dark, and I'd never hurt you."

It was a low blow. Alex had used and hurt her, but what overrode his picking at that old wound was the way he spoke of how he would treat her, as if it would definitely happen. It creeped her out, and she needed to turn his attention away from this fantastical future where she would ever be his queen.

"No, just try to kill everyone I love."

"Love is a weakness, Toury." His tone shifted, brooking no argument.

"Well, I think that is the first and only time I'll ever agree with you," Toury allowed. It was a weakness, but it was also strength; it was so much more powerful than all the magic in the world. But it would be foolish to tell him all the good things that came with love as well.

"You will come around to my way of thinking. You cannot think with your heart or for yourself. You must think for the greater good for all the people. I want to raise Fyr up into being the best sphere in the universe."

"Greater good?" She had heard that term in her Earth history books far too many times with terrible consequences. That's what Fyr would get with him, a tyrant, a mad one at that. He had to be stopped. Trying to kill him was not an option at the moment. Dare she try logic?

She picked at the food and, after the silence became stifling, said, "How? The necromancers will destroy the fire magic. Why would you work with them when you know their magic is bad, and they will snuff the fire out, *your* magic and power." There, make him think about self-preservation.

He scoffed at that and smirked. "They work *for* me, not with me. I've promised them their very own sphere, the one dying out with little magic left. I figure dark magic would reign well there. And then I'll have two of the four elemental spheres under my control."

Earth? Sure, she hadn't loved her life there, but Earth had been her home, and no human being deserved to live under the dark, sadistic nature of the necromancers. Unbelievable. He wasn't content with world domination, but wanted the entire galaxy.

"Why not go to Earth yourself, take over that one. Leave Fyr be. Alex and Mary have done nothing to you and want to improve Fyr too. Please, just spare them, and I'll...I'll go with you. I grew up on Earth—"

Henry stood so quickly, his chair flew back and tottered over. Rage contorted his face. His sapphire eyes flashed with a wrath she'd never seen from Alex, Mary, or even their father when he had lived. He leaned in on the arms of the wooden chair and was in her face. "Get this straight, Tourmaline Hematite: you will never own me. I'm not that lovesick whelp. And you will go with me and do what I demand because I will be your king, your master. You saw through my pretenses. It takes an actor to know one. You would never willingly leave the whelp for me, but because I make you."

At "your master," Toury was seeing red. At "make you," she lost it. She blasted him back away from her.

He slammed into the wall above the cot, making the entire shack creak. Then he fell onto the cot, stunned, gazing up at her in awe and fury combined.

"You get this straight! I am no man's property." With mad courage, she closed the distance between them, her finger pointed in accusation like a mother reprimanding a child. Fitting, because he was acting like one, yelling at his toys to obey. "There are people on Earth who were enslaved by others. People who looked similar to my mother, with skin darker than mine. And women were ill-treated for centuries."

He frowned, bemused, slowly sitting back up on the cot, his expression thoroughly guilty, reinforcing the child-parent situation they were in.

Having the upper hand on him, she continued: "I learned to never allow anyone to command me. You will never make me do anything. And I wasn't acting. I was being a martyr for my loved ones. I would resign my fate to be with you—as equals—if you spare them and you spare Fyr." Bile rose in her throat when she said it, but she needed Alex to live, and his people—her people—needed to live happy lives with the positive changes Alex would enact.

Henry was up again, his expression strange. His hands closed around her upper arms. She pushed away, but his grip bit into her flesh, making it painful. Then his lips were on hers, and she closed her mouth tightly and threw more light magic out. This time, he was ready with a curtain of fire between them. At least it got his lips away from hers.

"Tempting, Toury, but I'm unsure whether I want to keep you like this or to break you. You are so interesting and yet...unmanageable."

Toury ignored his "breaking" comment. She was sure he meant mental and physical abuse until she was a shell of a human being, just what they had done to his mother. "Well, you can't keep me here forever. I'll die, or Alex will find me."

"Finally, you talk sense. Anyway, I lost my appetite with your nonsense. I'll be back."

Then he was gone in a ball of flames. Toury collapsed onto her cot, crumpling into a blithering mess. She wanted to blame it on the hormones, but she was overwhelmed and terrified, dealing with this man and not knowing what would come next. She indulged in crying for a good five minutes before a huff in the doorway stopped her.

A blue dragon was there, smelling the room. Only the tip of its snout could fit in the doorway. Did it smell the food? It made a strange rolling lion-growl sound, but the tone was offering sympathy. Toury sat up slowly and wiped her eyes. The dragon backed its head out, and its eyes examined her. She swore she saw empathy in them.

"Good draca, draca." Toury cooed. She stood, inching toward the food on the table.

The dragon's eyes narrowed proclaiming, *Rude.*

What had Alex told her? They were smart but didn't speak man's language well and only telepathically with Sapphirians. Had Henry spoken aloud because he wanted Toury to hear? Or was he less powerful overall and couldn't connect his voice to theirs as well as Alex?

Of course she shouldn't treat it like an animal. "I'm sorry. You're the first draca I've ever met. I'm sure you don't see many humans either. I wish I could speak to you, but I'm not a Sapphirian by blood."

It backed up to view her better and made a huffing noise about not seeing humans often. The dragon could understand her?

"So, you don't like humans, huh? Neither do I, few of them at least."

The dragon smiled. This shocked Toury. It physically drew its lips back into a creepy grimace of sharp teeth and blinked its lids shut, which reminded her of the human expression of eye rolling; this draca apparently agreed with her. Then it sat back, staring in at her in a Sphinx-type pose, paws innocuously out in front on the doorstep, its regal head in the air, moving to and fro to fully scan for possible threats. Was it trying to protect her? It was definitely not in an attack position.

Toury ate some more hare. It was gamey and bland, but she was starving. Or the baby was. She was chowing down when she checked on the dragon. He was licking his lips. Toury held up a piece of meat.

The dragon nodded.

If she had a chance to get out of here, to have the dragons help her, she had to somehow befriend them—if that was possible.

Toury picked up the rest of her hare. She didn't want to set off Henry by giving away his food, and she could always pick at it if needed. She placed her food onto the porch and pushed it out with her foot.

The dragon examined it and then her.

"It's yours. Eat it. Thank you for not eating me."

The dragon edged up closer, slowly. Toury backed up. It stopped and cocked its head trying to understand her. Then it extended its neck and opened its mouth, about to eat it, but its teeth didn't close around it. Instead, the snout pushed the food back into the room. It licked its teeth, leaned up and swallowed, and nodded at her. Did it want her to eat?

"Me eat?"

The dragon nodded. Then it rolled over like a dog and patted its own belly and sat back up.

Toury was now cocking her head in wonderment. Did the dragon somehow know she was pregnant? The draca was trying to tell her to eat, rather than wanting her to share. Her limbs shaking, she sat and picked up the meat and ate some.

The dragon nodded, licking its lips to urge her on. She ate more. He watched her the entire time, making her feel oddly safe.

She relaxed. "Henry is a bad man. He is trapping me here. I have to get back to Alex, the king. Don't let Henry know about the baby. He will kill it, kill me. And the Sapphirian line and the fire could die out. I don't know how it all works, but I don't think you'd do well if the fire goes out, would you?"

The dragon just watched her.

"I must get out of here. Could you help me?"

The dragon perked up, alert. It clearly shook its head at her, staring her down, trying to impart something to her she could not hear or understand. Then it suddenly leaped up and flew away, leaving her bereft.

Henry reappeared an hour later with large duffle bags, throwing them on the ground. "There," he said, annoyed. He flopped onto the bed. "I need

170

to get some sleep, and if you hurt me in any way with some of those items, you'll be stuck here and die."

"I understand I'm at your mercy. I'm not stupid."

"Good." He rolled over to go to sleep.

Having nothing better to do, Toury opened the first bag to find all practical items: a bedpan, a couple short-sleeved dresses, soap, a bowl—she assumed it was for washing up—candles, a horsehair hairbrush, swine-bristled toothbrushes, washcloths, and a book. The second was filled with food: preserves, bread rolls, cheese, cured meat, carrots, spinach, four jugs of water, and dried dracaberries. She opened the bag of those and started eating them. Not as good as fresh fruit from the orchard, but it gave her some comfort.

Nothing could be used as a weapon unless she beat his head in with a bedpan. Tempting, but she needed to survive. Ugh, and she could finally pee somewhere. She opened the door all the way and slipped between it and the wall to create some privacy. Then she relieved her bladder and pushed the bedpan out the door with her foot and then closed it. Henry could dump it tomorrow.

Toury put the bowl and soap on the table and poured water in, washing her hands, face, and exposed arms. Then she took out her hair pins and removed her circlet out of her tangled hair. She brushed it smooth as best as she could and then climbed onto her cot.

Toury would bide her time. She would try to get the upper hand on Henry, and when he was gone, she would befriend dragons. She and her baby would get out of here.

24
A PLEDGE

Racine stood in his King's Room after Alex had summoned her, while he sat studying her. He was so desperate to find Toury, to know she was alive, but to trust Racine was another matter. Either she was breaking away from Henry's side, or this was a well-played intricate plot to get on his good side. And why? Alex had been groggy and almost unconscious, but he'd seen Racine turn on his cousin, Henry's surprise and rage, and then she'd saved Alex's life. He was still angry. Why not Toury? He resented her for not saving Toury instead.

"Am I the first woman in this room, Your Majesty?"

"No. Sit," he ordered, his voice barking more than he wanted.

She sighed, annoyed, and plopped most inelegantly into the chair.

Alex motioned with his hand. She was unladylike, so why not treat her like a gentleman? "How do you take your firewhiskey?"

"Huh?" She gaped stupidly, then recovered. "Half water, Your Majesty."

"You're a definitively different creature than the one I met," Alex said. He scrutinized her, hoping to somehow see the truth behind her cool exterior.

She shrugged. "People grow up."

"Meaning?" God and goddess, she was laborious to crack.

She mused, staring at the floor. "They experience grief, a broken heart, and become illuminated. I came to Fyr brainwashed. I can think for myself now. You see—"

"Spare yourself. Toury told me everything. Drink." He didn't want to hear some romantic drivel about Henry gone wrong. The man had used her as he did everyone else.

The servant presented them with drinks. "Good. I don't want to regale you with tales of my ridiculous naivety." She frowned at the thought. Of course, she would never want to admit a weakness. She was one hardened girl who would rather die before admitting her failings or shedding a tear. Racine sipped her drink and hummed. "How stupid of my parents to leave this comfort."

What an odd thing for her to say. She was changing the subject, but still. "You don't believe that. My uncles did terrible things to your parents. My family was horrific for the last couple generations." Not liking the subject, he inadvertently brought up, he added, "I'm changing that."

"I've seen. I've heard." she murmured, swirling the liquid in her glass. He knew she was uncomfortable being wrong, so this was all the apology he'd get from her for her former insults and actions. But then she continued, meeting his gaze, "I'm starting to see that it's not all fine speeches, but actual actions."

A silence formed. He had thought more was coming, but perhaps not. He watched as her face shifted into a softer expression, a frown formed, and her eyes pleaded—a very Toury-like expression that pierced his heart with desperate need to get her back.

Then she spoke. "Please don't make me repeat how wrong I have been. I simply believed what I was told. I was jealous of my sister's power. You don't seem the type to want groveling. I hope I've proven myself. It should be enough to just gain your audience, but I want to do more."

It was enough of an apology for that, but not for her most recent actions. "You proved yourself, but I have an issue with your conduct. Despite the fact I was clinging to consciousness, I saw all. You chose my life over Toury's. I'm having trouble forgiving that."

Racine drank another gulp of her drink, took a deep breath. He gave her a minute to admit her mistake, to beg forgiveness, but he should've known she would surprise him acting anything but sorry. "Get off yourself, Your Majesty. I told you she made me promise. I couldn't protect all three of you against him. He wanted you most, then Mary, then Toury. Part of my job was to seek information about you two from servants and the public opinion. I had downplayed it for a while to Henry, but Toury loves you as you love her. He saw it for himself when he was here. You two can't help but be so disgustingly sweet to each other."

Alex huffed. He resented her mocking his relationship with Toury.

"The point is, I wanted amends with her. If I let you die, that would never happen; I'd break that promise. Yeah, I'm the type to break promises, but in that moment, I chose you. I had to. Without you, my sister would be dead in spirit. Fyr would fall into Henry's hands and be destroyed."

"I'd rather be dead and Fyr lost than her be gone forever." It came out of Alex before he could control his emotions. His eyes stung.

Racine frowned. "I'm sorry. I did what was necessary. You won't see that now, but he won't kill her. I promise. He won't. Henry and I found a common bond. It was how he sucked me in. The jealousy. He covets everything you have, including Toury. He thinks she'll make a great queen. He was going to make sure if there was a baby between you two, it would be gone. If not, my guess is he'd pretend it was his after you were gone. He wants to keep her. That's how I know she is alive."

Weak and wanting to believe her, he dared to seek her assistance. "Concerning your request to do more, what do you suggest?"

"Give me one of your soldiers who is trained in covert operation to pose as my spouse, money to travel with and buy information discreetly, and a way to easily contact your army."

"What for?"

"I'm going to find my sister."

It was too easy, too good to be true. She wanted coin he couldn't care less about and one spy? There was nothing to lose on his side except false hope. "What's in it for you? I won't believe you're doing this out of the kindness of your heart."

"Of course not. I don't have one. I want a pardon. A life away from Fyr. I'm thinking Earth. I'm tired of fighting, and Fyr has nothing left for me. I killed a dragon and got hundreds of people killed. No one will forgive me. I want to do something good for myself for once. I want to like myself." The last comment made her blink back tears before shifting back to her stoic nature. There was that Hematite backbone he was familiar with.

"Pledge it then, on your life," Alex told her. "A fire oath."

Alex expected her to kick up a fuss, to bargain, to refuse even. He was not used to this broken-down rebel girl. She knelt in front of him, holding her hand up, ready to officially pledge.

He let his fire magic out slowly, letting it curl around her, not letting it touch her skin, controlling it similar to how he did whenever transporting David or Toury. He took a deep breath, having never done this type of magic before. "I, King Alexander Rowland Sapphirian, evoke this fire pledge ordering you, Racine Hematite, to find your sister, Queen Tourmaline Sapphirian and inform me of her condition and whereabouts in exchange for a full pardon of former crimes against the sphere and a one-way charged labradorite."

"I, Racine Hematite, pledge to locate my sister and inform His Majesty of her whereabouts and condition in exchange for the pardon and labradorite."

Once she was fully encased and the words were completed, the fire emitted sparks, telling him the deed was done. He pulled the fire back in.

Racine's hand trembled, and she sat in the chair, downing the rest of her drink. He didn't blame her. Racine would die if she did not fulfill her side of the pledge. If a fire oath bargain was broken, fire consumed the one who dared to enter such a pledge with a Sapphirian.

Alex penned a quick note, handed it to the servant in the doorway, and dismissed Racine. He would see she had everything she needed for her mission. Alex had the feeling a crafty Hematite rebel was the perfect person for the job. He could not put all his faith in her, though. It was another backup plan.

25
SPARKS

Henry left for so long the next day that she slept soundly until nightfall. It was a much-needed reprieve as she couldn't sleep the night before with him there, worried he'd try something while she slept. Another much needed reprieve was the weather. Although it was stiflingly hot still, she was sweating less. At first, she thought dehydration was the cause, but that wasn't it. She felt okay. She must be acclimating.

Henry returned at what she believed was the early evening, but she had no clock. He lit a candle with his magic and said very little.

He threw himself on the cot and stared outside. There were dark circles under his eyes; he was unwashed, and his clothes were dirty. Wherever he had been for hours, it wasn't in hygienic conditions.

"What now?"

"Huh?" He focused on her, his thoughts elsewhere.

"I can't stay here forever."

"I know that, so you can stop asking it," Henry snapped. "I have plans, and no, I'm not stupid enough to share them. You're stuck here until your whelp lifemate agrees to give me the throne."

"He can't give it to you. I read the edicts."

"He can offer his life up to save yours, though, can't he?"

"He won't." Deep in her heart, though, she worried he'd do something that foolish, particularly for their child. "And Mary's life?"

"Mary's easy to sweep aside. She drinks too much to be taken seriously as a ruler. Easily proven as unfit."

Toury wanted to defend her and point out to him that Mary had abstained for a while now and was taking her duties seriously, but that kind of info could threaten her life. Best let Henry think he knew it all. "Alex won't. He has never before. He will always choose his kingdom over me."

"Don't underestimate your effect, Toury. He's a lovesick pup right now who just was introduced to the flesh of a woman..."

He inspected her and backed up, envisioning her flesh, his eyes roaming up and down her body. "When a man experiences lust *and* love simultaneously...well, there's no better feeling in Fyr. A man does not give that up."

Toury said nothing more, not wanting the man's eyes roving over her or for him to try to make a move. She wanted to kill him and yet needed him for her survival. She flipped through the book to see it was a bunch of short stories of a romantic nature, but it was too dark in the candlelight to read.

"Why won't he go away?" Henry sat up, glowering at the blue draca outside who was standing guard. Toury had thought Henry wanted it to guard her, but Henry was utterly surprised. "Go away!" he shouted at the draca. "Don't you have some nest to guard?"

A moment passed.

"I'm sorry, fellow. Mine too." He paused. "This isn't a nest, but you can stay and protect her if it makes you feel better."

"What did it say?"

"Lost a mate, so there is no nest, poor thing. They mate for life, so it's downright tragic for them."

"It's tragic for humans too." Toury thought of Alex and if either of them had to go on without the other. Alex had once told her they were together for life, like dragons.

Too late, she realized Henry took it as sympathy for the loss of his own wife. He squeezed Toury's hand gently. "I must go," Henry said, his voice weak and thick. Then he vanished.

Had Toury known Henry's leaving meant he wouldn't return the next day or the following, she would've rationed her food better. Now she was running low on food and water. The dragon never left her. She often spoke to him, wishing he could talk back somehow. She was lonely. The book of short stories had lasted her a day and proved Henry had no taste in books. The fourth day, she went to bed hungry and woke up the fifth day parched. For dinner, she had licked the preserve jar clean, had her last bit of water. The dragon's head was resting on the porch, exhausted. She hadn't seen him eat either.

"Aren't you starving?"

Yes.

Toury sat bolt upright. She swore she heard the dragon speak. Had she gone insane? She decided to keep talking. "If you're hungry, go get us food."

Must protect you. The dragon's lips didn't move, but she could see in those glittering sapphire eyes that he was communicating with her. He was talking in her head. How? Was she hallucinating?

"You can't protect me if I'm dead. I need food."

The draca cocked his head thoughtfully, then backed up and took off. She panicked, feeling abandoned and unsafe, which was silly, but she had become used to her guard. If she could continue communicating with the draca, maybe she could convince him to help her out of the Firelands.

To keep her mind off food, Toury began forming a ball of light in her hand, forming it, molding it, and pulling it back in. She wanted to stay sharp so she could attack Henry once she knew her dragon guard would help her. She pushed even more magic out, trying to make a huge ball, but what came out was a flame, bright white with sparks crackling from it. She pulled it back in, afraid. What the hell was that?

She dared to try again, pushing most of her power out at once. Lightning shot out of her palm, hitting the ceiling, and white-hot flames danced around. In the center, she could make out her ball of light. She held onto it, even though it was taking a lot of strength to maintain. Electric bolts rippled around it. What the heck was going on with her? Then she pulled the power back in. Her tummy fluttered again in answer.

It was the first time she'd felt the baby move since the poisoning; it was small, like a butterfly wings flapping inside, but it was something. Her baby was alive. She slipped her hand down her abdomen and touched the spot where it was firmer. Her baby. She indulged for a moment before she let go. Henry could return any moment and see her touching her stomach in that loving gesture. All would be lost.

She lay down on the cot, thinking. Was she somehow using her baby's powers? How? And if so, why was the fire white instead of normal flames? What was this sparkling electricity coming out of her? Or had Ruby's power come to her in her time of need as her knowledge had against the necromancers? Even all these reasons together didn't explain it.

She peered up at the ceiling to see a charred spot. Apparently, the inside wasn't fireproof—or lightningproof. She hoped Henry didn't notice.

Her fear of him noticing was inane as he didn't come back that day. He needed her alive as a bargaining chip or for his cringeworthy future plans to make her queen, so where was he? Captured? Dead? Her draca did come back with a goat for supper. The dragon's favorite. Toury wasn't fond of the taste but had to eat, so she choked it down, being sure to hide her distaste. She didn't want to offend the creature. She went to bed that night with a full belly but a dry mouth.

Henry did not come the next day. Toury slept or lay there most the day, not having the energy to move. The dragon brought her some kind of bird meal, possibly a grouse or partridge? It was hard to tell under the charcoal. The dust of the charcoal in her dry mouth made her unable to eat. She almost choked twice, having no saliva to swallow it down with.

Eat, the draca said, his voice firm in her head.

Can't, she thought, unable to speak. She wasn't sure he would hear her. *I told you. I need to leave. I need water.*

Water is bad for fire. You are safer here. Humans bad.

Apparently, he could read her thoughts if she projected them at him.

They had this exchange a few times after she tried to convince the dragon to help her escape. The creature wasn't understanding that she needed to consume water to live. She wanted to keep arguing but had no energy to.

She changed the subject. *What is your name?*

Humans call me Sir Draca J.

Oh, well, what do you call yourself?

You wouldn't understand.

Tell me anyway.

The dragon made a series of short growls, purrs, and hisses.

It took her a moment to realize those noises were his name. *I see. Well, I can't say the latter, and the former feels rude. I'm going to call you DJ if that's okay with you.*

The dragon drew his lips back, which was very intimidating. She thought he was offended, but realized once again, it was a smile. He hissed smoke out of his teeth repeatedly; it was...laughter. *DJ. I like it.* DJ straightened up as if he had just been knighted. Obviously, nobody had given the dragons more personalized nicknames before.

She "spoke" to him for some time, but projecting her thoughts made her head ache. She wasn't sure how much time went by. She was aware she had slept. She whimpered in realization that Henry wasn't coming back, Alex wasn't saving her, and she was dying. She should have tried to run away through the Firelands and dealt with the heat and other dragons trying to eat her. Her draca may have even protected her, but now it was too late because she was too weak. She had thought Henry would've returned. Toury was his ransom. Perhaps Alex refused his demands, so

Henry decided to let nature take its course and for her to die. She'd rather he killed her quickly.

Something nudged her. *Flesh baby?*

I'm dying...water. It used up all her energy merely to focus her thoughts on communicating to the draca, and she fell back asleep. She didn't even have the energy to pray to wake up again.

26
A Death

Alex paced his study relentlessly, with Cobalt, Percival, and David watching. Cobalt's expression was taut with worry. Alex felt the soothing magic of his charismatic friend trying to alleviate Alex's anxiety.

"Stop," he commanded Cobalt.

"What?"

"I know you're trying to alter my mood. I don't want to be calm. I want to hear that Toury is alive. She's been gone for more than a week! Where is she?" A week since Henry had fled with Toury, and six days since Racine had left to find her. There was no word from anyone, no leads.

"Sorry, Your Majesty. It's a habit when anyone is distressed. I do it absentmindedly."

Alex was sure that had been Cobalt's excuse for when he'd made Toury kiss him. Alex withheld the comment on his lips that would needlessly bring up old grievances. Cobalt was not the enemy. "I just feel useless and trapped."

"Let me go," Cobalt begged for the umpteenth time.

"We already discussed this. You track well, but you cannot track someone who has transported. And you're too important now. They'll capture you, and Mary will do something ridiculous to save you." Like when she had gone back to Dragon Rock to save him. And Alex wanted to do that same desperate notion right now. He suppressed the urge. How easy it would be to transport to her if he knew where to go.

"Your Majesty. If you would just sit down, eat something, rest—" David tried.

"Rest!" Alex suppressed the urge to burn his servant. He took a deep breath, bracing himself on his chair. Alex had slept only when his body gave up on him. About every two days, he passed out on his settee, unable to face sleeping alone in his bed.

"Do sit, please, Alex," Cobalt pleaded. "Let us try to plan something. Even if it is futile, let's try something. Anything is better than this waiting."

Alex nodded and plopped into his desk chair, but it was only for the benefit of the two men in the room whom he deeply respected. The last thing he wanted to do was make pointless plans, but at least trying to come up with something would distract him and maybe, just maybe, lead to a solution.

After an hour of plans that didn't come to fruition, he gave in to eating to make David happy. After a couple bites of a roll, the door burst open. David and Percival were up, swords ready. It was an out-of-breath messenger holding up a missive. He was red-faced, sweating, and unable to talk. David crossed and took the missive and rushed it over to Alex.

"Get the man water," Cobalt told Percival.

The wax had no emblem stamped into it. Alex ripped it open and read quickly.

"What is it?" Cobalt demanded.

"Your Majesty?" David must've seen the look on Alex's face, for he rushed to him. On impulse, because they would stop him, and they couldn't go with him, he transported to the place Racine's one-word message told him to go: *Firelands*.

He knew it could be a trap. He wasn't stupid, but if Toury was there, she'd be trapped and suffering. He appeared and withdrew his sword instantly in case Henry lay in wait. No one was around, save a couple draca watching him with bored expressions. That meant Henry had been there. The dragons were always interested when a Sapphirian came, because it was usually a rare occurrence. Their boredom meant they had recently had human company. Alex ran for the shack, the only place Toury could be safe from the draca. He entered the shack. There were remnants of candles, a book, bones from food picked dry, a dress, an empty bedpan, an empty jug of water—she had been here.

"Toury!" He searched outside, rushed to the outhouse to see if she had hidden there, but it was empty. He shouted her name several times, then went back to the hut. He searched every square inch, noting a scorched spot on the ceiling, but not knowing what would cause it. Giving up on the hut, he burst outside.

A young draca waited, staring at him. A teen from the size, his colors were green: bearn Draca Q.

The woman who was kept in the hut, where is she?

Dead? He was unsure.

"Tell me what happened." Alex's knees grew weak. He didn't want to hear it, but he needed to know. He could not stand the torment of not knowing where Toury was. The only hope he had was the draca's uncertainty.

Sir Draca J didn't let us near her, guarded her.

Guarded? Or held prisoner for Henry? He had never heard of a draca guarding a human before, but perhaps Henry had commanded him to. That particular draca had lost his mate when Alex's father was a child. There was a skilled poacher who had gotten two draca and sold their pelts before he was caught and sentenced to death.

Henry? Other flesh baby? Gone for days. Left her all alone. Sir Draca J fed her, cared for her. Odd. Then he ate her.

Alex faltered, his hand going to his chest. There was pain there, his heart feeling as if it were physically shattering into pieces. He could not believe it. There was no way a draca would feed her and care for her to then eat her. It would've torn the shack down and eaten her at once. The thought made him sick. He forced the next question out of his mouth. "You saw this?"

He flew with her into the woods. She was like this. Being still a youth, he acted it out by flopping himself on the ground and lolling his tongue out, playing dead.

Alex bit back a tormented scream of anguish. Toury was dead. His child was gone. He went numb. The little draca sat up, waiting for him to laugh or to comment on his theatrics. Alex walked straight out of the Firelands, and when he hit the grass, he fell to his knees. He screamed out in agony. Toury was dead.

He looked to the woods. What would he find? Her bones? A gluttonous dragon he would slay himself despite it being a godly creature? He wanted to hurt something, someone. Mostly just himself. He pulled the dagger out of his boot and held it in his hand. Should he join her? Should he just give up on all this horror, this war, this deceit, this horrible sphere his father had handed him? *Why?* he asked the god and goddess. Why would they give him everything he ever wanted and snatch it away?

He shoved the dagger back in its sheath in the lining of his boot. What point would there be in letting Henry win? Alex was being stupid, impulsive, emotional. The seer had been wrong about Toury saving herself, but her other words returned to him: logic over heart. There were people who needed Alex, an entire kingdom. He couldn't afford to wallow. If Henry had left her, left his bargaining chip behind, he had switched his plans; he would make a move by attacking Celestia. Alex had to stop him. He had to forget his losses. He took a deep breath, then another.

Then a ball of fire appeared in front of him. Instinctually, he yanked the dagger out of his boot and moved it up to the Sapphirian's throat. It was parried away deftly by someone's sword.

Alex focused on his sister's face. "I'm sorry," he cried and fell forward into her stomach.

She caught him as he hid his silent sobs in Mary's dress, and she held his head tightly. "Are you wounded?" she demanded.

"No."

"You could've killed her!" Cobalt chastised him.

"He was right to attack me. I could've been Henry."

Alex saw Racine's note in Mary's hand. He must have left it behind in his haste, and they decided to get Mary. His sister. He had to get her out of here. The only two in the way of Henry ruling were together and out in the open. "Let us get back. We can't be out here together," Alex said, although it was the last thing he wanted to say or do.

They transported back to Alex's sitting room. He fell to the ground again, a mess. "A draca said Toury's dead."

"No," Mary said. "No. She can't be. Alex, I have seen you in the flames with her and children. She can't be gone."

With wild hope in his heart, he told them the story.

"She could be alive, Alex. Why would a draca carry her off like that?" Mary said. "And please, a bearn told you that. You trust him?"

"Mary, come. One more transport," Cobalt suddenly said, taking up her hand and leading her to the door.

"What are you doing?" Alex was lost. He made the commands around here.

"You can't think straight. Let me figure out the Toury situation. I'll delegate. I just need Mary to transport someone and come back."

"Who?" Mary asked.

"The firelasher. Who better? He proved himself." Cobalt said.

Alex nodded. Baron Firelasher had been given leave and gone back to his family after the siege of the fort.

"David, put him to bed," Mary told his valet.

"I make the orders around here," Alex said halfheartedly. His exhaustion, his anxiety, his grief—he could hardly stand.

"Today you don't. In the morning, Alex. You haven't slept in days and look awful," Mary said.

He took no offense, guessing his appearance matched his mood: horrible.

They left the room with their foolish hope. He wished they were right and that Toury was still here on Fyr with him in this life. He had absolutely no idea what to do without her.

After he drank the firespice tea David made him that he pretended not to know was laced with a mild sedative, Alex fell into a deep slumber.

27
WOODROW

Wet. Something wet was on the side of Toury's face. Dry. Her mouth was so dry, her tongue was glued to her cheek, and her lips were stuck together.

Drink.

Her face was prodded, and it was submerged, waking her fully. She opened her eyes and lifted her head with great effort. She was lying by the side of a brook, her face and shoulders leaning over the bank in the water. Water! She opened her mouth, cracking her lips in the process, and dunked her head into the warm but refreshing water. She took in mouthful after mouthful until she came up coughing and throwing some of it up. Realizing she was too dehydrated to drink too fast, she calmly dipped her shaking hands into the water and drank a few handfuls, letting it rest in her mouth before it trickled down her throat. Too weak to do more, she put her head on the bank and passed out.

She woke several times thirsty. It only occurred to her now that this water could be contaminated or have parasites, but she would die if she didn't drink, so she did. Throughout the day, she drank a few sips at a time. At night, the dragon brought back many birds, about ten. The dragon watched her eat, refusing to eat until she had her fill.

How can I hear you?

Bearn.

Toury had heard Alex say the term, so she was pretty sure it was the word for dragon baby. Her baby was allowing her to communicate with dragons? Why hadn't Alex told her about this possibility? *Is that normal?*

Never saw a Sapphirian with a bearn in belly. I sense it. I want to protect it.

You have. Toury reached out to touch the draca's snout, hoping he would not bite her. Her empathy for him not having a nest as Henry had said made her eyes prickle with tears. It meant the draca had lost a mate, and possibly a baby, from the overprotective manner she was seeing. *I can't thank you enough.*

Toury was full, pushing the limits of her stomach with food and water.

It made her sleepy. "Eat the rest. I'm done," she mumbled, half-asleep already.

The dragon inhaled four birds in one go, swallowed them, and then moments later, he sounded like he was hacking up a hairball. The tiny bones came out devoid of meat. Interesting and disgusting. She found the creatures to be more feline than reptilian, and now that nasty dining habit made him more owlish.

She slept yet again, not at all worried about anyone finding her—including Henry; no one could harm her with her draca guardian.

When she awoke, it was dusk. She had no idea if she slept half a day or a day and a half. She got up, steadying herself, feeling for the first time almost whole again. She felt stronger than she had in the shack, but not near her healthy potential before she had been taken. She walked by the brook, upstream, knowing that would take her away from the sea. Celestia was north and central in the land, so away from the ocean would be the right direction.

The sun was placed slightly different than on Earth, but it still rose in the east and set in the west. In the woods at dusk, it was too difficult to tell where it was setting, but the lightest spot was behind her. It was a guess, but she believed she was headed northeastward. If she followed the river, she would eventually get to Celestia. The heat told her they were still too far south to walk the whole way there, but people needed water, so there would be small towns along the river. All she had to do was get to one. Someone would help. She touched her head and realized during her weakness, she had slept with her circlet on, so whoever she found would recognize and help her.

Her guard-companion followed her without a word. The only noise in the woods was the draca snapping branches under his feet and when his wings—although folded onto his back—scraped branches.

She just needed to find a trustworthy person to take her back to the capital, to home, to Alex. What must he be going through without her? Was he hurt? Had Henry tricked him into giving up his life for her own? Had Henry attacked?

No farther. Smell humans. Humans are bad.

I'm human too.

The draca snorted at that.

Look, I can't take you with me. I have to go into town alone. Draca aren't supposed to leave the Firelands, and I have to be sneaky, hide in small places. You are too...conspicuous.

Don't like it.

I have to get home.

No. Get water jug, that bread stuff you eat. I take you back home safe.

Home? How could she let the draca know home was somewhere else away from the Firelands and its protection? Guilt crept over her. "I need you to stay here. I will come back if it is dangerous. If I find someone who can help me, I need to go back to Celestia."

No, come back. The dragon stomped, distressed. He again nudged her stomach with a gentle caress of his snout. *Get food. Come back. I'll take you to Celestia.*

Okay, she agreed. Could she really just fly to Celestia via dragon? Surely, an emergency like this would call for law-breaking, but she didn't want her trusty draca hurt. *I'll come back. Stay. Please.*

She walked on, and the dragon sat on its hind quarters, reminding her of a dog, but those vibrant eyes watched her the entire time until she turned away. He really cared about her wellbeing. On Earth, literature spoke of beastly dragons and untamable monsters. Even the ones who could think and communicate had some wild feral streak to them. DJ was all protection, kindness, and dare she call a draca chivalrous? They were definitely majestic, beautiful creatures.

The forest brush gave way to a wider walking path, which after a quarter mile or so merged into a dirt road wide enough for a carriage to drive on. She paused, tired. Spotting a thick stick, she picked it up and pressed it against the ground. It would serve as a good walking stick, or a weapon if needed. The lane merged with another, and that's when she saw the sign: Woodrow.

Toury recalled her geography. It was the largest village southwest of Celestia. She racked her brains about who lived there and what they would be like. It was one the closest places to the Firelands inhabited by many people, so Henry could've come here or near here. He could even be hiding out. Woodrow? Rebel or loyalists? They were a working-class village, self-sufficient and supplying the land with most of the wood. They didn't need rulers or rebels, supposedly undecided on their cause. The type of village to stay out of a fight. She was glad she'd paid attention to Madge's lessons but also wasn't sure if anyone here would help her. Best to stay incognito if possible. The circlet might be a problem, but she could not part with it. Alex had given it to her, and it meant everything. If she never saw him again... She would not think that way, but peering down at her short-sleeved dress, she had nowhere to hide it. Maybe if she could find a hat or shawl...

She reached the first log cabins, which looked empty, and left the road, moving behind them in the tree line. At the third house, she saw laundry drying outside. She hopped over a low stone wall and nabbed a gray cloak off the line and then ran back into the woods. She slipped it on. It was a bit long, dragging on the ground, but with it tied shut, the hood up, and with her walking stick, Toury would appear to be a hobbling old woman from afar. Her feet were so swollen from all the walking that she didn't even need to pretend her awkward gait.

She didn't see many people, only a couple kids playing in their yard, their frustrated mother calling them inside, then a man and his wife arguing. They were all too busy to notice her. Food! She followed the scent onto a side road. She was starving again. By the time she made it into the town center, it was dark. She had to go on the main road, for it was the only one lit by streetlights. She sat on a wall by the side of a pub, her feet hurting.

"Scram!" A man in an apron, perhaps the proprietor, said to her. "No beggars."

"Please," Toury pleaded, her voice feeble. "I need help."

"Don't we all, sweetheart. Move along."

"Please." Toury grasped his shoulder.

When he tried to shake her off, he saw her face. Recognition didn't cross his features, but something about her made him hesitate and steady her. "You speak strangely." He examined her.

Toury had forgotten her Earth accent was different than those in Fyr. She was so adapted here, they sounded normal to her, but she must still sound odd to people who had never heard it. It was like being the only American in a world of British-sounding people, only they'd never heard an accent other than their own before. "I need the post of the Sapphirian Guard. I'm noble and in danger. If you could just direct me—"

"There isn't anywhere safe anymore, love," the man said quietly. Toury was unsure if he was threatening her or warning her. "Come inside."

"No. I just need the guard. They will see me safe."

"I know they will, but you see, the guard has their own problems at the moment. They won't worry about you, Your Majesty." The man tightened his grip on her arm.

Alarm bells went off. He knew who she was and wouldn't take her to safety. Rebel or necromancer? "Let me go!" She shoved him.

His anger flared up, and so did the pupils of his eyes. They filled up the entire sockets until his eyes were black with dark magic. Toury staggered back, momentarily frozen in horror. A necromancer! Dealing with them brought the memories back afresh.

He reached for her again. Instinct took over, and she hit him in the face with her walking stick before she ran. She heard a whistle behind her but kept running. That was when a couple men stepped out of the shadows. Three of these men she vaguely recognized. They had been camped out with her parents in Mineria and must've gotten away when they were raided: rebels.

"We meet again." The man spat on the ground. Gross. It really was that guy. She remembered him spitting every time someone had mentioned a Sapphirian.

DJ! Toury thought then screamed, "DJ!" as loud as she could, in case he couldn't hear her mentally this far away. She didn't care if it drew attention; perhaps a good civilian would rush to her aid.

The spitting man grabbed her wrist. "DJ?" He laughed.

The bar owner laughed behind her. More people came outside to surround her. Half of them appeared to be merely curious civilians, a quarter had black eyes full of eagerness for catching the queen—the destroyer of darkness—and the other fourth drew weapons.

There was no way out, so she built up all the energy and power she had left inside of her.

"What are you doing?" The spitting man withdrew his hand from her wrist, wincing.

"What are *you* doing? Grab her!" someone said. "The commander will be pissed she escaped the Firelands. We have to lock her up."

"She shocked me, like electricity."

"That's impossible. Grab her, you idiot," a woman said. She moved forward, and before she could even touch Toury, she was shocked and blown backward onto her rear end, the air around Toury being charged.

Toury let her power loose. White fire burst out of her, blasting everyone around her away. They were on fire. She leaped over some, who were struggling on the ground, trying to put out the flames. She ran toward the woods. That's when she heard the screech. Everyone went silent, staring at the sky. Being close enough to the Firelands, they must've heard dragons from time to time.

"DJ!" Toury called, running to her draca savior.

He flew over her and torched everything that was a threat. People ran screaming. Toury had to remind herself they were mostly necromancers and rebels. Several rooftops were completely incinerated, the walls burning. Toury stopped, worried now about DJ's welfare and her own. She also worried whether or not she could rein in the draca before he torched everyone and everything, including the surrounding forests. He had saved her, yes, but this could get really ugly.

28
A MADNESS

When Alex woke, he didn't feel the despair he had the night before. It surprised him. Instead of raw agony, he was numb. Underneath his cool veneer was a boiling rage of revenge teetering toward madness.

This morning's missives on his bedside table reported Henry's troops on the move from all over, all heading to Celestia. And now he had an idea which verged on insanity. It would leave him possibly weak and vulnerable, but a move his cousin would never be able to foresee. Henry had always been a terrible firebrander anyway, but making this decision today would leave Henry no time to realize this move or stop his army and try another tactic.

Alex lit a fire, trying to see how his plan would come to fruition. Images were chaotic and hard to discern. There would be war—from the images that was obvious—but not much else was discernible. Alex could see an evenly matched battle occurring. Then he focused his mind on not making this rash decision, and the flames changed to show the castle almost razed to the ground, a lifeless Mary, and Alex with a sword at his throat. The images were clearer, crisper. He wouldn't let that happen. He would be reckless, because playing it safe would bring the end of his sister's and his lives. As his conviction built, the flames danced back to his army holding their own, Alex throwing fire across the undead, and the castle was whole.

What would Toury do in this situation? He had always asked her thoughts. She had wanted to kick Henry out of the palace with good reason, and she would trick the man. That was what Alex would do. She would tell him to use his head. Just like that blasted seer who let Toury die by telling him not to choose his heart. The woman had said she would save herself. What lies!

And then her image took shape in the flames, Toury peaceful in sleep—perhaps eternal slumber. Before he could make sense of the scene, it was gone, along with the future.

Outsmart Henry. Defend his kingdom. If Alex was successful, he'd figure out how to live life after that. One step at a time. First step, ring for David. Once he was outfitted in his armor and ate a quick breakfast—because David was throwing one of his guilt-tripping hissy fits—they transported to his study. He was surprised to see Mary and Cobalt already there, perusing more missives.

"Reading my messages again, Mary?" Alex quipped, although he wasn't mad. It was a poor attempt of a joke when his fiery nature was as cool as ice.

Mary also couldn't read his mood, for she stared at him, agape.

Cobalt side-eyed him. "What are you doing out of bed? And why are you dressed like that?"

"I have a plan."

"Oh, that mad look in your eyes and that creepy grin is scaring me, Alex. You're going to do something stupid," Mary whined much in the same tone as when she was a little girl. He couldn't help but see her that way always, his little sister whom he had to protect.

"Oh, I promise you it is both mad and stupid, but the flames tell me it must be done."

"Should I bother to even advise you against this plan at this point?" Cobalt groaned. The excitement in his friend's eyes belied his concern. Cobalt loved reckless, impulsive decisions, but as his advisor, he would be forced to tell him not to.

"I'm beyond listening, no worries," Alex retorted. The banter was making him feel a bit more alive again. He would fight for his sister, Cobalt, and their future children. He had meant it to Toury when he said he would have no one but her. Still, as long as Mary lived and had children, the Sapphirian line would continue. He had to protect the line and his people. "What is your plan of defense? What have you done while I was sleeping?"

Cobalt turned back into the serious advisor, convenient that he shifted his posture into a more proper one. Alex noted that. It would be better for their relationship as best friends, soon-to-be brothers, and officially his Ealder Advisor, for Alex to physically see which Cobalt he was dealing with. "I've ordered half the men of every fort to make haste to Celestia. I was about to issue demands to the outer posts—who could not reach us in a day's time—to send half their men to bolster those half-manned forts and to send more to Celestial if they could be spared."

Alex nodded. It was a sound defensive plan. Henry's armies would invade after Alex's first wave of reinforcements arrived, and the second wave would close around them. But the flames said this would not work. Perhaps with the necromancers and their dead, they would be overpowered before the outer bands could come through for them. His conviction grew stronger.

"Hold that order to the outer bands. Do not send it unless I don't return within the hour."

"What?" Cobalt asked.

With no time to waste, Alex grabbed David's wrist and transported to the Aberdane fort, where his uncle on his mother's side, Lord Jasper, resided while protecting the north.

Alex had been to all the forts as a child, so he knew to arrive in the General's chamber. However, upon arrival, several blades came their way, making him duck and David spin his sword around in protection. They had been on alert for Henry.

Alex blasted a fire ring to protect David and him, just in case he was wrong and Henry had control of that fort. The men backed away, then went down on bended knee, a salute of submission to their leader.

Alex pulled the fire back in then, and General Jasper stepped forward. "I'm sorry, Your Maj—"

"You were rightfully on alert for a traitor Sapphirian." Alex made a dismissive hand gesture, not having time for manners. "I want half your men suited up in the courtyard now. The bravest and best fighters. They're going to war. Celestia will be under attack."

At first, Alex's uncle didn't react. He was stunned, rigid as he took in what Alex said. He ordered several commands to the men in the room, and they ran out the door.

"And the rest of my men are to say here, Your Majesty?" General Jasper had a sound question, for what was the point in them protecting a fort if Celestia fell? But that was part of Alex's other plan.

"They march tonight toward Celestia."

His uncle smiled. "To come in behind and cut off their retreat. Sound plan, Your Majesty." Respect lit his features. Alex was now assured his armies would never surrender to Henry, even if Alex died.

The general led the way down to the courtyard, his squire grabbing his battle armor and scrambling after them. "How do you intend to get us to Celestia so quickly? How many times do you intend to transport today, Majesty? I have two hundred men altogether. You intend to get one hundred there today?"

This Alex knew. He purposely picked one of the smaller forts to test his limits. "I intend to try with one trip."

The general was wide-eyed. If Alex had transported fifty of his men before, and a massive and heavy draca, why not one hundred?

And he did, easily, opening his eyes in the front of his palace, traversing that many men from the far north end of his kingdom. The closest forts Mary was dispatching commands to would arrive that day, the further ones the next, and the ones Alex was visiting would be here today if he could keep transporting them. The other half of their troops would be a couple days and close up the rear. Only, Henry would never know how many men he would face at the start with Alex transporting men in. He could not estimate Alex's power. Even his stunt at Fort Emerald had only showed Alex's abilities to carry twenty men.

Alex ordered the wide-eyed men to set up tents on all the land, the generals and captains to see the dowager inside for lodgings. He would fill every inch of the palace and lands with men if his powers held out.

Alex lost count of trips. The only way he marked his progress was how much ground he had gained, starting in Aberdane and working his way around Fyr in a southwestward direction. Each transport took energy from him. When he was no longer able to make it in one go, he ate, got some light energy from Edwina and Aschen Hematite, and resumed. By nightfall, he had hit every major fort set near a coast, then inland for about twenty miles.

Barely able to stand, he leaned on his balcony's wall for support, seeing all the tents covering the expanse of his lands up to the front gates. David was by his side. "I can't believe what you accomplished today, Your Majesty."

"Neither can I."

Cobalt came out, giving a quick bow of his head. "I have rough numbers. Henry's forces are on the march and gathering in the north, south, and west. The east is his weakest front. Spies reported in their guesses, and when totaled, we are facing roughly fifteen hundred soldiers."

That didn't sound too daunting to Alex.

"The number of necromancers is unknown, but there are rumors of rebels who are backing out, then being slaughtered and raised from the dead, as well as Henry's armies killing on their way here and resurrecting your civilians. He will also have many powerful magicians and a few sorcerers who turned against you during the necromancer purge. There are some bitter nobles out there, but most are too spineless to join Henry's side but a few."

Well, that was becoming more of a problem. Alex would kill Henry with his bare hands if he had to. Killing his innocent people to create an army of undead? Alex was powerless to stop it. In fact, Henry would hope Alex would send his men, but dividing his Celestia forces would be a mistake. He had to act on the defense, surprise Henry with the men he had transported, and hope his wave of troops marching from the forts could stop some of it.

"How many men do we have?" Alex asked, bracing himself. His Celestial troops matched Henry's army, but the amount of undead could potentially keep growing to outnumber them.

Cobalt gave him a sly grin. "Thanks to your antics, we have doubled our forces and now have roughly three thousand men."

It was music to Alex's ears and the first bit of good news. It would be an even battle thanks to his foresight, even if the necromancers resurrected many. He was happy they did funeral pyres, or it would be impossible otherwise. They had a chance, and being the one on the defense, having walls and the palace for protection, they had the advantage. For the first time in weeks, a tiny hope grew in his breast. He couldn't save Toury from Henry Sapphirian, but he damn well would save Mary and his people. "Good. Go get some rest. Then set things up with Tobias and your father. We need soldiers, magicians, and sorcerers working together."

"I've got a few tricks up my sleeve, lots of ideas." Cobalt clapped his hands together gleefully. Before Alex knew it, Cobalt was launching a series of plans. Normally, he would shoot down the most ludicrous of them, but anything was on the table when it came to trying to save Fyr. Cobalt had always loved war, wanting to play soldiers when they were young. Little had they known their childish antics would become their adult reality.

29

A SIEGE

Alex was roused early in the morning by David. He was spent, his previous day's transporting exhausting him. Groggily, he sat up.

"What is it?" Alex grumbled. He was more than cranky, and it showed in his tone.

"Lord Cobalt says he has important news and must see you in person. Immediately."

Alex sighed and put off eating, bathing, and shaving—the latter of importance since his uneven stubble exposed his youth—and got dressed. With his father having been so proud of his full black beard, Alex knew he'd be judged as an inept novice if the men saw his poor attempt at a beard. A stupid little thing such as facial hair meant a lot. He would take after his lifemate's example—thinking of her was agony—and create change. He would be a beardless king by choice.

He transported to his study, instructed David to let Cobalt in but to also order the barber, breakfast, and tea.

"A draca!" Cobalt burst into the room, waving a missive in his hand. His face was animated, and his shout way too energized for this early in the morning. "Alex, a draca has left the Firelands. It torched part of Woodrow, killing hundreds of rebels."

Behind him, the elder Lord Cobalt and Tobias entered.

"It didn't kill enough of them. We're surrounded now, Your Majesty. The prince-to-be and Princess Mary need to escape. The sooner the better," Cobalt's father said. The strain on his face showed he and his son had argued about this prior to entering Alex's study.

"And let you have the glory, Father? I think not." Cobalt's voice was confident, and Alex saw the other men were bolstered by his friend's words, and his magical mood enhancers definitely helped. But when Alex saw the solemn conviction in Cobalt's eyes, he was telling Alex they would die together if needed. It made him snap into feeling, into caring again. There were still people he loved he could save.

"Is everyone ready?" Alex asked. He listened to each man's positive comments as Cobalt fidgeted, full of energy. Alex, too, wanted to talk about this draca and what it meant, but he was afraid to hope and to react in front of his elders. He dismissed Lord Cobalt and Tobias with orders.

"Alex, the draca. The firelasher said he was blue." Cobalt held up the missive.

Alex's head whipped around. "The Sapphire draca family, Sir Draca J?" The one who had supposedly eaten Toury was still out of the Firelands a day later? Why?

"Yes. The firelasher saw Racine but lost her in the chaos. He saw white fire and lightning. Alex, do you remember the legends we grew up hearing?"

"The edict prophecies? Cobalt, there is no savior after Toury helped banish the darkness. She was the savior, not this mythical Bladesung. No such person who can merge the powers of Fyr as one will save us now. Stop dreaming. What is real is out there. We are about to be killed, the castle taken, unless we fight our best. I can't believe in some dream of someone rescuing us. Doing that will get me killed."

"Just think about it...it could be. She has Ruby's power and her light—"

"She's *dead*!" Alex screamed at him.

Cobalt backed up a few paces, worried Alex might torch him, and Alex wanted to. How much he wanted to believe Cobalt was overwhelming. If Toury could be the savior, not of necromancers as she already had been, but of so much more, it would mean she was alive. He could not hope just to find out she was gone again.

"Alex," Cobalt ventured. The hesitancy in his voice proved how terrified he was to say what he would. "If you give up hope that she is alive, you give up the kingdom. I know you. You won't fight. You cannot give up on her. She would never give up on you."

That struck a chord. He wanted to lash out, but Cobalt was right. Toury would be disappointed in him. She was the type of person to fight until the end. She would deny his death until she saw his body. Why hadn't he searched the woods for Draca J? Because he had worried over Mary, but he should've gone back once Mary was safe in the castle. At the minimum, he should've transported some men there to search. Now, he needed every man here. With the enemy closing in on him, if Toury was alive in the far south with a draca, perhaps she was safer than Alex. He would not believe she would save him or was the Bladesung, but he would begin to believe again, until his last breath, that she and his child were alive.

"David, let us suit up for war."

Cobalt smiled, while David groaned.

"You will defend the inside of the castle," Alex directed to Cobalt.

His smile fell instantly. "But—"

"You are the best person to protect my sister."

"King Alex—"

"It is the most important job. Do you want me to listen to your father and have you sent away?"

Cobalt's mouth opened to protest, so Alex pushed on. "Cobalt, Henry will storm inside with a small retinue. You must stop him from opening the door and letting more in. He will do what I did, and he will believe I'm in here hiding, but I'll be out there. The army of the dead will die again by fire. My army needs me. And send a message back to the firelasher. He might arrive too late, but if he could come from behind the southern army, he could help take out necromancers, burn the dead he finds along the way to stop them being raised. After you do all this, Cobalt, arm yourself, and protect my sister and mother with your life."

"Yes, Your Majesty," Cobalt said with pride. He rushed out the door.

"You truly mean to fight out there?" David asked once they were alone.

"Yes, but I'm not asking you to die with me, David."

"I will fight for my kingdom, Your Majesty. I will not stay behind."

"I knew you'd say that. But I order you to take care of yourself out there and fight as a soldier, not as a bodyguard."

"But—"

"David, you will die quickly if you are worrying about my back and your own. You may fight by my side, but you will defend your life foremost. You are no use to me dead."

Before David could refuse or start groveling or whatever reaction he might have to his monarch telling him to worry about self-preservation, the barber entered, interrupting.

Alex and David stood on the balcony. The situation weighed more heavily upon him than all his scale-engraved armor, but he had to feel like the draca he appeared to be. Chills shot down Alex's spine as he saw the forms charging through the streets toward the barricaded gates. His men stood behind those walls and gates, steadfast and ready. The fools outside the walls carried torches and lanterns to light their way. Why had they attacked at night? It showed an impulsive and desperate carelessness on Henry's part. He couldn't get all his troops here in time and had chosen to attack in waves, instead of one massive force on the morrow. Alex's forces were prepared, thanks to Cobalt's knack for warfare. Henry's soldiers were in for a few surprises. Still, Alex was a ball of nerves. The war could go either way. Alex had more men, but what was to keep the necromancers from regenerating the fallen—his own men even? Only fire.

Alex concentrated on the faraway flames. He hadn't controlled fire over a distance in a long time. He pushed a little magic that way, and he saw lanterns burst, torches shoot up in the air, and men afire screaming and running. Apparently, he could do it very easily. The first wave in the front of the castle would be delayed.

Once the men were cleared from the gates, too quickly, new ones replaced them. They held no flames but pressed against the gate, many of them, piling on top of each other, so much they must be—

"The undead," David breathed.

Alex needed fire by the gates. He drew a line in his mind through the ground in front of his men, using his power to open the earth. It cracked and quaked. Alex's men backed up, glancing over their shoulders at him. He closed his eyes and homed in on the fire under the earth, pulling it out. He heard preternatural shrieks, like grotesque babies screaming. It brought the memory back of the time his father had burned a rabbit in attempts to make Alex thicker-skinned.

"Enough," David whispered, touching his shoulder.

Alex let go, gasping, trying to catch his breath and recoup from the effort and tried to dispel the memory. He was dispatching the already dead where they belonged, not torturing poor animals. He was not his father and would never be.

Alex opened his eyes to see the gates were completely inflamed. Too late did he notice shadowy-hooded forms dropping over the walls on either side of the fire, and possibly all around the palace. The men were scaling the walls, using the undead troops at the gate as a diversion. Alex itched to enter the fray, but he saw his commanders spreading the troops out and charging the intruders in classic formation—half stayed close to the palace as defense, the other half offense. He threw fireballs at groups of those who broke through the offense before they could get to Alex's defensive troops.

They were holding their own. Alex grabbed David's shoulder and transported them to the back balcony overlooking the orchards behind the palace to check on things there. The Magician's Guild and soldiers fought off mainly rebels. His side was winning easily back here. The undead couldn't get over the walls, and the necromancers were mostly up front. He transported to the east and west sides of the castle. They were holding the enemy at bay as well. Back to the front.

He shouldn't have left them, even though he had been gone only a few moments. His front line was pushed back and dwindling, his defense line battling—with magic and swords—the enemies that broke through. Balls of light or energy were blasting some men back, and other magic being used could only be felt, not seen—protection, courage, positivity, and more. Throwing fire might hurt his troops. Sure, they had fireproof gear, but he could still miss in the tangle of bodies.

A crashing sound drew Alex's attention to the gates. They were down. The undead army poured in like bugs running from water. Alex threw out fireballs and shot magma out of the chasm he had created. It took some out, but more and more poured in. They created a temporary bridge before the magma burned them to cinders, and some made it across. There were so many. Had they killed that many civilians merely to resurrect them?

"Your Majesty." David steadied him. "I would be honored to fight and die by your side."

"Don't get all sentimental on me," Alex chided, somehow finding a lightness inside himself. "But I am honored to die by my friend's side, my brother's side."

David blinked back tears.

"Don't you dare cry. That's an order. And don't confess your undying love for me either."

"You wish," David countered with a laugh.

"Ready?" Alex asked.

Right then, the balcony door burst open. A servant came out. "They're inside the castle!"

Alex was torn. Mary and Cobalt. "How many?"

"Only a dozen. The prince-to-be is trying to cut them off from opening the barbican," the servant replied. "He sent me to tell you and to say—forgive me, Your Majesty, these are his words, not mine—'Don't be stupid. I've got this. Fight.'"

Alex nodded. How well his people knew him, that he always wanted to help, to save, to spare others' pain. It was Cobalt's way of saying goodbye. Cobalt might fight off the men inside, the number might be downplayed for Alex to have hope, but his friend had sent the message because he was sure they might not see each other again.

Alex took a deep breath. David nodded, placing his hand on Alex's armor. They transported in front of the barbican. He would stop those in front of him, and if they made it out from within, he would take them out too. He wouldn't die without giving his people his all. And if Toury was somehow alive, he would live on through their child; if both of them were already gone, he would join them in the other sphere with the god and goddess themselves.

30
REDEMPTION

Toury was in a predicament. She was in the middle of a village that was half on fire because her dragon was overprotective. A crowd of people were gathering—some putting out fires, some staring at the dragon in fright and awe.

"I told you to stay put," she teasingly scolded at the draca aloud so the people could hear her. There was no hiding who she was or that she could control dragons now.

You'd be dead.

You got me there. She had been cornered, outnumbered, but the weird magic had saved her. Still, had the draca not come to save her when she'd called, she wouldn't have lasted forever.

"Get out of here," Toury heard someone hiss and realized the feminine voice was not the dragon's thoughts pouring into her mind.

She spun around and saw Racine in the doorway. Toury formed light in her hands to attack.

"Really? I'm on your side. I've been searching for you and traced you here. You were supposed to be in the Firelands. I sent your king there to save you. I couldn't find draca blood to get in there myself."

The dragon growled.

Racine went rigid.

Toury decided not to tell Racine the draca knew she was the dragon slayer and wanted to drag her back to Dame Draca B for dinner. Toury sent thoughts to him to yield, while trying to talk to Racine. "Alex is okay?"

"He's alive, yes, but there's an army heading that way that could very much wipe his out. So, not okay. Look, get out of here. Meet me in the woods. I'll follow the stream until I find you. Go. Get your draca out of here."

"I need supplies."

"I will bring them to you. Go!"

People were now staring at them. Toury awkwardly climbed up on her draca. His scales were hard as glass but smooth. People murmured and chattered, wondering how she was doing it, and she heard her name whispered. Some bowed down on bended knee, despite Alex getting rid of

203

that law for the cunning folk in hopes to promote equality among all people. The draca took off into the air, venting in disjointed phrases about her talking to the dragon slayer, asking if he could eat Racine, and then getting annoyed with being called Toury's draca.

Toury was too freaked out by the altitude and her awkward grip on the dragon's glassy and slippery spines. The wings flapping was so powerful, the wind pressed upon her. She carefully crept up his back closer to his head. The triangular shape of its skull was much wider than its neck, so it shielded the wind from her face. This must be the most secure place, right above its shoulder blades in front of the wings and spine, lying down across his neck, protected from the elements.

He landed in the first clearing by the stream that was large enough for his form. She slipped off on shaky legs. The dragon lay down in his feline Sphinx pose, then nudged her belly. Despite how huge the creature was, it was done gently. Toury put her hands to her stomach. There was a tapping against her hand, her child moving about wildly. Apparently, it was either a fan of dragon rides or absolutely terrified.

Baby needs food. I hunt. Will take evil dragon slayer time. No wings.

Toury didn't want to be left alone, and Racine would be a while, but what if someone or something worse was out here? She was afraid. *Please, don't leave me.* Toury fell onto her knees, exhausted. She just didn't have the energy she'd had before she was pregnant, kidnapped, and starved.

Not far. Not long. The dragon got up and awkwardly walked through the brush, breaking branches with his glassy hide.

True to his word, the draca came back a minute later with a smoking charred carcass in his mouth. He threw it down in front of her. Normally, this would be disgusting to Toury, but she was ravenous. She tried to touch the meat, but it burned her fingers, and she withdrew. It smelled of bacon and was round with short legs. A pig or boar. Toury thought of Earth bacon and wanted to burn her hands just to eat it.

"Please don't eat the dragon slayer. She did wrong, but she is my sister." She was too tired to project her thoughts toward the dragon and spoke.

You're a Sapphirian, not what that girl is.

"True," Toury allowed. She didn't want to argue it any further in case the dragon would withdraw protection. She stroked her stomach in realization: it was the Sapphirian inside her the dragon was protecting, not Toury. Or maybe it was Ruby's power essence helping too. Regardless, she was safe with her draca.

"I call you DJ, so it's only fair that you give me a nickname."

Bladesung. You are Bladesung, so I must call you that.

"What do you mean?" It sounded familiar. The book of edicts? That was it. It was a person in a prophecy she had read about, a savior. "I mean, what does it mean?"

Light and fire together and all that is good.

That was it. There was a prophecy of the savior who merges powers and would save the realm. "I don't think I'm some Bladesung," Toury said quietly. "But thank you. For everything, DJ."

Eat.

Toury remembered the food in front of her. She ripped off the charcoaled flesh to get to the meat. Then she picked up a steaming piece and bit into it. It tasted like a smoked pork chop, delicious and succulent. DJ watched her with those blue feline eyes and licked his lips. Toury, with effort, pulled off a leg and tossed it to him. He ate it whole. She hoped she was done eating when he spat that bone back up.

She wasn't. She was too hungry to allow the nausea to overtake her. When all four legs had been eaten and bones spit back up, she relaxed and enjoyed her food.

A twig snapped, stopping Toury mid-bite, and there was a little rustling of leaves. DJ perked up and sniffed the air.

"Toury?" Racine's voice asked as she came out of the shadows, her hands up in the air in peace.

DJ growled.

"Back down. If she attacks me, you can eat her. If she doesn't, you'll refrain," Toury told him.

Fine. DJ was not happy.

"Come slowly. Sit down. No sudden movements," Toury told her sister.

"Understatement," Racine muttered as she crept up cautiously, and she ended up sitting a good ten feet away from Toury on the side farthest from DJ. She took a duffle bag off her shoulder and put it onto the ground. She pushed it as far as she could toward Toury with her foot. "Food, but you have to share. It's all I have for a couple days. Some clothes."

Toury crawled the remaining feet and dug in the bag, thanking her. There was bread, cheese, and fruit. No dracaberry, their world's version of the apple, which reminded Toury of blue-raspberry candied Granny Smiths. There were men's clothes, so dragon riding would be much easier here on out. Now she wouldn't have to hike her dress up and have her legs be poked by scales.

"Here." Racine handed Toury her knife, the handle toward Toury. "Stop eating like a savage. Could I have some pork?"

DJ growled.

"Come on. She's being helpful, and there's plenty."

He huffed and went back to his Sphinx pose.

Toury handed her a slice but kept the knife. She broke the bread into pieces and cut the cheese. Toury made a cheese and pork sandwich and ate half of it before returning her attention back to Racine.

"Alex?" Toury said suddenly.

"You definitely are pregnant if you forgot about him for food." Racine's eyes peered at Toury's middle, likely gauging whether it was fuller or not.

Toury didn't trust her enough to confirm it. "I should be in the Firelands."

"If he went for you, he'll be gone by now, knowing you're not there. He shouldn't leave the palace, and he knows it. Henry will be attacking Celestia—"

"We have to stop him."

"No. We will die trying. Alex can beat Henry's army or at least hold them off. I already sent an express message about it. I will send another tonight that you are alive and safe, and just in case his scouts missed it, how the south will hit Celestia not far behind the northern armies." Racine sighed, foretelling Toury would disagree with her next comment. "But Toury, seeing how things lie, the safest place for you is with your draca in the Firelands."

DJ growled.

"Don't call him mine. It's offensive."

"My apologies," Racine said to DJ, bowing her head, and then she ate her sandwich, watching the draca warily.

Toury turned over Racine's comments. She was absolutely safe with DJ. Henry could get to her in the Firelands, but so could Mary and Alex. And she had this power that could fight Henry, possibly. It made sense, but all she wanted to do was go home.

"Why are you helping?" Toury stalled.

"I swore a fire pledge to the king to find you to get a pardon. I held up my side of the deal by finding you. My second missive will tell him you're alive, fulfilling my pledge. I've done so wrong, Toury. I've been so stupid."

Racine blinked back tears. "I'm sorry," she directed at the dragon. "I truly am, especially for hurting your kind."

"You found me. You'll be pardoned. What then?"

She wiped her eyes. "I can't stay here. Water was worse with rampant continuous civil war. Lyft sphere isn't much better with this young crazy empress who just took over, or so I heard. I was thinking...Earth. I think I could do well in a place without magic."

Toury didn't know how to respond. She understood how hard it would be for her sister to stay and deal with the backlash of her crimes. If the worst happened and Henry took the throne, Racine would be killed. She really had no options left. Part of Toury wanted to know Racine better, wondering how different things would be had they met under different circumstances or been raised together.

"You won't fight?"

Racine mused. "I wouldn't get there in time. I saw the firelasher, the *Baron*, just before I ran into you." She mocked his title. "He was heading back to Celestia. Maybe I could follow, go around the southern army. I'm not sure. I do need your king to live if I want some labradorite to go to Earth."

"Go, please," Toury begged. "I would feel better knowing you went to fight to save my lifemate because I cannot." She touched her stomach.

Racine smiled at her admittance that she was pregnant. "Do me a favor. If it's a girl, do not name her after me."

Toury laughed. Oh, how the people would be upset by that, her naming her child after a rebel and dragon slayer. "I won't."

Racine stood as Toury portioned off some food and put the rest back in the bag, as well as the knife. Racine took the bag, bowed to Toury, and before Toury could get a goodbye out, her sister had run off into the woods. Toury called it out after her anyway, but there was no response.

The draca prodded the boar for her to eat. Stuffed, she told him to eat it. He devoured it in pieces, his teeth so sharp, they cut through bone. She pondered if they cut through armor too. No, she could not fight; she must stay safe.

Toury changed into the men's clothes as the draca ate. Then she tied up her food in a bundle in her sundress and knotted it. *To the Firelands, DJ.*

With pleasure. The draca lay down so she could climb up onto his neck again.

After slipping the food bundle between her chest and tiny baby bump, she clung on. DJ took off carefully but, once clear of the trees, flapped his wings and sailed at a fast speed. She kept her eyes open this time, peering down at the village of Woodrow. The fires were almost out. Then there was nothing to see but trees that turned into a burnt and dried wasteland before they reached the Firelands. It wasn't too hot this time. It was warm, pleasant, a home away from home. She had acclimated to the lands completely.

31

A TIDE TURNS

Chaos surrounded Alex. This blasted helmet made it difficult to see. He and David were behind his men who were being pressed back toward the front doors. They had to stop Henry's soldiers from opening the barbican. If the inside fight joined the outside, Mary and Cobalt could be dead, and that meant Alex too, because the only way they'd get through him was if he were dead.

"You need a path." David entered the line of soldiers and barked orders to them without asking for approval. David always knew best.

Alex snapped out of his morbid thoughts. The seer had said if he used his head, he could save Fyr. He knew her message had been about that night he'd let Toury go, but it could also apply to all his choices hereafter. He had to stop his blasted sentimentality. A woman can save herself, a fact he knew reinforced by the seer's words. He had thought of Toury, but it could also mean his sister. It was every man and woman for themselves. Alex must worry about himself.

David had broken up the soldiers to give Alex an opening. Thinking they had broken the front line, the enemy started to funnel through the gap, and Alex torched them, unleashing too much power—he should conserve for a long night. The men turned to ash, so many of them in a row, unable to stop their inertia and being pushed forward from the men behind, who couldn't see what was going on. Alex's soldiers turned and stabbed the men who had made it through.

Some of his men risked a peep over their shoulder and saw Alex. They chanted "draca" over and over. The chants spread around the palace grounds faster than fire. Alex's eyes stung. His men, his people loved him and wanted his victory. It gave him the strength to push everything aside to protect as many of them as he could. His father would've called him stupid for joining the fray, his mother brave—stupidly brave—and his lifemate would chastise him with a smile, knowing he was doing the right thing.

He attacked now, pushing fire forward. Above him, light and energy in the form of air streaked across the sky into the enemy lines. Alex saw that sorcerers in the open windows of the castle had joined the war. His soldiers, his guilds, knowing he was with them, seemed rejuvenated and bolstered. They started to gain ground, slowly but surely pushing the enemy back. The front was secure for now. Alex edged his way down the line, checking there were no weak points. David shadowed him, protecting him despite Alex's orders.

"Told you to stop defending me," Alex said as he incinerated a man mid-air who had tried to propel himself over the line. Ash fell upon his stunned men.

"You are our greatest weapon, so sorry. Going to help that cause, plus I'll stay alive pretty long with you roasting anyone near me."

Alex nodded with a smirk. David smiled back. *Till the end,* their gazes said in unison.

A man broke through the line, diverting their attention, but three of Alex's soldiers simultaneously stabbed the man, and he went down. Alex looked for an opening. When he saw fire, he worried Henry was brave enough to enter the fray, but it was Tobias. He had ignited firewhiskey bottles, hurling them off the balcony into the fray. This meant the entire inside of the castle was not quite out of Cobalt's control. Cobalt's older brother was on horseback, swinging around a mace and screaming like a madman as he drove into the enemy line. Another horse broke through the line, but the poor animal fell to the ground, wounded. A soldier was thrown, his helmet flying off. It was Agate.

Alex helped him free his trapped leg. "What are you doing here? After the execution, I sent you back to Claymead," Alex scolded. He knew Mary couldn't have summoned Agate; he'd gotten here too quickly.

"Abandoned my orders, Your Majesty. Saw the troops marching in the south. You think I'd let my men miss this kind of fight? We rode on horseback round east and wiped out the troops there." He pulled out his sword, hungry for battle.

So that was why the east was Henry's weakest point. Alex had Agate to thank for that.

"This is my last fight. I had to make it a good one."

"What?"

The captain slapped him on the back. "After this war, I wish to hand in my resignation so I can retire."

Alex nodded, relieved the seasoned general wasn't writing them off as goners. "Deal."

"Stay alive so you can sign my retirement papers tomorrow." Agate laughed and swung his sword wildly at anyone who came near him. The man was old enough to almost be Alex's grandfather, but he had the vigor of a young man and the expertise and wisdom of a sage. Alex wanted to grow up into a king very much like that man.

Alex started to believe. They could win the day. Henry's men were getting farther and farther back. Alex nodded to David, who grabbed Alex's arm at the last second as he transported to the back of the castle. There were fights out in the orchards, but Henry's men were unsuccessful in getting close. Alex didn't dare move any troops out front, because the back was just as vulnerable. Satisfied he was unneeded, he transported into his mother's chambers to find Mary and her huddled inside. They jumped, worried it was Henry.

"Get out," Mary barked at him. "I think they've won the castle."

He gave her a despondent look. If the castle had fallen into Henry's hands, the remaining royals should part; being in the same place at the same time would help Henry end this in his favor. "Into the safeaway. We'll be back for you when we win it back." And if not, Mary knew to transport their mother to safety and get out of Fyr. They all had a charged labradorite with them for emergency purposes thanks to Tobias.

Mary clutched the corded pouch the stone was in to show him their unspoken thoughts aligned. He watched them run down into the bathing chamber where the entrance was before he transported away from his family. Logic, not heart, he told himself. If he started winning out here, he would draw his cousin away from Mary.

"You ready for a show?" he asked David.

"Oh god and goddess, what are you going to do now?" David moaned as he stuck his blade between two of their men to get a rebel in the gut.

"I need to get Henry out here."

David spouted out expletives. Alex took a double take, never having heard him curse before. David shrugged.

Turning his attention back to the battle, Alex saw the necromancers by the walls raising the dead. If he could take them out, the fight would be fair, live man versus live man. They were the source of the constant supply of soldiers. That's when he saw light magic out by them. Thinking it was Toury, he transported there, David barely grabbing hold in time. He was in the middle of a fray. It wasn't Toury but her uncle blasting multiple necromancers back, who were either knocked out or dead from his light magic. But he was outnumbered, and now their dead armies or live—it was hard to tell with the armor—were closing in. On Alex too.

He drew a line of fire around them. Gareth moaned in relief, caught his breath, and leaned over, resting his hands onto his knees for support. No one could get to the three of them for the moment. Those who were dead kept walking and combusting in Alex's flame shield.

"Why are you out here alone? And why are you back?" Alex asked Gareth.

"I came back because Toury was nowhere I could find, so she must be south. I almost ran into the southern army and raced back here. I was too late and hid with a shopkeeper until the gate went down. I saw the necromancers. I knew you needed my light," Gareth said.

"I'll take you back." Alex offered his hand.

"No." Formerly a cunning folk, Gareth looked frightened to have disagreed with Alex.

Alex tried to convince him. "We do need your light magic, so I need to keep you alive." And for Toury.

"The necromancers must be stopped. The rest will go down easy."

"All right then," Alex sighed. If the man would not retreat to safety, Alex would fight by his side and make sure he survived. He concentrated hard. He drew a line in his head, cutting this band of necromancers away from the rest of the fight. He heard David clashing swords and light magic whizzing by his head, but Alex focused on his objective. The ground quaked. He steadied himself.

David grabbed him, breaking his concentration. Alex saw the necromancers vaporizing less than a hundred feet from him in the molten chasm he created. It was way bigger than he intended. Understanding David's concern that he and Gareth would also burst into flame, he grabbed the Hematite and David and transported back to the front balcony.

Gareth hunched over, trying to gain his breath, covered in sweat. "Well...that was one way to do it."

Alex watched as the army of necromancers vanished, trapped between a wall and molten soil. He wished it was all of them, but he knew they wouldn't all be stationed together. The tide was turning in their favor, but Alex knew not to get "cocky" as his lifemate had once called him. He understood now what it meant.

He saw a flash of fire out by the broken-down gates: Henry.

Alex's instinct was to transport there and stab the cad, but he was showing himself because he wanted Alex to be reckless. Before he could move, he heard a warning call about arrows. Alex gazed up at the sky and saw hundreds of projectiles arching and heading toward his men. Alex sprayed the sky with fire. Instead of them burning to cinders as they had in the Siege of Fort Emerald, the fire went out, and they hit their targets. A few dozen of Alex's men went down. Another volley followed as Alex watched in horror.

"Metal-coated shafts," David said quietly. "They've learned."

More of Alex's men went down.

Next, a large rock came flying right toward Alex. He ducked, yanking David down. Toury's uncle lay next to him. Stone rained upon them as Alex stayed down, his arms folded over his head to protect it, despite his helmet. Gareth was cut up from the debris, having no helmet.

Alex and David looked at each other and then up at the massive rock lodged in the stone wall.

"Where'd he get a trebuchet?" Alex shouted. He had only heard of them in warfare books and had never seen one in action. His fire had given him away. He couldn't stay here.

They crawled toward the doorway of the castle, protected—for now—by the balcony's wall. Alex's mind was unable to focus on what to do next or even where to transport to. David poked his head up to get a better view and then dove down on Alex and Gareth. Another boulder smashed up ahead, stopping them from moving forward until the rock stopped raining on them.

Alex heard his men below ordering to fall back, but they sounded so close, they were likely almost up against the palace walls. The sound of more arrows zipping through the air rained upon them. A quick glance over the wall told him Henry was no longer by the front gate, hiding in safety, letting others die for him. It all seemed hopeless. What could be done?

Then it hit him. He *could* fight fire with fire.

"Hematite, give me power, and get yourself safely inside." Alex tore off his gauntlets to be able to get the power transfer. "When you feel up to it, shoot your light power at any necromancer you can find, but from within the castle, please. Stay safe. We'll need the light when all this is over."

Toury's uncle already pushed his light magic into Alex before he finished speaking by grabbing Alex's hands and funneling in the light power. Although a hazard to have his hands free, Alex needed them to be able to use his magic to its full extent. When Gareth was done, he crawled into the first door and shut it behind him. He was safe for now, hopefully.

"David, I have a plan."

"Will I like it?"

"Absolutely not."

The man groaned. "We're going out there?"

Alex gave him a wry grin.

"Are you mad?" David's eyes went wide.

Before David could convince him otherwise, Alex grabbed his servant's cloak and transported outside the safety of his army. He might be heading for an ambush, but he had to try to save his men and palace.

32
A COBALT PLAN

Alex and David appeared right where he had wanted, behind enemy lines but far enough behind them that they were not detected. The alleyway he envisioned was the one he and Cobalt had played in when they had snuck out of the palace as children. The woman who owned the tea room would have her lifemate keep an eye on them, feed them cakes, and let them frolic about for a good hour before they would report them to the palace guards. The idea of freedom had sent them back again and again. It was only fitting Alex would transport there to enact Cobalt's plan. The bonus was that Cobalt and Alex had made sport of never revealing the secret play area to Henry or Mary, who were always dying to know.

David said nothing but gave Alex a wide-eyed warning. They could not speak. He could hear men not far out of the alleyway. Alex just needed one shot, a glance in the right direction. He had to direct the fire. That was it, and he might turn the tide of this war.

Alex edged his way toward the mouth of the alleyway, but David crept faster, pushing Alex back. David popped his head out into the open and then flattened himself against the wall across from Alex, eyes wide. Alex gave him a perplexed stare.

David drew out his weapon slowly and quietly and jumped over to Alex's side of the alley. "Baron Firelasher and the other Hematite," he whispered.

Just great. Toury and Alex's family was between him and Cobalt's emergency plan. He couldn't in good faith hurt them, nor could he abandon them if they were in need. How had they gotten back from the south so fast? Mary, no doubt. Alex dared to take a peek. Twenty men had Racine and Craig cornered, and they were throwing light and fire only a hundred feet from the trebuchet and the walls. It was the worst possible place for them to be throwing around magic. They might spring the trap and kill themselves in the process. They didn't know, yet they weren't supposed to be here. He had been sure they would not make it back in time. He had to get them out of there.

David gave him a tilted don't-you-dare glare. Alex slowly unsheathed his sword. David swore under his breath and then threw himself out of the

215

alley first. Alex followed right behind. He rushed up and parried off a blade destined for his half-brother's neck. Craig distractedly met Alex's gaze.

"Stop the fire. Retreat," Alex commanded.

He hoped David was helping Racine, because Craig and Alex were batting away deadly blades. Sure enough, when Alex risked a glance, David had thrown Racine onto the ground. It was clear, so Alex threw his fire out, pushing all his rage into the flame. A dozen soldiers were thrown back, toppling into each other. The first few men vanished, their fireproof armor clattering to the ground. Like a real draca, his flames were intense enough to evaporate them. The few men far away enough to survive the blast didn't retreat, but stood, shaking, their clattering armor giving way their fright. Craig threw more fire, and the men cried out and ran.

"What was that?" Craig shouted.

"No time," Alex said, although he had no way to explain how his power was so profound. "Trebuchet. Racine."

"Yes?" The girl looked worse for wear but was now standing and nodding.

"Take it out with your light blasts. And Craig?"

"Your Majesty?"

"You and I are going to light things up."

"With pleasure, Brother."

Alex didn't correct him. He had questioned Craig's alliance, but here he was following Alex's every command. He had gone into enemy territory as a spy, tried to find the queen, and then returned to fight to the death for Alex. Craig noted his slipup, but Alex simply nodded. Craig smiled. How easy it was to make someone's life better with mere acceptance.

"Your Majesty," Racine said. "In Woodrow—"

"No time," Alex barked as a few braver men ran toward them.

Craig lashed them with fire enough to make them run and try to roll out the flames. David blasted back men with his energy and cleared the path for Racine, while Craig lashed fire around the back to cover them. Alex concentrated on the walls of his palace.

A huge blast broke his concentration. Racine had hit the trebuchet's wheel. It tipped it slightly. He needed to buy time, but they were being surrounded, this time by a horde of the undead. Racine blasted a few with her light magic, which broke them to pieces.

"No!" Alex commanded. "The trebuchet." Why would Hematite women never listen?

Racine glared at him but then blasted light ball after light ball at the weapon, frantically and erratically since the undead broke her aim. Finally, a ball took purchase, and the trebuchet went down.

"Close in!" Alex commanded them.

He concentrated on the wall, while he hoped the others listened; if Cobalt's plan worked, they would have to get away fast. He lit the rope on the wall, and it took. Having been dowsed with firewhiskey earlier under Cobalt's command, the rope along the entire front wall ignited past where he could see on both sides. It burned a moment while they fought to survive, and then Alex heard the screams of the undead. He risked a glance, and the spike shields Cobalt had invented to keep people out gave way. Bottles fell everywhere, and Alex ran his fire down the line. Everything went up, the enemy coated in firewhiskey and flames. As hands grabbed his shoulders, he transported to the back of the palace by the orchard.

David, Craig, Racine, and Alex watched wordlessly as the walls ignited down the sides and around the back, surrounding the castle. They were protected by a wall of fire that had dumped the castle's entire stock—including vintage—bottles of alcohol. They were not safe from Henry, but from his army. It was only momentarily. Once the whiskey burned off, another wave of Henry's army would charge. These dead would not be resurrected, though, being given a not-so-traditional form of a pyre.

An army of men raced at them, but from the jerky and clumsy way they moved, they were the undead. He watched the army run at him as his two companions backed away, trying to get into the castle. Only David stood by his side, ready to strike down as many as he could, willing to protect Alex until his last breath. Alex placed his hand on David's chest and prodded him back. The bewildered man lowered his weapon and backed up, misreading his action as Alex giving up.

Oh, he was far from done. He waited until they were ten feet from him and lit the ground on fire. Unlike the walls, the grass was saturated with the rest of the whiskey, and the flames were strong. The army crumbled under the inferno. Thanks to his companions, flames, energy, and light killed the ones that got through.

Moments later, they were alone in the silence. A crash behind him made Alex turn. Craig had broken a window to gain access inside. Alex grabbed his arm to stop him.

Craig said, "Our aunt, your mother, our sister..."

Alex let him go.

"Ugh," Racine said, acting as if she had been ordered to help. She went to slip in after Craig, but Alex grabbed her wrist to stop her.

"How'd you get back so fast?" he asked. Alex was too afraid to ask the most important question he was longing to know.

"Princess Mary. Don't you waste time scolding her. She came for Craig, sensing his blood and knowing he was needed here or maybe wanting to save him—it's all the same these days—I had caught up with him on our way to Celestia. I'm here by happenstance."

Alex fished under his collar to grab the cord of the pouch, the one Tobias insisted he take even though Alex would never use it: his escape route. He pulled it out from under his breastplate and over his helmet. Alex would die before abandoning his people for Earth, but he had taken it from the man for this exact moment, this chance to fulfill his bargain to Racine.

"Take this. You held up your bargain and found her." Alex refused to meet her gaze, not wanting to see the confirmation in her eyes.

"I arrived before my latest letter, I assume from your expression. I thought you had known, or if not, you'd demand the truth." Racine said. She didn't appear morose, so shock loosened his grip on her as she tried to slip away. "She was alive and guarded by a dragon when I left her. I ordered her to the Firelands to stay safe, to keep your heir safe. I mean, I'm still alive, so why would you doubt she wasn't? I took the oath to die if I failed to find her."

"Was a little busy trying to stay alive back there to even think. What's in the pouch is your ticket to Earth. The oath is fulfilled on both ends." With that comment, he let go of her. An energy between them severed, telling them both that the oath had been satisfied and Racine was free of Alex's magic.

Racine clutched the pouch to her chest, and she slipped into the castle. Toury and their baby were alive with a draca. There was hope yet. Alex wanted to transport to the Firelands instantly. It would only take a minute to see her, to see she was alive. But to what end? If a draca was keeping her safe for some reason, why bring her here to a war? As much as Alex needed to see the truth, her safety overrode that. He would believe: Toury was alive. His baby was alive. He must survive this for them.

"Listen," David said.

"Dra-ca! Dra-ca!" chants were coming from the front of the castle. The walls of fire had emboldened his men.

Alex thought of them, his people. He could go inside and fight to win his home back but be trapped in it while his men died, or he could join his men and win outside.

If he would die, he would die on his own terms. He would fight, not hide inside his fortress and be captured and killed. He would die with his men. He would protect his lifemate and unborn child.

David touched his shoulder, and Alex transported to the front of his castle. It was absolute mayhem.

33
DRACA

DJ watched Toury's pacing in the Firelands with a wary eye. When any other draca came near, he growled low in his throat in warning, but none of them seemed to want to hurt her. They were curious, trying to smell her, figure her out like docile dogs would. The temperature didn't bother her, and she refused to be confined in the hut. She had returned, listening to her sister, knowing Alex would want her safe. Then again, Alex wouldn't sit here safe. He would foolheartedly run into battle to save her. Or his people. He was the type to die among his men just for the principle of it. The thought terrified her.

She had slept like a baby in the hut, which surprised her. Pregnancy taxed her energy. The near starvation and dehydration weren't helping either, but it possibly was this weird magic she had never used before exhausting her.

She tried to busy herself. There was nothing but charred remnants all around her. In the distance, she could see rippling heat and a red glow of what DJ told her was the nesting area. She saw the looming silhouettes of the male dragons protecting their eggs or babies. The females were off hunting food or roaming around chasing after the bigger offspring.

Time seemed endless and dragged on. She could vaguely guess off the sun's position and how many meals the draca fed her—although DJ was likely overfeeding her. When the sun started to dip down toward the horizon, she could no longer stand the wait. It was taxing on her nerves with no word, not knowing how her lifemate was doing. Toury touched her stomach. Alex. It didn't matter what was going on or if there was a war on their front steps. She needed him, which meant he needed her. *I have to go back.*

You can't. She heard DJ's voice in her mind.

She had simply thought it to herself, not projecting it, but the draca heard her nonetheless. She tried to clear her mind and not think, so she spoke. "What's the point of me surviving if Alex dies and Henry takes over the sphere and ruins it all? He'll destroy this entire world, and he'll kill my bearn. He already tried to."

DJ growled deep in his throat and huffed out his nostrils, sounding like a horse. She knew she was swaying him. The draca's thoughts were rampant with anxiety and images of human carnage from the flames of Henry.

"You had a mate, a bearn on the way, from what Henry was saying to you. They died, didn't they? This will happen to me. And if I don't help Alex, he will die too. I don't want to be left alone forever without my mate like you have been. You know how unfair it is to live without a mate. Please don't do that to me." She knew it was an unfair amount of pathos she was plying on the creature, but it was the truth. Alex needed her, and she needed him: mates for life. She had to help him. If Alex died, Henry would kill her and her baby.

I will not let him kill you or your baby.

You can't stop him.

You can't get there in time. One human can't turn the tide of war.

"I can. You have to let me try." Toury stood there, closing her eyes, concentrating. For some reason, she had the wild idea that if she could make fire and talk to dragons, maybe she could do the dragon's trapdoor trick the Sapphirians could. She tried to remember what it felt like when she had transported to escape the rebels. She imagined the place she wanted to be: her bedroom in the palace. She let the fire magic roll over her. Her body was covered by the same weird tickling sensation as when Alex would take her somewhere. Then she opened her eyes. She wasn't in her bedroom or the palace, but she had moved fifty feet away.

DJ whirled around, his frantic eyes locking on her. He stormed over to her, stomping. Was he angry? *You stay put.*

The dragon was scolding her, really? On Earth, she'd never imagined dragons truly existed, let alone that she would see one, speak to one, and then be scolded by one.

"I'm the queen. I don't really think you can tell me what to do." Toury barbed back.

DJ stopped and stared at her, cocking his head in thought or trying to really see her for whom she was. *Please?* he tried. He leaned forward and brushed his snout gently against her abdomen, reminding her through the gesture of why she should stay put.

She wanted to laugh at DJ and herself. That was such a Toury-Alex exchange, and why in Fyr did she think she could challenge a dragon? *I have to save him.*

It'll take you ages to get there if you can only move a bit at a time. Stay safe. Here.

But you could get me there much faster. Toury gazed up into the sapphire eyes and petted his glassy scaled hide. He was a brilliant dark blue, eyes only a shade lighter, a glass dragon adorned with sapphires—beautiful, majestic. *Help me.*

Draca cannot enter the capital.

I don't think the king will punish you since I'm the queen and I permit it. You can eat the bad guys if you want. I won't complain. Toury was half joking, but a red dragon came loping up, a baby trailing behind her. Toury patted the little draca as he rolled around on the ground like a puppy. She rubbed his belly because you couldn't really scratch glassy scales. The bearn seemed to love it.

Eat human. Oh yes, I want to eat humans, the red dragon said, making Toury stop touching the dragon's baby and step back a couple paces.

Leave the Firelands, spread my wings? I'm there, another one thought. Then more thoughts bombarded her mind, and she couldn't tell which dragon was saying what.

What does human taste like?

Gross.

No good.

You wouldn't know.

I want to see everything. I never saw a building thing.

Okay, Toury might've started a draca revolution she couldn't contain if she wasn't careful. "Wait!" she shouted. "There are bad humans and good humans. You can't go around just killing and destroying for sport. That's what Henry's army is doing. I'm on the good team, the Sapphirian team, team draca. I want you to help me win Fyr back from these bad guys. We have to stay organized, stay careful, and you must listen to me."

Organizing a bunch of excited dragons was more difficult than Toury could imagine. This was a very bad idea. If she couldn't control them, they might torch everyone and everything in Celestia. Except Alex. She could not afford to be so selfish and reckless risking others' lives for him. The sad part was, she wanted to. Nothing mattered but getting back to him, fighting by his side. She could flee if her life was in danger, but she had to see, to help. They were partners.

Toury closed her eyes and took a deep breath. *STOP!*

The sound of shifting wings and some soft surprised hisses reverberated around her.

She knew what she had to do, although it was an unnatural thing for her. She opened her eyes and turned, refusing to be intimidated by the draca herd—or whatever they were called when together. Her trepidation was for nothing; they sat on their hind quarters, staring at her wide-eyed like a bunch of reprimanded cats. Massive cats who would kill the mice if she asked them to.

"Draca!"

Even the young ones stopped frolicking and paid her attention.

"I, Queen Sapphirian, now of your kin through marriage and blood..." She paused to touch her belly, thinking of her child.

DJ moved closer, his tail wrapping around her, giving a deep growl that spoke of protection.

She patted his glassy-scaled tail to soothe him. "I will not command you to leave the Firelands, but ask for volunteers. No, to be honest, I beg for your help. I will invade Celestia to save my lifemate, our king, and our land, and secure a future for this sphere that will allow the fire continue to burn. There are those who want to snuff out the fire and light. They will rule through powerful darkness, and there are others who want to dismantle Sapphirian rule, and now they have joined forces. It is a difficult fight. Without being there and seeing it firsthand, I fear the side of fire is losing. Unfortunately, one of ours, Henry, the 'flesh baby' who has kidnapped me and tried to kill my bearn with poison—"

The hisses and disruption caused by her speech rattled Toury, but DJ was not accepting anything and went into full protective mode, screeching and breathing fire at the crowd. Despite the fact fire would not burn them, they had backed off, cowering.

Who dares attacks his own brethren? A voice rang in Tory's head.

The draca crowd parted. DJ's throat purred in that creepy growl that made her feel safe. His paw—for lack of a better word since it was mostly claws—gently wrapped around her chest and drew her against him. His warm glassy scales at her back was a security she hadn't had since she was out of the palace.

Have to protect bearn, DJ said in defense.

Not yours, the voice rang out in raspy command. This was a draca in charge who shuffled forward with careful steps, the others bowing their heads. A bluish-gray draca stopped before Toury, its eyes clouded with age. The shine of the scales was long gone, making Toury ponder over how old this dragon was and how long they lived.

Mother. DJ bowed, making Toury bend down too.

Queen, the draca corrected.

"Queen?" Toury whispered.

You thought you were the only queen?

No. Toury fumbled on formulating and projecting her thoughts; she had no idea there was a draca queen. *But I am the queen of the people, and I need your help.* Toury thought a request would be better than a demand.

Queen of the people, you say? The queen sniffed the air, and Toury felt a pull, a tug at her light magic. *You smell nothing like a Sapphirian.*

But you sense the blood in her, Queen. DJ, who had appeared so strong, was now cowering under his mother's rule.

What is blood? The old draca scoffed.

Toury knew this type. She had seen that dismissive attitude for the sake of it from old folks on Earth.

You think Henry will let you live? Protect you? He plans to win a throne, only the people helping him get there will quickly usurp it. You will be slain for your blood—either by those who fear you or by others who will seek the fire to save the sphere. My queen, it is time we unite. We must join human and draca fire together. It will be the most powerful weapon.

You'll ask for our help and then banish us back to the Firelands? That is the way of man. I've lived long enough to see it. Two hundred years I've watched these fools fight and kill each other off, like bearns fighting over a carcass when there's plenty of meat going around.

I ask for volunteers only. A few willing draca could turn the tide,%% Toury told the queen. So much relied on their help, for all Toury knew—everything.

And what would we get in return?

To kill and devour the enemy. Toury hoped that was enough and not an insult.

Including your sister, the dragon slayer? Parents who helped her? The little boy who watched it all happen and did nothing?

Her brother. Racine. She could not offer them up in reward.

Toury braced herself. The queen would not take kindly to her words: *Unlike my enemies, I cannot offer up a life that is not mine to give.*

You are no draca! The queen's voice reverberated in Toury's head, jarring her, and she felt dizzy.

The warmth hit her before the queen's spout of flames. DJ's roar made her jump, and instinctively, she threw up her arms in protection, closing her eyes and tucking her head under them.

Something crackled and hummed. Toury strained and fought against the urge to fall down. Hot and oppressive power was pressing against her, pushing her down. She was so tired, so weak, so distraught. She would not die after all this. She would not let Alex die. She pressed up with all her light power. The pressure eased off enough for her to risk opening her eyes.

All around Toury were flames, white hot flames—her magic together with Alex's, or their baby's or Ruby's—she had no idea how it was happening or what was going on. Within that cocoon of light and flame, she felt safe. Toury stared at the draca queen, whose milky eyes had grown wide. She might be half blind, but the old bat could see *this* light.

Anger roiled up in Toury. She was wasting time clashing swords with another queen when her lifemate was fighting—possibly dying—for their kingdom. She'd had enough. *I'm taking DJ and whoever else wants to go kick some ass, torch, and eat some evil folks full of darkness.* Her anger leached out into her flames, making that lightning, that electricity she somehow had conjured before, rise to the surface. Now was not the time to test it, so she tried to pull in her rage and frustration.

Bladesung, the queen said quietly. She bowed her blue-gray head, much like dust-covered sapphires, making Toury's jaw drop.

Toury's protective shield flickered out, and the powers drew back into her.

She has come to free the draca.

"Wait, no—" but a roar of triumph drowned out Toury's voice. Then the legend in the edicts came back to her. Bladesung would unite his or her powers to save the world. It wasn't just about Alex winning the kingdom over and extinguishing darkness. It was about liberating people and dragons too. The legend was about the world of Fyr returning to a proper balance where every human and creature could live the life it wanted, unhindered and with choices, opportunities. The evil of the world was not just darkness, but also trapping beings—humans by limiting their power and wealth, and dragons by boxing them into a limited domain.

"Wait, listen. We need a plan." Toury tried to talk to them, but the draca were wild with excitement.

The Draca Queen's face came close to hers, and Toury had to try hard not to flinch. She recognized that look, the one her Earth mother had given her that pretty much told her to be quiet and know her place. *Don't take this the wrong way, dear—is that what you call one another? I'm the one in charge, and I am the only remaining draca who has seen battle and fought in wars. I know how to crush a human army.*

225

Feeling overwhelmed in many ways, but particularly how all the draca were telepathically communicating simultaneously, turning everything to cacophonic drivel to her, Toury leaned on DJ.

Climb on. We take you home now.

How many draca? Toury asked. She climbed onto his neck.

The bearn will stay; and some adults, to guard them and the eggs. Don't know human number things. DJ lifted to his hind legs, ready to take off.

Tonight, we steal our freedom! the queen said with fervor as she took flight.

Toury swallowed the lump in her throat, wondering if what she had just started was a good thing. She had very little control over any of it.

As they left the Firelands, the cool wind whipped at her face, forcing her to close her eyes. With DJ's wide jaw breaking the wind, she was more comfortable hunched down, and she could hear all the dracas' thoughts. Overpowering them all were the queen's directions—formations, instructions, and description of whom not to kill. Toury began to believe. They could do this. They could turn the tide and save Alex. She just prayed it was not too late. She also sent a prayer to the god and goddess, although she wasn't quite a believer, that the draca queen knew what she was doing and wasn't senile.

34

AN END

Alex was in front of his palace. The chasm he'd created earlier pushed his own men back, and although it cut off his enemy from both their reinforcements—if Henry had any left—it forced everyone into hand-to-hand combat. A quick glance at what lay before him, Alex judged they could win this battle. It was only a battle. If there were reinforcements, the battle would continue once they had a break, but it would give Alex time to bolster up his men, care for the wounded, and pyre the dead before any remaining necromancers could reanimate them. If Henry had no more reinforcements, Alex would still have to win his castle back by fighting his way through the inside.

The clashing of swords brought Alex back to the moment. His men were protecting him, barely allowing him to fight, so Alex stabbed the enemy between his men when he was sure his blade would not miss. Wherever the line was pushed too close to the castle, he'd blast it with fire. His men were in fireproof gear—as were some of Henry's surely—but Alex's men were better trained. They heard and felt the heat of the flames coming and would duck down. He had commands when he unleashed a great spread of fire so they were never caught in unawares. He wondered how long his powers would stay this strong with all his efforts and energy being used up.

The inky evening sky giving way to full darkness was the only indicator time had gone by, and neither army had made any progress. His power stayed high, but Alex's physical energy began to dwindle along with the battle. He was running on pure adrenaline, his body exhausted, his sword arm heavy. His men—except David—had to give up protecting him, and Alex had to limit using his power. For, after every time he had, Henry's army had attempted to push their forces toward him, figuring if Alex were slain, it would be over. Fools. They did not know the dedication of his soldiers. Unlike Henry's misled, purchased, or blackmailed alliances, Alex's men fought for the crown. His death would simply mean they would fight for Mary. But he had no intention of dying this night.

They were holding their own, although it felt like three to one. The defensive edge he had counted on no longer existed if Henry won the inside; if that happened, they'd be sandwiched between the enemy. They were vulnerable, and watching his men get slain was ripping Alex to shreds inside.

Fire lashed out of the window near the balcony, and it whipped around, striking Henry's men. Light balls larger than he had ever seen flew across the sky and landed, taking out huge clusters of men in bright explosions. Craig and Racine had made it to the front of the castle. The magicians and sorcerers rejoined them on the balcony.

Alex made his way to the front doors of the palace, daring to hope the inside had been won back. The doors to the palace opened, and the barbican rose. The Cobalts would never open them, instructed by him not to do so even if they won or kept control of the palace. Alex watched, hoping to see his friend. He did not. The rush of soldiers that came out were on both sides. A confused Alex took out a few of the enemy as he got out of the way. There was no Cobalt, but there was Henry. Through the crowd between them, Henry's gaze met his. Vain as ever, he wore armor with flames etched into them as a bold statement that he was the true fire king. He might have fire, but Alex was the Draca, and *his* armor showed it.

Alex fought his way toward the flames with renewed vigor. And the flames fought their way toward him. Henry and Alex were done with this fight. They were both ready to end it. Then the ground cleared for a moment. He and Henry paused, staring at each other. Powers were useless. It would come down to swords. Alex had more strength and power than Henry, but Henry was a great swordsman who had fought through real battles, not simulated training as Alex had done until recently. Henry was cunning as well. Alex reminded himself to fight with his head, not his heart. When Henry was dead, Alex could live by his heart for the rest of his days with his queen by his side. The crowds of soldiers noticed what was occurring, beating each other back on both sides to clear the path between them.

Always a gentleman, Alex lifted his sword to officiate a proper challenge. Henry slowed his steps and held his aloft in acceptance. Despite the war and what was on the line, they understood each other. This was about the throne; Alex had to not think about this battle on a personal level. He swung with all his might. Of course, Henry blocked it. Sparks flew from the power behind his blow. Henry staggered back, surprised, but then he smirked. Alex had shown him his newfound strength, put Henry on alert. He would use his skill rather than brawn now to try to defeat Alex.

Alex was no fool, though; he did nothing by accident. He was exploiting Henry's weaknesses: his conceit and narcissism. He knew Henry thought he had this won already. Alex focused on all of Henry's moves, the way he pointed his toe ever so slightly in the direction his sword would fly, how his eyes would flicker to the spot where he wanted to hit Alex. These things weren't easy to see, but Alex had grown up with him, idolizing him, studying his fighting skills. Henry never had time for anyone but himself. He knew nothing of Alex's form. And it showed.

Alex parried and blocked move after move and slipped in nips of attack when he could, getting oh-so-close to the joints of the armor where Henry would be most vulnerable. Wanting to take him off-guard, Alex smacked him with the broadside of his sword and then planted a flat-footed kick to his abdomen. Henry went down hard. Alex took advantage and swung his blade at Henry's pizaine, the vulnerable mail under his helmet and above his plates. Henry had his sword up just in time to glance off Alex's, shifting Alex's sword higher. The inertia still ripped off Henry's helmet, cutting Henry's face. He blasted Alex with fire. The power pushed him away enough for Henry to scramble a few feet away. His eyes were wild until they fixated on Alex, filled with fright, his mouth agog.

Good. Henry finally realized this wouldn't be as easy as he had anticipated.

Blood ran down his face. Henry wiped it away with his shaky hand.

Someone ran at Alex from behind. Without taking his eyes off Henry, he blasted fire behind him. The screams told him he took out Henry's soldier.

"That's cheating." Alex added a *tsk* for effect.

Furious at the taunt, Henry screamed and ran at Alex. It was too easy. He was leaving himself vulnerable, so Alex went for it. He dropped down onto one knee as Henry swung his sword where Alex's head had once been. Alex thrust his sword up under the armor plate into Henry's abdomen. Then, on instinct, Alex reached up, grabbed Henry's sword arm, and twisted it the wrong way until the blade fell to the ground.

Alex hadn't wanted it to end this way. The Sapphirian race was dwindling, but he had to kill his own kind. The wound was mortal, his sword in Henry almost to the hilt. His cousin stumbled backward, inadvertently sliding Alex's sword out of his abdomen. Henry put his hand on his stomach, half laughing, half sobbing. Alex couldn't differentiate the sound.

"You...you've killed me. You'd always been a spineless little whelp not fit to rule. Look at you now."

"It was only your mother's curse that held me down."

Henry fell onto his bottom. The battle was still going on around them. The men nearest had stopped to stare, but the others were unaware their leader was dying.

"Mother? What will you do to her?" Henry peered up at Alex. Finally, the manically hateful expression slipped away from his cousin, and he was clear-headed and worried about his mother.

"Tell me what you did to Toury," Alex demanded. "Confess your crimes against my queen, and I will make sure no harm comes to your mother. I have her in the palace...for now."

"That piece you have is a queen all right." Henry sighed, and jealousy rose up in Alex. His cousin spoke of her with a kind of admiration. Alex didn't like that, not one bit.

"Did you try to kill my child?" Alex shouted.

This unfortunately attracted the attention of some of Henry's men, but David was there, using powers and two falchions in alternating arcs to stave them off. More of Alex's men crushed in closer, noticing Henry and wanting to protect Alex since the end of this battle could be near.

"I left her in the Firelands. There was no child."

"There was and, from what I have been told, still is," Alex growled. He took his boot and pressed it against Henry's wound.

He screamed in agony. "Impossible! I gave her black draca root. It should've killed it."

Alex took his foot off him, noting the blood pooling under Henry. There wasn't much time left, and his cousin was pale, his lips blue. Alex could not feel guilt or despair as he had when he'd taken his uncle's life. This was the last person between his kingdom and peace, the person who had taken his lifemate and sister, left Toury for dead, and tried to kill his child. He prayed to the god and goddess Racine was not mistaken.

Henry gathered his breath, speech becoming difficult for him. "I hadn't meant to abandon her there...trapped, without food or water. I tried to...find a new place, but had to come here. I...I wanted her to live..."

"Just not my heir. You wanted my medallion more," Alex finished for him.

Henry nodded. For the first time, Alex believed him. The actor was gone, and a scared and upset man lay before him.

"Your father forced your mother to curse my father and me. He admitted this much. Your mother lost her mind for her crimes. I think that is punishment enough. I will not harm your mother. I will have her healed if possible," Alex told him, crouching down to Henry's level. "I never wanted to hurt you, Henry."

"Oh, but you had to," Henry said in a mere whisper. "I was...going to be king one day, no matter what. I wouldn't have ever stopped... I won't stop." He lunged at Alex with a dagger.

Alex caught his wrist easily and twisted it. It was a poor last-ditch effort to kill him.

Alex let go, and Henry fell onto his side. "Won't...stop." Belying his words, the breath left Henry, and he did not inhale again. His face went blank, and his eyes became unfocused and glassy. Blood trickled out of his nose and slack mouth, and he was still. Then his body started to twitch, and Alex had to stand and turn away.

Only, what he saw around him was worse. The rebels—oblivious their leader had fallen—were pummeling his men. He had just killed his cousin and now would have to fight his way out of this. Alex searched the vicinity for necromancers, but seeing none, he had hopes they were all dead and that Henry would stay that way too.

Alex threw himself into the fray, knowing that this was the end. If they did not get the castle back this night, the Sapphirian rule would be over. He most likely would be slain, and then they'd kill Mary. Rebels or necromancers would reign, or there'd be more war until someone stepped up to control the chaos. Henry might have issued orders to continue the attack if he died; there could be a commander-in-waiting for all Alex knew.

White light made him freeze. Surely, it was Toury's uncle, but Alex's heart leaped at the thought of her. Racine came bounding into view, dispelling his fantasies.

Alex froze when he saw David go down. The culprit came straight for Alex afterward, and he hardly got his sword up in time to block the blow. Pain vibrated through his arm, his foe being much stronger than he was. The soldier swung at his head, but Alex ducked in time. It was too close for his liking, so he lit the man on fire. The man ran about screaming and bumped into a couple other soldiers, who caught on fire.

Before Alex could pull David aside and ascertain his wounds, he heard a high-pitched screech that made his heart pump faster and his energy level skyrocket. The power reverberated through him, his negative energy left him, and he could conquer the world. He was only bolstered and energized in this way around them: the draca. He peered up into the sky to see not only one dragon, but at least a dozen circling the castle. On one draca, he saw someone riding on its neck. He had no time to ponder who the figure was above—noting he was on the small side and wore pants. The downward slope of the dragons alarmed him, along with their thoughts. They were coming in for an attack. His men!

"Fire down!" Alex screamed at the top of his lungs.

His soldiers dropped to the ground instantly, being trained to do so, for when a Sapphirian made that command, soldiers knew what would ensue. The call echoed throughout the battlefield as his captains and generals passed it on. It was much different with draca; the heat of their flames could melt metal.

The enemy hesitated, confused, and the fire consumed everything in its path. At the last second, Alex threw himself over David to shield him from the flames. The dragons screeched and circled around again with another monsoon of fire. He looked up amidst the flames and saw a few rebels who had been trying to run for it fall to the ground, enveloped in fire.

Then the attack stopped. Alex hoped his men's fireproof armor spared them from serious burns.

He pushed himself up and gazed down at David. David's face was stunned, but he was alive. "You saved me, Your Majesty?" David asked in awe.

A bit embarrassed, Alex moved off him and deflected the question: "How bad is your wound?"

"I will live, Your Majesty."

The men started to scatter and back up, trampling on the injured. Alex had to get control of them, or they'd create absolute chaos. Then he saw what was frightening them. The dragons were landing. In Celestia.

"Steady men! Weapons pointed down and heads bowed!" he shouted.

His captains shouted the orders down the line again, and he heard it reverberate around. The largest dragon landed in front of him with a thud, quaking the ground. Everyone and everything went silent. Dragons had not been in Celestia in a millennium. There were gasps as a dragon dipped her head down and nuzzled Alex's cheek in greeting. He petted her glossy snout.

Commander B reporting. It was the ruby-scaled Dame Draca B, apparently with a military title.

Commander, no harm to the blue men, and eat as many of the ones in black as you desire. An organized draca army—tales and legends were coming true right before his eyes.

The draca's attention was drawn to a figure trying to sneak off: Racine. Alex gave her a loaded, wide-eyed silent command. Racine needed to leave.

Draca slayer! Dame Draca B screeched both in Alex's head and aloud.

Racine reached into her shirt for the pouch, struggling with shaky hands to get the labradorite out. Alex could not stop the Draca; she would never understand—she might eat him. Dame Draca B sent fire in the direction of Racine. She vanished in the nick of time. She had gone to Earth, forever. That was much too close.

She's gone, Alex soothed. *Time to fight. Eat the other rebels, the ones who ordered her to kill your mate.*

Dame Draca B then called out to the others, raising her neck high, communicating mentally and in their other way—growls, purrs, and hisses. Another draca came in to land, and Alex's men backed away, allowing the draca to land by Dame Draca B's side. The rebels started running.

This draca had been blue once, now grayed with age. Alex hadn't known the matriarch of the J family was still alive.

Queen. Thank you.

We will clean up your mess, little flesh baby. In return, we will not stay in the Firelands, but we will only hunt the humans you ask for.

Alex hesitated. Draca roaming the lands? Eating farmer's cattle, rampaging on humans if they hurt draca? And humans would hunt them, poach them for their scales and blood, use the blood against them. *You would not be safe.*

What kind of king are you who cannot control his people? It stung in its truth.

What kind of queen are you to not control yours? Is one draca's life worth hundreds of innocent humans? He referred to the havoc Dame Draca B had unleashed onto the town of Hollyhaven after her mate had been killed.

It really was a stupid thing to say, to challenge the most powerful draca in Fyr, who could eat him. She growled and then spit fire at him. Alex's men dove out of harm's way. Alex had to admit it was pretty hot, draca fire, but it would not kill him, and the queen knew that. He let her throw her hissy fit.

When she was done, she said, *Well then. We leave.*

I'm sure we can negotiate something, no? How can you resist these tasty evil rebels running away from you right now? They want you dead as much as they want me.

This isn't over, flesh baby. We will talk.

Looking forward to it. It was thinly laced with sarcasm, but draca didn't understand human nuances in this Sapphirian thought-speak.

With one command from her, the draca went to town on any remaining necromancers and rebels. The draca raced around like a game of cat and mouse, toying with his enemy before they charred and ate them. His men at first were afraid, then astounded, and lastly comfortable enough to help corner the stragglers who were trying to flee.

Through the crowd, a figure strode toward him.

"Cobalt!" Alex hugged his friend, squeezing him as tight as armor allowed. "You're alive!" He thought he'd never see him again, not after Mary had said the castle had been taken.

"Almost not!" He pointed to a nasty deep gash that ran down his head and face. "What a victorious day!"

"Get to a healer, man. Mary will kill you if you scar."

Cobalt placed his hand on Alex's shoulder, his eyes alight with the same mischief he had as a child when he'd get Alex into some sort of trouble. "And let you take all the notoriety? Not a chance. Let's get you inside and kill the last few standing between you and your throne. I secured the inside as best as I could, but they got to the doors, and some got in. Mostly to hide. Cowards." He rolled his eyes and smiled at the thought.

"I'll let you take all the glory if you get yourself to a healer. I trust you to see to it and to assure me my mother and sister are well. I must find Toury."

Cobalt gave him a two-handed slap on the back, the closest thing to a hug they could have with the armor in the way. Then Cobalt headed toward his men, and they were off into the castle to fight some more. He better actually see a healer and not be reckless; Alex knew he'd do neither.

Alex gazed down to David with regret. "I can't take you with me, but I have to find Toury."

For once, David did not argue with his decision, even though it was dangerous and he had so much to do here. He knew Alex needed Toury. David's mouth dropped, and his eyes were fixed up in the sky. "Look no longer, Your Majesty."

Perplexed, Alex followed David's gaze. Up atop the castle roof, a dragon stood, Sir Draca J, the queen's son whose mate and bearn had been poached. The rider Alex had seen slid off his back onto her own two feet: Toury.

He was about to transport to her, but before he could subdue his awe and wonderment about how she could ride a dragon, she vanished into white flames and reappeared in front of him. Now he was rendered speechless. She ripped off his helmet, tossed it to the ground, and threw her arms around his neck and kissed him. He finally snapped out of his shock and responded with what felt like a lifetime of saved up rigor, even though she had only been gone ten days.

Relief. That was all he could feel. His lifemate was alive in his arms. Alive. He wound his arms around her, unable to get close enough due to the armor. She was alive.

When the crowd of soldiers started catcalling and whistling at them, they broke apart, embarrassed at their display of affection. He knew if the army had time to heckle him, the battle outside was officially over.

"How?" was all he could muster. A mixture of overwhelming relief and exhaustion muddled his mind.

"Long story," she said. When he took in her features, he then realized she was dirty, exhausted, and ready to crumble.

She cringed in his arms, and he followed her gaze to see his men covering a body in a sheet. He turned her away but too late. Her face lost its color, and he knew she had seen the dead body of Henry. The scoundrel who'd put Toury through Alex didn't want to know what.

He had so many questions, particularly about this white-flamed transporting power, but duty called. "Can you wait a moment, love?"

"I'm home," she sighed. "I have the rest of my life." She rested her forehead on his shoulder.

He held her up, bracing her weight, for he was afraid she might fall if he did not. "Captain Lightspeare!" he called to the first captain he saw, who jogged over. He gave him instructions to pass to a general. His soldiers were rounding up those who dropped their arms and begged for mercy.

Healers poured out of the castle to help the wounded. He signaled a healer over to David. Once David was tended to, Alex transported Toury into their bedroom. Toury sank into him, and he scooped her up and gently laid her down on the bed.

"How, Toury?" he asked, but he knew the answer already and placed his hand on her abdomen. "Our heir somehow helped you?" Or was it something more? Cobalt's theories came to mind, but there were more pressing matters to tend to. He didn't even know if bringing her in here was the safe thing to do.

"I'm not sure."

He leaned down, kissing the stomach of her shirt, which was fuller than it had been the last time he'd beheld her. "That's...unheard of." He leaned in and kissed her once. "We'll puzzle this out, but..."

"Duty calls," she said with a resigned sigh.

"No." He shook his head. "I'm going to go out there to make sure there is no threat to you and that Cobalt has it under control, to make sure Mother and Mary are okay. And then, Toury, nothing, not even duty, will come before you and our child."

Toury smiled and wept at the same time. He felt terrible about leaving her when she was overwrought and her emotions high, but as soon as Madge burst in, his hesitation dissipated. Toury would be in good hands and well protected.

35
BLADESUNG

Madge checked Toury for wounds and would have fussed over her beyond Toury's patience could handle, but Alex reappeared with two healers before he winked and vanished. She could do that too now. Was Alex right that her child had helped her transport, or had she become this Bladesung legend? She couldn't wrap her mind around the latter and clung onto the former: her baby protected her as she had protected him or her from the poison.

The healers poked and prodded her, asked her questions, and *tsk*ed her for letting herself get malnourished—like it was her fault—and placed stones everywhere to take inventory of her health. For once, she actually felt the power in the stones. Before, she had let the healers do their ministrations, inwardly thinking the practice ridiculous and wishing they had pain relievers on Fyr. Now, she could feel their power envelop her, a cocoon of health and ease.

All her worry shifted off herself and remained on the one thing she feared for the most: was her baby okay? She tried not to think about the poison Henry had made her drink and the starvation and dehydration they had gone through.

"Is the baby okay? Tell me it's okay."

"The baby is perfectly fine, the perfect size, but your body is weak. You must rest in bed for a fortnight, eat, and then you can resume normal duties."

She cried from relief, covering her face. Madge tried to dismiss the healers, but they were told the door was not to be unbarred until the king did it himself. Madge nodded. Great. Toury was trapped in her quarters, crying like a child in front of others, feeling far from a heroic queen who had just led an army of draca into Celestia.

At some point, she fell asleep during her sobbing, because before she knew it, she was being prodded awake, a spoon pressed to her lips. She instinctively drank what tasted of chicken broth. As soon as she was coherent, she demanded more food.

"It is dangerous to leave the rooms. Our healer risked her life to go fetch your broth." Madge was trying to soothe her, but Toury found it irritatingly condescending.

"I want food, and I want it now." Toury had no idea where the command came from or why she said it with such vicious intent. All she knew was she was famished, and she couldn't go on this way.

"You must take it easy, build your appetite back slowly, or you could be sick," the healer warned.

It was exactly what Henry had said to her about the water, which struck an angry chord in her. She'd hardly had any morning sickness and was starving. She wanted a feast. "I don't know how it'll affect you or how many people you'll need to fight, but I'm going to get food," Toury told Madge.

"Your Majesty—wait, what affects me?"

Toury gave her a wry grin as she grabbed her servant's hand in hers and closed her eyes. Toury thought of the kitchens and let the fire and light magic transport her there.

Madge stood wide-eyed and stumbled back until she regained her footing. She shook her hand, cringing in pain. "You shocked me!" Madge's face was priceless.

Toury stifled a laugh, for her servant seemed more offended than amazed. Before Toury could explain, a shout and footsteps down the hall put Madge into protective mode, searching the kitchens and the hallway for enemies.

"They're gone, they are. You're hearing them round up the last few," a raspy voice said.

Toury turned to see an weathered old woman stoking the fire. She pulled out a fresh loaf of bread from the oven and placed it down, and Toury had to refrain from trying to eat it immediately.

"The soldiers came, but no one would dare harm an old lady. That, and I have me some sharp knives," the old lady said.

Unable to resist the temptation, Toury ripped a hunk of bread off, blowing on it and then inhaling it despite how hot it was. Madge and the old woman stared at her, the first bugged-eyed and the second with a knowing grin.

"Come, come. In the cool locker, I have cheese and all sorts of meats."

Toury's stomach turned at the idea of meat. The charcoaled meat her draca had given her had sustained her, but it was not what she would've preferred. "Dracaberry," Toury said.

"Yes, got a ton of those. When you went missing, that lil' forager of yours gathered almost all of them in hopes you'd come back. Told him not to as I was worried they'd go to waste. No need to worry now. I'll be right back." The old lady shuffled off.

"Your Majesty, how...what..." Madge couldn't form a question.

Toury decided to answer what she thought Madge would need to hear. "I don't know the cause, but I can now transport, obviously. And I'm pregnant, as you guessed accurately ages ago, and so really freakin' hungry, okay?"

"O-kay," Madge hedged, making Toury realize she was over-the-top with her tone.

"Sorry. I need a lot of food if I'm trapped in that room."

"Fine. Dracaberry. What else?"

"Huh?"

"We are momentarily in the clear, but our quest for food might lead to a skirmish if we don't hurry." Madge pointed to the inkpot, quill, and parchment the old woman used to draw up shopping lists for the market.

Toury grabbed it up and started writing. She was so engrossed by her food demands that she didn't turn upon the door opening or take much notice of Madge's sword clashing with someone else's, but when the body thudded near her feet, Toury squeaked and took a step back, continuing her list.

A sword clashed against Madge's again as the old woman entered, saying, "Oh, my."

Toury diverted her attention to the intruder—a sweaty Cobalt lowering his bloodied sword. His face was covered in dried blood, but she could see a long puckering line down his face. He had been wounded.

"We have almost won the castle, and you're out of bed?" He hesitated and observed what Toury was doing. "Making a list for tomorrow's menu?" Cobalt asked her incredulously.

Realizing the ridiculousness of what she was doing out of her room—but it was absolutely necessary to her—she retorted with every fiber of austerity she could muster, "I am making the list of demands for the menu tomorrow, yes." She ran her hand down her nightgown, resting her hands under her small baby bump.

Cobalt stared at it, then gave her a wry smile.

"If you would be as good as to guard the door for my safety before you chase the last of them down, that would be much appreciated."

"I will escort you back as well, with honor, my queen." He bowed his head.

"She transported here, milord," the old kitchen-scullery maid told him.

Bug-eyed and slack-mouthed, Cobalt gawked at her, and his face shifted to a knowing look. He went to speak, but a noise right outside drew his attention, and he was out the door before he could say anything or she could even ask about the others.

The old woman had a basket of dracaberry.

"I need this—all this—and as fast as possible, so let us help you."

Madge was annoyed she couldn't stand guard, but Cobalt was right outside. No more clashing of swords or fights happened while they loaded four more baskets of food. Toury was ravenous, but she was also thinking of Alex, and both of them needed to stay in their room until it was completely safe. It was enough food for both of them to eat over two days without spoiling, but she had an inkling that if left to it, she could eat it all on her own.

Laden with baskets in their arms, Toury transported Madge and herself back to the safety of her barred quarters. She thought she heard the old lady shout she'd send more up as soon as it was deemed safe, but that might have been Toury's wishful thinking.

Toury inhaled four pear-sized dracaberries, two wedges of cheese, and two slices of bread before Madge insisted she should take it easy. The healers were angry. To escape them, she let Madge pamper and bathe her. For the first time, she indulged in actually enjoying someone washing her. She was so exhausted, she allowed Madge to scrub her arms, hands, face, and hair while she half drifted in and out of sleep. She was so filthy, it took a good part of an hour to get her clean.

Then she ate more, the veggies since the healers were still grumbling about her diet. She could not help it that Henry had starved her, dehydrated her, and left her for dead. Plus, veggies and fruit were not part of a draca's diet.

Once Toury was clean and fully fed, Madge forced her back into the bed. She had so many questions, but she was still so tired. "How long was I gone? I lost count of days and nights."

"Over a week. Felt like years." She gave Toury a wry smile that said a lot: Toury had been missed; Madge had worried over her, and she was exhausted. The blood spatter on the woman's draca mail and a healing wound on her neck proved how hard she had fought for Toury both that night she had been taken and tonight.

"Is everyone alive? Mary and the dowager? What of my aunt, uncle, brother?"

Madge pressed her shoulders firmly to the bed. "You were told to rest, to not worry yourself, so relax, stop asking questions. As far as I know, their rooms were never breached. Your king can tell you everything later."

"But now the castle's almost secure?" She worried for Alex. He should have stayed safe in here with her.

"It will be soon. The fight is over outside, thanks to you and your draca. The king slayed Lord Sapphirian, but you won this war, Your Majesty. With what you've done and what you can do now, I've failed, and I'm ill-equipped to protect you. As soon as the king finds someone better suited for the role, I want to hand in my resignation—"

"Request denied."

Madge was shocked.

"No one could protect me from Henry Sapphirian, and Madge, I think I don't want to—nor will be allowed to—leave these walls for six more months. You are the best protector, and I would have no one else."

"Your Majesty." Madge grabbed up Toury's hand and kissed it, making her feel weirdly worshipped. "Thank you." The woman was about to cry, making Toury's eyes well up. They had been through so much together, her and Madge. She was a friend more than a servant, a confidant.

"Stop it." Toury wiped away tears. "I order you, no crying."

Madge laughed and wiped her eyes before pulling herself back together. "I will let you sleep." She rose to leave and stationed herself at the bedroom door.

"No, stay here." Toury was afraid to be left alone, even if Madge would be right there in the sitting room. She also wanted to stay awake. She was exhausted but couldn't imagine sleeping until Alex was back. "Indulge me, Madge. I'd love that slice of cake"—she ignored the healer's *harrumph* as the woman changed powerless stones for ones charged with more magic—"and for you to read to me."

Madge nodded.

Toury took stock of the four baskets. She had eaten so much. She shouldn't eat more, or she might be sick, but she had a strong longing and urge for the cake with icing the old kitchen-scullery maid had insisted on putting in the basket, so large a pang for it, she thought she'd cry if she didn't get it. Ugh, this was pregnancy.

She wasn't sure how long Madge read to her after she ate a slice of cake, but her eyes grew heavy, and she fell asleep.

Toury woke up when someone touched her cheek, but when she smelled Alex's soap and a subtle sooty smell he could never wash off, she sighed dreamily. "Alex." She reached for him.

The bed pressed down with his weight, and his arm wrapped around her. He pulled her flush against him, unable to be close enough to her. "All is well. The family is well. Every traitor and rebel is out of the castle. We have won our home back, thanks to you, the savior of our world."

She turned around under his arms to face him. "Hardly."

"I mean it, Toury." His expression was earnest; his eyes, despite his fatigue, became illuminated. "We were holding our own, but there's no way we'd win if you didn't wipe most of them out."

She touched his face, trying not to cry, her voice thinning. "I saw so many of them around you, and I was afraid to hurt your men, but I couldn't let anything happen to you."

He gave her a tired smile, took her hands off his face, kissing each of them, and then gazed upon her. "How, Toury? How were you commanding dragons?"

"It's a long story." She didn't want to talk or think about these weird powers. She just wanted to rest in Alex's arms and marvel over how they both were alive.

"I'm not going anywhere." He punctuated his vow with a kiss.

Despite the exhaustion upon his face, he eagerly sought out answers. She sighed, giving in. Perhaps staying awake to explain everything to each other would help them get past these horrific events sooner.

They traded tales, filling each other in on what had happened while they were apart and realizing they had just missed each other in the Firelands. She downplayed the fear and trauma of thinking she and the baby would die, and knew Alex must have been doing the same when he described a war that didn't sound very death-defying. When their tales came together with her draca fleet saving the day, they both went silent for a moment.

"Toury, the dragons accepting you makes sense. They can sense Sapphirian blood miles away, so they'd sense our child's blood inside of you. But this doesn't explain your powers. I've never heard of anyone taking on Sapphirian powers, not even during motherhood."

She met his gaze and saw how concerned he was. "I was warned Ruby could've imparted more than knowledge into the stone you unlocked. I don't know for sure or if it's lasting, but maybe the baby and Ruby's power are what made this happen. I won't know until after the baby is born to see if the powers fade away or not."

"Regardless of the how, you are the prophesized Bladesung."

Toury didn't want to admit it, but a memory returned. "My father somehow knew. He tried to say I wasn't the savior because of the necromancers, that I was destined to do much more. He knew something and never got to tell me."

"Well, he was right." Alex lazily twirled his finger in her hair. "Thank the god and goddess he was. Throughout it all, Toury, I missed you to distraction. The worst was not knowing whether I'd ever see you again. When I thought you were dead and the baby..." His voice broke off, heavy with emotion.

"Don't think about that," she said.

"The baby," he marveled, touching her abdomen. "I didn't want to think about the future because becoming a father kind of scared me, but after I thought I lost both of you, I realized how much this baby means to me. And how much I need you, Toury."

"Me too." Then she kissed him, with a conniving plan. She pressed up against him and opened her mouth to deepen their kiss. When he moaned, she thought she had won.

All too soon, though, he pulled away. "Toury, no. You need to rest."

"I need my lifemate," she growled at him, trying to divest him.

He laughed breathily and kissed her soundly.

"I promise to stay in bed all day tomorrow and rest," she told him, running her hands through his hair. He needed a haircut.

"Deal." His lips were eagerly upon hers.

There never could be enough of this feeling. She'd keep the fact she was already on ordered bedrest to herself. When Alex found out, he'd be a little mad. It would be worth it regardless.

36

THE WORLD

The first few days of her recovery were fine. Toury needed rest. She was ravenous and exhausted. But after the third day, Alex started rising early and leaving their quarters. There was a kingdom to run, shambled pieces that needed to be put back together. He came back often, and the queen dowager and Mary visited daily, but even they had duties to attend to, especially in her stead. Her family visited, but they became bored after a few minutes because she had nothing to add after her tales were told. Being in bed so long was driving her crazy. Alex still came to her room often, bringing his work with him when he could or just to see her. He was truly making an effort to put her first.

On the fourth day, an excited Alex came into her room with Tobias. "Tobias figured it out!" Alex was a kid at Christmas with excitement—not that Fyrians would understand that holiday reference.

"What?" He had to give her more info than that.

"Your powers. Go on, tell her." Alex nudged Tobias. His sapphire eyes were illuminated with this frenzy of excitement, like he'd burst if the old man didn't get on with it.

"Your Majesty." Tobias bowed his head. "I have been searching through my ancient texts in the old language and found more about the prophesized Bladesung. You see, one of the texts explains Bladesung as a descendant of healers of light magic, while another explains Bladesung as a probable powertaker, but other sources suggest a powermender—now this one is interesting. A powermender—"

"Is a person who can fuse powers together," Alex interrupted, unable to wait. "Permanently. So your new powers should last." Alex was glossing over so much, she was lost.

"First you were given Ruby's magic," the more patient Tobias explained. "Then you must've taken some of your baby's power—"

"What?" Toury took from her child? What did that mean? Was the baby okay?

"The name is misleading. A powertaker trades powers, giving and taking. If your baby ends up with white flames, don't be alarmed—to get the baby's fire, you gave it your light."

244

Toury thought of how she protected her child, using healing powers by encasing her womb in her light.

"Now, the rest is guesswork as there are few powertakers and fewer powermenders left in Fyr, and never has anyone been able to do both, but you also swapped powers with Alex when breaking his curse."

Toury was trying to keep up with terms, feeling very much like she was back at Madam Mage's Finishing School, being drilled about a world she was ignorant of. Her, Alex's, Ruby's, and the baby's power fused...

Tobias continued, "Then at some point under duress or frustration—something made you inadvertently mend those powers." He pulled his hands together for a visual effect which didn't quite help as she grappled over the terms still. She seriously had preggo-brain—or woolgathering, Madge would tell her. "You 'healed' them together, in a sense fused them, linking light and fire permanently together."

In the shack, Toury had made a spark, accidentally learning—she supposed—how to put the two powers together. And then, when overwhelmed and surrounded in... "Woodrow," she told them. Toury was Bladesung, a savior as her father had said. How he knew would forever be a mystery. Racine, who might know more, was gone, but Toury was glad her sister was safe living a new life. She must be descended from these powermenders or -takers, and her father had known.

"I took on both my parents' powers, but my siblings didn't," Toury thought aloud.

Tobias's eyes gleamed as a teacher would toward an apt pupil. If on bedrest, maybe she should get him to tutor her. "Yes, Your Majesty. You had to have powermended in the womb before you could even control your powers, just as you fused Ruby's unknowingly once His Majesty unlocked that labradorite."

Alex and Tobias discussed it further while she tuned them out, her mind spinning. Amazing how so many things had to have happened in the way they did for her to be this Bladesung. Her parents had to marry and have her so she could save Alex, but then Ruby had to find her first and give her the boost of power and knowledge to save him. Her father had to have limited the curse to Alex's heart so that she could win it and save him. Breaking his curse and then carrying his child added to her powers, and then the death-defying situations made her instincts do the rest.

So much happenstance for Alex to be here alive and her to be a savior. Or dare she admit to divine, god of fire and goddess of light, intervention?

It took about three days for her to wrap her mind around this Bladesung thing, and she let Tobias read his books to her; aside from that, she was half-mad with boredom. She was eating seven small meals and reading a book a day. Alex returned to give her written grievances to sort through and answer. It kept her busy, but it was work. She was healthy, well-rested, and didn't understand why she had to stay in bed. Alex insisted for the sake of the baby. When he put it that way, she could hardly argue.

The following week, she refused bedrest, but the healers insisted she stay in her quarters. Toury was dying for some real fresh air—more than open windows on one side of the room. Madge sighed as Toury paced the room.

"What?" Toury asked irritably.

"Only three more days if you actually rest. You're wearing a hole in the carpet," Madge said.

Toury glared at her. How bored the woman must be too. After a war, she supposed boring was good for her bodyguard, but still.

"Your draca is still on the roof. The people are terrified and in awe of it. The king has left him there on purpose as a warning to any rebels or necromancers remaining. After the king negotiated with their queen, the other draca returned to the Firelands, which I think means it is safe to say most of your enemies are dead. He intends to send him back to the Firelands soon, but I think he knew you'd want to say goodbye."

Poor DJ, sitting bored on the roof, trying to protect her. Then something popped in her mind.

"I know that look," Madge groaned.

Well, Madge should've never told her this. "I can let him go, and the healers will never know."

"My Queen—" Madge tried to talk her out of it, but Toury let the white fire trickle out of her and consume her. Madge grabbed her arm at the last second.

They reappeared on the roof, feet from the sleeping draca. His feline eye opened and regarded her. Then his head shot up with a purr.

Madge shook her hand due to the transport's shock. "I think I'll need gloves for this." She backed up away from the draca warily.

"Sorry," Toury said and then turned back to her dragon. Madge had a valid point. She couldn't keep electrocuting her bodyguard. "DJ." She petted his snout. *As you can see, I am well again. Thank you for all your service and everything you've done for me. You saved my life and my baby's. But it is time to go home. The enemy is vanquished, and I am safe.*

246

Come visit?

If I can, I will.

Promise?

I promise I'll see you again. She ran her hand over her stomach. *I'm sure you'll see my child in a few years too.*

DJ gently nuzzled her stomach and then rose up slightly to press his glassy scaled cheek against Toury's. The hard scales did not make it a very gentle action, but Toury knew it was showing affection draca rarely bestowed on mankind.

Goodbye, Toury said, her eyes beginning to brim with tears. Her emotions were annoyingly high.

She watched him take off, his wings creating wind that blew her hair about. Then he was off. Like a soundless airplane, he circled the castle, cried out what she realized was a goodbye in his language that she could not speak, and he flew away toward the south, his scaly body lighting up in a sparkling blue from the sun. When he was just a speck on the horizon, a fireball ignited next to her. She jumped, all thoughts centered on Henry out of habit, but he was dead and the man she loved stood before her, David his shadow.

"Are you up here to scold me back into bed?"

"Not at all." Alex watched the horizon as well until the dot vanished. Then he turned his attention to Toury. "I was wondering when you would use your powers to cheat the healers' protocol. In fact," —he pulled her into his arms, stealing a chaste kiss— "you're wanted downstairs. You must dress well, I warn you. We have company."

Together, they used both their powers to return to their quarters. Poor David, too, was shaking off the shock, but Alex seemed immune. He frowned.

"They'll need gloves. I'm electric."

"Yes, you are." Alex stared her down, his thoughts clearly naughty, from his insinuating tone of voice. Then he shook his head and ordered the servants to ready them. It had been so long since Toury had worn her circlet or something other than bedclothes that she almost enjoyed being pampered and primped like a living doll. She didn't even care that she might be overdressed for a few friends visiting.

When she came upstairs to the waiting Alex, who looked ever the king in his finery and adorned with his king medallion, he turned, a smile spread across his face. How lucky was she? She had come to Fyr as an abandoned and neglected girl, and now she was a married woman who was expecting a baby with the most powerful and attractive man in the land. And she was queen, the apparent Bladesung heroine.

"Something came for you, but there was no indication of who sent it." Alex handed her a box with a simple bow on it. Toury untied the bow, curious, and then opened the box. Inside, there were many precious stones, but when she went to lift one, she realized a thin metal wire attached them all together. She pulled it out.

Alex had gone to the shelf and grabbed something else. "What is it?" he asked distractedly.

"My wedding necklace!" Toury held it up, smiling. She had never thought it would be returned after she bartered it for her escape from the rebels. "Misty returned it."

Alex came back to inspect it. "There's a note." Alex lifted it out of the box.

For your first daughter.

Toury had to blink back tears, wondering if she was carrying a girl.

"I could wear it," she mused.

"Actually, I was wondering if you might wear this, if you are okay with that?" Alex held the golden prince medallion.

"But people will know."

"Don't take offense, my love, but I think they'll notice without the medallion." Alex ran his hand gently across her belly. The cut of the dress under her chest inadvertently accented the little bump.

Toury's hand covered his so he could feel the baby's flutterings. Her other hand took up the medallion, one she would only wear until her baby was born. Then, she was told, it would adorn the baby's cot—called a crib on Earth—until he or she was old enough to bear it.

"Ready?" Alex prompted, taking her hand. "*I'll* transport us. We don't want to shock our servants."

Toury rolled her eyes but smiled at the lame play on words he had used several times over a couple days until she'd thrown a dracaberry at him last night in hopes it'd stop him.

Alex took them to the Great Hall instead of the Sapphirian Tea room as she'd thought their small gathering would've taken place. All around her stood people: her family; his family; the Cobalts; her waiting maids, whom she hadn't seen in ages; all the lords and ladies they were well acquainted with, but no more. Every face was friendly and familiar. For a feast or ball, it was a small gathering, but in times just after everything they had been through, it was safe and comfortable. Quite a few shocked faces gawked at her medallion and stomach.

Then she saw Tobias Firebrand and Baron Firelasher by the back wall. They bowed their heads to her instead of going down on bended knee—Alex's new laws promoting equality embraced at court.

Alex had held a pyre for the fallen soldiers while Toury was on bedrest, but had not let her see the list. He did admit that the man he had admired as almost a father, Captain Agate, had died in the battle. Toury could tell it affected him deeply—as well as losing so many men—but she would let him talk about it in his own time. Alex had honored them by having all their names engraved on the new walls that replaced the parts knocked down in the war. She would visit the wall and then give personal condolences to the fallen soldiers' families once it was deemed safe.

She scanned the room, taking stock of who was present as they applauded. Her friends and family were alive, although many were dressed in black for their personal losses. After missing out on a family and losing loved ones, she was happy the people she was closest to were still with her. It was a selfish thought, for so many had died to keep Fyr alive, to keep her family safe; for this moment, she would indulge in the thought of who was still with them.

When the people stopped their applause, Alex led her to the high table. Mary was there with Cobalt. Toury ignored the cheering to greet them and tried not to stare at the large scar down Cobalt's face.

He smirked at her. "It'll fade with time, the healers say, but will scar. I was too attractive for my own good anyway."

Mary let out a laugh but grasped his arm, her eyes agreeing. "I think scars make a man more attractive."

Cobalt had eyes for nothing but his engagee. Good. He'd finally grown up and would be faithful, Toury hoped. Nothing like thinking you may never again see the person you loved to make one faithful.

Toury sat at the center of the table next to the dowager. Then the rest of the high table sat, followed by everyone else present.

The dowager squeezed her hand. "I forgive you for not allowing us to be present at your hasty wedding, but you won't begrudge me a wedding feast."

"Is that what this is?" Toury asked.

"Why yes, dear, what did you think it was?"

"A celebration of being alive."

Alex ran his hand down her hair, twirling his fingers in the locks that were down. "That too, my love, that too, but a wedding is a happier occasion. The end of war is rarely celebrated, but a wedding and a prince on the way deserves a party."

"A boy?" The dowager gasped. She beamed with grandmotherly exuberance.

Toury gave Alex a mock glare, but truly she had wanted to know. He shrugged, admitting he or Mary would've slipped up at some point.

Mary, on the other side of Alex, leaned over, "You'll have to wait a while for girls."

"You just wait until it's your turn, Mary," Toury retorted.

"What should I put Cobalt through? A couple kidnappings, a few scandals, and some death defying adventures?" Mary teased Alex, Toury, and Cobalt simultaneously.

"Haven't we all been through enough?" Cobalt groaned.

Alex raised his glass to that, and they both had a sip.

Then Alex stood, and all went silent, awaiting a speech. Regal as ever, Alex was now a man in the role of king that she'd doubted the boy she had met could've risen to. Perhaps, without the hardships he'd faced—likewise her as queen—they never would have made it here. Alex addressed the room: "Thank you all for coming here in celebration of our marriage. It was a much-delayed feast, and I apologize wholeheartedly. We were a bit busy winning a war."

The people laughed.

"We celebrate my heir, and we celebrate our victory—"

There was too much cheering for him to continue. In the pause, he pulled Toury's hand, asking her to stand. "We mourn for the dead and will remember their sacrifice. We have won the war, but not without cost to us all. We will rebuild, flourish. We are safe, and the flames have told us of a golden age that will follow." He looked to Mary, who met his gaze and nodded.

Alex's orating skills were unmatched. To Toury, *that* was attractive.

"But most of all, today is truly about our savior, our Bladesung Queen." Alex did something she never expected. He took her hand in his and bowed his head to *her*.

The entire room then stood and bowed to her. Toury was overwhelmed. Her emotions ran rampant, and tears filled her eyes.

He pulled her closer than normal propriety would allow, then whispered, "You come first from hereafter. That is my wedding vow." Then he kissed her in front of everyone.

Whoops, hollers, and clinking of glasses broke them apart. Alex gestured for her to sit, and he followed in suit. Everyone else sat.

"Let the feast begin."

The first course came out. Toury devoured the salad, but when the soup came out, she had to turn it away. Her baby wasn't a fan of seafood, and the chowder was full of it. Right away, Alex noticed and waved a hand. Madge grabbed it and handed it to a servant.

"Did you see the gift table?" Alex asked her.

At first, she thought it was simply him making idle talk to occupy her nauseous mind, because why would they care about gifts? She had everything she needed.

"I'm impatient. It can't wait," Alex said.

He flagged down a servant and whispered orders. The servant returned carrying something off the present table that shone like it was made of glass.

"This is just a little something. I've done a few other things I'm sure you'll approve of—I had the King's room redecorated to be more neutral so any business there can be my queen's as well; I've had a desk brought in to my study because when you wish, I'd love for you to work by my side. Toury, these people, our enemies, they kept trying to get you into their power—the necromancers, rebels, Emeralds—they knew you were my greatest weakness. We won because they didn't realize you are really my greatest strength."

Toury, who had still been bitter about all the kidnappings, melted at those words. She yanked Alex by the neck and kissed him hard.

He laughed against her lips, then pulled away. "Look."

Toury saw an exquisite blue glass sculpture about the size of a dinner plate. It was a draca made in such detail, she could tell it was DJ. The spines, the scales, the teeth over the lips, the feline eyes.

"How?" Toury voiced her wonder.

"I told you once that if I weren't a prince—"

"You'd sculpt sand into glass."

"Yes, I tried to make you a castle as I had made them as a kid, but this came out instead, and I went with it. You already have a castle anyway. We'll see him again, my love, your draca, but I wanted you to have a piece of him here with you." He let her examine the glass sculpture for a moment before he continued. "The Draca Queen insisted on a few things in exchange for their help, one being that we build a house for us to visit right outside their land and we build her one for royal visits."

"How big would a dragon house be?"

Alex laughed at the thought. "You know they don't live indoors. I'll turn part of the front drive into a charred pile of rubble, make it homey."

Toury laughed at this and looked down the table. Cobalt and Mary were whispering and smiling to each other.

"They have no idea what they are getting into," Toury whispered.

Alex had followed her gaze. "No, but they'll learn soon enough."

"It was all worth it, no?" She playfully elbowed him in the ribs.

"Every excruciating moment of it," Alex teased.

They silently stared at each other as their laughter fell.

"Thank you." Toury was trying to keep her tears of happiness at bay, but Alex's natural gestures and playful jokes were almost too much.

"Toury, you are carrying my child. I can never repay the gifts you'll give me in life. I promised you the world, my love. I will give it to you."

Toury grabbed his chin in her hands and turned his lips to hers. She said, "You already have," and kissed him soundly, despite all the people in the room.

Toury had lacked a family on Earth, and then some of her family had been taken from her in Fyr, but now she and Alex were creating their own family, better than any of the dreams she'd had of one in the past. There were no more dreams she had left from her Earth days; they had all come true. Like the land fighting against darkness and corruption and winning, she fought for what she wanted, and now she had the world. Fyr.

COMING JULY 2024

TOURY AND ALEX HAVE FOUND THEIR
HAPPILY EVER AFTER.

BUT PRINCESS MARY HAS HER OWN STORY...

CELESTIAL SPHERES
WUNDOR

ACKNOWLEDGMENTS

First, I'd like to acknowledge my husband, without whom, my dual careers and fulfilling my dreams would not be possible. The amount of support given during the pandemic, while I tried to edit this and a second novel, write and submit a third, and be the best lecturer and mother I could be, was only possible with him taking on more than his share of life's duties.

I'd like to thank my parents for stepping in and quarantining as a family of five so that we could have the childcare and homeschooling needed to be able to maintain both careers. Your help was tremendous, necessary, and much appreciated. On top of them, I want to acknowledge all of my family's support, belief, and pride in me.

Most of all, I would like to acknowledge my son. At times, writing this novel was a struggle when describing things that dredged up difficult memories, but his constant love of life always brightens my days. I will continue with my positive thinking mantras: "we are alive," so troubles are nothing, and seeing each obstacle he works so hard to overcome shows me that I can do anything too. *I love you so much, my little Draca D.*

I'd like to say to my friends, thanks for still being there, despite hectic pandemic schedules. It takes true friendship to support someone who is so busy juggling so many hats that sometimes friends fall to the wayside; for that, I apologize but am thankful for the continuous understanding. I cannot wait to start seeing you all again in person. I particularly want to throw a shout out to the Lewis family: Kelly, Stu, Taryn, and Dylan. You single handedly helped us through the social draught of the pandemic. The online hangouts and chats across the sea were instrumental in maintaining positivity through trying times. Your interest in this trilogy was the fuel that kept the Fyr going to finish it.

I'd like to thank Authors 4 Authors Publishing for taking a chance on an online pitch that propelled us into this long journey of multiple books together. I thank you for putting up with my stubborn and questioning ways, and appreciative of your collaborative process. It truly brings the best out of my writing.

Last, but most importantly, I must thank my readers. You stuck through the trilogy the whole way with me. Thanks for the support. You are why sharing my writing with the world is worth it. And if you feel yourself bittersweet at the end of all this, I am not quite done with the Sapphirians. They'll be back one day.

ABOUT THE AUTHOR

LISA BORNE GRAVES

Lisa Borne Graves is a YA author, English Lecturer, wife, and supermom of one wild child. Originally from the Philadelphia area, she relocated to the Deep South and found her true place of inspiration. Her love for all literature led her to branch out from the academic arena to spin her own tales. Lisa has a voracious appetite for books, British television, and pizza. Her inability to sit still makes her enjoy life to its fullest, and she can be found at the beach, pool, or on some crazy adventure.

Follow her online:

lisabornegraves.com
Twitter: @lisabornegraves
Facebook: @lisabornegravesauthor
Instagram: @lisabornegraves

ALSO BY LISA BORNE GRAVES

THE IMMORTAL TRANSCRIPTS I

QUIVER

What would you do if you could live forever? Could you hide it from the one you truly loved, especially if her life depended on it?

Thanks to his dysfunctional Olympian family, Archer Ambrose finds out firsthand how difficult this can be. He never falls in love but bestows it on others—until he meets Callie.

When Callie Syches moves to the Upper East Side to prepare for her father's impending death, she doesn't expect to meet the boy of her dreams. She also never believed her father's harebrained theory about myths, but her uncanny ability to "see" uncovers godly secrets Callie can hardly fathom.

With an immortal family demanding absolute obedience, how far will Archer go to protect his love from the storm the gods will unleash upon them?

In this reinvention of Cupid and Psyche, experience an electrifying series where familial and romantic bonds are at war, and knowledge could mean the end of everything...or a new beginning.

books2read.com/quiver

Authors 4 Authors Publishing

A publishing company for authors, run by authors, blending the best of traditional and independent publishing

We specialize in speculative fiction: science fiction, fantasy, paranormal, and romance. Get lost in another world!

Check out our collection at https://books2read.com/rl/a4a
or visit Authors4AuthorsPublishing.com/books

For updates, scan the QR code or visit our website to join our semi-monthly newsletter!

Want more romantic fantasy? We recommend:

KISS OF TREASON
by Brandi Spencer

Two forbidden lovers share the rare gift to heal others with a kiss—but at a cost. Odelia's life has been a lie. When the queen tries to remove her from the palace, Odelia uncovers the truth. Now she must decide whether to forsake her people or embrace a destiny that would pit her against the current heir to the throne...her best friend. Though her only hope of avoiding a civil war lies in winning his heart, revealing her secrets too soon could cost both their lives. And a kiss might not be strong enough to save them...

books2read.com/kisstreason

www.ingramcontent.com/pod-product-compliance
Lightning Source LLC
Chambersburg PA
CBHW020611110726
47899CB00002B/471